HOME LIB
CE
D

9781405649117

D1140976

DORSET COUNTY LIBRARY

100399675 /

THE AFFAIR OF THE MUTILATED MINK

The Earl of Burford can't believe his luck; Rex Ransom, his favourite star from the 'talkies', and his hot-shot producer, Haggermeir, want to film their next feature at Alderley, the family's seventeenth-century country estate. Somewhat less enthusiastic is the Countess, who suddenly finds herself hosting an impromptu house party for the incoming Hollywood crowd. And before long the guest list grows to include two of their wilful daughter Lady Geraldine's dubious suitors, a long-lost cousin, a sultry femme fatale, a bespectacled librarian, an eccentric screenwriter, and a professional blackmailer. It's almost too much for poor Merryweather, the family's imperturbable butler, to cope with. And that's before there's a murder in the dead of night...

THE AFFAIR OF THE MUTILATED MINK

James Anderson

WINDSOR
PARAGON

First published 2008
by Allison & Busby Ltd
This Large Print edition published 2008
by BBC Audiobooks Ltd
by arrangement with
Allison & Busby Ltd

Hardcover ISBN: 978 1 405 64911 7
Softcover   ISBN: 978 1 405 64912 4

Copyright © 1981 by The Estate of James
Anderson

The moral right of the author has been asserted

All characters and events in this publication, other
than those clearly in the public domain, are
fictitious and any resemblance to actual persons,
living or dead, is purely coincidental

All rights reserved.

British Library Cataloguing in Publication Data available

Printed and bound in Great Britain by
CPI Antony Rowe, Chippenham, Wiltshire

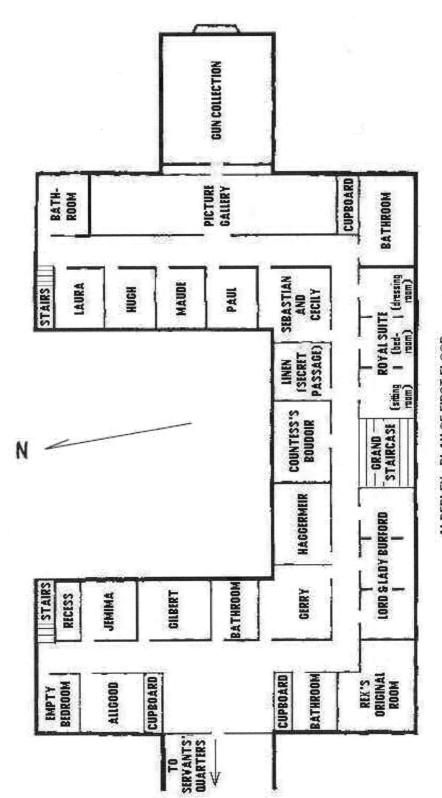

ALDERLEY - PLAN OF FIRST FLOOR

PROLOGUE

'You murdering fiend!'

She hissed the words. Then she hurled the magazine to the floor and kicked it across the room.

This made her feel a little better, and after a minute she calmed down. She retrieved the magazine and again stared at the face that smiled out at her. There was nothing in the features to indicate the ruthlessness lying behind them. Could she possibly be mistaken? It had all happened a long time ago. And they'd only met once. Nevertheless, she was almost certain—

Almost. It wasn't enough. She had to be sure. And to be sure she had to see this face in the flesh—ideally study it at leisure, converse with its owner, lay little traps . . .

Could she arrange to spend such a time in the company of her suspect—preferably staying under the same roof? It ought to be possible—if not socially, then professionally.

She glanced at the second subject of the photo. What was the relationship between these two? A casual one? Or were they closer than that? Accomplices? Hunter and victim?

She reread the caption beneath the picture. Then she put the magazine safely away. As she did so, her mind was working furiously.

CHAPTER ONE

'On Guard!'

George Henry Aylwin Saunders, twelfth Earl of Burford, took up a fencing stance and thrust. The ferrule of his umbrella stopped one inch from his butler's waistcoat. 'Yield, villain!' the Earl exclaimed.

'Certainly, my lord.' Merryweather, the butler, relieved his master of the umbrella and his overcoat. 'An enjoyable cinematographic entertainment, my lord.'

'Tophole. Errol Flynn is terrific. You really ought to go and see it.'

'Thank you, my lord, but I prefer to pass my leisure hours with an improving book.'

'I can't honestly believe you need any improvement, Merryweather.'

'Thank you, my lord.' Merryweather vanished into the background.

'You know, Daddy, you'll have to stop doing things like that to Merry. I'm sure he feels it's lowering to his dignity.'

Lady Geraldine Saunders crossed the big oak panelled hall and tucked her arm through her father's. She was petite, vivacious, red-haired, with a tip-tilted nose and deceptively innocent large hazel eyes.

'Don't know what you mean, my dear. Never done anything like that before.'

'Maybe, but last month you were calling him an ornery horse stealer and pretending to beat him to the draw, and before that threatening to squeal to

1

the cops about his bootlegging operation in the cellar.'

'Ah, that was during my cowboy and gangster periods. I've gone off those now.'

'Well, can't you go off swashbucklers, too?'

'No fear! Couldn't if I wanted to just now, anyway. The manager of the Bijou's booked the new Rex Ransom for next week—especially for me. Uncommon civil of him.'

'He's just trying to keep you away from the Odeon.'

They went into the drawing-room. Gerry flopped down on the sofa, while Lord Burford poured himself a whisky and soda.

Gerry said, 'I honestly think the talkies have taken the place of guns in your affection.'

'Oh, no. Basically my collection'll always come first. I admit my enthusiasm was dampened a bit after one of 'em was used to commit a murder. But it'll come back. In the meantime I'm very much enjoyin' having something else to do. And I must say, they're remarkably hospitable in these places. Manager meets you in the foyer, shows you to your seat. Pretty little gal brings free coffee in the interval. Amazin' how they can keep up such a service.'

'They only do it for you, Daddy.'

Lord Burford looked surprised. 'Really? You sure?'

'Quite. You wouldn't know. As a rule, most of the other customers are in by the time you get there. But you happen to be a peer of the realm. And they don't get many. It must do wonders for the box office in a little place like Westchester— especially when you turn up in a chauffeur-driven

Rolls in full evening dress.'

'Bless my soul.' Lord Burford squared his shoulders. 'You think people still care about that sort of thing in the 1930s?'

'Certainly they do.'

'Well, that reporter chappie certainly seemed interested.'

'Reporter?'

'Yes. Young feller from the *Westshire Advertiser,* waiting for me when I came out. Said they wanted to do a piece about the county's newest film fan. Asked how it was I'd only recently started going to the movies. I explained no one had ever told me how good they'd got. I saw those jumpy old silent things when I was a boy and didn't think much of them. So I never bothered again—'

'Until a few months ago you found yourself with a couple of hours to kill in London, noticed a cinema showing the latest Garbo, felt curious, went in—and were hooked. You told him all that?'

' 'Course. And he wanted to know all about the pictures I most enjoyed and my favourite stars. Most flatterin'.'

'Well, make the most of it. I don't suppose you'll be going so often once Mummy gets home.'

'Don't see why. Harmless enough hobby. Deuced cheaper than popping off to the Italian Riviera, too.'

'She did want you to go with her.'

'Don't like seaside resorts. Borin' places. Rather watch Errol Flynn or Rex Ransom any day.' He crossed to the massive fireplace and warmed his hands at the blazing fire.

'Cold out,' Gerry asked.

'Decidedly chilly.'

3

'I was talking to old Josh earlier. He says we're in for what he calls a 'real shramming winter'.'

'Well, I've never known him wrong about the weather in forty years. Suppose you'll be clearing off to warmer climes before the real winter hits us, will you?'

'No, I'm not going away for a bit.' Gerry suddenly spoke absently.

Her father looked at her closely. 'Oh, lor', don't say you're going off into another brown study. You still ditherin' between those two young fellows?'

She nodded.

'I wish you'd make up your mind and marry one of 'em.'

'*Marry*? Who said anything about marrying?'

Lord Burford frowned. 'But—but that's what it's all about, isn't it? This moonin' all over the house, kickin' things?'

'Not at all. I simply can't decide which of them to become engaged to.'

The Earl raised a hand to his brow in bewilderment. 'Look, forgive me if I'm dense, but doesn't one follow the other?'

'Usually. But not always. Not the first time. Every girl should have one broken engagement these days. All my friends have.'

'Now let me get this straight. You want to get engaged to one of these boys—Paul or . . . Hugh, is it?—solely in order to break it off again?'

'Well, not *solely*. It's conceivable I *might* marry him. But that's not the main object of the exercise.'

'Then I can't see what all the fuss is about. If you're not going to get hitched to him, what's it matter which one you choose?

'Daddy, surely you wouldn't want me to get

4

engaged to just *anybody*? This is serious. They've both proposed and I can't keep them waiting much longer. Do advise me.'

'Certainly not! You'd immediately pick the other one and always hold it against me. No, you've got to choose for yourself. Who d'you like best?'

'Oh, that's easy. Paul.'

'Then what's the problem?'

'Just this: I always feel happy with Paul. Relaxed. We get on fine. We can talk about anything. We're jolly good *pals*.'

'But?'

'But perhaps I get on a bit too well with him. He's not really exciting.'

'In spite of careerin' all over the place climbing mountains, running for Britain in the Olympics and so on?'

'In spite of that. Because I'm really not a part of that side of his life at all.'

'But Hugh *is* excitin'?'

'Mm. He fascinates me. But he frightens me rather, too. I'm always sort of on the edge of my seat, wondering what he'll say or do next. And he's thoroughly beastly to me sometimes. But he does make me think—about the only person I know who does. But usually he also makes me unsettled, disturbed or downright angry, too.'

'Sounds thoroughly uncomfortable. He's the painter, isn't he?'

'That's right.'

'Make any money at it?'

'Shouldn't think so; he lives pretty frugally. But he won't discuss it. Or anything about his background. I think he's a bit ashamed of his family, actually.'

5

'Well, I don't think that's very nice.'

'I'm sure there's a good reason for it.'

'Sounds rather mysterious. Is that part of his appeal?'

'Could be, I suppose. Paul is so open about his background.'

'Yes, I remember, he told me. Rather amusin' actually. "Of course, sir," he said, "I've got no breeding at all; *nouveau riche* you'd call me, I daresay." I quite warmed to him.'

'Yes, that's Paul all over. The *nouveau riche* thing is rubbish, of course; he went to Eton, after all, even though his grandfather did start life as a factory hand.'

'Mill owner eventually, wasn't he?'

'Iron foundry. Paul's mother was his only child. She and Paul's father were killed when Paul was a baby, and his grandfather brought him up. Then, when he died about ten years ago, he left Paul his entire fortune.'

'Well, families like ours can do with a stiffenin' of tough working-class backbone every other generation. Stops us becomin' effete.'

'Daddy, remember we're only talking about an engagement.'

'Sorry. Must admit, though, that I'd rather you got engaged to a chap with a bit of money than a penniless artist. Not that you need it, but I fancy you might always have the uneasy feeling he'd married—er, got engaged to you for your money.'

'I'm certain Hugh wouldn't do that.'

'You've talked to your mother about this, I suppose.'

'Definitely not. As far as Mummy's concerned they're just casual boyfriends, two of the crowd. If

6

she knew I was thinking of becoming engaged to one of them she'd start vetting his background and finances for husband-suitability. And that would be too shaming. I'll tell her as soon as I make up my mind. OK?'

'So long as you promise not to go running off to Gretna Green to get married or somethin'.'

'As if I would!'

'You wouldn't be the first member of the family to try it. Remember your great grandfather Aylwin.'

'I don't want to remember the old scoundrel. I want to think about Paul and Hugh. I've had a sort of idea that might help me decide. I thought I might have them both to stay for a bit.'

'You've had 'em both to stay before. Didn't help much apparently.'

'No, I mean have them at the same time. It occurred to me that if I could see them side by side over several days it would be easier to compare them. What do you think?'

'That it would be highly embarrassin'.'

'Yes, it would be if we had *just* the two of them. It would be pretty obviously a sort of audition. But if we were to throw a little house party, then—'

'No!'

'I don't mean straight away. After Christmas.'

'No, Geraldine! Good gad, I thought after what happened last time you'd have had enough of house parties for the rest of your life. People getting bumped off all over the place, jewel robberies, detectives, spies, secret agents, me nearly being arrested. I never liked having crowds here—stuffin' the place with people, mostly perfect strangers to each other. Always leads to unpleasantness. Your mother and I've agreed: in future we have at most three or four guests at a time. Understood?'

CHAPTER TWO

'Rex, baby, come right in.'

Cyrus S. Haggermeir, head of the Haggermeir Pictures Corporation, strode beamingly across the expanse of deep carpet and gripped the hand of the bronzed, handsome man with the thick blonde hair, who had just been shown into his Hollywood office.

Rex Ransom blinked in surprise at the warmth of his reception and allowed himself to be ensconced in an armchair. Haggermeir went to a cocktail cabinet. 'Scotch on the rocks, isn't it, Rex?'

'That'll be fine, Mr Haggermeir.'

'Cyrus, Rex, Cyrus. Surely we been buddies long enough now for you to call me by my first name?'

'We have? Oh—I mean, yes, I guess we have.'

Haggermeir handed Rex a glass, went behind his huge desk and sat down. He was a big man with a frankly homely face, like an unsuccessful prizefighter's. 'Why I sent for—asked you to stop by, Rex, is to discuss your next starring vehicle.'

Rex breathed a sigh of relief—which did not escape Haggermeir's shrewd brown eyes. 'Sumpin' wrong?'

'Oh, no. It's just that it's always good to know another one's being planned. I know the box office receipts of my last picture weren't too hot, and—'

'That wasn't your fault. It was a lousy script. A

8

complete change of setting is called for in your next picture. Recently you've played a Corsican pirate, a Spanish conquistador, and an Arabian prince—all with your hair dyed. Time you got back to an Anglo-Saxon type. You're gonna be an Englishman.'

'I did Robin Hood six years ago, so—'

'English Civil War. Cavaliers and Roundheads. You'll be playing a nobleman, the best swordsman at the court of King Charles, who tries to get the king to safety after the Battle of—of . . .' Haggermeir glanced down at a script lying on his desk. 'Er, one of them battles. But you're also in love with the daughter of a Roundhead boss, the one that's leading the search for Charles. In the end he finds you guarding him and orders you at sword-point to hand him over. You gotta choose between fighting and perhaps killing your girl's pa, or betraying your king.'

'Certainly sounds like a strong story line. Is that the script you have there?'

'Yeah.' Haggermeir slid the sheaf of oddly yellowing typewritten papers across the desk.

'*The King's Man,*' Rex read aloud, 'a scenario by Arlington Gilbert.' He turned the pages. 'This looks awfully old.'

'It's been hanging round the studio for years. We commissioned it from some English writer. It was back when we were trying to sign Douglas Fairbanks, and this was the bait.'

'I see. But Douglas apparently didn't like it.'

'Sure he did. But then he formed United Artists with Mary and Chaplin, and—'

Rex's eyebrows shot skywards. 'We're talking about Fairbanks *Senior*?'

9

'That's right.'

'But UA must have been formed fifteen—twenty years ago.'

'Nineteen nineteen.'

'So—this is a *silent* movie script.'

'Sure. But a mighty good one. And it'll adapt just fine for sound. Now, my idea is to make the picture on location—in England.'

'Oh, swell. The exteriors will look far more realistic. What about the interiors, though? Going to rent some studios over there, or shoot them here?'

'Neither.'

'Neither?'

'Nope. I mean to shoot the whole picture in genuine British settings: castles, stately homes and the like.'

'Gee whiz. Is that feasible, technically?'

'Oh, I guess the sound guys'll crab a bit, but I gotta hunch this is going to be the normal thing in a few years.'

'I see. Have you got your stately homes and castles fixed up?'

'Not yet. But I got my eye on several joints. Here.' Haggermeir picked up a large and heavy book, which he passed to Rex. Rex opened it and saw that it consisted of photographs of old English country houses and castles, each accompanied by a page of descriptive text.

Haggermeir said, 'We'll need several places, but the most important will be the one that serves as your home. Look at page four.'

Rex turned the leaves until he came to several pictures of a lovely house set in tree-dotted parkland. It was built basically in the form of three sides of a rectangle, was three stories tall, but with two-storey extensions projecting from the east and west wings.

He read aloud: 'Alderley, Westshire, home of the Earls of Burford since the late seventeenth century. Alderley houses valuable collections of stamps and first editions, together with the present Earl's famous collection of firearms. Commenced in 1670—'

Haggermeir interrupted, 'It's got everything—including a ballroom, a big oak panelled hall with a grand staircase that'd be swell for a sword-fight, and a secret passage, which'd be just right for the king's hiding place.'

'But what makes you think this Earl would let us shoot there? These English lords are kind of particular about their stately homes, I should imagine.'

'That, Rexy, is where I'm counting on your help. Get a look at that.' Haggermeir took a small piece of paper from his drawer and pushed it across the desk. It was a newspaper clipping. 'As you probably know, the studio subscribes to press clipping agencies in most countries—which means that whenever our pictures or stars are mentioned in any paper, no matter how small, we get a clipping of it. That one was a real stroke of luck. It arrived just when I was gonna start making enquiries about old English houses, so I at once sent for all the dope on this Alderley dive. It's from a paper called the *Westshire Advertiser*.'

Again Rex read, 'One of the newest and most avid patrons of the Westchester cinemas is the Earl of Burford. In an exclusive interview at the Bijou cinema, given before he returned to Alderley, his

11

historic seventeenth century home, his lordship told me that he had only recently "discovered" the talkies, and is now a most enthusiastic "film fan". The pictures he most enjoys are historical adventures, with plenty of swordplay. His favourite stars are Errol Flynn and Rex Ransom. "I should love to meet them," his lordship added. His lordship hopes that Lady Burford, who does not, incidentally, share his enthusiasm, and is at present holidaying in—'

Haggermeir again broke in, 'You needn't bother with the rest.'

Rex looked up and grinned. 'Well, I'm sure flattered. And you figure the fact that I'm going to be in the picture will persuade his lordship to let you shoot it at Alderley?'

'That's part of it, but there's a bit more to it. We gotta convince her ladyship as well.'

'Who does not share his enthusiasm.'

'Exactly. And I been reading up about her. She sounds a tartar—and real crazy about that house. Then there's a daughter, Lady Geraldine. She's a live wire, always in the gossip columns. Very much a mind of her own, too. That's the first point. Second is that I gotta check the house for suitability before actually committing myself to shooting there: make sure there are no snags— things that don't show up in the photos. So what I thought I'd do is write and ask if I can come and make a feasibility study for a day or two, bringing my leading man, Rex Ransom. That should make sure the Earl don't say no out of hand. Then if the place does turn out to be OK, it'll be your job to put all the famous Ransom charm into persuading the old dame to agree. OK with you?'

'Sure it is. It'd be dandy to stay in a genuine old English country house. Should be real relaxing.'

*   *   *

'Good gad!' Lord Burford goggled at the letter he was holding.

Lady Burford glanced up sharply from *The Tatler*. 'What *is* the matter, George?'

The Earl gazed at her, wide-eyed with excitement. 'Rex Ransom wants to come here?'

'Who?'

'Rex Ransom, Lavinia. The film star!'

'Oh.' The Countess was unimpressed. 'Why?'

'To look over the house.'

'What's to prevent him? Plenty of open days. I suppose he can afford two shillings.'

'You don't understand. He—or rather his producer, this fellow who's written the letter, er, Haggermeir—wants to come here with Rex and go all over it, examine it at length.'

'What on earth for?'

'You'll never guess.' Lord Burford seemed to have swollen visibly with pride. 'It's a tremendous honour.'

'Oh, I suppose he wants to make one of those absurd talkies here. Really, the insolence of these people!'

The Earl's jaw dropped. 'Eh?'

'Naturally, you will write and tell him that it's not convenient.'

Lord Burford gave a squawk of dismay. 'I can't do that! Turn away Rex Ransom? When I've just been made Honorary President of the Westchester Film Society?'

'Oh, dear. Well, I suppose if you want the man here you'll have to have him. But only him. We can't have this Hog man crawling all over the place, treating it like some second-rate film studio.'

'I can hardly write to the chap and say Ransom can come but not him. It would be most insultin'.'

Lady Burford sighed. 'I suppose you're right. But you must make it clear that filming here is out of the question.'

'Yes, yes, of course, my dear. I will—er, after they arrive.'

*   *   *

The telephone buzzed in Cyrus Haggermeir's suite at the Ritz Hotel in London. He lifted the receiver. 'Yep?'

'This is the desk, sir. There is a—a gentleman wishing to see you. A Mr Arlington Gilbert. His business relates to your forthcoming motion picture.'

'OK, I'll give him five minutes. Send him up.'

Three minutes later there was a loud and peremptory rapping on the door. Haggermeir opened it. Then he blinked. The man standing on the threshold was over six feet tall and of considerable girth. His hair was long. He was wearing a tartan cloak over a black and somewhat grubby polo sweater; black and white check trousers; and on his feet sandals over mauve socks. In his hand he was clutching a newspaper.

For a moment Haggermeir stared at the visitor, then said, 'Er, good day. Mr Arlington Gilbert?'

'I have that honour.'

14

He had a deep and plummy voice. Then, uninvited, he stepped into the room, almost forcing Haggermeir to stand aside. With a swirl of his cloak he swung round and gazed at Haggermeir. His expression was of a man looking at some interesting but rather repulsive exhibit in a museum.

Haggermeir said, 'I'm afraid I haven't had the pleasure to know—'

'A pleasure it most certainly ought to be. But I'm afraid you are not going to find it so.'

'Mr Gilbert, if you could kindly state your business—'

'My business, sir, is this.' Gilbert thrust the newspaper under Haggermeir's nose. It was folded to show a photo of a smiling Rex Ransom, surrounded by autograph-hunters. The caption beneath it read:

Rex Ransom, the American film star, who arrived in London yesterday. Mr Ransom and the well-known producer, Mr Cyrus Haggermeir, are in England to make arrangements for their next picture, a Civil War drama to be called 'The King's Man.'

Haggermeir said: 'Yes, I saw that. What about it?'

'*What about it?*' Gilbert cast his eyes heavenwards. 'Jupiter's teeth! It may interest you mildly to know that this film you so blithely announce you are going to make is my property. I own the copyright. I wrote it.'

Haggermeir snapped his fingers. 'Of course! Arlington Gilbert! I thought the name rang a bell.'

Gilbert gave a snort of disgust. 'Absolutely

15

typical. One sweats blood creating a work that they tell you is 'great' or 'the cat's whiskers,' and which is then locked away for years in some vault. When they do eventually deign to produce it they've forgotten your very name.'

'Well, it has been a long time. And I don't think we ever met—'

'True. You sent your underlings to deal with me—assistant producers, associate producers, lawyers—all the faceless men. But I fought them all and I retained the copyright. What's more, I obtained a contract which states that any rewrites necessary shall be done by me.'

Haggermeir scratched his chin. 'Well, it seems our script department may have goofed on this, and I'm sorry you had to read about it in the papers.'

Gilbert waved the apology aside. 'I am interested in only one thing: how much are you going to pay me for adapting the scenario into a talkie?'

'Ah.' Haggermeir looked a little embarrassed. 'Well, that's something that'll have to be discussed. Will you take my word that—'

'No. I won't take your word for anything, Mr Haggermeir. I want everything down in black and white.'

Haggermeir flushed. 'I don't know what you expect to gain by insulting me—'

'Insult you, sir?' Gilbert drew himself up to his full height. 'How is it possible for *me*, a creative artist and therefore one of the noblest of earth's creatures, to insult you who by definition are a villain of the deepest dye?'

'Look here, you've no right to say things like

16

that—'

'I have every right. I have learnt from bitter experience that every film producer—and every theatrical impresario, publisher, editor, literary agent, accountant, lawyer and tax inspector on earth—is a rogue and a vagabond. A bloodsucker. A leech.'

Thoroughly angry by now, Haggermeir stepped forward and jabbed a finger into the other's chest.

'Now, get this, Gilbert—'

'Sir, my friends call me Arlington. Others call me *Mr* Gilbert.'

There was a pause. Then Haggermeir chuckled. 'If your writing's as plagiaristic as your speech, you got a fat chance of doing the script. That was a straight lift from Oscar Wilde.'

For the first time Gilbert looked disconcerted. Haggermeir spotted this. 'Oh, I read sumpin' else besides screenplays and balance sheets.'

'Congratulations. Now to revert: my fee.'

At that moment a knock came at the door. With some relief, Haggermeir called, 'Come in.' Gilbert swore.

The door opened and the head of a middle-aged man peered diffidently into the room.

'Yeah?' Haggermeir barked.

'Oh.' The head's eyes blinked. 'Mr Haggermeir?'

'Yes, yes.' Haggermeir spoke irritably.

'Ah, capital. Er, spare a moment?'

'I'm very busy. What's it about?'

'Well, I wondered if I could talk to you about—'

'Well, come in, man! Don't yell at me from the doorway.'

'Oh, thanks.' An untidily dressed body followed

17

the head into the room. 'Sorry to interrupt, my dear chap, but I wanted a word about *The King's Man.*'

Haggermeir groaned. 'Not another one! I suppose *you* wrote it, too, did you?'

'What's that?' Gilbert gave a roar. He stepped menacingly up to the newcomer. 'Let me tell you that I am the *sole* writer of *The King's Man,* and—'

'Really?' The other beamed and held out his hand. 'I'm delighted to meet you. I suppose that means you'll be coming down to Alderley, too, will you?'

Gilbert stared at him. 'Eh?'

Haggermeir goggled. 'Who—who are you?'

'Oh, sorry. Should have introduced myself. I'm Burford.'

Haggermeir's jaw dropped. '*Earl* Burford?'

'Of, as a matter of fact.'

'Uh?'

'Earl *of* Burford's the correct form. Not that it matters.'

'Oh, my lord, I'm so sorry. I had no idea. Do forgive me.' Haggermeir was red-faced. 'Please, sit down.' He ushered Lord Burford to a chair. 'Will you have a drink, sir?'

'Ah.' Lord Burford thought for a moment. 'I'll have a bourbon old fashioned.'

'Oh, I'll have to send down for that. I only have Scotch.'

'No, no, Scotch and soda will be fine.'

'Sure?'

'Quite. Er, prefer it, actually. No offence. Just thought, you being American . . .' Lord Burford tailed off.

Gilbert said: 'Whisky'll suit me, too, thanks—

Cyrus.'

Haggermeir, crossing to a makeshift bar, cast him a dirty glance.

Gilbert flopped into a chair near the Earl's. 'Why should you expect me at Alderley, Lord Burford?'

'Well, as the producer wants to look over the place to see if it's suitable for filming, I assumed the writer would want to, as well.'

Gilbert nodded, as though a light had dawned. 'Ah, yes, of course—I will want to. I was just surprised you, a non-professional, realising the necessity of that. Cyrus and I were hoping you'd include me in the invitation. That's settled, then. Now, let me see, Cyrus, you're going down when?'

Haggermeir came hack carrying two glasses. He looked grim. He handed one to the Earl and the other to Gilbert, saying, 'Thursday. But on second thought, I'm not sure it's necessary for you to come—until I've decided if the place is suitable.'

'Oh, nonsense. If you do decide on it, the script will need a lot of adaptation. I'll have to start the rewrite as soon as possible.' He downed his whisky and got to his feet. 'So Thursday it will be. I'll make my own way down, Cyrus. See you there. Thanks for the invitation, Lord Burford. I should be there for lunch. Bye.' And Gilbert ambled from the room.

Lord Burford said: 'Interestin' feller.'

Haggermeir grunted grimly.

'Unusual personality. I didn't catch the name.'

'Arlington Gilbert.'

'Oh.'

'Earl, it's an honour to have you here, but is there anything you particularly wanted to talk

19

about?'

'Well, just this: it's my missus. She isn't at all keen on having this picture shot at Alderley. Didn't want you to arrive assumin' everything was cut and dried.'

'Oh, I won't be, my lord. I anticipated that situation. Now, firstly, so her ladyship doesn't object to my looking over the place, I recommend you tell her I want to do it because I'm thinking of building a replica of Alderley in Hollywood. It's quite true. If it turns out it's impractical to shoot at Alderley, I may well do that. Then, if I do find the house is OK, I suggest we leave the next stage to Rex. He has a very persuasive manner.'

'Ah, I see.' The Earl looked knowing. 'Oh, that's splendid. Right ho. Er, he around, by any chance?'

'No, afraid not. He's out seeing the sights. Naturally, we didn't expect you to call . . .'

'Course you didn't. I'll see him Thursday. Must say it's a real thrill.' He stood up. 'Better be toddlin' off now.'

Haggermeir got up hastily. 'Well, my lord, it's been a real pleasure. And I do apologise for that little misunderstanding.'

'Think nothing of it. Sort of thing that's always happenin' to me. Lavinia says I lack an air of authority. Funny name, that.'

Haggermeir looked blank. 'Lavinia?'

'No, no—Arlington Gilbert. Backwards. Like that singer chappie.'

'Er, I'm afraid I don't—'

'Feller who sings with the MacDonald gal. Always think he ought to be called Eddy Nelson. Well, toodle-oo, my dear chap. Till Thursday.'

CHAPTER THREE

The telephone rang at Alderley. The Countess, who happened to be near, answered it. 'Alderley One.'

A woman's voice said, 'Is Lady Burford there, please?'

'Speaking.'

'Oh, Lavinia. It's Cecily.'

'Cecily?'

'Your cousin. Cecily Bradshaw as was.'

'Good gracious! Cecily! It must be twenty-five years. I can hardly believe it. Where are you?'

'London.'

'I thought you were still in Australia. How long have you been home?'

'Just a few days. We're here for a fortnight, then going on to America.'

'We? Oh, that is you and, and—' Lady Burford groped unsuccessfully for a long-forgotten name, 'and your husband?'

'That's right—Sebastian.'

'How is Sebastian?'

'Thriving. Lavinia. I was hoping we could get together?'

'That would be very nice. When were you thinking of?'

'Well, we're fully engaged for the next few days, but we're free from Thursday until Monday. Could you come up to town?'

'Unfortunately, that's impossible. We have guests. Next week perhaps?'

'No, we're off to Norfolk to stay with some

friends of Sebastian's on Tuesday. Oh, what a shame! I did want to see you again. You're one of the few relatives I have left in England.'

Lady Burford thought rapidly. There was no help for it. 'Would you like to come here?'

'You mean to stay? Oh, I wouldn't want to impose, if you have other guests.'

'Oh, that's no problem. We have plenty of room.'

'That's really very kind.'

'It's settled, then. When will you be arriving?'

'Well, we've hired a station wagon, so we'll be motoring down. We could leave Thursday morning and be there by lunchtime, if that's convenient.'

'Perfectly. Very well, Cecily, we'll look forward to seeing you then. Goodbye.'

'Goodbye, Lavinia, and thank you so much.'

Lady Burford put down the receiver and was turning away when it rang again. She answered it.

'Gilbert here.'

'Who?'

'Arlington Gilbert. Listen, I've got a message for the Earl or his old woman. Tell them I'll be bringing my secretary.'

'I beg your pardon?'

He gave a sigh. 'You deaf? I said I'm bringing my secretary, Maude Fry, for the weekend. I'll need her if I'm to work on this screenplay. She shouldn't be any trouble. She's a big woman, but she doesn't eat much and she's quite respectable— won't dance on the table or anything. Tell him we'll be arriving sometime Thursday morning. Mind you don't forget.'

Gilbert rang off.

'Really, George, the man was insufferably rude.'

'Obviously thought you were a housemaid.'

'That makes it no better.'

'Well, you should have told him no.'

'He didn't give me a chance. And it's getting out of hand. First there were to be two of these film persons, then three, now four.'

'At least they're all friends together. It's you that's turning it into a confounded house party by bringing in outsiders at the same time.'

'My cousin can hardly be referred to as an outsider.'

'She is to Haggermeir and Co. And her husband is to all of us. Even Cecily's virtually a stranger to me; I only met her two or three times.'

Gerry, who was sitting by doing a crossword puzzle, looked up. 'I remember hearing you mention cousin Cecily years ago, but I don't exactly know who she is.'

'She's the daughter of my Aunt Amelia, mother's sister. Aunt Amelia was considered to have married beneath her. She died when Cecily was born. Her father brought her up and she never had much to do with us—her father moved in rather different circles from us. But she came to stay sometimes. Later on she decided to go on the stage. She didn't make much of a success of it, and ended up in a chorus line. Lived a rather fast sort of life, I believe—stage door johnnies, and so on. Which naturally was quite beyond the pale to my mother. She decided we wouldn't have anything more to do with Cecily. But I still met her occasionally in town. Your father and I were engaged by then, and one weekend I brought her to see Alderley. Then a few months later her father died and she told me that as she had nothing to keep her here she was going to try her luck in Australia. I had some letters from her over the next few years. She said she was doing quite well on the stage. Eventually she told me she was getting married—to a sheep farmer. I can't remember his surname, so I don't know what hers is now. She was going to send me her new address, but she didn't do so and I've never heard from her since—until now.'

'You'll certainly have masses to talk about,' Gerry said.

Lord Burford gave a grunt. 'Well, as long as no one expects me to talk to this husband about sheep, I don't mind. I'm going to be fully occupied with Rex and Haggermeir. Stupid creatures.'

Gerry grinned. 'Rex and Haggermeir?'

'No—sheep. Anyone seen my copy of *Photoplay*?' He went to the other side of the room and started vaguely picking up cushions.

Gerry said, 'Mummy, did you remember her husband's *first* name?'

'No; fortunately, Cecily supplied it—Sebastian. I wonder what he'll be like. And what can I do with him all weekend?'

'I don't expect he'll be any trouble: a stable for his kangaroo, an open space to practice his boomerang throwing, plenty of billabongs to eat—'

'Don't be silly, Geraldine. It's just that sort of facetiousness that irritates colonials—quite justifiably.'

'Sorry. You mean you don't want him to be unoccupied all weekend?'

24

'Well, I can see your father monopolising this Ransom man, and I can't imagine Sebastian having a lot in common with Mr Haggermeir or the Gilbert person.'

'So you'd like there to be additional manpower here?'

'It might be convenient.'

'Mm.' Gerry was silent for a moment. Then she said, 'Excuse me,' and left the room.

She was back in ten minutes. 'Problem solved,' she announced. 'Paul Carter and Hugh Quartus are both willing to help out.'

'Lady Burford jerked her head up. 'You've invited them both—for this weekend?'

'Yes. Wasn't it lucky they were free?'

'Really, Geraldine! That's very naughty of you.'

'But you said you wanted extra manpower.'

'One extra man—not two. And certainly not two who are almost strangers to me.'

'It doesn't matter if they're strangers to you. They're not coming to amuse you. I've made it clear that their main function will be to entertain my wild colonial second-cousin-in-law-once-removed Sebastian. It was necessary to invite both because we don't know what he's like. Now, Paul can discuss lowbrow things like sport and the London shows, and Hugh can talk about literature and art. Paul can play him at billiards, Hugh at chess. You ought to be grateful you have a daughter who can supply a man for every occasion.'

*   *   *

Paul Carter put the receiver down and gave vent to

25

a loud whoop of joy.

It had to be a good sign. It had to be. True, it was short notice to be invited for a weekend—almost as though he was a last-minute addition. But he *had* been invited. It must mean something—other than merely helping with the Australian relative.

He'd been rather uneasy lately about Gerry. At one time things had been hunky-dory between them. Then she'd seemed to cool off and he'd started to have horrible misgivings.

But now this. Glorious Alderley. A long weekend with Gerry. And surely a chance to win her. She must at the very least be meaning to give him that opportunity—an opportunity when she would be free from the presence of that twerp Quartus.

*   *   *

Hugh Quartus hung up and stood gazing at the telephone, a suspicious frown on his pale, slender-featured face. His dark, deep-set eyes were thoughtful.

Why now, at this late date, had she asked him? Was he a replacement for somebody who'd cried off? No—she must know dozens of socially gifted young toffs, who would fill that bill much better than be would. Like that rotter Carter.

So why? For there was certainly more to this invitation than met the eye. She didn't really want him to entertain this Australian cousin.

Hugh ran a thin hand through his rather long black hair. What was the matter with the confounded girl? Hot—cold, on—off, yes—no.

26

She was really infuriating. He just didn't know why he bothered.

Yes, he did. He knew quite well.

Not that he had any real chance. Once or twice he'd thought there was a glimmer of hope. But they always seemed to end up bickering.

He wished now he'd refused the invitation. He had half a mind to call back and tell her he'd forgotten a prior engagement. There'd be no pleasure in the visit. The bucolic Australian cousin sounded utterly grim. That idiot film star would be preening himself all over the place. He'd seen a Rex Ransom film once. Never again. Gerry hadn't said who the other guests would be; no doubt they'd all be equally ghastly.

One thing held him back from cancelling. Curiosity. He had to find out why she'd invited him. Though he was going to hate every minute of it. The only consolation was that the fact she'd asked him certainly meant she wouldn't be seeing Carter for a few days.

CHAPTER FOUR

Thursday dawned bright, crisp and very cold, with a coating of frost silvering the lawns of Alderley and tracing fantastic opaque patterns on the windows. A thin layer of ice covered the lake.

In the house the atmosphere at breakfast was markedly strained. The Earl—nervous as a schoolboy at the prospect of meeting his idol—managed only one egg, two rashers of bacon and three slices of toast. Gerry, who, at the last minute, had been beset by Terrible Doubts as to the wisdom of inviting her two beaux at the same time, spoke hardly at all; while the Countess was feeling decidedly disgruntled at the prospect of entertaining eight people, all of whom had been more or less foisted upon her.

After breakfast the Earl decided to try and calm himself by spending half an hour with his beloved gun collection. On his way upstairs he encountered Merryweather.

He stopped. 'Ah—everything ready for the guests?'

'Quite ready, my lord.'

'Where you puttin' people?'

A close observer would have noticed a momentary expression of astonishment appear on the butler's impassive and august features, it being the first time in thirty years that Lord Burford had taken the remotest interest in domestic matters.

'You wish me to appraise you of the disposition of guests in relation to sleeping accommodation, my lord?'

'That's it.'

'Well, my lord, Mr Haggermeir is in the Cedar bedroom, Mr Ransom in the Grey, Mr Gilbert in the Blue—'

'Who's Mr Gilbert?'

'Mr Arlington Gilbert.'

'Oh, yes, of course. Go on.'

'Miss Bradshaw and her husband in the Oak, Mr Carter in the White next door, the secretary person in the Regency, and Mr Quartus in the Green.'

'No one in the Royal suite.'

'No, my lord. It is not usually occupied except by special guests.'

'But we've got a special guest! Mr Ransom.'

Merryweather closed his eyes. 'Your lordship is not suggesting we should accommodate an *actor* in the Royal Suite?'

'Not *an* actor, Merryweather—a Great Star. Why not?'

'May I ask, my lord, if this is also her ladyship's wish?'

'Not exactly. You think she'd object?'

'It's hardly for me to say, my lord. But I should recommend that your lordship consult with her before taking such a radical step.'

Lord Burford rubbed his chin. 'P'raps you're right. Very well, better leave it.'

He moved off. Merryweather breathed a sigh of relief.

*   *   *

Paul's manservant, Albert, brought him his early tea at six-thirty in his Park Lane flat. After drinking it, Paul rose, donned a track suit, and went for his usual run in the park. By the time he'd returned, glowing with health, and had shaved and showered, Albert had his breakfast ready. Paul sat down to eat it, saying, 'Better pack my traps now. And put my running kit in. May do a bit of cross-country training.'

By the time he'd finished breakfast, Albert had stowed the cases in the car. Paul gave him a few last minute instructions—he had decided not to take Albert with him on this occasion—and by eight o'clock was on the road. He'd be at Alderley comfortably before lunch. And then for a long, long weekend with Gerry.

29

'Happy days are here again,' Paul carolled lustily as he drove.

*   *   *

Hugh Quartus groaned thickly as the alarm clock clanged stridently a few inches from his ear. Without opening his eyes, he reached out an arm and knocked it from the table. It stopped. He lay still, trying to remember why he had set it. He usually slept till he woke. So there must be something important on this morning.

Then it came to him. Alderley. Oh, lor!

Hugh dragged himself out of bed, staggered to the washbasin, splashed tepid water over his face, shaved, and ran a comb through his hair. He made some tea, cut and ate a couple of thick slices of bread and jam, shoved some clothes and a few necessities into an old army kit-bag, and wrapped his only decent lounge suit in brown paper. Like it or lump it, they'd have to put up with one of their guests not wearing formal dress in the evenings.

Next he filled a Thermos flask with tea, dressed in two pairs of socks, thick corduroy trousers, three sweaters and his old, moth-eaten fur-lined flying jacket, and went down to the lock-up garage he rented.

He opened it and wheeled out his motorcycle and sidecar. He threw his luggage into the sidecar and took from it a scarf, goggles, cap and gauntlets. These donned, he was ready. Wrapped up though he was, it was going to be a fearfully cold trip. He was tempted, even at this stage, to go by train. But no; this way he'd have independence of movement. Without the bike, he'd be stuck in

30

the heart of the country and utterly reliant on his hosts for transportation. Besides, he'd save a few shillings this way—always an important consideration.

The superbly tuned engine of the little motor-bike started at first kick. It really had been a bargain, this machine.

Hugh remembered he hadn't washed the breakfast things or made the bed. They'd be waiting for him when he got back.

Something else to look forward to.

*   *   *

It was a little after eleven o'clock when Merryweather threw open the big double doors of the morning room at Alderley and announced, 'Mr and Mrs Sebastian Everard.'

Thankful at last to know her cousin's surname, Lady Burford went forward to greet her.

The woman who led the way into the room was small, somewhat plump, had a round, good-natured face and blonde hair done in lots of small tight curls. She stopped, staring at Lady Burford, her head tilted to one side. There was something birdlike about her.

'Lavinia?'

'Cecily?'

'My dear, how lovely! You're looking wonderful.'

'And you, Cecily.'

They kissed. Lady Burford said, 'You remember George?'

'Why, of course.' Cecily turned and presented her cheek as the Earl stepped forward. He brushed

31

it with his lips, a little uncertainly.

'Well, well, well,' he said, 'this is splendid. Splendid,' he added dogmatically, as though someone had contradicted him.

Cecily said, 'And this is my husband, Sebastian.'

Sebastian Everard was slight and thin, with a round, clean-shaven pink face and a bland expression. He smiled. 'How—how—how de do?' He spoke in an exaggerated drawl, offering a limp hand to the Earl and Countess. 'Jolly—jolly decent of you to ask us.'

'Delighted to have you,' Lord Burford said.

'Really? Oh, jolly good.' He gave an amiable titter, gazing round the room vaguely at the same time.

'Now, George,' Lady Burford said briskly, 'why don't you give, er, Sebastian a drink? Cecily and I have a lot to talk about. There'll be some coffee shortly and if I remember rightly that's what she'll prefer.' She led her cousin to a chair by the fireplace.

'Thank you, dear.' Cecily said. 'Now, there's so much I want to hear about you and George and Geraldine. And you must bring me up to date on twenty-five years of gossip. I want to know all about Lucy and the twins and Margaret and Reggie and Bobo and the Pearsons—and, oh, dozens of people.'

'My, that's a tall order.'

Lord Burford meanwhile had plucked at Sebastian's elbow. 'Come across here and let me pour you something.'

'What? Oh. Right. Jolly good.' He followed the Earl across to a sideboard where drinks were laid out. 'What'll you have?'

32

'Oh.' Sebastian frowned. 'Don't know, really.'

'Sherry?'

'Jolly good.'

Lord Burford poured and handed Sebastian a glass.

'Cheers.'

'Oh, yes, rather.'

They drank. There was a pause. Lord Burford cleared his throat. 'Chilly today.'

'Oh, rather.'

'Good drive down?'

'Jolly good.'

'Capital.' There was another silence. The Earl said, 'Er, I keep a few sheep.'

'Really? Oh, jolly good.' Sebastian peered out through the window, as though expecting to see them dotted about the lawn.

'Oh, not personally, of course. At the home farm. Have a good man running it. Must admit I find 'em rather irritatin' creatures. No offence, I hope?'

'No, no, not at all.'

'Always getting lost in the snow or caught in hedges, lambing at the most inconvenient time of the year. No doubt you feel quite different about 'em.'

'Well, I—I haven't given it a lot of thought, actually.'

'Really? You surprise me. I imagined it would be unavoidable.'

'No, never found it necessary. Partial—partial to the odd chop, don't you know. And useful for insomnia, eh, eh?'

'Countin' them jumping over a fence, you mean? Even that doesn't work with me. They

33

always refuse to jump. Not that I'm often troubled by sleeplessness. Clear conscience, I suppose. How many thousand you got?'

The nearest thing so far to animation or surprise came over Sebastian's face. 'How—how—how many thousands?'

'Just roughly.'

'Oh.' He stared at his sherry glass. 'Don't know, really.'

'But you must count your stock sometimes.'

'Count? No. I get statements from the bank and my jolly old accountant keeps tabs on my position.'

Lord Burford's eye bulged. 'Your accountant counts your sheep for you?'

Sebastian blinked. 'Oh, no. Thought you meant money. I don't own any sheep.'

'You don't? You mean you ain't a sheep farmer?'

'Oh, no. Not at all. Never. Sorry.' He smiled.

'Great Scott! I could have sworn . . .' He turned and raised his voice a little. 'Lavinia, you said Sebastian here was a sheep farmer. He's nothin' of the sort.'

Cecily said gently, 'Oh, I'm sorry. I should have explained. It was Philip, my first husband, who was the sheep farmer. He died many years ago. Sebastian's not even an Australian. He was just visiting when we met. But then he decided to stay on.'

The entry of Gerry at that moment caused a welcome diversion. After introductions she said, 'Well, I suppose you know all about our expected VIP guest?'

'No, dear,' Cecily said. 'Who's that?'

'The great Rex Ransom, no less.'

34

'The film star? Really? How exciting. Did you hear that, Sebastian?'

'Oh, rather. Jolly good. When—when's he expected to arrive?'

'The train should be getting in to Alderley Halt in about five minutes. Hawkins has gone to meet it in the Rolls. Actually, there's quite a party of film people coming, isn't there, Daddy?'

Lord Burford nodded happily. 'Biggest thing to happen at Alderley since Queen Victoria stayed here in 1852.'

'Jolly good,' said Sebastian.

*   *   *

By the time Hugh reached Alderley village at about eleven-thirty and started on the final stage to the house he was stiff with cold. This last part of the journey did nothing to improve his mood. The estate was surrounded by a positive network of narrow lanes, and like all of them the one he had to follow wound irritatingly, several times approaching to within a mile of the house, which could be clearly glimpsed through the trees. Then the lane would suddenly turn away, without apparent reason, on another long detour.

Hugh's mind was filled with thoughts of blazing fires and hot coffee, and as bend followed bend he became more and more frustrated and began to push his machine ever faster.

At last he reached the final bend before the straight stretch of wider road that ran past the entrance to the drive leading up to the house. He twisted the throttle grip, leaning over so that the wheels of the sidecar actually left the ground.

One thing, however, which he had not allowed for was the heavy overnight frost that had resulted in icy roads. Until he'd reached the village he'd been travelling on main roads, on which grit had been laid. But this twisting, little-used lane had not been treated.

Suddenly Hugh felt the bike start to slip from under him. The next moment he found himself rolling over and over on the road. It seemed as though he was never going to stop. But eventually he did, and when his head had cleared he sat dizzily up.

After a few seconds he decided he wasn't hurt and got unsteadily to his feet. Suddenly he no longer felt cold. He walked over to his cycle and sidecar, which were apparently undamaged. Hugh tried to get the contraption upright. But it was heavy and his feet kept slipping on the still icy surface.

He was making another attempt when he heard a car approaching from around the bend. It had the deep-throated roar of an expensive sports model. Hugh started to run towards the bend. But his feet went from under him again. By the time he'd scrambled up, a long, low scarlet drop-head tourer had appeared round the curve.

Hugh yelled and waved his arms. He saw the driver brake and the car start to skid. Hugh threw himself to one side, and in a graceful spin the sportscar's nearside rear wheel went over the front wheel of the motorcycle.

*   *   *

Paul felt the bump and a horrible crunching

clatter. Then the car had stopped and there was a great calm. He got hastily out and saw that the front wheel of the motorcycle was badly buckled. The driver, only his nose showing between goggles and scarf, was standing on the grassy shoulder, staring mutely at the wreckage.

Paul walked towards him. 'I say, old man, I'm most frightfully sorry—'

Without taking his eyes from his injured machine, the motorcyclist raised both arms skywards in a gesture of fury and shouted, 'You reckless imbecile!'

Paul said, 'Now, steady on. I only—'

'*You only*? You only wrecked my—' He looked at Paul for the first time and stopped short. '*You*?' he said.

Paul felt a sudden chill of alarm. He said, 'What?'

'Carter! What are you doing here?'

'I'm afraid I don't—'

The other suddenly tore off his goggles and scarf, and Paul's eyes widened. 'Quartus! Hullo. I didn't recognise you in that get-up.'

'I said, what are you doing here?' Hugh snapped. His face was white.

'I'm on my way to Alderley.'

'I gathered that, you fool. But just *why* are you on your way there?'

Paul frowned. 'I've been invited for the weekend.'

Hugh was breathing hard. 'By Geraldine?'

'Yes, of course.'

'The little beast!'

'Look here, don't you speak about Gerry like that.'

'What's it to you how I speak about Gerry?'

'I think a lot of her. I won't stand by and listen to her insulted.'

'Then don't stand by. Clear off. I'll stay here and insult her to my heart's content.'

Paul swallowed and managed to control himself. He said, 'I'm sorry about the bike.'

'So am I!'

'But I'm not really to blame—'

'Not to blame! I suppose you think my machine dived under your car—decided to commit suicide!'

'I came round the bend and it was in the middle of the road.'

'A driver should be prepared for obstructions in the road. He shouldn't drive so fast that he can't stop if—'

'Oh, for Pete's sake! Normally I could have stopped, but the road's icy—'

'The road's icy! He's telling me the road's icy! Why do you think I came off?'

'I wouldn't know,' Paul retorted. 'It could have been sheer incompetence—or, to judge from your manner, drunkenness. However, I have no wish to continue arguing. Although I admit no legal liability, I'm naturally prepared to pay for the repairs—'

'I don't want your confounded charity.'

'As you wish. But if you change your mind, the offer stands. Now, as the bike obviously can't be ridden, I suggest we drag it to the side of the road and then call up the local garage to come get it. I'll give you a lift to the house. Er, I suppose you are a guest there, too?'

'I was.'

'Was?'

'I wasn't looking forward to the weekend before. Now I doubt if I could stomach it.'

'Well, that's up to you. But you'll have to come to the house to use the phone. Hop in the car.'

'No, thanks.'

'But it's pretty well a mile—'

'That's my business.'

Paul shrugged. 'OK. What do I tell the Burfords?'

'Tell them to—Tell them what you like.'

'As you wish. So long.'

Paul walked to his car. Really, that chap was insufferable. What on earth did Gerry see in him?

He drove the last hundred yards, turned in past the lodge, and sped up the tree-lined drive to Alderley. Even his brush with Quartus couldn't take from him a delightfully pleasurable anticipation. His last visit had been in summer. He and Gerry had gone for long rambles in and outside the estate. He remembered his sense of pride when she'd presented him with a key to the small doors set into the walls that surrounded the park—a traditional mark of esteem in the family. This time there'd be few rambles, but plenty of time alone with her indoors; he'd make sure of that.

He pulled up before the impressive seventeenth century façade of the house, got out and started up the steps. As he did so, Gerry emerged from the front door. He grinned.

Gerry stopped, feeling the warm glow she always experienced when she saw those pleasantly rugged features, the deep blue eyes and the curly light-brown hair. He was so *nice*. She really liked him better than anyone else she knew. Why, oh why, could she never be quite sure she was in love with him?

He ran up the last few steps and kissed her. 'Hullo, my sweet.'

'Oh, Paul, it's good to see you! Thank you for coming at such short notice.'

'Try and keep me away.'

They went indoors as a footman emerged to unload Paul's luggage. As Paul was divesting himself of his overcoat in the hall, Gerry said, 'Paul, I have a confession to make. Hugh's coming for the weekend, too.'

'I don't think he is, actually.'

'What on earth do you mean?'

He explained what had happened.

'Oh, golly!' she said, when he'd finished. 'Where is he now?'

'As far as I know, still standing staring at his bike.'

'Why didn't you bring him to the house?'

'I tried, darling. He wouldn't come. He's very angry with me—and with you. And with the whole world.'

'But what's he going to do?'

'He wouldn't say. Honestly, darling, I did my best.'

'Oh, I'm sure you did, Paul. He's quite impossible sometimes.'

'Sometimes?'

She grinned. 'Now if *I* said that about a *girl*, you'd probably say "meow." '

'Sorry. All the same, Gerry, I think you might have told me he was going to be here.'

'I thought you wouldn't come if you knew.'

'I'm not scared of Quartus.'

'I know that, chump. But you know you can't stand him.'

'That's not true. I could get on all right with him if he gave me a chance. I admit I have been apprehensive about your interest in him, but I'm convinced now that it's merely a sisterly concern for the chap because he's a failure.'

'He's not a failure!'

'Oh, come off it! How many pictures does he sell?'

'Well, that's immaterial. I've got to do something. I can't just leave him down there. I must go and investigate.'

'Oh, send one of your countless minions.'

'No, no—*noblesse oblige* and all that rot.'

He sighed. 'OK, get your coat and I'll drive you back down.'

'I wouldn't hear of it. Go into the morning room and get some coffee. You must be frozen. Besides, you're needed in there. Our tame film star has arrived, together with his producer.'

'Rex Ransom? Great. I've been looking forward to meeting him. What's he like?'

'Very nice. No pretence to him at all. But the producer is very much out of his element. Daddy's been struck dumb with awe, and Mummy, who doesn't approve of them, is being frostily formal and polite. As the only others in there are Mummy's cousin Cecily, who hasn't been here for twenty-five years and keeps asking after people who are dead, and her idiot husband, who does nothing but grin inanely and say 'Jolly good,' the atmosphere is rather sticky. I've been doing my best to keep the conversational ball rolling. You can take over.'

41

'Oh, gosh, Gerry, it sounds frightfully grim.'

'It is. But to someone who's climbed Everest—'

'The Matterhorn.'

'—it will be child's play. So come on.'

*   *   *

Ten minutes later Gerry, driving her beloved Hispano Suisa towards the village, drew up by a lone figure, kit-bag over his shoulder, who was trudging along the road.

She leant over and opened the passenger door. 'Hop in.'

Hugh looked at her. 'Why?'

'I'll give you a lift to the station. There's a train to London in about ten minutes. You'll never catch it otherwise.'

He hesitated, then threw his kit-bag into the back and got in next to her. She drove on. He said, 'I won't be able to catch that train, anyway. I've got to stop at the garage about my bike.'

'I'll see to that.'

'No, thank you.'

'Well, there's not another train to town today.'

'Then I'll have to stay till tomorrow. I suppose there's a pub where I can get a room.'

'There's the *Rose & Crown,* but I doubt if they'll give you a room.'

'Why on earth not?'

'It's a highly respectable house. And they're very particular about who they take in. Of course, I could come and put in a good word for you.'

'Very funny.'

'Look, as it seems you've got to stay overnight in the area, why not come to the house? You needn't

42

see Paul, or any of the guests. We'll put you up in the servants' quarters, if you like. You can eat with them and everything. I don't suppose they'll mind.'

'Again, no thanks.'

'*Why*, Hugh? What's the matter?'

'I don't like being made a fool of. Inviting me at the same time as Carter, without telling me, when you know how I feel about him?'

'I didn't tell *him* you were coming, either.'

'That makes things no better.'

Gerry was silent for a moment. She said, 'You're quite right. It was thoughtless. I'm sorry.'

He looked at her in surprise. 'My word, that must have taken some effort.'

'Don't rub it in.'

'Why did you do it, Gerry? You must have known we'd both be annoyed.'

'Paul's not annoyed.'

'Want to bet? He just doesn't show his feelings.'

'A trait you might well try to emulate.'

'Why?'

'It's a sign of good breeding.'

Hugh gave a snort. 'That's just the sort of talk that repels me about all your class.'

'In that case I can't think why you accepted the invitation in the first place.'

'Because I thought you wanted me here.'

'I did. I do.'

'But why? Why now—with Carter and all those other people? You must have realised I wouldn't exactly be the brightest company.'

'I—I wanted you to meet Rex Ransom.'

'*What?* You thought I'd want to meet that prancing purveyor of mindless mush!'

'There's not only him. There's Arlington

43

Gilbert.'

'Who is Arlington Gilbert?'

'A writer. A creative person, like you.'

'Never heard of him. What's he write?'

'Film scripts mainly, I think.'

'For Ransom, I suppose?' Gerry didn't answer. 'Geraldine, this just won't do. You're up to something. I want to know your real motive for inviting me.'

'I don't admit there is one. But if there were, there'd be only one way you could find it: by staying for the weekend.'

'And have to watch you ogling and smooching with Carter all the time?'

'Ah! Now we come to the true reason you don't want to stay. You're jealous.'

'Of course I'm jealous! I'm in love with you.'

'Most of the time you behave as though you hate the sight of me.'

'I hate a lot of the trappings you surround yourself with—the privileges of rank and unearned wealth. I hate the inane conversation of your friends, the Philistine outlook on life of your whole circle.'

'I don't think I'm a Philistine.'

'No, I couldn't love you if you were. You've got a good brain. With a free hand I could mould you into something special.'

'What an utterly ghastly prospect,' she said.

They reached the village. Gerry said, 'Well, how about it? Coming back?'

There was a pause before he replied. 'Oh, all right. I suppose so.'

Gerry said, 'Thank you *so* much for the invitation, Geraldine. It's *awfully* kind of you. I really *do* appreciate it.'

Hugh said, 'Don't forget the garage.'

She drove on to Jenkins' Garage and pulled up in front. Hugh got out and disappeared into the workshop. Gerry sat and waited for him. But she could never sit doing nothing for long, and she suddenly grabbed a duster, got out and started vigorously—and rather unnecessarily—polishing the windshield. She was hardly conscious of the car that drew up alongside her, so she didn't raise her head when a voice nearby said sharply, 'Hey! You!' It was not a form of address she was accustomed to.

But then the voice repeated irritably, 'You! Girl! With the duster,' and she turned in surprise.

She saw a very small baby Austin car, driven by a very large man with long black hair. Sitting next to him was a severe-looking middle-aged woman. It was the man who had spoken, and now he did so again.

'Yes, you, girl. How do I get to old Lord Burford's place? Look lively. I haven't got all day.'

Gerry felt herself start to flush and she opened her mouth, prior to letting him know what she thought of him. Then she paused. Of course. This had to be Arlington Gilbert. She had had a full report of his appearance and conversation from her father. So she'd better watch her tongue.

Then an idea struck. She let a vacant expression come over her face and she strolled towards the Austin, wiping her nose with the back of her hand. In a broad west country accent she asked, 'What 'ee say?'

Gilbert said again, 'How do I reach Lord Burford's residence?'

45

Gerry leant up against the car. 'What 'ee wanna know for?'

Gilbert gave a bellow. 'It's no business of yours, but I happen to be spending the weekend there.'

With an exaggerated gasp, Gerry stepped hurriedly back from the car. He looked startled. 'What's the matter?'

Gerry made her eyes big. 'Do 'ee be gonna stay at the big 'ouse? Sleep there? Cor, mister, Oi wouldn't like to be 'ee. Nor 'ee, missus.'

The woman glared at her. 'Miss.'

Gilbert said sharply, 'What on earth do you mean?'

Gerry looked furtively over her shoulder, stepped right up to the car again and whispered, 'Things 'appen at big 'ouse.'

'What are you talking about? What sort of things?'

'Moighty queer things. They d'yu say folks bain't never the soime again arter a noight at the big 'ouse. Those that leaves at all, that is.'

'I've never heard such utter balderdash!'

Gerry shrugged. 'All roight, mister, 'ave it your way. Only don't say 'ee ain't been warned.'

'Just tell me how to get there.'

At last Gerry told him. He gave a curt nod and thrust the car into gear again.

'One more word, mister,' Gerry said.

He glared at her. 'Well?'

'D'yu 'ee watch out for that there Lady Geraldine.'

'Watch out? What the deuce are you talking about, girl?'

'That's all I be gonna say. Just 'ee be careful, that's all.'

46

And Gerry turned away and went on with her polishing. Behind her she heard Gilbert give an exclamation of disgust and the car drive quickly away.

A few seconds later Hugh reappeared. 'All set?' she asked.

He nodded, 'They'll pick it up straight away.' He pointed after the disappearing Austin. 'Who was that?'

'A very remarkable man.'

'Oh? In what way?'

'He's even ruder than you are.'

*   *   *

In the Austin, Gilbert said, 'What a very odd young woman.'

Maude Fry said, 'And remarkably well-dressed for a garage hand.'

'Was she? I didn't notice. Probably her father's a smuggler.'

'Thirty miles from the sea?'

'Well, a coiner, or whatever branch of villainy is the most popular down here. What did you make of all that rigamarole?'

'About the big house? Bad hats in every old family. Legends grow up around them. Don't die out for generations.'

'I was really thinking of what she said about Lady Geraldine. Do you suppose she's insane, or something? Dabbles in black magic? Takes drugs?'

'I would guess nothing so dramatic. Probably she's just a maneater—one of those depraved young women one reads about, around whom no male is safe.'

47

'I see.' Gilbert nodded slowly. 'Yes. That's quite possible.' He unconsciously raised a hand and patted his hair. 'I wonder if you're right. It'll be interesting to find out, won't it?'

Maude Fry sniffed.

CHAPTER FIVE

Arlington Gilbert and Maude Fry arrived at the house fifteen minutes later. Merryweather conducted them to the morning room. But before he could announce them, Gilbert marched past him into the room. Rather more slowly, Maude Fry followed him.

Just inside the door, Gilbert paused and stared round appraisingly. 'Yes,' he said with a decisive nod, 'this would be ideal for the proposal scene. Though all this Regency stuff will have to go. Make a note, Miss Fry.'

'Yes, Mr Gilbert.' Maude Fry took a pair of blue-tinted spectacles from her bag, put them on, got out a notebook, wrote in it, then put both glasses and book away.

Meanwhile, the Earl, seeing his wife begin to swell visibly, hurriedly stepped forward, holding out his hand. 'Ah, Arlington, how are you?'

Gilbert's eyebrows rose slightly. 'Tolerably well, thank you, er, George. Nice place you have here.'

It was Lord Burford's turn to look decidedly surprised. 'Oh, thanks. Let me introduce you.'

'Don't bother, George. I'll soon find out who everybody is. Jupiter's teeth, though, I could do with some coffee! I'll help myself.' He strode across to where the coffee things were laid out.

The Earl rejoined Rex Ransom and Haggermeir, while Lady Burford, taking sudden pity on the rather lost-looking Maude Fry, went across and spoke to her.

Lord Burford lowered his voice. 'Strange feller, that,' he murmured to Rex. 'Called me by my first name.'

Rex said, 'Well, actually, you did call him by *his* first name.'

'I didn't. I called him Arlington.'

'That's right. Arlington Gilbert's his name.'

The Earl snapped his fingers in irritation. 'I keep thinking it's Gilbert Arlington. Dash it, it ought to be! Oh, drat—suppose I've got to keep it up now. It'll seem as if we're bosom friends.' He turned to Haggermeir. 'Do you know him well?'

'Not at all. But I made some inquiries after he called. He's quite well-known as a solid all-around writer. Had a couple of successful plays in the West End some years back and wrote quite a few film scripts. Hasn't done anything recently. Said to have made enough to live on and is working on a big epic novel.'

'And you'll be using him on *The King's Man*?'

'Looks like I may have no choice,' Haggermeir said grimly.

'I see. Still, I suppose if he can provide Mr Ransom with a good script we'll have to put up with him.'

'Surely,' Rex said, 'if you call him Arlington, you're going to call me Rex, aren't you?'

Lord Burford's face lit up. 'Really? May I? Oh, I say. I'm, er, George.'

Rex bowed. 'Glad to know you, George.'

49

By the time Gerry and Hugh arrived at Alderley the little party in the morning room had broken up, the guests having mostly retired to their rooms to unpack. Hugh went straight to his room and Gerry sought out her father.

'Did Gilbert arrive?' she asked.

'Arlington? 'Fraid so. Why?'

'Did he ask about me?'

'Yes, wanted to know when he'd be meeting you. Why?'

'What did you say?'

'Probably for drinks before lunch. Why?'

'Good. Mummy won't be there then, will she?'

'Doubt it. Why?'

'You'll see.'

'Look, what are you up to?'

'Never mind. Just don't be surprised at anything about me.'

*   *   *

'Ever thought of trying to make it in pictures?' Rex asked.

Paul laughed. 'Good heavens, no.'

'Why not think about it? You've got the looks and the physique.'

'For one thing, I can't act for toffee.'

'Don't let that stop you. It didn't stop me.'

'Oh, no false modesty, my dear chap,' Lord Burford said. 'You know you're one of the world's great actors.'

Rex gave an exaggerated start. 'Jumping

50

Jehosophat! Hey, Cyrus.'

Nearby, Haggermeir, a dry martini in his hand, was conversing with Cecily. He looked up. 'Yeah?'

Rex said, 'Just say that again, will you, George—slowly and distinctly.'

'Certainly.' He did so.

'D'you hear that?' Rex asked triumphantly. ' "One of the world's great actors." George, you've made a buddy for life. You're the only person—apart from my ma—ever to say that. And she doesn't say it too often. Just once in a while to try and convince herself.'

'Be careful, Lord Burford,' Haggermeir said, 'that's the way to wreck his career. If Rexy once gets it into his head he can act he'll want to start proving it. And *Hamlet's* box office poison.'

Lord Burford scratched his head. 'I don't understand. You mean *you* don't think he's a good actor?'

'Wa-all.' Haggermeir shrugged.

'But you amaze me, my dear fellow. To me he's every bit as good as Errol Flynn.'

'Can't hold a candle to Rin Tin Tin, though,' Rex said with a grin.

Quite perplexed by this, the Earl looked round the room. Cecily had moved away and was talking to Maude Fry, while Gilbert had cornered Sebastian and was holding forth on the iniquities of literary agents, emphasising his points with a series of prods to the chest, at every one of which Sebastian took a little step backwards. Standing alone, his face set in a scowl, was Hugh.

Lord Burford was wondering if he should go across and talk to him, though the young man's demeanour didn't suggest he'd welcome this. The

51

Earl was just wishing Gerry would come in when the door opened and she entered.

Everyone glanced automatically towards her— and there was an abrupt silence.

Gerry had changed out of the tweed suit and brogues she'd been wearing earlier and was now attired in a slinky, tight-fitting dress of black satin and very high-heeled shoes. Her face had been almost free of make-up before, but now her eyes were painted with mascara and her cheeks were rouged. Her hair was swept upwards to the top of her head. She was smoking a cigarette in a six-inch holder. She crossed the room in a sinuous, undulating walk.

Lord Burford closed his eyes, Paul coughed into a handkerchief and Hugh stared in horror.

Gerry made a straight line for Gilbert. He watched her approach with the fascination of a rabbit watching a snake. Gerry stopped in front of him, gave him a long, cool stare, slowly exhaled a lungful of smoke and said softly, 'Arlington Gilbert.'

She held out her hand in a regal gesture. Uncertain whether to shake it or kiss it, Gilbert compromised by taking it and giving a sort of half bow. 'At your service, Lady Geraldine.'

'I have long been an ardent admirer of your work, Mr Gilbert—'

Then, as he straightened up, gazing at her with a mixture of gratification, alarm, admiration and bewilderment, she broke off and said in a decidedly frosty voice, 'Mr Gilbert, you are looking at me as though I were something the cat had dragged through a hedge backwards. Why?'

Gilbert gave a start. 'I beg your pardon, Lady

Geraldine. It's just that—there was a girl in the village earlier . . . Jupiter's teeth, it's incredible!'

'I see nothing incredible. There are many girls in the village.'

'But this one was—forgive me—the absolute image of you. In a bucolic way, of course.'

'But naturally.'

'I'm sorry . . . ?'

'Mr Gilbert, my family has held sway over this district for hundreds of years. Until quite recently they virtually had powers of life and death over the peasantry. Even today there are hundreds of them dependent on this estate. My father is certainly the first lord of the manor of whom—unfortunately—the great majority of them are not absolutely terrified.'

For a moment Gilbert looked blank. Then comprehension dawned. 'I see. And you mean that your ancestors exercised this power, er, liberally?'

'Of course. You could no doubt find half a dozen girls in the vicinity who bear a resemblance to me.'

Gilbert chuckled. 'That sounds as though it would be a very worthwhile pursuit. But why did you use the word 'unfortunately' just now?'

Gerry took his arm and drew him to one side. She spoke softly. 'My father cares not a fig for power. If he did, the mere terror of our name would mean we could control these people as our forefathers did.' Her voice grew harsher. 'They could not get away with their present laziness and insolence.'

'Insolence? Well, I must admit that girl I mentioned was unusually cheeky.'

'Tell me: was she employed at the garage?'

'That's right.'

'Pah!' Gerry banged a nearby table with her fist. 'That hussy is one of the worst. And they say she is the one most like me in appearance. She no doubt made disparaging remarks about me. The things I'd like to do to that girl! Oh, for the power my great-great-grandmother had! Do you know what she did once to a serving wench who'd displeased her?'

Gilbert shook his head.

Gerry put her head close to his and whispered in his ear. As he listened, Gilbert's expression changed. He gave a gulp. Gerry drew back and gazed at him with satisfaction.

'And you'd, er, like to do the same to that garage girl?'

'Actually, I can think of some interesting refinements.'

Gilbert gave a sickly grin. 'I must say I'm sure your peasants don't appreciate just how lucky they are to be so free.'

'They'd better enjoy it while they can.'

'Oh, yes?'

'Yes. You see, I know of several ways in which our—or rather, *my*—dominance over them could be asserted as in old times. Absolutely reasserted—body *and* soul.'

For a moment Gerry's eyes shone with a fanatical light. Then suddenly this faded and she was giving Gilbert a warm smile. 'However, that's enough of me. Mr Gilbert, did I say how very great an admirer of your work I am? I do feel I'm going to become just as keen an admirer of you as a man. Do come and sit down and tell me all about yourself.'

And she put a hand on his and drew him unprotesting but bewildered across the room to a sofa.

*   *   *

Over lunch the atmosphere at Alderley grew considerably easier. Lord Burford, basking in the fact that he and Rex were now 'buddies,' had lost all his nervousness and was his usual self. Rex meanwhile concentrated on exerting all his considerable charm on Lady Burford, and in spite of herself the Countess could not help gradually softening under the impact.

The fact that Gerry was playing a hoax on Gilbert had also got round among the other guests, and everybody was waiting with anticipation for the next development. However, for the time being she contented herself with remaining largely silent and throwing him long and meaningful looks from under her lashes.

It was towards the close of the meal that Merryweather entered, bearing a silver salver on which was a telegram. He took it to Haggermeir.

As Haggermeir read it his eyebrows went up. 'What in tarnation . . .? This doesn't make sense. Lady Burford, it seems you may be having another guest shortly. I think you'd better read this.' He passed it to her.

Lady Burford picked up her lorgnette and read aloud, 'Invitation accepted. Arriving Alderley Thursday afternoon. Lorenzo.' She gazed at Haggermeir. 'Who is this person?'

'Search me.'

'You don't know a Mr Lorenzo?'

He shook his head. 'And if I did I'd certainly not invite him here without your permission.'

'How very strange,' Lady Burford said.

Gerry said, 'May I see?' She took the telegram. 'Handed in at a London post office. No address of sender. Quite a mystery.'

'Well, we certainly won't sit around waitin' for the chap,' Lord Burford said. 'What d'you all want to do with yourselves this afternoon?'

'Well, I know what I want to do,' Rex answered, 'and that's to see your famous gun collection.'

Haggermeir nodded. 'Me, too.'

The Earl looked delighted. 'Oh, capital. Great pleasure. Anybody else? Arlington?'

Gilbert nodded condescendingly. 'I don't mind.'

'Sebastian?'

'Oh.' Sebastian looked doubtful. 'Guns? Will—will—will they be going off? Can't stand bangs, you know.'

'There is a firing range up there, and I may demonstrate one or two. But I'll give plenty of advance warning, so anyone who wants to leave can do so.'

'Oh, right. Jolly good.'

'Am I invited?' Cecily asked.

'Oh, of course, my dear. Didn't think you'd be interested. Ladies aren't very as a rule.'

'I can't say I am normally. But your collection *is* world famous, and I would like at least a glimpse of it.'

'Splendid. Any more for the Skylark? Hugh?'

'I don't like guns,' Hugh said shortly.

'Oh, as you wish, my boy. Paul—you saw it last time you were here.'

'Yes, but I didn't do it justice. I'd love to have

56

another look.'

Hugh glowered at him, 'On the other hand,' he said loudly, 'I understand the craftsmanship on some of these old pistols is very fine. I'd like to see them from that point of view.'

Lord Burford looked pleased. 'That's everybody, then. He glanced round the table, counting on his fingers. 'No, that's wrong. Who did I leave out?'

'Me, I think, Lord Burford.' It was the quiet Maude Fry who spoke.

'Oh, I'm sorry, Miss Fry. You're very welcome, of course.'

'Thank you. Like Mrs Everard, I should be interested in at least a glimpse.'

It was therefore a party of eight which, half an hour later, Lord Burford led up to the first floor. At the top of the stairs he turned right. Halfway along the eastern corridor he opened a pair of double doors on the right and led the way through a long gallery, which ran most of the outer side of the wing. It was lined with painted portraits and was unfurnished, except for a number of sofas and upright chairs against the walls.

The Earl crossed the gallery to another door opposite. This was the entrance to the top floor of the eastern extension, the ballroom being beneath it. Lord Burford unlocked it with a key attached to his watch chain, saying as he did so, 'Live ammunition in here as well as the guns, so I always keep it locked.'

Immediately beyond the door was another one. The Earl unlocked this one also, then stood back and ushered his guests through.

They found themselves at the end of a long,

57

delightfully proportioned room, with French doors leading onto a balustraded balcony at the end, beyond which the lake could be seen.

But the visitors noticed practically nothing except the hundreds of guns with which, apart from a clear path down the centre, the room was filled. Pistols were in display cases, rifles slung around the walls, while at the far end a number of cannon and other large guns were standing. One section of the room was partitioned off to form a firing range, and there was a large cupboard where Lord Burford kept ammunition and various accessories.

Except for Paul, the visitors each gave a little gasp as they entered. Then they just stood, staring round in amazed disbelief.

The years had given Lord Burford a great deal of experience in showing his collection. He knew well what interested people and had a fund of anecdotes concerning his exhibits, which—to their own surprise—kept even Sebastian, Hugh and the two women attentive. Two hours in fact passed quickly for everybody, and it was past four when they all trooped out, the Earl carefully locking up again.

They were making their way along the corridor when Cecily said, 'Oh, by the way, George, don't I remember something about a secret passage here?'

'Yes, I'll show you.'

He turned into the main corridor and opened the second door on the right. This was a room used for linen storage. As the others crowded in after him, Lord Burford crossed to the far wall, put his hands against one of the wooden panels, and pushed to the right. The panel slid sideways, revealing a large black square.

'There you are,' Lord Burford said. 'Comes out in the breakfast room downstairs. Anybody feel like going down through it? No takers?'

'Well, you know,' Cecily said, 'I really wouldn't mind. I used to love stories about secret passages when I was a girl. Sebastian—shall we?'

'Oh,' Sebastian looked dubiously at the black hole in the wall. 'I hardly think so, precious. Awfully dark and dirty, what?'

'Dark,' the Earl said, 'but there are flashlights. And it's reasonably clean.'

'No—no—no, I'd much rather not, actually, if you don't mind,' Sebastian said. 'Spiders, you know, moths and things. Unpleasant generally.'

'Yes, I suppose you're right,' Cecily said, a little wistfully. 'I certainly wouldn't want to go on my own.'

'Madam, pray allow me to act as guide.' Paul stepped forward. 'I know this passage like the back of my hand. Been along it on at least—oh, one occasion.'

'Why, thank you,' Cecily said.

Paul stepped into the gap, reached for the shelf above his head and found the flashlight that was kept there. He switched it on. 'Very well, Mrs Everard, if we're to make camp by sundown, we'd better get moving.'

'Oh, right.' Cecily gave a giggle and stepped in.

'Mind the doors,' said Lord Burford, and he slid the panel across.

The Earl was waiting in the breakfast room when Paul and Cecily emerged into the light of day a few minutes later. 'Well, how was it? Rather borin', eh?'

Cecily blinked. 'Well, perhaps a little. But at least I can say I've been along a secret passage now.'

* * *

When Gerry came into the drawing room for tea she had transformed herself. She was wearing a simple jumper and skirt, sandals and bobby socks. All make-up had been removed and she had done her hair in two plaits tied with ribbon. She practically skipped about the room, prattling girlishly, and eating a great number of cream cakes, which she pronounced 'scrumptious.' Eventually she sat down by Gilbert and began plying him with questions about his work, such as didn't he find it terribly difficult spelling all those horrid long words?

Except for Maude Fry, everybody else—even the Countess—was now in on the joke and all behaved perfectly normally, making no comment on the transformation. Gilbert, however, was plainly utterly perplexed—and alarmed. At last, finding it increasingly hard to keep a straight face, Gerry retired to the window seat and curled up with a book entitled *The Most Popular Girl In The School*, which she'd brought in with her.

Gilbert immediately sidled over to Rex and tugged at his sleeve. 'What do you make of that?' he hissed.

'What?'

'Lady Geraldine. She was so different! You must have noticed.' He lowered his voice still further. 'I think she's a—a *schizophrenic*.'

Rex frowned sharply. 'Don't say anything, man.'

60

Gilbert's jaw dropped. 'You mean she is, *really*?'

Rex just put his fingers to his lips.

Gilbert walked shakily away and started whispering furiously to Maude Fry.

*   *   *

'Just been thinkin',' Lord Burford said. 'Haven't given you much time to start your inspection of the house, have we?'

'Oh, that's OK, Earl,' Haggermeir said. 'I wouldn't've missed your collection for the earth. Maybe, though, I could make a start after tea.'

'By all means. What exactly do you want to do?'

'Well, I'd just like your permission to wander all over the house. I want to measure the rooms and corridors, make rough sketches showing the positions and sizes of all the doors and windows, take some photos—all so I can figure out distances, camera angles, lighting and sound problems, decide which rooms could be used for the various scenes, and so on.'

'That's fine by me, old man. Go wherever you like.'

Before Haggermeir could reply, the conversation was interrupted by the entry of Merryweather, who approached them, said 'Excuse me, my lord,' and addressed Haggermeir. 'A visitor has arrived and is asking for you, sir.'

'Ah, is it our friend Lorenzo, by any chance?'

'That is the name, sir.'

Haggermeir said, 'I'll come out.'

Lord Burford said, 'No need, my dear chap. I'm sure we all want to see this mysterious stranger. Is this person presentable, Merryweather?'

61

'Eminently so, I should say, my lord.'

'Then let the stranger be presented.'

Merryweather bowed his head and withdrew. Half a minute passed and then he reappeared, to announce solemnly, 'Signorina Lorenzo.'

There was a stunned silence as a magnificent figure swept imperiously into the room. She was about thirty-five, tall, with long, jet-black hair, dark flashing eyes and a flawless complexion. Her features, bold and regular, were more striking than beautiful. She looked as though she might have a superb figure; however, at the moment, it was obscured by a sumptuous mink coat, which made the eyes of every woman present widen. On her head she wore a toque in matching fur.

She stood, regally surveying the room.

Rex muttered, 'Holy mackerel! It's *Laura* Lorenzo.'

Haggermeir stepped somewhat hesitantly forward. 'Signorina Lorenzo? This is, er, indeed a great . . .'

She eyed him up and down. 'Who are you?'

'Oh—sorry—I'm, er, Cyrus Haggermeir. I believe you—'

'Ah.' She gave a satisfied nod. 'You are Haggermeir. So, Meesta Producer, you want Laura Lorenzo, eh? Well, here she is. Perhaps you will have her—if you can sateesfy her. But it will cost you. Oh yes, it will cost you many dollars.'

For several seconds Haggermeir gazed at the woman, speechless. At last he managed to stammer, 'I—I see. Well, that's—that's certainly a most interesting . . . Do I—er, understand that you're offering me your services?'

'That is what I am here to talk about, is it not?'

'You are? I see. Well, in that case, perhaps . . .'

She said, 'Are you seek?'

'Seek? Oh, *sick*. No, I'm fine.'

'Then why you behave like an imbecile?'

Haggermeir's eyes bulged and Rex gave a snort of suppressed laughter. Laura bestowed on him a crushing glance—into which puzzled semi-recognition could be read—before turning back to Haggermeir. 'I have met many producers. Some have been peegs, others Pheelistines or creeminals. But never have I met one who was a fool. Now, do you or do you not want me for your talkie.'

Haggermeir coughed. 'Gee, that'd be swell. I hadn't given the possibility any thought, but—'

'*You have not given the posseebility any thought?*' Laura positively screeched the words. 'Do you dare say that after you send me the telegram pleading with me to come here and talk about it?'

'I sent you no telegram.'

Laura froze. Then she spun on her heel and strode out of the room. As she did so she called loudly, 'Eloise! My handbag. Quickly!'

For seconds nobody spoke. There was a general letting out of breath. It was Lady Burford who found her tongue first. In a voice touched with ice, she asked of anybody who cared to answer, 'Who is that woman? She is, I take it, an actress of some sort?'

'Just about the best dramatic actress in Italy,' Rex said, 'perhaps in the whole of Europe.'

Hugh nodded firmly. 'Certainly among, the top half dozen. And she's actually considering signing with Haggermeir . . .' He gazed at the producer with an expression of incredulity.

'Must say I've never heard of her,' Lord Burford

remarked.

Rex said, 'Well, she's not done any English-language pictures for years—not since she made her name. In the States you can only see her movies in little art houses in the big cities. But she's the darling of the highbrow critics. And most of the Hollywood moguls have been trying to sign her for years.'

At that moment Laura again sailed into the room. She was carrying a telegram. This she thrust into Haggermeir's hand with a triumphant gesture. Haggermeir stared at it for a few seconds, then said, 'I know nothing of this.'

Laura scrutinised his features in silence for a moment, her own face darkening, her fingers twitching, her body almost seeming to pulsate before them. It was, as Gerry later remarked, like waiting for Vesuvius to erupt. Then she suddenly burst into a stream of impossibly rapid and passionate Italian. Her arms flailed, her eyes flashed. Vehemently she addressed the ceiling and each corner of the room in turn. There was clearly only one thing to do, and that was wait for her to run down. Gradually she did so, and then just stood, panting.

'So,' she said to Haggermeir, 'somebody play the—what you call—practical joke, yes?'

'It would seem so.'

'When I find him he will know what practical jokes really are.'

Paul said, 'May I see that telegram?'

Haggermeir passed it to him. 'Better read it out, son.'

Paul read aloud, 'Signorina Laura Lorenzo, Savoy Hotel, London, WC2. Offer starring role my next movie stop. Great English civil war extravaganza stop. Top payment stop. Cordially invite you come stay weekend Alderley to discuss stop. Cyrus S. Haggermeir.' He looked up. 'Handed in at Westchester post office five p.m. yesterday.'

'At that time I was still in London,' Haggermeir said.

Lord Burford said, ' 'Straodinary thing.'

Almost for the first time, Laura seemed to become aware of the other people in the room. She looked round at them vaguely. She said, 'I am sorry I will not have a chance to meet all you folks. But I go now.' She turned back to Haggermeir. 'Goodbye.' She started for the door.

Haggermeir said hastily, 'Now, hang on, signorina, please. The only reason I've never offered you a part is because I never figured you'd be interested. Can't we discuss it some more?'

She eyed him appraisingly. 'So, you do invite me to stay, after all?'

Haggermeir looked embarrassed. 'Well, I can hardly do that—'

She stiffened. 'May I ask why not?'

'Well, I'm only a guest here myself.'

She looked blank. 'Only a guest? I do not understand. Have you not taken this house? Rented it?'

'Good grief, no. I'm just staying with Lord and Lady Burford here.'

Laura's face was a study. She seemed quite disconcerted. She turned towards the Earl and Countess. 'Oh, Lord Burford, Lady Burford, I am so sorry. I took you all to be members of Signore Haggermeir's party—feelm people.'

'Well, I for one am flattered,' said the Earl. 'Just what sort of film person did you think I might be?'

'But an actor, of course.'

'Really?' Lord Burford preened himself. 'Hear that, Lavinia?'

'Yes, George. Signora, allow me to make some introductions.'

She went round the circle. Laura was now all charm, smiling bewitchingly at everybody. When Lady Burford came to Rex she said. 'And I'm sure I don't have to tell you who this is?'

Laura puckered her brow. 'The gentleman's face is familiar, but I regret I do not . . .'

Lord Burford interrupted. 'This is Rex Ransom!'

'Ah, yes, of course.' Laura held out her hand. 'Do forgeev me, but I have not seen any of your peectures—er, unfortunately.'

Rex shook hands and gave a stiff smile. 'That's quite OK. I haven't seen any of yours either.'

Lady Burford said hurriedly, 'Mr Hugh Quartus.'

Hugh said, 'While I, on the contrary, have seen all your films, Signorina Lorenzo. May I say it's an honour to meet one of the world's great actresses.' Then, in Italian, he added: 'This has made the weekend worthwhile.'

Laura looked delighted. 'Grazie, signore. Siete davvero troppo gentili.'

When Lady Burford had completed the introductions she said, 'Now I do hope that you'll stay for the weekend.'

'Unfortunately, that will not be possible. I must be on the set in Roma early Monday, and I go back to London first to see my English agent. I would like to stay two nights, but is vital I leave here by meed-day Saturday.'

'Then that's settled,' said the Countess. 'Now, will you excuse me?' She rang the bell, then went outside to meet Merryweather in the hall. 'Merryweather, Signorina Lorenzo will be staying two nights. Where do you suggest we put her?'

'Apart from the Royal suite, my lady, on the first floor the Spangled and Lilac rooms in the west wing, and the Dutch in the east are free.'

'Not the Royal Suite. And both the Dutch and the Lilac are rather small.'

'Yes, my lady, but on the other hand, the Spangled bedroom is where the—the'—he cleared his throat—'the sudden death took place. It occurs to me that if Signorina Lorenzo should become cognisant of the fact it might disturb her.'

'Yes, quite right. Put her in the Dutch. And have a large fire lit and make sure the room's kept really warm. I imagine as an Italian she finds our winter rather hard to bear.'

CHAPTER SIX

Rex Ransom's brow puckered as he made his way to his bedroom to dress for dinner. He was worried. Had that telegram to Laura Lorenzo just been a hoax? Or was Haggermeir, in spite of his denial, responsible for it? Had he wanted to invite her, but not liked to ask the Burford's permission—or, more likely, not wanted him, Rex, to know he was after her for *The King's Man*? Either way, it seemed on the cards that she would sign. And Rex didn't like the idea at all.

For years his name had been the only one to appear above the title of his pictures. Laura Lorenzo, however, would certainly demand at least an equal billing—perhaps even top billing. Moreover, her first Hollywood picture would undoubtedly be something of an event. The top critics would attend press screenings in force. Haggermeir might even give it the full publicity treatment of a gala premier. Rex could see himself being reduced to the level of a supporting player.

His lips set tightly. He would not stand for it. He'd fight for his rights. And he had one trump card: Cyrus needed *his* cooperation to get this picture off the ground. It was *him* the Earl was a fan of. It was *his* charm that was going to win over the Countess.

As Rex reached his room on the corner of the main block and the west wing, he looked right and saw Haggermeir—camera round his neck, a tape measure and writing pad in his hands—leave an empty room at the end of the corridor. Rex was tempted to go and tackle him immediately. But then Haggermeir disappeared up the stairs to the next floor, and Rex opened the door of his room.

As he did so, he was hit by a blast of cold air. He switched on the light—and stopped.

Where the window had been was a gaping black hole. And the floor was littered with broken glass.

Rex stood hesitating, wondering what Emily Post would say was the correct thing to do under the circumstances. He shivered. Well, he couldn't pretend it hadn't happened. He'd freeze to death in here.

He went in search of his host.

*   *   *

Lord Burford stared round Rex's bedroom. He scratched his head. 'How very peculiar. I meantersay, if one of the maids had got careless and backed a broom through the window, you'd hardly expect her to do quite such a wholesale job. Likewise if small boys are trespassin' and started throwing stones.'

Rex said tentatively, 'I have heard of big birds—geese and suchlike—smashing into windows in the dark.'

The Earl looked impressed. 'That's a thought. You may—ah!' He bent down and picked something off the rug. It was a grey feather, two-inches long. 'Looks as if you may have hit the nail on the head, old man. Wonder if the creature killed itself. I'll send a servant to look outside in a moment. But what are we going to do with you? That's the problem. Of course!' He snapped his fingers. 'The Royal Suite.'

'Oh, I couldn't possibly—'

'Nonsense, Rex. We don't keep it exclusively for royalty. Besides, you've been a prince and a king in your time, so you ought to feel quite at home.'

'I've also been a pirate and a highwayman. All the same, I'm surely honoured.'

'Good. I'll arrange with Merryweather to have it made ready.'

Lord Burford smiled.

*   *   *

Dinner that evening was a great success. The food

was a highly traditional English menu, most of it the actual produce of the estate; mushroom soup, grilled trout, roast beef and Yorkshire pudding, apple tart and cream and Cheddar cheese, with an excellent selection of wines.

But it was as a social gathering that the occasion turned out far better than could have been anticipated. This was due largely to the presence of Laura. She looked exquisite in an extra-tight sheath gown of black velvet, split over emerald satin; and although she didn't herself speak much, she seemed to act as a sort of catalyst on some of the others.

Lady Burford, for example had quite forgiven Laura's earlier behaviour on learning of the misconception she had been under; and was, in fact, secretly delighted to have a Serious Dramatic Actress added to the party. She had learnt that the highly respectable and respected magazine *The Londoner* had recently devoted a long and fulsome article to Laura, who was clearly a fit person to be entertained at a house where Sarah Bernhardt had once stayed—and who would provide a most useful camouflage for the other film people; they could now be represented to friends as having been merely necessary appendages to Signorina Lorenzo. Consequently, the Countess was far happier with the house party than she had been.

Laura also brought out the best in Rex. Determined not to be outshone by her, he put all he had into making an impact, and compliments, jokes and anecdotes of the stars flowed from his lips throughout the meal.

The third person affected by Laura's presence was Hugh. It was obvious to everybody that he'd been deeply smitten by her, and to his delight, found himself sitting next to her. He talked animatedly to her all through dinner, mostly in Italian.

Gerry was rather irritated by his attentiveness, but she was honest enough to realise that she could have no real cause for complaint. Anything was better than the way he'd been behaving since his arrival.

Having run out of ideas for new characterizations, Gerry had decided just to be herself this evening. However, as this was a personality Gilbert had not previously seen, it was to him as much a new side of her as the others had been. Sitting opposite her, he stared at her with a fearful fascination.

It was during dessert, when Rex had just completed an amusing story concerning a backstage incident at the previous year's Oscar ceremony, that Lord Burford addressed the company at large.

'By the way, talking of prizegivings reminds me: wonderin' if you'd all care for a little jaunt tomorrow evening.'

'I'm game for anything,' Rex said. 'What do you have in mind?'

'Well, it may be a bit of a bore for you, Rex, but ever since the village learnt you were coming they've been agog, wonderin' if they were going to get a chance to see you.'

Rex grinned, 'I'm happy to display the old visage, sign a few autographs.'

'Actually, there's a little more to it than that. You see, each year about this time they hold a talent contest. Everybody turns out, and I usually

71

act as one of the judges and present the prizes. Well, this year's contest is tomorrow night—seven o'clock—and I was wondering if you'd hand out the awards.'

'I don't want to steal your job.'

'I've done it dozens of times. No it'll be a nice break for me, and a real thrill for the village.'

'Then I'll be glad to.'

'Oh, fine. As a matter of fact, the committee put the contest back a week when it first got round you were coming, in the hope you'd agree, and I said I'd do my best. Now, how about you, Haggermeir? Care to be one of the judges?'

'Me? Oh, I don't think so, thanks—'

Rex interrupted. 'Now, come on, Cyrus, you might discover a new Shirley Temple.'

'I'm afraid that's highly unlikely,' the Earl said. 'Most of 'em are pretty ghastly, actually, though there are usually two or three who aren't too bad.'

'Well, I guess they couldn't be much more lousy than some of the screen tests I see every week. OK then.'

'Splendid. I'll telephone the chappie who's organising it in the morning and tell him to expect a couple of VIP guests.'

Gerry said, 'Daddy, don't forget we have more than just two VIP guests.' She inclined her head slightly towards Laura.

However, as she did so, Arlington Gilbert said, 'Thank you, Lady Geraldine, but I can think of no more revolting way to pass an evening than witnessing the cavorting and caterwauling of bucolic *brats*.'

Gerry bridled. 'Personally, I wouldn't miss it for the world. It can be the most spiffing fun. Paul, you'll come?'

'Certainly. Try anything once.'

'Hugh?'

'Thanks, but I'd rather not.'

Lord Burford, who'd got the gist of his daughter's hint, turned to Laura. 'Forgive me, signorina, for not including you. 'Fraid it just didn't occur to me that you ...'

Rex said lightly, 'Oh, I can't imagine that such a distinguished and intellectual actress would find such an event at all amusing.'

Laura smiled at him sweetly. 'You are quite wrong, Mr Ransom.' She looked at the Earl. 'I should enjoy much watching the dear leetle bambini performing, and helping you judge them.'

Avoiding the eye of Rex, who was looking very slightly disgruntled at this, Lord Burford said, 'Well, we're going to have quite a party. Anybody else who'd like to join us, of course, will be more than welcome.'

Hugh said, 'Thank you, Lord Burford. I think I'll change my mind and come along.'

Now it was Paul's turn to look displeased. He said, 'Come with me in my car, Gerry?'

'Yes, of course.'

She glanced a little anxiously at Hugh. But he was looking at Laura.

*   *   *

When coffee was being served in the drawing room after dinner, Rex suddenly said, 'Do you know, George, what I've been looking forward to ever since I knew I was coming here: learning something of the history of Alderley and of your ancestors. There must be quite a few interesting stories in nearly three hundred years.'

'Oo, don't know about that. Pretty dull lot, actually. Most of 'em just hung around here, looking after the estate and collectin' things.'

'Surely, they can't *all* have been dull?'

'Well, there was the fifth Earl. He was very mechanical. Built a flying machine. Powered by gunpowder. Tried to take off from the roof of the east wing. People still fish bits of the machine out of the lake from time to time. And the Earl, for all I know. Then there's the business of the seventh Earl and the Westshire Declaration of Independence. Got the idea from the American colonists. Proclaimed the county an independent republic, with himself as president. Couldn't get anyone to take him seriously. So he went to London, bought up several tons of tea and dumped it in the East India dock. But nobody took any notice. He couldn't understand it. Said it had worked for the colonists. His wife came and took him home then.'

Cecily said, 'George, wasn't there a ghost at one time?'

'Oh, you mean Lady Elfreda.'

'That sounds interesting,' said Paul.

'Not especially. Daughter of the eighth Earl. Shut herself up in her room for the unrequited love of a dancin' master and swore never to eat again.'

'What happened?' Cecily asked. 'Did she die?'

'Oh, yes.'

'She starved herself to death for love?'

'Just the opposite. Kept it up for three days, then crept down in the night and stuffed herself with a rather doubtful game pie they'd been going to throw away. Died of food poisonin'. We still hear her voice sometimes. Calling for castor oil.'

'Wasn't your grandfather something of a character, sir?' Paul asked.

'Oh, old Aylwin. Well, I agree, you couldn't call him dull.'

'Tell us about him,' said Haggermeir.

'He wasn't exactly an admirable character.'

'So much the better,' said Rex.

The Earl collected his thoughts. 'Aylwin was a holy terror from the start. Always in scrapes—playing practical jokes, taking up dares. Got through dozens of nursemaids. No viciousness in him, mind. Just high-spirited, with a keen—if not very subtle—sense of humour. And apparently quite fearless. When he was eleven they sent him to Eton. There he was constantly in trouble for fighting, being out after hours, and was eventually expelled after being found playing cards for money in a public house. He came home for a few years, made life miserable for a succession of tutors, and was generally thoroughly pestilential throughout the neighbourhood. By the time he was eighteen he already had a county-wide reputation for drinking, gaming, wenching, fighting, and all kinds of wild stunts.

'Then, for the first time, he fell in love. The girl was a Lady Mary Carruthers, the daughter of a large landowner, with an estate ten miles away. She was as different from Aylwin as chalk from cheese—small, pretty, demure, shy—but he proposed after knowing her a week. And she accepted. However, her parents wouldn't hear of it. For one thing she was only sixteen, and although

75

it would have been a very advantageous match for her, his reputation was just too bad for them.

'Aylwin, though, wasn't going to let that stand in his way. He asked Mary to run away with him. She agreed, and accompanied by Aylwin's manservant—a fellow called John—they eloped. They were making for Gretna Green in Scotland, to be married over the anvil as the saying went. 'Course, it wasn't long before Mary's parents found out what had happened, and her father and Aylwin's set off in pursuit—though not, I imagine, with much hope of catching them in time.

'But, by sheer luck, they did run them to earth, at an inn just short of the Scottish border. The youngsters gave way to the inevitable then. Explained that they'd been held up when the carriage had gone into a ditch.

'Aylwin and Mary were taken home in disgrace. But Mary's parents were so relieved to find that Aylwin had behaved as a perfect gentleman throughout, and her virtue was unblemished, that they didn't take the matter any further and a scandal was avoided.

'But Aylwin's father had by then taken just about all he could take of his son. He gave Aylwin five thousand guineas and told him to clear off. He never wanted to see him again.

'Aylwin didn't argue. He took the money and left, again with the faithful John in tow. He spent the next couple of years in London and Paris, until eventually he had just a few pounds left. With most of this he bought two tickets to America. He and John set sail in August, 1842.

'Now, he succeeded in winning about twenty pounds at cards on the voyage. It was the only money-making skill he had, and it seemed to him that his best course was to try and earn a living at it. After a few weeks in New York, though, he decided that he'd have a better chance of doing this out West.

'Aylwin took to the West like a duck to water. He loved the free and easy atmosphere, the opportunities for adventure and excitement. He was tough, knew how to use his fists, and was a first-rate horseman. As a result, he seems to have got on famously, and for the next six or seven years he roamed far and wide. Exactly how he kept himself all that time I don't know. He certainly made a living as a professional gambler for a spell; but he also went fur trapping, acted with a touring theatrical company, and had a few bouts as a professional prizefighter. He fought Indians, shot a man in a gunfight at Dodge City, and became a close friend of Kit Carson.

'Then in 1849 came the California gold rush. Aylwin was actually in Sacramento when the first strikes were made and was among the first at the gold diggings. What's more, he made a strike. Not a fabulously rich one, but it made him money enough to live on for at least a couple of years. So, still accompanied by his servant John, he made his way to San Francisco for a holiday.

'Meanwhile, back here, his father had been in failing health for some time, and had been told by his doctor that he couldn't expect to live for more than another year. He wanted to see his son and patch up their quarrel before it was too late. Now, Aylwin had been writing tolerably frequently to his mother—care of her sister, so that the old man wouldn't hear of it—and consequently she at least knew that he was in San Francisco. So an employee of the family solicitor was sent to try and trace him. After several weeks he at last tracked Aylwin down.

'Aylwin, I imagine, had by then had about enough of the life he'd been leading. He knew his cash wouldn't last indefinitely and then it would be back to the old ways. However, he still had enough left to return home in some style, so his pride wouldn't suffer if he did go back. The short of it was that he arrived home early in 1852 and was quickly reconciled with his father. The old man died six months later, and Aylwin succeeded to the title as tenth Earl. That's just about the whole story.'

There was silence for a few seconds before Paul said, 'But what happened to him? What did he do for the rest of his life?'

'Nothing much. Ran the estate, became a pillar of the Tory party, took his seat in the House of Lords.'

'Whom did he marry?' Cecily asked.

'One guess.'

'Not Lady Mary?'

'The same. She'd waited for him and she was only twenty-eight or -nine when he came home. I think they were very happy. Had four children, my father being the eldest. Sorry if the end's a bit of an anticlimax.'

At that moment Merryweather entered. He approached the Earl. 'My lord, the window of the Grey bedroom has been boarded up.'

'Oh, fine.'

'No bird's body was discovered outside, but there were some more feathers.'

78

'I see.'

'And a thought has just occurred to me, my lord. The burglar alarm: I fear it will be impossible to turn it on. The contact will have been broken when the window was smashed. If the current is now switched on, the alarm bell will be automatically activated.'

'Lor', I suppose you're right. Oh, well, can't be helped.'

Merryweather departed and Lord Burford hastened to explain to his guests. 'Few years ago we had a very complex alarm system installed—too complex, really. Supposed to be foolproof, but it means that after it's switched on you can't open an outside door, or any window more than two inches, without setting it off. In fact, your bedroom windows have got stops fixed, though they can be forced easily enough in an emergency. However, as it would be pretty inconvenient if nobody could go outside during the evening without setting off the alarm, we don't usually switch the system on till the very last moment. Tonight, though, seems we won't be switching on at all.'

'Well, at least the burglars don't know,' said Gerry. 'That's the main thing.'

*   *   *

It was when the party was breaking up two hours later that Rex drew Lord Burford aside. 'In view of what's happened, I wonder: could you lock some money in your safe for me?'

'Of course—delighted. Go and get it now. I'll wait for you in my study.'

Three minutes later Rex entered the study to

find Lord Burford ready with the safe open. He took a bulging billfold from his pocket and handed it to the Earl, who raised his eyebrows. 'Quite a bundle here, by the feel of it.'

'Something over two thousand pounds.'

'Great Scott! D'you always carry that much cash around with you?'

'Mostly. Psychological thing, I suppose. Makes me feel secure. Didn't always have a lot of dough. And I'm a country boy, raised not to trust banks. Don't mention it to Cyrus, will you? He thinks I'm crazy enough already.'

'Oh, shan't tell a soul.' Lord Burford put the billfold in the safe, closed the door and spun the combination knob. Together they left the room.

CHAPTER SEVEN

Cyrus Haggermeir looked at his watch, wound up his tape measure, left the room on the top floor of Alderley and made his way down to his bedroom. He went in—and stopped. Sitting in the room's only chair was Laura. In her hands was the script of *The King's Man*. She looked up with a smile.

'Do forgeev me, Meesta Haggermeir. I thought I would like to see the screenplay of the movie. I was going to ask to borrow it, but as you weren't here I deed not like to take it away.'

'Oh, that's OK.' He took his camera from around his neck and put it down.

'Will you be wanting this tonight, or may I take it to my room to feenish it?'

'You understand that's only the old silent

version?'

'Of course, but the plot of the sound version will not be much deefferent, will it? Though naturally I understand that it will have to be, er—what you say—adapted to feet me.'

'Ah. Yeah.' Then he said a little awkwardly: 'Signorina, I, er—well, I'm not sure I can use you on this movie.'

She drew in her breath. 'What is it you say? *You* cannot use *me*?'

'Well, not—that is—'

She jumped to her feet, again breaking into a torrent of Italian.

Haggermeir held up both hands. 'Please, no, signorina. No understand Italiano.'

Eventually she ran out of breath and stood staring at him, her eyes flashing. 'Signore, you eensult me. Do you not know the big Hollywood men, they all—Goldwyn, De Mille, Warner, and Korda in England—they all want to sign up Laura Lorenzo. They go on their knees. They grovel in the dirt. But always I say no. Until now. I offer you my services. And you? *You* turn me down. I not forget this!'

Haggermeir ran his hands through his hair. 'Don't get me wrong, signorina. I'd be tickled pink to sign you up. It'd be a terrific feather in my cap. But for another movie, not for *The King's Man*. It's not your sort of picture. It's a crummy old story—'

'*Sciocchezze!* Nonsense! It is a fine story.'

'It is? You think so?'

'Of course.'

'Well, maybe for Rex. But there's no part in it that would suit you.'

'No part? You are mad. The part of Anne-Marie

81

might have been written for me. It just needs to be—what you say—written up, made bigger. True, she is French, but she can be Italiano just as well. Call her Anna Maria. Where is the problem?'

'I'm not sure Arlington Gilbert would go along with that.'

'Geelbert? You let your writers deectate to you?'

'Not normally, but he's a touchy guy. Now, look, what I'd like to do is commission a screenplay from a really first-rate writer—S.N. Behrman, say, or Llllian Hellman—just for you.'

'Fine words, Meesta Producer, but disguising the seemple fact that you do not weesh to have me in your movie. Well, do not fear that you will have to. Do not imagine that you will ever get the opportunity.'

And she flung the script at his feet and swept from the room.

*   *   *

Gerry stood in her room, surveying herself in a full-length mirror. She gave a satisfied nod at what she saw. She was wearing a plain white sleeveless nightdress. She had combed out her hair, so that it fell straight to below her shoulders. She had applied a very pale, almost white, face powder and a bright scarlet lipstick, very thick. The effect was dramatic.

She opened her dressing table drawer and took from it a long-bladed carving knife, which she'd sneaked from the kitchen earlier, and practiced holding it in various positions, rubbing her thumb lightly along the blade. She rehearsed several different kinds of smiles. At last she felt ready.

She'd realised earlier that it was nearly time to abandon her hoax on Arlington Gilbert. However, she couldn't just let it fizzle out. It had to end with a bang. This last personality was going to be her *piece de résistance.* Afterwards she'd tell him the truth.

She opened the door and went outside. Brr, but it was cold. She must get this over as quickly as possible.

She turned right and hurried past the intervening bathroom to Gilbert's room. She paused outside, then gently turned the knob and pushed the door open an inch. No light showed, nor was there any verbal challenge. Gerry slipped in, silently closed the door behind her, and stood quite still, her heart beating fast.

She took a deep breath and stepped forward. The knife was held behind her back, ready to be brought forward at the crucial moment. What she was going to do after he saw it she didn't know. It would depend on his reactions.

When Gerry judged she was in the middle of the room she stopped. Then she spoke, softly and wheedlingly, in the voice of a little girl.

'Oh, Mr Gilbert.'

There was no reply. Gerry raised her voice. 'Mr Gilbert, would you like to play with me? I'm so lonely. Do wake up and play. I have a lovely toy here.'

But still there came no response.

Suddenly Gerry grasped the truth. She stumbled back to the door and switched on the light. The bed was empty.

She gave an exasperated exclamation. All for

nothing. What a waste!

Then abruptly she realised how very relieved she was. She'd been behaving extremely childishly—not at all like a mature young woman with two prospective fiancés under her roof. So, back to her room quickly, before he returned.

But, she wondered, returned from where?

He hadn't just gone to the bathroom. It had a fanlight over the door and the light was out.

She looked round the room again and took in the fact that the bed had not been disturbed and that a pair of pyjamas were folded on the counterpane. It must be nearly forty minutes now since she'd seen him come in here, and it seemed he must have left again almost immediately. Perhaps he'd gone to talk to somebody. Haggermeir—about the script for the film, say?

Then Gerry saw something else. On the bedside table was a glass. And in it was a set of false teeth.

She pondered. Surely no one would go to talk to somebody and leave his false teeth behind. He might have gone to the library to get a book. But he'd never have stayed all this time. So—where was he?

Gerry thought hard. She didn't trust Arlington Gilbert, and she found herself consumed by an intense urge to know just what he was doing. For Alderley contained many valuable things. The burglar alarm was out of action. And if Gilbert was light-fingered, tonight would present a fine opportunity for him to do some thieving, fake a forced entry and put the robbery down to some mythical burglar.

Gerry knew she had to try and find out what he was up to.

84

Hastily she returned to her room, donned a woollen dressing-gown, wiped her face free of make-up, put a flashlight in her pocket, and left again. She was still carrying the knife, which she intended to return to the kitchen. This time she turned left, went to the main stairs and started down. It was quite dark, but she didn't turn the lights on, just flicked her torch on and off occasionally. She knew the house intimately. Gilbert didn't. So the darkness would give her a big advantage. Besides, she didn't want to risk being seen herself, apparently spying on a guest.

It was just as she reached the bottom of the stairs that she heard the sound.

She couldn't be sure exactly what it was, for it was muffled. But she knew where it came from.

Her father's study.

Gerry stared towards the study door, which led directly off the hall. She felt a prickling up and down her spine, which had nothing to do with the cold.

What on earth could he want in there? Her father kept no valuables in the study. Only a few pounds in a cash box, family and estate papers, account books, correspondence. Of course, Gilbert might not know that.

Well, there could be no innocent reason for him—or anyone else—being in there. So there was no cause now for concealment.

Gerry marched to the study, paused for a moment, threw open the door and reached for the light switch just inside. She pressed.

But the room remained in darkness.

Only then did it occur to her that with the alarm out of action a real burglar could have got in. Her heart gave a lurch. But she'd shot her bolt. In a voice that quavered only slightly, she said:

'Who's in here?'

At that second a thin beam of light from a flashlight pierced the darkness, hitting her full in the eyes.

Gerry groped frantically for her own flashlight. But before she could get it from her pocket she was aware that someone was coming towards her.

With a great effort she held her ground. In her right hand she was still gripping the carving knife. She raised it, holding it out in front of her like a sword, and said loudly, 'Keep back. I've got a knife.'

With her other hand she at last managed to get out her flashlight. She was fumbling desperately to switch it on, when it was wrenched from her grasp and fell to the floor.

Now very frightened indeed, Gerry slashed with the knife. She felt the blade make contact with something and heard the man give an exclamation of pain. But he drew back only momentarily, and the next instant he'd grabbed her wrist, forcing her to drop the knife. She opened her mouth to scream, but he must have anticipated this, for as she did so he released her wrist and clapped his hand over her mouth. She struggled furiously.

Then, unexpectedly, he pushed her to one side. She staggered, tripped, and sat down hard on the carpet. She drew her breath for a shout. Then she froze.

All was quiet—and there was complete darkness.

He'd turned off his flashlight. He was just standing silently, waiting to pounce as soon as he knew her exact position.

At that moment she heard another noise. But it wasn't in the room. It sounded like some sort of scuffle, maybe a fall or hurrying footsteps. It was from above, probably from the top of the stairs.

Gerry sat quite still, holding her breath.

*   *   *

Rex Ransom sat before the dying fire in the magnificent bedroom of the Royal Suite, sunk in gloomy forebodings. At last he stirred and gave a little groan. Keeping up his gay manner throughout the evening had really taken it out of him, and on coming to his room he had flopped down without even removing his evening jacket. Now he felt awful. He had let the room get cold, and he was stiff, uncomfortable and more depressed than ever. There was coming over him, too, that dreaded feeling of oppression, the sense of something pressing in on him. He had to do something about it quickly. He stood up, took off his coat and started to remove his cuff links.

Three minutes later, stripped down to shorts and undershirt, Rex stared down at the two objects he was holding. How he hated them. Yet they were so necessary to him. He couldn't carry on without them.

At that second, to his alarm, he heard a slight sound from the next room.

The Royal Suite consisted of three connecting rooms: a sitting room, nearest to the grand staircase; next to it the bedroom; and then a dressing room. Rex had told Merryweather to have a fire lit only in the bedroom. It was from the sitting room that the noise had come.

There was nothing sinister about the sound—just a sharp tap, as though someone's foot had knocked against a piece of furniture. But why should anybody be in there, creeping about in the dark?

Rex swung round towards the adjoining door and saw to his consternation that it was open a couple of inches. He took a step towards it. Then he stopped. For there appeared through the crack a black-gloved hand.

Taken utterly aback, Rex stood momentarily transfixed as the hand, followed by a black-sleeved arm, moved like a deadly snake along the wall. Suddenly he came to his senses, gave a shout of anger and took two hurried steps towards the door. But he was too late. The hand had reached the light switch and the room plunged into darkness.

Rex stood motionless. In the blackness there was not much else he could do. In his best actor's voice he barked, 'Who is that? What are you doing here?'

There was no reply.

Rex backed a little towards the bed. Able to see nothing, dressed as he was and barefooted, he felt uncomfortably vulnerable. He spoke again, with a brash confidence he was far from feeling, 'OK, the joke's gone far enough. Clear off and I'll forget about it.'

He felt a rush of cold air hit him as with a creak the door opened wide. He heard footsteps approaching.

He shouted, 'I know who you are—'

Then a blinding light seemed to engulf him. Rex gave an exclamation and staggered back, dropping the objects he had been holding, as the room again went black.

For a second he flinched, waiting for an attack. But suddenly a sense of the indignity of his situation swept over him. Was this the way for the great Rex Ransom, dashing hero of thirty swashbuckling adventures to behave—skulking in a darkened room, waiting submissively to be set upon?

Never!

Rex gave an exclamation of rage and strode blindly forward, swinging random punches. For seconds he punched the air. Then one of his fists made contact with a face. It was a glancing blow, probably in the vicinity of the eye. But it gave him a surge of satisfaction, especially as it drew from his adversary a muffled gasp.

Rex gave a yell of triumph, 'One for all and all for one!'

The words were quite inappropriate, but they were the only ones he could think of. Then he realised that the intruder was retreating before him, making for the door. Since extinguishing his flashlight, he must be as blind as Rex himself. There was a chance of collaring him.

Rex kept moving forward. But then he heard the door to the sitting room slam, and a second later his outstretched fingers touched the door panels. He fumbled for the knob and pulled the door open. He heard somebody blundering across the sitting room, towards the corridor door. Rex groped for the light, but before he could get it on he heard that door in turn open and close.

About to go after him, Rex instead paused. He couldn't possibly go outside in this state, not at

Alderley. He turned and went back into the bedroom, switching on the light. As he did so he thought he heard some sort of commotion from the corridor or landing outside. He grabbed for his dressing gown.

*　　　*　　　*

Gerry sat on the study floor. She had heard not a sound since the small rumpus from upstairs a minute before. Very quietly she let out her breath. He was gone; she was sure of it. Carefully she got to her feet, felt her way to the desk, groped for the reading lamp and switched on.

Apprehensively she peered round. The room seemed in order. She'd been half expecting to see the safe door open and the desk drawers on the floor. But there was no sign at all of the intrusion, or of her titanic struggle with the intruder. Which was, in a way, rather irritating. She crossed to the window and examined it. It was intact and locked—virtual proof that it was no outsider she'd been dealing with.

The bulb from the centre of the room had been removed and was on the desk. Gerry fetched a chair to stand on and replaced it. Then she found her flashlight and left the study, switching off the light. She went to the kitchen, replaced the knife and made her way upstairs in the dark. For the moment she couldn't quite think what to do next. The obvious thing would be to rouse her father and take him to confront Gilbert. On the other hand, a scene of that sort would upset the Earl terribly. And Gilbert wouldn't try any more funny business tonight. Perhaps, then, it would be better to do nothing now and make a decision about her next move in the morning.

Gerry had nearly reached the top of the stairs when the light on the landing above her went on. She gave a start and blinked upwards, fearfully. Then she said, 'Mr Ransom!'

Rex gazed down at her, in obvious surprise. 'Lady Geraldine.'

She said, 'I—I thought I heard a noise.'

'Yes, so did I.'

He looked immaculate in an elegant mohair dressing gown, not a hair of his head out of place—and certainly not like someone who'd just got out of bed.

'It sounded like a sort of scuffle,' she said. 'But I expect it was just somebody stumbling in the dark.'

'Probably. Well, in that case I think I'll get back to bed. Good night, Lady Geraldine.'

'Good night, Mr Ransom.'

Rex returned to his room and at last got into bed. He lay on his back, staring up into the darkness. But it was a long time before he slept.

CHAPTER EIGHT

On Friday Alderley awoke to an even colder day. In addition; there was a strong north wind and the sky was a surly grey. The weather had none of the crisp, bracing quality of the Thursday.

Somehow this change seemed to be reflected in the atmosphere indoors. So, at least, it seemed to Lord Burford at breakfast. He was down early and had only just started his meal when to his great surprise the first person to join him was Gerry.

'Good gad!' he said. 'You all right?'

'Couldn't sleep.' She sat down and started buttering a piece of toast.

Her father looked astonished. 'No bacon and eggs?'

'No, I'm not hungry.' She spoke absently.

'Can't sleep and off your feed? You must be sickenin' for something.'

But Gerry wasn't listening. She was staring intently at the door, which was just opening. Then she visibly relaxed as Rex came in. He said good morning and sat down. There were dark circles under his eyes, and though he responded cheerfully to the Earl's remarks, his good humour was clearly forced. He too kept his eyes fixed on the door.

Sebastian and Cecily, Haggermeir, Paul and Hugh arrived during the next ten minutes and all seemed strangely preoccupied. Each was subjected to the closest scrutiny by Rex.

Then the door opened again and Gilbert entered. Lord Burford looked at him and gave an exclamation. 'My dear chap! What have you been doing to yourself?'

His words drowned Rex's quick intake of breath, and no one noticed the sudden expression of triumph in Gerry's eye. For down Gilbert's left cheek ran a long strip of bandage. And his right eye was a most magnificent shade of purple.

Gilbert said nonchalantly, 'Two quite separate mishaps. I walked into a cupboard door and then, while shaving with my old cut-throat, I slipped, and gashed myself. However, they say suffering is good for the creative artist.'

He went to the sideboard and helped himself to two large kippers.

Rex said, 'If you'll excuse me.' He stood up and strolled out. So now he knew. Gee, that punch he'd landed must have been harder than he'd realised. And thank heavens for it, for now he could act.

Gerry left the breakfast room a few minutes later and returned to her bedroom to think. The cut on Gilbert's cheek proved beyond doubt that it was him she'd slashed at in the study. But what was she going to do about it? She couldn't bring herself to tell her father. After so much apprehension, the Earl was now enormously enjoying the house party. To be told one of his guests was a crook would be to rekindle his fears of a repeat of that other disastrous weekend—and take away all his pleasure at the visit of Rex Ransom. What was more, without absolutely cast-iron proof, Lord Burford would certainly not just send Gilbert packing. He would merely worry. And if she told her mother, the Countess would undoubtedly go straight to the Earl.

Gerry was tempted to ask Paul's advice. But it seemed hardly fair to invite him to stay and then involve him in her problems.

No, she had to resolve the affair on her own. And really there was only one straightforward course: to confront Gilbert privately and give him the opportunity to make some excuse and leave. It would be a horrible task; bad enough at the best of times, but now complicated by her idiotic behaviour toward him the previous day. Whether or not she now revealed that she had been the girl at the garage, he'd have good grounds for putting round the story that Lady Geraldine Saunders was a candidate for the looney bin. And any accusation she made about his searching the study would just seem additional evidence of this.

However, there was no way out. Gilbert was up to no good, and had to be got rid of. At least he didn't, thank heaven, know about her nocturnal visit to his bedroom.

Gerry went downstairs again, deciding to wait outside the breakfast room and waylay Gilbert when he came out. She'd been there for five minutes when she saw Laura Lorenzo, who'd breakfasted in her room, descending the stairs,

Laura this morning was wearing a lettuce-green tweed jacket and corduroy trousers. She smiled charmingly. 'Ah, *buongiorno,* Lady Geraldine.'

'Good morning. I hope you slept well.'

'Oh, *si*, I did, *grazie*.'

'Sorry you've got such a pokey little room, right down at the end of the corridor.'

'Oh, that does not matter. It is a beautiful room. And such a lovely fire! For the first time since I arrive in England I am warm enough.'

Then over Gerry's shoulder she exclaimed. 'Signore Geelbert!'

Gerry swung round to see Gilbert emerging from the breakfast room. But before she could speak to him, Laura had swept past her. '*Scusatemi*, Lady Geraldine. Signore Geelbert, a queeck word with you.'

'What? Oh, of course, pleasure.'

Laura took him by the arm. 'Perhaps we can go somewhere quiet.' She led him away.

*   *   *

'So, Signore Geelbert, that is quite definite?'

'Quite.'

'*Bene, bene.* I'm glad we understand each other. I just wanted to make quite sure. Now I must leave you. I have not long here and there is much that I must see to. Goodbye.' She went out.

Gerry saw Laura leave the small music room, where she'd been having her tête-à-tête with Gilbert, and walk off. She waited a moment and entered the room herself.

Arlington Gilbert was seated at a table near the window. He looked up as Gerry entered and his face took on an expression halfway between alarm and excitement. Gerry said, 'I want to speak to you, Mr Gilbert.'

He stood up. 'Oh?' His face now displayed a kind of apprehensive attentiveness, as though he was trying to work out which of Gerry's personalities was on display this morning. 'What about?'

'I think you know quite well.'

'I assure you, I—'

'Let's stop playing games. That cut on your face: you didn't get it shaving; I did it.'

He positively boggled at her. '*You*?'

'Oh, don't pretend you didn't know who it was!'

'I had no idea!'

'Well, now you do. And I want an explanation.'

'*You* want an explanation? Don't you owe me an explanation—and an apology?'

Gerry gave a gasp. 'Me apologise to you? What on earth for?'

'Well, do you normally go around attacking your guests in the middle of the night?'

'No—just defend myself when they sneak

around in the dark and manhandle me.'

He gave a roar. 'I did not manhandle you! You ran into me.'

'I did nothing of the sort!' Then Gerry took a grip on herself. This was most undignified, and not at all as she had envisaged the conversation. More quietly she said, 'Who ran into whom is immaterial. What I want to know is what you were doing there.'

'I can't answer that.'

She said incredulously, 'You refuse to tell me?'

'I do.'

'But you had absolutely no right to be there!'

'*No right*? Jupiter's teeth, what sort of place is this? Alcatraz? Do you set a curfew, make certain areas off limits to your guests?'

'No, of course not! But we don't expect them to go snooping around in the dark.'

'I was not snooping!'

'Then why didn't you switch the light on?'

'Why didn't you?'

'You'd taken the bulb out!'

'I had not!' He said this with such vehemence that for a moment she couldn't manage to argue; after all there was no way to prove it.

Rather lamely she said, 'Well, somebody did.'

'Not me. And anyway, what were you doing spying on people in the middle of the night?'

'I wasn't spying.'

Suddenly his face cleared. 'Oh, I see?' He chuckled slyly. 'Date with one of the boyfriends, was it?'

'Certainly not!'

'Tell that to the marines.'

'I was looking for you, you fool!'

96

She could have bitten her tongue off as soon as the words were out, but simply stared dumbly at him.

Gilbert gave a start. 'Looking for me?'

'Yes, but—'

'Well, well, well,' he said slowly. 'I must say this puts a different complexion on things. And I won't say I'm not flattered. I am, of course, attractive to women, and I'm quite familiar with these sudden irresistible urges they get.'

Utterly speechless, Gerry just stood, her mouth open, the dozens of scathing words she wanted to utter stuck in her throat like a log jam on a river.

Gilbert continued thoughtfully, 'Now, I must try and work out just what happened, because it's all very confusing. I take it you went first to my room?'

Gerry gulped. 'I—'

He smiled. 'I can see you did. Don't be embarrassed—it's quite natural. You found my room empty, and, of course, were bitterly disappointed.' He took a step towards her. 'I'm terribly sorry, Geraldine, but I couldn't know you were coming. And now that I understand the situation, I don't mind telling you what I was doing. But one thing first: when we ran into each other, you must have realised you'd found the person you'd been seeking. Why then did you claw my face?'

At last, presented with a straight question, Gerry managed to reply. Through clenched teeth she hissed, 'I did not claw your face!'

'But my dear, you said—'

In a sudden bursting of frustration, anger and humiliation, Gerry yelled, 'I didn't claw your face. I

97

did it with a carving knife!'

For seconds Gilbert didn't react at all; his face wore the same slightly pulled but patiently indulgent expression. Then it was as though something clicked. His jaw dropped.

He said hollowly, 'You came looking for me with a—a carving knife?'

'Yes! Now listen—'

But Gilbert had gone pale. Hurriedly he stepped back. He said, 'Keep away.'

Desperately Gerry shouted, 'You great imbecile, you don't understand—'

'Oh, yes, I do—only too well. I was warned about you, Lady Geraldine. I didn't know what the warning meant. But I do now. You're mad. Certifiable. You ought to be locked up!'

'Will you listen?' Gerry screeched. 'You've got it all wrong. I want to know what you were looking for. Either tell me or leave this house at once.'

'Well, I wasn't looking for a victim to stab! And don't worry, I'm going. Now. Nobody's safe with you around. It's monstrous that you're walking about free. The power of the aristocracy! Disgraceful! I shall show it up!'

And being careful to remain facing her, Gilbert sidled round her, backed to the door and went hurriedly out.

Gerry sank helplessly into a chair. She felt exhausted. Oh, crumbs, what a ghastly mess she'd made of that!

But at least he was going. To spread abroad heaven knew what sort of rumours about her. He'd make her out to be a maniac certainly—but whether on reflection he'd paint her as merely a nymphomaniac, or homicidal as well, she wasn't

98

sure.

Suddenly Gerry's lips started to twitch. Then she gave a giggle. Next a chortle. Within seconds she was bent double in her chair, helpless with laughter.

*   *   *

Laura opened the door to the library and looked in. The only person inside was Paul, who was kneeling on the floor, peering under a chair.

She said, 'Oh, *mi scusi.*'

'It's all right.' Paul stood up. 'I was just looking for my fountain pen. Thought I might have dropped it in here yesterday. But no luck. It's rather a nice one: gold, twenty-first birthday present from my godmother.'

'Ah, then it would be a peety to lose it.'

'Were you looking for somebody in particular?' he asked.

'It is no matter. I am seemply exploring this beautiful house.' She looked round her. 'Would it be eendeescreet of me, signore, were I to ask whether perhaps one day it will be your home?'

'Mine?'

'Forgeev me, but I got the impression that you and the Lady Geraldine were—were . . .'

'Oh, I see.' Paul grinned. 'Well, I'd certainly like to think we were. But I'm not banking on it.'

'Ah, you have a rival?'

'You could say that.'

'Signore Quartus, I think? And you hate each other, yes?'

'Great Scott, no!'

'But if you are both in love with the same

99

woman . . .'

'That doesn't mean we hate each other. After all, we're not Latins, who—' He broke off, in confusion. 'I'm sorry, I didn't mean—'

Laura laughed, a rich appreciative laugh. 'Not crazy, hot-blooded Italianos? No, Signore Carter, you are certainly not that. You especially are very English, are you not? And so you stay in the same house as your rival, and you are very polite, and if the Lady Geraldine eventually chooses him you will smile and shake him by the hand and tell everyone what a frightfully decent chap he is. Right?'

Paul laughed. 'I sincerely hope the situation doesn't arise. But if it does, it wouldn't do any good to cut up rough. Just have to grin and bear it.'

'And suppose veectory should go to you. Will Signore Quartus also green and bear it?'

'I expect so. I mean, what else could he do?'

'Oh, quite a lot of theengs. You see, signore, you say you do not hate Hugh Quartus. But I look at his face once or twice last night, and I theenk very much he hate you.'

Paul felt decidedly embarrassed. 'I say, steady on.'

'You theenk perhaps that because I am an actress I seek the melodrama everywhere, eh?'

'Oh, I wouldn't presume to say such a thing.'

'Which means you do theenk it. Perhaps you are right.' Laura leant forward and helped herself to a cigarette from a box on a nearby table. 'Will you have one?'

She pushed the box towards Paul.

'No, thanks, I don't smoke.'

'Ah, no, of course not: you are an athlete, are

you not? Deed I not hear it said that you competed for England at the Olympic games?'

'That's right.'

'And deed you ween a medal?'

'No, just missed out: I came fourth.'

'What was your event?'

'Three thousand meters steeplechase.'

'Steeplechase? Ah, yes, that is the one where they jump over the hurdles, yes?'

'That's it. But I shan't be doing much more serious competitive running.'

'I'm sure a boy so feet and active will not be content to seet around and do nothing, though?'

'No, as a matter of fact, I'm very fond of climbing.'

'Indeed? But that is a very dangerous hobby, no?'

'It needn't be if you take reasonable precautions.'

'So you have never fallen?'

'Touch wood.' He tapped on the table with his knuckles.

'It would be a terrible death, I theenk.'

'I can think of worse. Very quick.'

'But eemagine those few seconds while you were actually in the air.'

'I'd rather not imagine them, thanks!'

'You have never known anyone fall to their death?'

'No, never.'

She stubbed out her cigarette half-smoked and stood up. 'I have to go. I do not have long here and I must make the most of the time. There are people I must speak to. *Scusatemi.*'

'Of course.' He stood up, too.

She smiled, crossed the room and opened the door. She was just going through when from outside a voice spoke, 'Oh, signorina, I've been looking for you. Can we talk privately? It's important.'

Paul remained standing after Laura had gone. For some reason he felt strangely uneasy. There seemed something in a way sinister about that woman. He gave a sudden shake of his shoulders. Oh, he was being ridiculous!

Now. His pen. Where could it be? He hadn't used it since he'd arrived. So, it must have fallen out of his pocket. And that could only happen when he was bending over. Had he had occasion to stoop at all since he'd been here?

Of course, the secret passage! The roof in there was very low in several places.

Paul went upstairs and a minute later was again making his way along the passage, carefully scrutinising the floor as he went. However, he met with no success, and by the time he'd reached ground level and knew he could be only yard from the end, he'd more or less given up hope.

Then by his feet he saw the slightest gleam. He knelt down. Yes, there it was. What a stroke of luck! The trouble was it had slipped down a deep crack between two bricks and looked as though it might be tricky to extract; if he knocked it, it could easily slip even further down. He felt in his pocket for something to hook the pen up with and brought out a comb. He was gingerly trying to slip the end of it under the pen clip when he gave a start that nearly made him lose them both.

From close beside him he heard a voice.

It took Paul a few seconds to realise what had

happened. Having nearly reached the end of the passage he was now behind the breakfast room panelling. The person talking must be standing very near the wall.

It occurred to Paul he was eavesdropping. But for the moment there was no avoiding this. So precarious was his hold on the pen that he couldn't relax his concentration for a second, or he might lose it altogether. So he remained quiet, gradually drawing the pen out and listening with half an ear to the slightly muffled voice.

At last he got his fingers on the pen and lifted it clear of the crack. He was about to stand up and make his presence known by banging on the wall, when he heard some words that caused him to jerk his head up in utter amazement.

Paul remained frozen as the voice went on, saying incredible things. He knew listening like this was a caddish thing to do. But he couldn't help himself.

Occasionally the voice paused, the 'silences' occurring obviously as the other person in the room spoke. But Paul could hear nothing of this; plainly only the one speaker was near enough to the panelling to be audible.

For two or three minutes Paul remained where he knelt. Then the voice simply stopped in mid-sentence, though Paul couldn't tell whether the speaker had left the room or simply moved to the far side of it. He made his way to the end of the passage, slid back the panel, and peered cautiously into the breakfast room. It was empty.

CHAPTER NINE

After leaving Gerry, Arlington Gilbert hurried up to his room. He was breathing heavily. He threw open the door, burst in, and stopped. Standing by the mantelpiece was a grim-faced Rex Ransom.

Rex said, 'At last. I've been waiting to have a little chat with you. You know what about.'

'I assure you I don't.'

'Don't play the innocent with me. Just tell me what your little game is.'

'Game? Are you mad?'

Rex stepped forward menacingly. 'Listen, buster, I'm warning you: spill the beans, unless you want me to black your left eye like I blacked your right last night.'

Gilbert gave a start. 'You—you did that?'

'Who the blue blazes did you think it was?'

'Now, listen to me—'

'No, you listen. I've got a good mind to beat you to a pulp.'

'Do so, and I shall sue you for assault. Fine publicity for you. I can't see the Burfords agreeing to the movie being shot here after that sort of behaviour.'

Rex closed his eyes for a few seconds and got a grip on his temper. Then be said slowly, 'I just want to know what you were up to last night.'

Gilbert turned away. 'I refuse to discuss the matter.'

Rex was silent. He dared not push Gilbert too hard. He might just make things worse for himself. So it seemed the only course now was to play for time, in the desperate hope that his worst foreboding was not about to be realised.

He said, 'You may not be able to keep that attitude up for long. I advise you to think over what I've said. I'll give you until tomorrow morning to come clean.'

'I shan't be here tomorrow morning.'

'What do—'

'I'm leaving. *Now.*'

It was Rex's turn to give a start. 'Oh, no, you're not!'

Gilbert stared. 'What's that?'

'I'm not letting you out of my sight until I get to the bottom of this business.'

'You can't stop me leaving.'

'Yes, I can.'

'How?'

'If you leave this house, I shall use my considerable influence with Haggermeir to make sure you do not write the revised screenplay for *The King's Man.*'

'I've got the copyright.'

'Haggermeir's attorneys aren't at all sure you have. Apparently it's a moot point, legally. And if he cuts you out, could you afford to fight it through the courts?'

'That's a filthy trick.'

'So's whatever you're up to.'

Gilbert said slowly, 'If you want me to stay you'll have to arrange it with Geraldine.'

'Geraldine?'

'It's she who's given me the push.'

Rex's eyes narrowed. 'But why?'

'That is between her and me. However, if I'm to remain you'll have to convince her my presence is vital to the success of the movie—something like that.'

'All right, I'll speak with her. And if she agrees, you stay here. Understood?'

'Very well.'

Without another word, Rex left the room.

*　　　*　　　*

Haggermeir said, 'So that's the whole story. Satisfied?' Laura smiled. They were in his bedroom. She had been somewhat reluctant to go there, but with so many guests, and servants busy everywhere, it was hard to get privacy downstairs.

'And Signore Ransom does not know this?' she asked.

'Not likely!'

'He will be very angry, I theenk.'

'What of it? It's you I want. So, can you forget what I said last night and let me see your agent about a contract?'

She inhaled deeply on her cigarette. 'I theenk it may be arranged. It will have to be *very* remunerative.'

'I've already said it will be. I'll top any other offer that's made. Just so long as it's firmly agreed that we do have—have . . .'

'An understanding?'

'Yeah.'

'Very well. You've gotten yourself a deal, Meesta Producer.'

*　　　*　　　*

Sebastian Everard stood at the edge of the lake, his

hands in his overcoat pockets, and stared at the dull grey water. After a few minutes he gave a shake of his head, turned and began to retrace his steps along the gravel path to the house. Shortly, he reached a point at which the path forked, one branch leading to the front of the house, another round to the side, ending eventually in the stable yard. Sebastian took the latter.

The Burford family these days kept only a few riding horses, and all the old stalls on one side of the yard had long ago been converted to provide covered parking space for half a dozen cars. Now Lord Burford's Rolls, Gerry's Hispano, Sebastian and Cecily's station wagon, Paul's red tourer and Gilbert's Austin Seven were standing side by side in a row in order of descending size, like a family group. Sebastian went to the station wagon, took a key from his pocket and opened the rear door. The luggage space was nearly filled with a number of bulky objects, all covered with a rug. Sebastian was about to pull the rug back when be heard a woman's footsteps behind him. He straightened and turned.

Maude Fry was approaching from the direction of the house. She was carrying a stamped and addressed envelope, and was in the act of putting on her glasses.

Sebastian said, 'Ah, good—good—good morning.'

She nodded stiffly. 'Good morning, Mr Everard.'

'You—you—you going out?'

'Yes, to the village. I have to mail a letter. I wonder if you'd mind helping me get my car out.'

'Your car?'

107

'Yes, the Austin is mine.'

'Oh. Thought—thought it was old Gilbert's.'

'No, his is being repaired. If you could just stand behind and guide me out. There's not a great deal of space and I don't want to scrape Mr Carter's car. Simply call out 'right' or 'left' as the case may be.'

'OK, then. Let me think. This is my right, isn't it?' He held up his left hand.

'On second thought, please don't bother.'

'No bother. Pleasure, and all that. Spot of point duty, eh? Quite exciting, really.'

Maude Fry said, 'What on earth's that?'

For some seconds they'd been conscious of a sound growing in volume, and now it had become very loud. The next moment a motorcycle combination came speeding through the archway at the end of the yard, closely followed by a small van bearing the name Jenkins' Garage. The two vehicles skidded to a halt in the centre of the yard.

The rider of the motorcycle, a lad of about eighteen, jumped off and came across to them. 'Name o' Quartus?'

'No, actually,' Sebastian said. 'Sort of know him, though.'

'Brought his motor-bike back.'

'Ah. Jolly good.'

'Tell him, will you?'

'Oh, right.'

'Ha. Here's the bill.' He handed Sebastian a manila envelope. 'Quite a machine he's got there.'

'Oh, has he?'

'I'll say. Really been souped up. Terrific turn o' speed. And acceleration. Oh, well, so long.'

He strolled jauntily over to the van, which had

108

turned while they'd been talking, and jumped into the passenger seat. It drove off.

*   *   *

Immediately after leaving Haggermeir's room, Laura walked along the corridor to the east wing and opened the door of the picture gallery. She went in, looking interestedly around her.

'Hullo,' said a man's voice.

She turned to see Hugh. He was sitting on one of the sofas, a few yards to her right.

She smiled. 'Good morning.'

'Do you honestly think it's a good morning?' he asked in Italian. 'Can you really stand our weather at this time of year?'

'One puts up with what one has to.' She closed the door.

'But do you have to? Couldn't you at least have remained in a nice centrally heated London hotel?'

'I received an invitation from a producer. Naturally I came.'

'Tell me: you still believe Haggermeir sent that telegram?'

'Of course. Or had it sent.'

'But why should he lie?'

She shrugged. 'Maybe he did not want me to think he was too eager. Or perhaps he didn't want the Earl and Countess to know he had invited me without their permission.'

'Sly dog. May I ask an impertinent question?'

'If it's not my age.'

'No, it's this: Why should you, one of the world's great dramatic actresses, want to sign up with a man like him? He's got no reputation as a serious

109

filmmaker.'

'I felt it was time to branch out, You see, I am not widely known outside Italy, As a result I've never made much money. I knew where the big money was to be earned—Hollywood. Yet for years I held back. I was nervous. My English wasn't good. But then I asked myself: If Garbo had stayed in Sweden, where would she be today? So I took English lessons. At last I thought I was ready. Then I received Haggermeir's telegram, while on a visit to England. I believe in fate. So I came to see him. He will, at least, make my face known to millions of people. Then again, he would love to please the intellectual critics. Now he will have a chance to do so, because they like me. He will not want to lose the opportunity. So he will be—amenable. I will be more likely to get my own way about all sorts of things than I would with a Zanuck, say.'

'Signorina Lorenzo, why do—'

'Call me Laura.'

'May I?' Hugh's pale face flushed with pleasure. 'My—my name's Hugh.'

'I know. You were saying?'

'Just—why do you tell me all this?'

'Perhaps because you're the only person here who speaks Italian. Also—well, I am always conscious of atmosphere. When I arrived yesterday there was only one person present whom I sensed was sympathetic, glad to see me. You. I was grateful.'

'I can't imagine anyone not being glad to see you,' he said simply.

She smiled. 'You're very sweet. But enough of me. Tell me about yourself. You are a painter, I know. What kind of paintings do you do? Very

110

avant garde?'

'On the contrary. My specialty is portrait painting.'

'And you enjoy that?'

'I would if I could get some decent subjects. You should see some of the people I've had to paint.'

'Would you like to paint my portrait?'

Hugh gave a start. 'You?'

'Yes, me. Don't look so frightened. Am I so hideous?'

'Are you serious?'

'Perfectly. Oh, I would pay you a proper fee, of course.'

Dazedly Hugh said, 'I can't believe it. It would be absolutely wonderful!'

'Good. Then that's settled.'

He said eagerly, 'When do you want me to start? Now? Today?'

She looked surprised. 'You have your equipment with you?'

'No, but I can start on the preliminary pencil sketches.'

She said thoughtfully, 'I would like some time to sit and think. There are decisions I have to make. Or again, perhaps . . . Can you talk while you work?'

'Oh, yes.'

'Good. I may want to ask your advice, Hugh. I have a problem.'

'Well, if you think I can help . . .'

She gave a decisive nod. 'We'll start after lunch.'

He leant forward and took her hand. 'Laura—'

The door opened and Gerry came in. 'Hugh? I—' She stopped short. 'Oh.'

Hugh got hurriedly to his feet. 'Gerry. I, er, just

111

came up to browse among the paintings.'

'Yes, I thought I'd find you here.' She looked at Laura. 'And you are an art lover, too, signorina?'

'But naturally, Lady Geraldine.'

'Did you want me for anything particular, Gerry?' Hugh asked.

'I wondered if you'd like to come riding this afternoon. If so, I must tell the groom to get the horses saddled up.'

'No, I'm sorry, I can't. Laura—Signorina Lorenzo—has asked me to paint her portrait. We're making a start after lunch.'

'I see.' Gerry looked a little taken aback.

Laura said, 'Oh, please, Hugh, do not let me keep you from going riding.'

'Oh, I can go riding any time. It's not often I get a chance to draw a beautiful woman.'

There was a pause. Then Gerry looked at her wrist watch and said brightly, 'Twelve o'clock. There'll be drinks in the morning room now, if anyone's interested.'

'I am. Very,' Hugh said.

Laura said, 'And I must go to my room and fix my hair, to be ready for my seeting. It looks awful today.'

'It looks much the same as it did yesterday to me,' Gerry said pleasantly.

They left the gallery together. In the corridor they saw Sebastian approaching his room. He came strolling towards them.

'Ah, er, Quartus. Been—been—been looking for you, old man. Chappie just brought your jolly old motor-bike and thingummy back. Said to tell you. Said I would. Have.'

'Oh, fine.'

112

'And there was this.' Sebastian produced a crumpled manila envelope and handed it to Hugh. 'Jolly old bill—what?'

'Thanks.'

'Seemed quite impressed—garage chap. With the bike, I mean. Said it had a real turn of speed.'

'I believe so. I bought it from a chap who used it for competitions and made a number of modifications. Quite a genius with engines, I believe.'

'What's its top speed?' Gerry asked.

'I wouldn't know. What about those drinks you mentioned?' He started to walk away. Gerry followed him.

Sebastian gazed after them, a vacant expression on his face. Laura said, 'You are eenterested in motor-bikes, Signore Everard?'

'What? Oh, no fear. Frightfully dan-ger-oos, eh?'

'You do not like a leetle danger now and then?'

'Me? Not likely. Safety—safety first, that's my motto.'

'Signore Everard, we have met before, have we not?'

'What? Us? No, don't think so. Sure I'd have remembered. Don't meet many film stars, unfortunately.'

'But I have an excellent memory for faces, signore. You have been in Italy, I theenk?'

'Never at all. Sorry and all that. No offence.'

'But at one time you were in the limelight—the publeek eye?'

Did his eyes flicker slightly at that, she wondered, or was it just my imagination?

He answered after a couple of seconds. 'Me?

113

Famous? Golly, no. Never done anything interesting. Just kept myself to myself.'

'You have a profession?'

'No fear! Don't need one, happy to say. Couldn't hold one down, I'm sure.'

'Have you never thought you would like to try?'

'Why?'

'Don't most men feel the need to achieve something, to make some contribution to society?'

He scratched his head. 'Did help the Fry woman back her car out earlier. 'Fraid she bashed the fender. Wasn't pleased. Best I leave things alone, really.'

'One of the other gentlemen—I cannot remember who, now—was saying you were an old friend of his, I theenk.'

'Me? No, never clapped the old peepers on any of 'em before yesterday. Ah, well, must go and have a snooze before lunch—make sure the old gastric system's fresh for the fray. Pip-pip.'

*   *   *

'You have a high performance machine and you've never bothered to try it flat out?' Gerry said incredulously as she and Hugh went downstairs.

He shook his head. 'Why should I? I've never been in that much of a hurry to get anywhere.'

'Haven't you any sense of excitement, adventure?'

'Not really. To get a cheap thrill out of speed for its own sake is simply juvenile.'

'Then why buy a hotted-up machine?'

'Because the owner was getting married and wanted a quick sale, because I needed a bike, and

114

because it was obviously in first-class condition. Satisfied?'

Gerry said, 'You infuriate me. You know that?'

'Yes.'

'You're so dashed superior!'

'I can't help that.'

'Oh, go take a running jump at yourself!'

They went into the morning room. Lady Burford, Cecily and Rex were already there. Rex immediately came across to Gerry.

'Ah, Lady Geraldine, a word in your ear?'

'Of course.' They moved to one side.

'I've just discovered Gilbert's planning to leave, at your request,' he said. 'However, it's very important for this film that he does stay at least a little longer. He's reluctant to do so, but said he will if I clear it with you. I hate to interfere in private matters, but I have to ask if you'll relent. If it wasn't really important, I wouldn't impose.' He smiled persuasively.

Gerry hesitated. After all her efforts to get rid of Gilbert, this was annoying. On the other hand, he had probably learnt his lesson by now and would be too scared to try any more funny business. Moreover, she *would* rather like a chance to correct some of his misapprehensions about her.

So she gave in with good grace. 'Oh, if it's that vital, I certainly wouldn't insist on his leaving. Tell him it'll be all right.'

'Thank you. I really appreciate it.'

Just then Paul entered the room. She said, 'Oh, excuse me, Paul.'

He came across, looking a little preoccupied. 'Hullo?'

'Like to come riding this afternoon?'

115

'I don't think so, Gerry, thanks, I'm hopeless on a horse.'

'Come on! I'll put you on Sally. She's a lovely placid old mare.'

'I'd really rather not, Gerry. Actually, I thought I'd go for a long run. I'm entered for the English cross-country championships shortly and I must get some training in.'

'Oh, well, please yourself,' she said a little huffily.

Rex said tentatively, 'Lady Geraldine, I should love to go riding with you, if I may.'

She looked surprised. 'Do you ride?'

He smiled. 'You've obviously seen none of my movies.'

'Oh, I have. Only I always thought they used a double for the horseback scenes. I didn't know they let their stars actually *ride*.'

'Oh, yes, except for the stunt stuff. I've been riding since I was about three. I was raised on a farm.'

'Then I'd be delighted to take you riding. I can show you the estate.'

'Great. I only hope the snow doesn't start and prevent us.'

'I think you'll be all right,' Paul said. 'I was talking to the local weather forecaster, old Josh, earlier, and he says it'll come late tonight—a heavy fall—but not before. He's infallible, isn't he, Gerry?'

'Just about.'

At that moment Haggermeir entered. He had his camera around his neck and was carrying the inevitable tape measure and writing book.

Rex said, 'Been at it all morning, Cyrus?'

'Pretty well.'

Gerry said, 'Mr Haggermeir, you look as if you could do with a drink. What can I get you?'

'A Scotch on the rocks would be fine, Lady Geraldine. Thank you.'

'Mr Haggermeir, you'll soon have as good a knowledge of the interior of Alderley as the family.' It was Cecily who spoke, from a seat by the fire.

'I doubt that, ma'am.'

'What about some exterior shots, Cyrus?' Rex asked. 'Shouldn't you get a few to show folks back home?'

'What? Oh, yeah. I'll wander round outside tomorrow morning and snap off a roll. Carry on indoors this afternoon, though, if Lady Burford still doesn't object.'

'Not at all,' the Countess said.

Cecily cleared her throat. 'Excuse my asking, but isn't it unusual for the head of a studio to undertake this sort of work himself? I don't know much about movie-making, but don't you have designers and photographers and so on to handle that sort of thing?'

'Why, yes, that's right. But I figure I know every side of the business. I've acted and scripted and directed; I can light a set, operate a camera, do most everything except compose the music. So I couldn't send deputies to *Alderley*. Be kind've insulting not to come myself.'

Lady Burford bowed her head. 'Thank you, Mr Haggermeir. I appreciate that. And have you decided whether it will be possible to make your film here?'

'Oh, so far I'm thinking primarily in terms of

building a replica—'

'That's what George told me. But please stop the pretence. You want to film here. That's really why Mr Ransom is here. He's been trying to soften me up.'

Rex grinned engagingly. 'All is discovered. But tell me, Countess, have I succeeded?'

'Hardly, Mr Ransom. Not in twenty-four hours.'

'So it's no go?'

'It's not actually for me to say, Mr Ransom. I'm not the battle-axe everyone seems to think. It's George's decision, ultimately.'

'He won't agree to anything that'll make you unhappy.'

'No, but I needn't be here when it happens. Promise your people won't do too much damage, and I won't, er—is "kick up a stink" the correct term?'

CHAPTER TEN

As lunch was finishing the Earl said, 'Oh, by the way, everybody, as the talent contest starts at seven, we're having a sort of high tea at five-thirty today instead of dinner. Then, after the contest, Sir James and Lady Needham, friends of ours, have asked us all back to their place for supper. I took the liberty of accepting provisionally, on behalf of everyone. Anybody else who wants to have second thoughts and come along will be most welcome.'

'Thank you, George. I think I'll take you up on that.' It was Gilbert who said this.

Trying to conceal his surprise, the Earl said, 'By

118

all means, Arl—er, Gil—er, my dear chap. Delighted.'

Gerry looked at Gilbert pensively. Just what, she wondered, was the reason for this change of mind?

After lunch Rex made his way to the library for a smoke and read before setting out on his ride. He'd been there only a few minutes when Laura came in. He got to his feet.

Laura waved him down again, seated herself next to him, looked at him keenly and said, 'Signore Ransom, what is it that you have against me?'

'I have nothing against you.'

'Yet your manner, it has been hostile ever since I arrived.'

'I'm sorry you think that.'

'Why are you frightened of me?'

'Frightened? What in the world do you mean?'

'I have never done anything to harm you. We have never met before.' She paused. 'Have we?'

'Of course not!' He spoke sharply.

'Well, when in such circumstances one person is hostile to another, the usual reason is fear.'

'My, quite the little female Freud, aren't we?'

'Prego?'

'Skip it. No, signorina, I'm not frightened of you. If you feel I've been cool to you, I apologise. Let's put it down to the fact that I don't want the picture ruined. Oh, don't get me wrong: you're a fine actress. But completely unsuited to *The King's Man*. To accommodate you the story would have to be changed beyond recognition.'

Laura gave a quiet chuckle.

'Why do you laugh?'

'Oh, no reason. What you said: it struck me as

119

funny.'

'I fail to see the joke.'

'Skeep it. But tell me, is it only that which concerns you? It could not be you are also afraid that I peench your thunder?'

'Steal my thunder?' Rex threw back his head and laughed. 'You're kidding. My fans are tremendously loyal. It's me they'll come to see. Your name will mean nothing to them.'

'Maybe not, when they arrive. But when they *leave* . . . You said I was a fine actress.'

'The finest actress on earth can be miscast.'

She nodded slowly. 'Ah, well. We shall see. Or perhaps not.'

'What does that mean?'

She just shrugged.

He said, 'I'm only concerned for the success of the picture.'

'So you say, signore. But I theenk there is something else. Something else that you are afraid of. And Signore Ransom, I eentend to find out what it is.'

*   *   *

Paul started on his training run in one direction just before two, and a few minutes later Gerry and Rex set out in the other direction on horseback. Laura commenced sitting for Hugh, Haggermeir again disappeared into the further recesses of Alderley, Gilbert and Maude Fry retired to do some work, Sebastian went to have another snooze, Cecily announced her intention of driving to the village to do a little shopping, and the Earl strolled off for a talk with Mr Briggs, who ran the home farm. Finding herself alone, Lady Burford seized the opportunity to go to her boudoir and write some letters.

It was four o'clock when there came a tap on Lady Burford's door. She called 'Come in.'

It was Maude Fry who entered. She said, 'I'm sorry to disturb you, Lady Burford, but could you spare a few minutes?'

'Yes, of course, Miss Fry.'

Maude Fry came somewhat hesitantly across the room. The Countess asked her to sit down and she did so.

'Is there something I can do for you?' Lady Burford asked.

Maude Fry didn't answer for a few seconds. She was staring down at the carpet, looking decidedly embarrassed. Then she glanced up, and the light glinted on the blue-tinted spectacles that concealed her eyes as effectively as sunglasses. 'I wanted to apologise.'

'Er, for what, Miss Fry?'

'For being here. You see, I gather from certain things Mr Gilbert has just let drop that he foisted me on you, without warning or your permission. I really do feel extremely embarrassed.'

As she said these last words there was a sudden catch in her voice. It occurred to the Countess that this plain, competent and apparently self-possessed woman was in fact extremely shy. She said hastily, 'Oh, not at all. It's often assumed that a busy man will want to take a secretary wherever he goes.'

'But I am correct: he did simply announce he was bringing me—without even a by-your-leave?'

Lady Burford smiled. 'It was rather like that.

But please don't worry. With eight other guests, one more makes no difference. Besides, nobody could possibly take exception to your presence in their home. Don't give the matter another thought.'

'You're very kind, but under the circumstances I cannot possibly remain.'

'But surely your leaving would inconvenience Mr Gilbert very much?'

'No doubt. But that does not concern me unduly. He has treated me very badly in a number of ways.'

'You intend to leave his employment?'

'I do.'

'Well, far be it from me to try and dissuade you. But please accept that it is no wish of ours that you leave this house.'

'That's understood. Thank you very much. Now, if you'll excuse me, I must go and pack.'

'But you can't possibly leave *now*. You came in your own car, I believe. Very soon it'll be dark, and snow is forecast. To drive all the way to London this evening would be most unpleasant. Why not wait until the morning?'

'That's very kind of you, Lady Burford. I'd be tempted to accept, if I could be sure of not seeing Mr Gilbert again. We—rather had words.'

'Well, there's no reason why you should see him. Your rooms are at opposite ends of the house. He'll be going out with the others this evening, and I imagine that our party will not be back until quite late. I suggest you remain in your room until they've left. I'll have a tray sent along to you. Then, afterwards, perhaps you'll join Mr and Mrs Everard and me downstairs. Tell me, do you by any

122

chance play bridge?'

'Why, yes, I play quite a lot.'

'Oh, excellent. Then we can make up a four. I must admit I've been wondering what to do with them. My cousin and I have virtually run out of "Do you remembers".'

Maude Fry said doubtfully, 'Mr Everard can play bridge?'

'It is rather surprising, isn't it? Apparently he had the rudiments drummed into him at an early age by a fanatical bridge-playing mother. It remains to be seen what standard he plays to; however, it will pass a couple of hours. So you will be doing me a favour.'

'In that case, Lady Burford, I shall be delighted to stay.'

*   *   *

The two horses thundered across the field under the lowering sky. Gerry's cheeks were aglow as the wind whipped them and she bent over her horse's head, urging him on. For a few seconds she managed to keep level with Rex Ransom's mount, but her eyes kept watering and at last she gave a laughing gasp. 'Whew, that's enough for me,' she said as she slowed her horse to a canter.

Rex reined in and waited for her. He grinned. 'You need goggles for galloping in this weather.'

'Yes, you do. Sorry it's been such a dismal afternoon. You haven't seen the estate at its best.'

'Oh, it's been great. I've thoroughly enjoyed myself. And this feller's got a real turn of speed.'

'You certainly got the best out of him, Rex.'

'How far are we from the house?'

123

'Less than a mile. Better walk them the rest of the way home.'

He said, 'Gerry, before we get back, there's something I want to ask you. It's a bit awkward, but it's about your requesting Gilbert to leave.'

'I've withdrawn that.'

'I know. Would you think it impertinent, though, if I asked why it happened?'

'Not impertinent, but I'd rather not say. Sorry.'

'That's OK. But would I be right in assuming you have been having trouble with him? I have a reason for asking.'

'It depends what you mean by trouble. It's not what a girl would normally mean by that. But, in a sense, yes.'

'I see. Well, you're not the only one.'

She stared. 'You mean you—? I don't follow. *You* wanted him to stay.'

'I know. It's a complicated situation. And rather worrying.'

'Do you want to talk about it?'

'I'd like to tell someone. Fact is, he's been prowling about my room.'

'Good heavens.'

'There's rather more to it than that, though. I'd like to tell you the whole story. I didn't know who to talk to before this afternoon, but in the last couple of hours I feel we've gotten to know each other. However, it'll take rather a long time to explain properly.'

'Well, we'll be home in a few minutes, but if we go off for a tête-à-tête after being out all the afternoon it'll look a bit odd. Then there'll be tea and changing and leaving for the village. Could we have a chat late tonight, after we get back?'

'Fine. Perhaps you could come to my personal sitting-room. I've not entertained anyone in it yet and I must do so before I leave.'

'OK, pardner,' Gerry said, 'you've got a date.'

*   *   *

Cecily turned into the drive on her return from the village and was surprised to see Laura Lorenzo waving her down. She stopped and Laura got in. Wearing a scarlet boxy top coat, she was nonetheless shivering. '*Grazie*,' she said. 'A leeft back will be most welcome.'

'I'm surprised to see you out in this weather, signorina.'

'I have been seetting for Signore Quartus and I got rather steef. I decided I needed some exercise, but I did not realise how cold it was.'

'They say it'll be snowing by tonight.'

'Which will be an unusual experience for you, will it not?'

'Oh, yes. We don't get much in Australia. It'll be like old times.'

'When you and the Contessa were girls together, in those days you and she were very close, yes?'

'Well, fairly close.'

'It must be nice for you to meet her daughter.'

'Yes, Gerry's a lovely girl.'

'I understand, though, that in the past she has had rather a bad reputation?'

Cecily frowned. 'I don't think so.'

'Oh, *mi scusi*. Bad was the wrong word. Reckless, undisciplined perhaps?'

'Oh, I see what you mean. Yes, I believe she went through a rebellious phase, got in with a rather wild set. Her name was always appearing in the gossip columns.'

'*Ma per Dio*, if her name appear in the gossip columns in Australia she must have been really notorious!'

'Oh, no. I have the English papers sent out to me.'

'Ah. But she appeared in court more than once, did she not?'

'I believe so.'

'Do you know what for?'

'Snatching a policeman's helmet and running off with it. And wading in the fountains in Trafalgar Square.'

'Oh.' Laura looked pensive. 'But of course as the daughter of a nobleman, nobody would charge her with anything more serious.'

Cecily said stiffly, 'That sort of thing does not happen in England.'

'You say you never see Lady Geraldine before yesterday. Your husband—he did not know her either?'

'Sebastian? Oh, no.'

Laura said suddenly, 'I have seen your husband before.'

'Oh? When?'

'Some years ago. But he seems not to want to talk about it.'

'He's rather shy with women, particularly film stars. So don't be offended.'

'I am not offended. But before I leave here, he will admit it. Oh, yes.'

*   *   *

After returning, showering and changing, Paul found Gerry in the drawing room with Merryweather, who had just brought her a pot of tea.

'Hullo,' she said. 'Want a cup?'

'Please.'

'Can I get you anything to eat, sir?' Merryweather asked.

'No, thanks. Not with high tea so close.'

'No doubt you are wise, sir,' Merryweather said. He sighed.

Gerry said, 'You don't approve of high tea, do you, Merry?'

'It is not a meal I recognise, your ladyship, though I acknowledge the need of it on occasions.'

'You coming along to the show, Merryweather?' Paul asked.

'Thank you, no, sir. I attended one year. The daughter of Hawkins the chauffeur was performing and I felt an obligation. It was an experience I would not wish to repeat.' He withdrew.

'Good ride?' Paul inquired.

'Yes, thank you. Rex is a fine horseman, and excellent company.'

'Oh, it's Rex now, is it?'

'Why not? If you choose to let us spend the afternoon together, while you go off on your own . . .'

'Oh, don't be like that, Gerry. I must do a certain amount of training. And I'm really not good on horseback. Besides, I wanted to think.' His face was troubled. She looked at him closely. 'Is anything wrong?'

'Well.' He stopped. 'I don't know what to do.'

'About what?'

'A conversation I overheard this morning.'

'What's the problem?'

'I can't decide whether I ought to take it further. You see, I was eavesdropping—quite accidentally, of course, and unavoidably.'

'Then I don't see how you can do anything about it.'

'Normally that's what I'd say. Except—what I heard was so *fantastic*.'

'Oh?' She looked intrigued.

'It's so unbelievable that I think the person may have been joking. But the words were spoken so seriously. And if they were true, then I can't help feeling that I ought to tell your father about it.'

'Why Daddy?'

'Because it means one of the people in this house is here under completely false pretences.'

'Oh. Then why don't you go to him—or her— and ask straight out?'

'Yes, I think I'm going to have to do that. But I feel such a fool. They're sure to deny it, or claim it was a joke, or that I misheard or misunderstood.'

'*Could* you have?'

'That's what I've been asking myself all afternoon. I just don't know.'

'Is it important you do something immediately?'

He looked thoughtful. 'I suppose not.'

'Then why not give it a few more hours? Maybe the truth will come to light without your having to do anything.'

His face lightened. 'Yes, perhaps you're right. Oh, Gerry, you always give such good advice! You've got so much common sense.'

'Don't be beastly! That's a horrible thing to say about me. Someone like Hugh's got common

128

sense, not me.'

'Ah! So Quartus is horrible, is he?'

'I didn't mean it like that! In certain people common sense is all right.'

'Only 'all right'? Gerry, do I detect a slight change in your attitude toward friend Quartus?'

'You—you may. You're not to read anything into it, though.'

'But this must be the result of your having had a chance to study him at close quarters, and compare him with me.'

'Don't flatter yourself.'

'But I shall. I love to flatter myself. After all, nobody else does. And you've got to admit I am much nicer than he is.'

'The conceit of the man!'

'No. I've been weighting myself up—and him. I *am* nicer than he is. Not that there's anything very exciting about niceness. I'm not as clever as he. In addition I'm lazy, rather selfish, and—at least where you're concerned—unscrupulous. Anything I can say to put you off him I will.'

'At least you're honest.'

'I try not to be, but with you I can't help myself.'

'The influence of a good woman,' she murmured.

'I know. It's awful. I've never experienced it before and it's ruining my life. Gerry, are you in love with Quartus?'

Gerry looked at him for a moment, then stood up, crossed to the window and stared out over the park. It was now nearly dark and the trees were gaunt grey skeletons against the only slightly lighter grey sky. She said, 'Snow any time now.'

Paul joined her at the window and gently turned

129

her to face him. 'You didn't answer my question.'

'Am I in love with Hugh? I don't know.'

'Oh, sweetheart, you must!'

'I don't, honestly, Paul.'

'Well, do you love me?'

She nodded. 'Oh, yes!'

His face lit up. 'You do? But that's marvellous! Gerry, I don't know what to say. It's like a dream come—'

She interrupted. 'I love you, Paul. But I don't know if I'm *in love* with you, either.'

'Oh, that's splitting hairs!'

'It's not, really.'

'Well, then: you don't know if you're *in love* with Quartus. But do you love him?'

'Oh, no! Sometimes I hate him.'

Paul gave a mock groan of despair. 'Women! Ye gods! I'll never understand them.'

'Surely you never expected to, did you.'

'In my innocent youth I think I did.'

'I'm sorry, Paul. I've treated you badly. You *and* Hugh.'

'Oh, forget Hugh! He doesn't love you.'

'I think he does. In his own way.'

'A deuced funny way. I suppose he's still with Lorenzo, is he?'

'I imagine so.'

'At least I did spend the afternoon on my own, and not slobbering over another woman. If you ask me, he's got it bad.'

Gerry didn't answer.

CHAPTER ELEVEN

At six-thirty the male section of the party had assembled in the great hall.

Rex looked at his watch. 'Seems we're short a couple of ladies.' He'd been ready to leave before anyone else and had been waiting patiently in the drawing room for twenty minutes as the others trickled down.

'No, you're not.' Gerry spoke from the stairs.

The Earl looked up. 'Where's Miss Lorenzo?'

'Still in her room, I expect.'

'Someone better tell her we're ready to leave.'

'I'll go.'

Gerry retraced her steps to the top of the stairs, made her way to Laura's room and tapped on the door. '*Avanti.*'

Gerry went in. Laura, wearing her velvet evening gown and a matching cartwheel hat from which drooped an emerald feather, was seated at her dressing table, writing a letter. Without looking up, she said, 'Oh, Eloise, I—'

She raised her head and saw Gerry. 'Oh.' With a sudden, rather furtive movement, she closed her writing case. 'Lady Geraldine, *mi scusi*. I thought that would be my maid.'

Gerry smiled. 'Just to say that we're ready to leave.'

Laura glanced at a tiny jewelled wristwatch. 'It is later than I thought. I, er, was hoping to feenish a letter—just a reply to a fan—before we leave so I could post it in the veellage.'

'I'm afraid the last collection in the village was

131

at six. We could have somebody take it to Westchester.'

'No, please, it does not matter.'

She opened a drawer, slipped the writing case inside and closed it. Then she crossed to the wardrobe, took out her magnificent mink coat and put it on. She and Gerry went downstairs.

A few minutes later the party left. The Countess and Cecily waved them off and went back inside.

'Well, my dear, we might as well start our bridge, don't you think?' Lady Burford said.

'Oh, so soon?'

'Not if you have something else—'

'No, no. I'll just go up and fetch Sebastian. He's having a nap.'

'Very well. Would you look in on Miss Fry, please, and bring her down? Tell her Mr Gilbert's left the house and we're ready to start our game.'

* * *

News of the personal appearance of Rex Ransom had obviously spread far and wide. The village hall was ablaze with light, and a crowd of about seventy people, ineffectually controlled by the village constable, was gathered outside. The Rolls drew up and a cheer broke out as Rex alighted. He grinned and waved. Autograph books were thrust into his hands, and as a photographer from the *Westshire Advertiser* popped flashbulbs, he made his way slowly up to the doors, the rest of the Alderley party following like a train of courtiers.

Across the entrance to the hall a banner, bearing the words WELCOME REX, had been hung, and Rex stood beneath it, waving to the crowd before finally going inside.

The hall was packed, and there was another great cheer as Rex was spotted and, with the rest of the party, made his way to reserved seats at the front. Shortly afterwards the entertainment commenced.

*　　*　　*

Sebastian Everard stared at his cards. 'Now, what did I say? Was it Two Clubs? Ah, yes—you said One Heart, didn't you, Lavinia? I nearly said One No Trump, though I hadn't quite got the count, and then you said One Heart, so I had to go Two Clubs. I always find it jolly difficult when one has two short suits.'

Lady Burford sighed. She wondered how soon she could put an end to this farce. Really, Sebastian might just as well lay his cards face up on the table. She looked apologetically at Maude Fry, who, from the expression on her face, would clearly rather be elsewhere. For a skilled player, this must seem an utter waste of time.

However, it wasn't long before there came a welcome diversion. Merryweather entered.

'Excuse me, my lady,' he said, 'a Miss Jemima Dove has just arrived.'

Lady Burford looked surprised. 'Jemima Dove? Who is she? And what does she want at this time on a Friday night?'

'I think, my lady, that she is expecting to stay. She has a suitcase.'

'Does the woman think this is a hotel?'

'She did ask me to tender her apologies for arriving at such an inconvenient hour.'

133

'Well, find out what she wants, Merryweather.'

'Yes, my lady. Naturally, I should have done so, only I assumed from the young lady's manner that she was someone you were expecting and had omitted to mention.'

He started back towards the door, but stopped when the Countess suddenly said, 'Oh, my goodness, I believe I am—expecting her, I mean. But not yet, surely.'

Cecily said, 'A guest arriving ahead of schedule?'

'Not exactly. I think she may be the woman who's coming to recatalogue the library. I've never met her; it was arranged through an agency. But I'm certain she wasn't due until the week after next. Merryweather, if she is the lady, show her in please. And send somebody to fetch the desk diary from my boudoir. I suppose you'd better have another bedroom prepared, as well—the Lilac, I think.'

'Yes, your ladyship.'

Merryweather withdrew, to return a minute later, accompanied by a small, fragile-looking girl. She had soft brown hair and big grey eyes behind large and strangely masculine-looking glasses. She was pretty, in a quiet, demure way. She had a slightly lost air.

The Countess said, 'Do come across to the fire, Miss Dove. I'm sure you're cold.'

Miss Dove crossed the room, 'Oh, thank you. Yes, I am. Lady Burford, I'm terribly sorry to arrive so late. It's the weather. The roads are terribly slippery and I got lost three times. I've been driving for hours.' She had a soft, rather musical voice.

The Countess said, 'You drove yourself? From

134

where?'

'Cambridge.'

'My, my, you must be tired.'

'I am, rather. And I had hoped to start work before this. I do trust the delay hasn't inconvenienced you too much.'

'No, not at all,'

Just then Merryweather returned with the Countess's desk diary.

'Thank you, Merryweather.' Lady Burford flicked through the pages, then gave a nod. 'As I thought. Miss Dove, I haven't been inconvenienced, because—and you'll find out sooner or later—I wasn't expecting you until the week after next.'

Miss Dove's face fell. 'The week after next!'

'Yes; Monday the nineteenth.' She held out the diary for the girl to see.

When she looked up there was an expression of dismay on Jemima Dove's face. 'But I'm sure the agency said the ninth. Here, I wrote it down at the time.'

She delved into her handbag and drew out a small pocket diary. She found the date and handed it to the Countess. 'You see.'

'Yes, I see. Well, no doubt the agency is at fault. I shall get in touch with them on Monday. But in the meantime—'

'In the meantime, I must leave at once.' Jemima Dove was pink with embarrassment. 'I'm so terribly sorry. And thank you for being so kind.' She moved towards the door. 'I'll come back on the nineteenth, of course.'

'Don't be silly, child. I couldn't turn you out on a night like this. Besides, it's better to be early than late, and there's no reason why you can't stay and commence work as soon as you wish.'

'Oh, Lady Burford, are you sure? It won't be inconvenient?'

'Not at all. It's true we have a number of guests at the moment and they tend to wander in and out of the library, but if they don't disturb you, I'm certain you won't disturb them. Now, take your things off and let me perform some introductions.'

Jemima Dove shook hands shyly with Sebastian, Cecily and Maude Fry, and then said, 'I'm afraid I interrupted your card game. Please do carry on.'

'We had just finished a rubber,' Lady Burford said. She addressed the others. 'I don't know whether you want to continue . . .'

'Well, if you don't mind, I'd rather—rather like to pack up now,' Sebastian said. 'Always find bridge jolly exhausting.' He yawned. 'Fact is, think I'll have an early night, if no one minds. Pretty wearing sort of day all round, actually. 'Night, all.' He ambled from the room.

'I'm sorry about that,' Cecily said. 'I'm afraid Sebastian's not really a very good player. I rarely get the chance of a decent game.' She sounded quite sad. Then she looked at Jemima. 'You don't play, I suppose?'

'Bridge? Well, yes, I do.'

Cecily brightened. 'Really? Then perhaps we could have a proper game. What do you say, Lavinia?'

'By all means, if Miss Fry and Miss Dove would care to play.'

They both expressed their willingness, Maude Fry adding, 'But I would like to slip up to my room for ten minutes first.'

Jemima said, 'I'll come with you and find my room. I'd like to freshen up.'

'It's on the right at the end of the west wing,' Lady Burford told her. 'The Lilac room. You'll find your things have been taken up.'

Jemima and Maude Fry left the room. At the top of the stairs, Jemima hesitated. 'West wing: now which way would that be?'

'To your left.'

'Are you near me?'

'No; I'm in the east wing, halfway along.'

'I see.'

They went their separate ways.

Maude Fry was the first to return to the drawing room, ten minutes later. It was a further five minutes before Jemima came in.

'Oh, I hope I haven't kept you waiting,' she said a little breathlessly. Then she saw that Lady Burford had had some refreshments sent in, and started to express her gratitude. Lady Burford stopped her—not, however, adding that Jemima's arrival was really a godsend. What she would have done with Cecily and Maude Fry for several more hours she just didn't know.

*   *   *

The children's talent contest was a great success. Most of the entrants rose to the occasion, and the committee had created so many classes of competition that the judges were able to make some sort of award to every entrant. Meanwhile Rex, handing out the prizes, was in top form— radiating charm, good humour and an air of innocent enjoyment.

One person who, at the beginning, was plainly unhappy with this situation was Laura. She was clearly unused to taking a back seat. However, her striking looks quickly attracted attention, and after the Earl had quietly explained to the MC who she was, she was introduced to the audience and then assisted with the presentations. If Rex was not altogether pleased about this, he didn't show it.

The proceedings ended with more photographs and autograph signing, after which the Alderley group retired backstage for coffee with the committee and other village VIPs.

They eventually left at nine-thirty and arrived at the Needhams' to find that quite a party had been arranged, with about twenty other guests, a huge supply of drink (at the sight of this, Arlington Gilbert, who'd been sunk in a morose gloom all the evening, immediately brightened) and piles of foodstuffs.

It was nearly half past twelve before the Alderley group finally got away. Gilbert had to be gently guided out to Lord Burford's Rolls.

As Gerry was climbing into Paul's car she felt the lightest of tickles on her forehead. She glanced up and felt several more. 'It's come at last,' she said.

Thick snowflakes were starting to fall.

She got in, shivering slightly and glancing a little wistfully at the Rolls, which was already sweeping down the drive. A convertible sports car was not the warmest form of transport on a winter's night.

*   *   *

Paul peered through the cloud of whirling

snowflakes, which were being driven against his windshield. He swore softly.

Gerry, her eyes closed, sunk down in her seat, her hands in her pockets and her coat collar up, murmured, 'What's the matter?'

'I've lost the taillight of the Rolls.'

'Well, you know the way, don't you?'

'Hope so, but there's such a maze of winding lanes round here that I'm not too confident. Do you know where we are?'

'Of course I don't!'

'But this is your country.'

'I was asleep until woken by your foul language and the bitter cold. I don't even know how long we've been driving.' She peered into the gloom. 'There are three or four routes Hawkins could have taken. All these narrow country roads look exactly alike in the dark, particularly in a snow storm. If I could spot some landmark . . .'

'Oh, don't worry. I know roughly where we are.' Gerry closed her eyes again. Five or ten minutes passed. Then she sat up with a start as the car suddenly gave a sort of shudder. She said, 'Oh, no, I don't believe it!'

The engine cut out.

Between clenched teeth Gerry said, 'Paul, is that what I think it is?'

' 'Fraid so, old girl.'

'You're out of petrol! Honestly, of all the blithering idiots!'

Paul didn't reply as the car glided to a halt. He bent forward and peered at the fuel gauge. He muttered 'Knew I was low, but could have sworn I had enough to get back.'

'The important thing is: what do we do?'

'We could walk.'

'But you don't know how far it is.'

'Must be several miles.'

'Me walk several miles in these shoes in this weather? I'd have frostbite in a hundred yards!'

'Then you'll have to wait here, darling, while I go and get some petrol. Luckily, I've got an empty can.'

'But where will you go? Jenkins' won't be open.'

'I'll go the other way, to the main road. With any luck I can get a lift from a truck to that all-night filling station outside Westchester.'

'I don't fancy staying here alone.'

'But what's the alternative?'

'Can't we both just wait here? They're sure to come back for us when they realise.'

'Yes, but how long will that take them? And then they won't know exactly where we are. There've been several forks or crossroads since I last saw the Rolls, and I could have gone wrong at any of them. They could drive round for ages.'

'Oh, really, Paul. Of all the prize chumps, you take the cake!'

'I know, don't rub it in. Well, what about it: do I go?'

'How long will it take you?'

'Hard to say. Perhaps three quarters of an hour.'

'Well, all right, but be as quick as you can.'

'Oh, no, I'm going to stroll—enjoy the scenery, pick flowers.'

He took the key from the ignition, got out and went to the back. Gerry heard the rumble seat open and a moment later slam shut.

He called, 'Chin up, sweetheart. I'll do my best.'

Then came the sound of his footsteps on the

road for a few seconds. They gradually faded away and, but for the wind, all was silent. Gerry sat huddled down in the seat and shivered.

*   *   *

'Two Spades,' said Maude Fry.

'Pass,' said Cecily.

'Two Hearts,' said Lady Burford.

'Three Diamonds,' said Jemima Dove.

Maude Fry hesitated. Her face was flushed and she was breathing more heavily than usual. It was remarkable what a change had come over her since Sebastian had left and they'd started playing seriously. Not, thought the Countess, that she was a very good player. It was fortunate they were not playing for high stakes; Maude Fry would already have lost quite a lot of money.

Lady Burford's reflections were interrupted by the sound of tires outside. She said, 'Oh, they're back. Sooner than I expected.' She glanced at the clock. 'My word, it's nearly one! I had no idea.'

'Good gracious!' Cecily exclaimed. 'I've never known time to pass so quickly.'

Maude Fry got hurriedly to her feet. 'Oh, Lady Burford, do you mind if we stop now and add up tomorrow. I'm sorry to break off in the middle, but I did explain about Mr Gilbert.'

'Yes, of course.'

Jemima said, 'I'll come now, too, if nobody minds.'

They both said good night and left the room together.

Lady Burford and Cecily went out to the hall to welcome the others. They came in shivering and

141

giving exclamations, the men removing their outer things and handing them to the footmen. Hugh especially looked particularly cold and hurried straight into the drawing room and across to the fire.

The Earl brushed some snowflakes from his hair. 'Brr—what a foul night!'

'I expect you'd all like something warming,' Lady Burford said.

It was Laura who answered first. 'Not for me, Lady Burford, thank you. If I may I will go up to my room in just a few meenutes. I am very tired and I have a slight headache. But may I make a telephone call first? I must ring my London agent at his home and tell him what time I arrive tomorrow.'

She smiled as she saw Lady Burford glance at the grandfather clock. 'Is all right. He keeps very late hours.'

'You know where the telephone room is?'

'*Si, grazie.*' Laura walked off.

Arlington Gilbert meanwhile was smiling benignly, swaying slightly as he did so. He said, 'Did I hear you talk about something warming? Does that mean rum, by any chance?'

Haggermeir said, 'You've had quite enough for tonight, feller.'

Gilbert raised his eyebrows. 'I have?'

'You have. It's bed for you, pronto. I'll see you up.'

He took Gilbert by the arm and led him to the stairs. Over his shoulder he said, 'I'll say good night, too, Lady Burford. Thanks for the outing, Earl.'

'Glad you came, my dear chap. 'Night.'

142

Haggermeir and Gilbert proceeded a little unsteadily up the stairs.

Lord Burford said, 'That fellow Arlington—much nicer when he's had one over the eight. Not that he seemed to me to drink all that much. All the same, we'd better keep him tanked up the rest of the time he's here.'

The Countess said, 'I take it the evening was a success?'

'Capital. Rex here was simply splendid. Great hit.'

Rex smiled. 'I enjoyed myself.'

'Fancy somethin' before you turn in?'

'No, really, thanks. Your friends the Needhams did us very well. I'll go straight to my room, if you don't mind.' He said good night all round and ran lightly up the stairs.

Cecily said, 'My turn now, I think. Good night, Lavinia. It's been a delightful day.'

'Good night, Cecily.'

They kissed and Cecily in her turn ascended the grand staircase.

Laura reappeared.

'Did you get through all right?' Lady Burford asked.

'I'm afraid not. The phone seems to be dead. Perhaps the lines are down.'

'Oh dear, how tiresome! I am sorry.'

'Is no matter. I can send a telegram from the veellage in the morning.' She gave an elegant little yawn. 'Well, if you do not mind I will go to bed now. *Buonanotte*.' She made her way up the stairs.

As she did so, Hugh emerged from the drawing room again. 'Gerry and Carter in yet?' he asked.

The Earl hook his head. 'No. Why?'

'I wonder what's happened to them. They were right behind us when we left the Needhams.'

The Countess looked alarmed. 'George, didn't you say the roads were difficult tonight?'

'Bit slippery.'

'Oh, my perhaps they've had an accident! Somebody must go and look for them.'

'Oh, lor', Lavinia, let's give it a bit longer. I don't like to get Hawkins out again on what's almost certainly a wild goose chase. He's probably turned in already.'

'George, we're talking about your daughter.'

'You know I can't drive.'

'I'll go, Lady Burford,' said Hugh.

'Oh, would you, Hugh? I'd be so grateful.'

'That's all right. I want to know what he's up—I mean, I want to know what's happened to her.'

The Earl said, 'Thanks, my boy. You'll have to go and get the car keys from Hawkins.'

'Oh, I wouldn't risk driving the Rolls tonight— bit too big and heavy for me. Do you know where the keys to the Hispano are? Gerry's often let me drive that.'

'You'll probably find she's left them in the ignition. She nearly always does.'

'Oh, right.' He fetched his flying jacket, scarf and cap from the cloakroom and pulled on his gloves. 'Got a flashlight?'

'Should be one in that table drawer.'

Hugh found it and opened the front door.

'Be careful, Hugh,' Lady Burford said.

'Don't worry.'

He went out. The storm was worse than ever and only the gale had so far prevented the snow forming a carpet underfoot. He stumbled to the stable yard, his mind full of black thoughts. He didn't for one moment believe there'd been an accident. Carter was up to some dirty business. Exactly what wasn't clear. But for him to disappear with Gerry at this time of night couldn't be chance. Hugh just hoped against hope that the little idiot hadn't let him persuade her to run away with him, or anything really drastic.

In the yard he made straight for the Hispano Suisa. To get to it he had to pass his motorcycle combination. The beam of his flashlight happened to fall momentarily on the sidecar. He noticed that it seemed to be leaning over at a strange angle. He directed the beam straight on to it. Then he stopped dead and gave an exclamation.

The motor-bike was gone.

Hugh stood, gazing blankly. The sidecar apparently hadn't been damaged. But the bike had been neatly detached. There was no sign of it.

Hugh's thoughts whirled. It didn't make sense. It had certainly been here just a few moments before they'd all left for the talent contest. He'd come out to fetch his scarf, which he'd left in the sidecar.

No one would come right up here just to pinch a motorcycle—or, if they did, be so insane as to stop and remove the sidecar first. It could only be some sort of hoax. But by whom?

However, this wasn't the time for speculation. He hurried on to the Hispano and opened the door. Yes, the ignition key was there. He got in and a minute later was on his way down the drive. Hugh gripped the wheel tightly and peered through the driving snow.

145

CHAPTER TWELVE

Gerry sat huddled in Paul's car. Her teeth were chattering. She'd never been so cold in her life. Surely, Paul ought to be back by now. She reluctantly drew her left hand from her pocket and squinted at the luminous dial of her wrist watch.

Oh no! He'd been gone less than twenty minutes. It seemed at least an hour. Why hadn't she been missed at home? Did she mean so little to her parents that they didn't even notice whether she was there or not?

There was a terrible draft in this car. She groped in the direction from which the wind was coming and gave a gasp of annoyance at finding the soft top of the car wasn't closed properly. There was a gap of at least an inch immediately above the windshield and the passenger door. She reached up and tried to close it. But it wouldn't budge. She leant to her right and felt above the driver's door. Here there was no gap. Obviously when Paul had last had the top down he'd closed it crookedly afterwards. The only thing to do was open it and re-close it—making sure it was straight.

Gerry jerked at the handle and the top flew back. Snow swept in. She heaved forward again. Nothing happened. She knelt on the seat and had another go. But it was hopeless. The top was well and truly jammed.

Gerry nearly wept. If there'd been a draft before, there was now a howling gale around and she was colder than ever. She threw herself back into the seat, staring dismally into the darkness.

The next moment she stiffened. Lights—surely? Yes, a car was approaching. Slowly it drew closer.

Then Gerry knew a twinge of unease. It wasn't the Rolls—the lights were wrong. Suppose it wasn't from home at all? It might be—anybody.

The car came nearer still, and stopped about ten yards in front of her. Then a figure was suddenly silhouetted against the car's lights. It began walking towards her. She held her breath. The next moment a light was shining in her eyes and a voice was saying, 'Gerry? Are you all right?'

'Hugh! Oh, thank heavens!'

She opened the door and got stiffly out. 'Oh, Hugh, am I glad to see you! But what are you driving?'

'The Hispano.'

'Oh.' Of course, she'd never seen her own car approaching her in the dark, so it wasn't surprising she hadn't recognised it. 'How did you find me?' she asked.

'Followed the tracks of the Rolls until they got covered with snow. Then just kept straight on. But what happened?'

'It's Paul. He—'

Hugh grabbed her by the elbow. 'What's he done? Where is he?'

She pulled away. 'Hugh, please. It's ripping of you to have come for me, but this isn't the Old Bailey.'

'Gerry, has he hurt you? In any way?'

'Certainly not.'

'Then why's he run off?'

'He hasn't run off. He's gone to get petrol. We ran out.'

He gave a snort. 'Oh, come off it! Don't tell me

147

you fell for that old chestnut.'

'It's true!'

'Gerry, for Pete's sake stop defending the rotter.'

'He's not a rotter!'

He grasped her roughly by the shoulders. 'Don't say you were in on it!'

'In on what?'

'This whole shoddy scheme. For the two of you to—to be alone. Where no one could see you.'

She gave a gasp. 'You're not serious! You don't honestly think we'd *choose* to stop—out here, in this!' She gestured to the elements.

'I think he'd do absolutely anything to get you. And I think you're so besotted with him that you'd let him.'

'Why, you utter beast!' And Gerry slapped him hard across the face.

He started shaking her, shouting to make himself heard above the wind. 'Gerry, come to your senses! The fellow's a cad. Give him up!'

Gerry's teeth were rattling so much that she couldn't speak. Then, when she was sure that if he continued any longer her head would fall off, there came the sound of hurrying footsteps, muffled by the snow, and then blessedly Paul's voice:

'Gerry? I've got the petrol. Didn't have to go to the garage. A truck driver let me siphon some out of his tank. Gerry? What's happening? Who's that with you?'

Hugh let her go as Paul loomed up from the rear, carrying a can. 'What's going on?' he said urgently. 'Quartus!'

Hugh spun to face him. 'Right, Carter, I want a few words with you.'

148

Paul took in Gerry's distressed condition. He put down the can. 'What have you done to her?'

'Nothing, except give her a well-deserved shaking. The question is: What have I prevented you doing to her?'

Gerry stepped shakily towards Paul and fell into his arms. 'Oh, Paul, he's been saying horrible things about us: that we arranged all this so we could—could be alone.'

Paul drew his breath in sharply. 'You unmitigated bounder.'

'*You* call *me* a bounder?' Hugh shouted. The next moment, without any warning, he swung a wild right hook in the direction of Paul's head.

Paul easily evaded the blow, and Hugh's fist landed with a clunk against the windshield of the car. He gave a yelp of pain.

'Right,' Paul said grimly, 'if that's the way you want it.' He drew back his fist.

Gerry screamed, 'No, Paul!' and he stopped in mid-movement. 'No fighting, please!' she said imploringly. 'Let's get home before I freeze to death.'

He hesitated, then dropped his fist. 'Oh, all right. He's not worth it, anyway. I'll get the petrol in.'

He turned, and for the first time took in the appearance of his car. 'Why by all that's wonderful have you put the hood down?'

She stammered out an explanation.

He groaned. 'Stuck! Oh, marvellous! It's happened before. I'll never be able to put it right out here.'

'Well, I'm sorry,' she said tearfully. 'I didn't do it on purpose.'

149

Muttering to himself, Paul picked up the can and walked to the rear of the car. Gerry turned back to Hugh, who was nursing his knuckles.

'Is it bad?'

'What do you think?'

'It's your own fault.'

He jerked his head at the tourer. 'You going back in that?'

'I suppose so.'

'Why not come in the Hispano? At least you'll be dry.'

She looked longingly in the direction of the other car. 'No, I'd better go back with Paul. It is my fault the top's down, after all.'

'That's crazy reasoning—'

Paul came up. 'What's the matter now?'

'Hugh's suggesting I should go home in the Hispano,' she said. 'I say, let's all go in it.'

'I'm not leaving my car here,' Paul said. 'The inside would be sodden by the morning. You do what you like.'

'All right. Thanks. I'll go with Hugh. I'm so *cold*.'

'Is that settled?' Hugh asked irritably. 'Good. Then come on, Gerry. You drive. My hand's hurting.'

'All right, so long as *somebody* drives.'

They were about to move towards the Hispano, when suddenly and unexpectedly Paul gave a yell. 'Stop ordering her around!'

Hugh turned. 'What?'

'You heard, you insolent little twerp! 'Do this, Do that.' Do you think she's a scullery maid?'

Gerry said despairingly, 'Oh, Paul, it doesn't matter!'

'It matters to me. I won't have you spoken to

150

like that by anybody, let alone this insufferable, jumped up pip-squeak.'

He stepped up to Hugh. 'You took a poke at me just now. Want to try again?'

'All right.'

Hugh jabbed out his fist. Paul effortlessly parried the blow. Gerry gave a yell and stepped forward.

'Stop it, both of you!'

But at that second Paul let fly with a left hook. It was a textbook punch, except for one thing. As he threw it his feet slipped on the icy road surface. He spun wildly, his arms flailed in the air, and his clenched fist caught Gerry square on the jaw.

Without a sound she collapsed on the road and lay still.

Paul stared at Gerry in abject dismay.

'You fool!' Hugh gasped.

Paul fell on his knees beside her and raised her head. Hugh shone his flashlight on her face. With immense relief in his voice Paul said, 'It's all right. She's breathing easily. She'll be round in a few minutes. Let's get her into the car.'

They lifted Gerry and manoeuvred her through the door of the Hispano and onto the passenger seat. Paul closed the door. 'Are you capable of driving this thing?'

'I'll manage.'

'OK.'

Splendid,' Paul said ironically, 'then, follow me.'

It was less than five minutes later that Gerry gave a little groan and opened her eyes. 'What happened?' she said thickly.

'Carter socked you on the jaw.'

'Don't be silly,' she murmured.

'He did, I tell you. Unfortunately, I'm forced to admit it was a pure accident.'

She fingered her jaw. 'Ouch. Oh, I remember now. The clumsy oaf.' She started to sit up.

Hugh said, 'Keep your head down a bit. You'll be groggy for a while yet.'

She did as he advised. A few seconds later she said, 'Gosh, I'm colder than ever.'

'You'll have to put up with it a bit longer.'

'Where are we?'

'I don't know. I'm following Carter. But you were about four miles from home when I found you and we've done a mile or so since then. If only this snow would ease!'

'Paul will be frozen solid with the top down.'

'How sad,' said Hugh.

*   *   *

When Gerry eventually walked stiffly into the house she was blue with cold. Her mother fussed around, plying her with questions, as she made her way thankfully to the fireplace and sank down in the chair closest to it.

'Don't laugh,' she said, 'but Paul ran out of petrol.'

The Countess brought a cup of coffee across to her. 'Oh, thanks, Mummy. I need that.'

Her father asked, 'Where are the boys?'

'Just putting the cars away.'

At that moment Hugh came in. Lord Burford said, 'Ah, the good Samaritan. Come and have some coffee, Hugh.'

'No, thank you, Lord Burford. I'll go straight up. Just looked in to say good night.'

152

'Thank you very much, Hugh,' Gerry said.

'That's all right.'

He went out, closing the door. A minute later Paul entered. He avoided Gerry's eye, refused coffee, but accepted a whisky and stood chatting to Lord Burford while he drank it. Then he too said good night and left the room. The Earl followed him upstairs a couple of minutes later, after bolting the front door.

Gerry and her mother remained talking for a further ten minutes, until Gerry had thawed out a little; then they also made their way rather wearily upstairs.

After kissing her mother good night and going to her room, Gerry stood hesitating, trying to decide whether to have a bath. She did need one in order to warm up fully. On the other hand, it was very late—nearly ten past two—and she was extremely tired.

Golly, what a day it had been! First that row with Gilbert—Oh no! Thinking of Gilbert had made her recollect the appointment she'd had with Rex.

She wondered if he could conceivably still be waiting for her. It was surely unlikely. But, on the other hand, he might have been expecting her any minute for the last hour and not have liked to go to bed.

Gerry sighed. She'd have to go and knock on the door of his sitting room, just in case. If he had turned in, that wouldn't disturb him. She left her room again.

There was no reply to her tap on Rex's door and, relieved, she started to turn away. She'd done her duty.

153

Then suddenly the door was pulled open with great force and Rex stood in the doorway.

*　　　　*　　　　*

He was still wearing evening dress, minus the coat, and for a moment there was an utterly unfamiliar expression on his usual cheerful countenance. In that second Gerry saw the face of a worried, even frightened, man behind the actor's mask. Then he was smiling.

'Why, Gerry. This is an unexpected pleasure.'

She stared. 'Unexpected? You mean, you weren't waiting up for me?'

'No.' He looked blank. 'Should I have been?'

'We had an appointment. Granted I'm absurdly late.'

Recollection came into his eyes. 'Of course! Come right in.'

'Just for a few seconds.'

Gerry went in and he closed the door. She said, 'It's a bit late to talk tonight. I'm at fault, though not really to blame. Paul had car trouble. So could we have our discussion about Gilbert tomorrow?'

'Gilbert?' He looked dazed and his manner was so odd she wondered if he'd been drinking. 'I don't want to talk about Gilbert. You must have misunderstood me.'

'I did no such thing!' she said indignantly. 'You asked if I'd been having trouble with him, as you had been. He'd been prowling about your room, you were worried and wanted to tell me a story.'

'Oh, I must have been exaggerating—professional failing, to dramatise situations.' He gave a decidedly unconvincing smile. 'We had a

154

few words about the script, but's all sorted out now.'

She gazed at him incredulously. He looked back, smiling stiffly, and there was silence.

At last she said, 'I see. Well, if you're sure there's nothing—'

'No, nothing,' he said sharply. 'Nothing at all.'

'Whatever you say.' She went towards the door. 'Good night, then.'

'Good night.'

Her hand touching the doorknob, on a sudden impulse she turned. 'Rex, are you all right?'

The eyes that met hers looked almost wild. Then, unexpectedly, he gave a harsh laugh. 'All right? Well, how would you feel if a career you'd spent all your adult life building up looked like it was over? Oh, yes, I feel just dandy!'

'I—I don't understand.'

'Well, I shouldn't try. I'm sure you've got your own problems. So why don't you go sleep on them?'

On the verge of demanding a fuller explanation, Gerry changed her mind. This wasn't the time. So she just said, 'Very well, if that's what you want. Good night again.'

This time she did go out, closing the door behind her. She made her way slowly back towards her room. What had happened to change him so? *Could* he have been drinking? There'd been no smell of it. If not, it really seemed he might be on the verge of a nervous breakdown.

She went into her room and sat down on the bed. Suddenly she felt wide awake. She decided to have a bath, after all. Perhaps a good soak would help her think. Her maid was long in bed, so Gerry

155

left her room again to go and run the bath. Not wanting to disturb Gilbert, she decided not to use the next-door bathroom, but the one across the corridor.

She had just entered it when, in the distance— but definitely indoors—she heard an utterly unexpected but quite unmistakable sound.

It was a gunshot.

Gerry's heart gave a leap, and for seconds she stood quite still, as the report reverberated through the corridors.

Rex. Could it be? Had that been his meaning when he'd talked about his career being over?

Gerry ran from the bathroom and sprinted along the main corridor. She reached the door of the Royal Suite. But as she got there the conviction came to her that the shot had come from farther away. She ran to the corner and stared along the east wing. At the far end a shaft of light streaming into the corridor showed that a door on the left was open.

Gerry started to run again. She was conscious of doors opening beside and behind her, of voices calling—alarmed, questioning. Then she saw that the light came from the end room, Laura's room. She arrived in the doorway. She gazed fearfully through it, then hesitantly stepped inside. The heat from a huge fire in the grate hit her, but she was hardly conscious of it. Her legs turned to jelly.

Lying on her back in front of the fire, her beautiful eyes staring sightlessly at the ceiling, was Laura. Just visible on the breast of her evening gown, looking like a ruby brooch, was a small dark red stain.

And standing near her, staring down, an

156

expression of blank horror in his eyes, was Paul. In his hand was a revolver.

CHAPTER THIRTEEN

At Gerry's cry Paul jerked his head towards her. For perhaps six or seven seconds they stood motionless, staring at each other, both quite unable to speak. Then Paul got out just two words:
  'She's dead.'
Automatically Gerry gave a jerky nod. She was barely conscious of the footsteps outside, or of Hugh's voice in the doorway. 'What's up?'
Then he came into the room and stopped short. He didn't speak.
'Is anything wrong?' It was Maude Fry's voice, slightly alarmed. Then the older woman, too, had entered the room. She gave a gasp.
The next moment everybody seemed to be there. There was a buzzing of questions, exclamations, muted screams. And then suddenly everyone was silent. As if at a given signal all eyes turned to Paul.
For a few seconds he met them, unflinching and wide-eyed. He said, 'I just—' Then something in their faces seemed to hit him. His expression changed from one of uncomprehending horror to appalled realization.
He gasped, 'You don't think I—?' He broke off, then shouted, 'I found her dead, I tell you!'
No one spoke. Seconds passed. Then Lord Burford stepped forward. There seemed a sudden new authority in his manner, as he held out his

157

hand and said quietly, 'Better let me have that, my boy.'

Paul gazed at him blankly. Then his eyes followed the Earl's downwards and he seemed, almost for the first time, to become aware of the revolver in his hand. He looked up again and his expression altered once more. Suddenly he looked frightened. He took a step backwards, and as he did so he raised the gun.

'No,' he said.

There was an instantaneous ripple of movement among the others. Cecily gave a little scream. Gerry gasped, 'Paul!'

He spoke hoarsely. 'Listen, all of you. I didn't do it. The gun was on the floor.'

Lord Burford, the only one present who hadn't moved when Paul had raised the gun, said, 'We can talk about that later. Give it to me now.'

Paul hesitated. His gun hand dropped again. There was the slightest relaxing of tension in the room. Then a thought seemed to occur to Paul. He swallowed. 'Wait, just a minute.'

He looked quickly round the room and in a few strides crossed to the dressing-table. He picked up an inlaid mother-of-pearl jewel box and opened it. It was empty. He placed the gun inside, closed the box, locked it, removed the key, and handed the box to Lord Burford. He said, 'My fingerprints are on that gun. But just possibly somebody else's—the killer's—are as well. They mustn't be smudged.'

With the pistol now safe, the Earl turned his attention to Laura Lorenzo. He knelt down by her and took her wrist, then looked up and shook his head. 'Dead, all right. Not that I doubted it, but must go through the formalities.' He got to his

158

feet. Avoiding Paul's gaze, he said, 'Better try and get hold of a doctor, I suppose, all the same. And the police. I'll go and ring up. We'd better lock this room—not touch anything. Look, do you mind all, please, moving out?'

Desperately, Paul said, 'Listen, I beg you all. You've got to believe me. I didn't do this. I was walking along the corridor when I—'

Haggermeir interrupted him. 'I don't know what you want to say, son, but take my advice and don't say it.'

'But I'm innocent.'

'Innocent or guilty you're in a tight spot. I know a bit about the law. Don't say another word until you've spoken with an attorney.'

Gerry moved near Paul and took his arm. 'He's right, darling.'

Paul closed his eyes and breathed deeply. Then he said, 'OK, except for one thing. A few minutes ago the real murderer was in this house. By now he may have got away. Or he may still be in the building.' He looked round the assembled throng. 'Or he may even be in this room.'

Lord Burford said, 'Let's go outside.'

Everybody shuffled slowly out, several people casting backward glances at the mortal remains of Laura Lorenzo. Most of those present seemed anxious to keep their distance from Paul. Only Gerry stayed close to him, even tucking her arm through his.

The Earl let everybody leave, then removed the key from the keyhole, closed the door and locked it. He addressed Paul again, 'I've got to call the police. You'd better go to your room and wait there. I don't want to have to do anythin' undignified like locking you in, so will you give me your word you won't try and do a bolt before they get here?'

Paul licked his lips. Then to everyone's alarm he gave a shout, 'I can't! I won't see the police!' He backed a few paces down the corridor. There was sweat on his brow. 'They'll arrest me. And I'm innocent. I've—I've got to get away. Now.'

And before anyone could even attempt to stop him, he turned and sprinted down the corridor.

Gerry screamed, 'Paul, no! Don't be a fool!'

She ran as fast as she could after him. But by the time she'd reached the corner of the corridor he'd disappeared down the stairs. She followed and caught sight of him, scrabbling with the bolts of the great front door. Before she'd got to the bottom of the stairs he'd heaved it open and vanished into the storm.

Gerry ran across the hall and out through the doorway. The driving snow was thicker than ever, and seemed to have swallowed Paul up. She called his name twice at the top of her voice, but the wind whipped the words from her lips. She stood helplessly, staring into the darkness.

Then, from the direction of the stable yard, she heard the familiar roar of the Hispano Suisa's engine. A few seconds later she saw the blaze of its headlights, and the next moment the car shot past her. As it did so, she heard Paul's voice, calling one word:

'Sorry.'

Then the car, sliding on the snowy surface, disappeared down the drive.

Forlornly, Gerry retraced her steps indoors, to meet the others, who'd descended in a body, in the hall. 'He's gone,' she said dully.

The Countess hurried forward and put an arm round her shoulder. 'Come and lie down, my dear.'

'I don't want to lie down, Mummy.' Then she burst out, 'Oh, the idiot—the stupid, stupid idiot! Why did he have to bolt? They'll never believe him now.' She gazed at her father. 'Will they?'

The Earl looked awkward. 'Well, er, couldn't say, my dear. Doubtful, I should think. No point in speculatin', though. I must go and phone them now, tell 'em exactly what's happened.'

'Daddy, you will tell them, won't you, that in spite of all the appearances, we don't believe he did it?'

Lord Burford avoided her eyes. 'Don't think I could actually do that, sweetheart.'

Gerry was white-faced. 'But—but you don't really think he killed her, do you?'

The Earl didn't answer. Gerry gave a gasp. 'I don't believe it!' She stared round the circle of faces. 'Tell him, somebody. Tell him Paul couldn't have done it.'

But the appeal got no response. Some eyes met hers squarely. Others fell. But in none was there any sign of agreement.

Gerry burst into tears. She shouted, 'You're a lot of beasts!' Then she turned, ran across the hall, up the grand staircase and out of their sight.

Hugh took a couple of steps to go after her, but the Countess put a hand on his arm. 'Leave her alone for a while. She'll be all right.'

Lord Burford turned to his wife. 'While I phone the police, will you ring for Merryweather, Lavinia? Explain what's happened and let him tell the others, if he thinks fit.'

The Countess nodded grimly. 'He won't like it, you know, George; he won't like it at all. None of them will.'

'Can't say I'm absolutely overjoyed about it myself, Lavinia.' He started to move away.

Lady Burford said sharply, 'Oh, George, I've just remembered. You can't use the telephone. Signorina Lorenzo tried to make a call. The line's dead.'

The Earl gave a groan. 'Oh, of course, I remember. Gad, that's all we need. Well, then Hawkins will just have to drive to the village.'

He turned away a second time, only to bump into Jemima Dove, who'd been witnessing everything with large, frightened eyes. She gave a little squeak.

'Oh, sorry, my dear,' Lord Burford said absently. Then he stopped and looked at her. 'Who the deuce are you?'

Lady Burford said hurriedly, 'Oh, this is Miss Dove, George. In the anxiety about Geraldine earlier I forgot to tell you.' She made a hasty explanation.

'Well, sorry you've had such an inauspicious welcome to Alderley, Miss Dove,' Lord Burford said. 'Should explain: this sort of thing—murders and suchlike—doesn't happen here often. Only every few months.'

*   *   *

Merryweather entered the library, crossed to the hearth and coughed discreetly. Lord Burford abruptly stopped snoring. Merryweather coughed a second time and the Earl's eyes opened sleepily.

162

'Mm?' he said.

'Another police officer, my lord.'

'Oh.' The Earl sat up, rubbing his eyes. 'Expect he's got news. What time is it?'

'Ten a.m., my lord.'

'Any of the guests up yet?'

'No, my lord.'

'Good. Hope they keep out of the way as long as possible. All right, show him in.'

Merryweather went out. Lord Burford stood up, ran his fingers through his hair, and blew his nose.

Merryweather reappeared in the doorway. 'Inspector Wilkins, my lord.'

He stood aside and hesitantly into the room came a short, plump man with a drooping moustache and worried expression.

Lord Burford gave an exclamation. 'Wilkins.'

He held out his hand as the other came across the room and with a somewhat diffident air shook hands.

'Good morning, my lord,' he said in a deep and mournful voice. Then he added, 'Though, perhaps not.'

'Not?'

'Not good, my lord. Another melancholy occasion, I fear. However, not without some nostalgic appeal, I must admit. Quite like old times, as they say.'

'Yes, well, come and sit down, Wilkins. Merryweather, coffee, please.'

The Earl and Wilkins sat down as Merryweather went out. Lord Burford gave a huge yawn. 'Excuse me. Been up all night. Not strictly necessary, I suppose. But seemed a bit heartless, just to turn in. All the rest of the household stayed up till about

163

five, too. Think they all felt the same. It was quite a night. Constant stream of people: first the village bobby; then those plain clothes men of yours—they were here for hours, taking statements from everybody; then your photographers and fingerprint men all over the place; doctor, ambulance men. And every time the door opened a howling gale sweeping through, snow coming in. Has it stopped?'

'Yes, my lord, a couple of hours ago. A slight thaw has already set in.'

'Thank heavens for that. Then there was the—' He broke off. 'Sorry. Wafflin' too much. Always do when I'm sleepy.'

'That's all right, my lord. Anyway you'll only have to put up with me and Sergeant Leather from now on.'

'Good. Sure if anyone can clear the business up quickly it's you. Not, of course, that it's going to present the problems of the last affair. Open and shut case, what? Just a question of catching Carter, really. Haven't done so yet, I suppose?'

'No, my lord, but it's only a matter of time.'

'You know he took my daughter's car? Oh, yes, of course, you're bound to.'

'Yes, my lord.'

At that moment Merryweather entered with coffee. When both he and Wilkins were gratefully sipping from steaming cups, Lord Burford said, 'Just how much *do* you know, Wilkins?'

'Well, my lord, I've seen all the officers who were first on the scene and I've had their reports. They were all very comprehensive.' He seemed to find this fact vaguely depressing.

'Ah, so you've got a pretty clear picture of what's

164

been going on?'

'I couldn't really say that, my lord. Must admit I find it all rather confusing. So many people on the scene. All made statements. Just names to me, except Mr Ransom, of course. Difficult to get them all sorted out, as it were.'

'Well, I can explain exactly who everyone is, if you like.'

'No, my lord, please don't bother. Hardly think it's going to be relevant. Just a few points about events leading up to the incident, if you don't mind. As I understand it, you all—or most of you—went to some function in the village. Got home about one, all except Lady Geraldine and Carter.'

'That's right.'

'All the others, including Signorina Lorenzo, went straight up to bed, only she tried to make a phone call first, but was unable to on account of the telephone being out of order. Then Mr—er, Quarter, is it?'

'Quartus.'

'Ah, yes. He went out to see what had happened to Lady Geraldine and Carter, and found them out of petrol about four miles away. Carter got some petrol, however, and they all arrived home the same time, about one-fifty. Carter and Mr Quartus went up immediately, followed by yourself, and the Countess and Lady Geraldine ten minutes later. The shot was heard another ten or twelve minutes after that, at about two-twenty. Lady Geraldine, who hadn't retired, was first on the scene, and then everyone else in a sort of rush.'

'That's about it. And there he was, Wilkins, just standing by the body, holding the gun.'

'Yes, my lord, I think that part of it's clear enough. What I haven't got is much information about either Carter or the deceased lady herself. If you could just tell me what you know about them . . .'

'All I can tell you about Paul is that he seems just a nice, pleasant-mannered young chap. Don't know a lot about his background. He's comfortably off, athletic type—ran in the Olympics, climbs mountains, and so on. Gerry's known him a year or so. He's stayed here once before.'

'And would I be right—excuse me—in assuming that there is—er, was—something more than mere friendship between them?'

'Oh, he's in love with her all right.'

Wilkins coughed delicately. 'And Lady Geraldine? She, um, reciprocates?'

'Oh, I think so. That other boy, Hugh, was by way of being a rival.'

'That would be Mr Quartus—the young gentleman who went out on the errand of mercy last night?'

'That's right. Seemed quite anxious. Must say he and Paul both appeared to be in a bit of a temper when they did eventually get back. Unusual for Paul. Hugh, on the other hand, tends to be rather temperamental. But then, he's an artist. Where was I?'

'Saying Mr Quartus was by way of being a rival.'

'Oh, yes. And I think *was* is the operative word. I've seen Geraldine definitely swinging towards Paul over the past few days. She's terribly cut up about this, of course, swears he couldn't have done it. Trying to convince herself, I think.'

'Now, what can you tell me about the signorina,

166

my lord?'

'Virtually nothing. Had never even heard of her until Thursday.'

'Yet you invited her for the weekend?'

'Didn't. Mystery about that.' He explained the full circumstances surrounding Laura's arrival, together with the reason for the visit of Haggermeir, Rex, and Gilbert.

When he'd finished, Wilkins rubbed his jaw thoughtfully. 'And this Mr Haggermeir denied all knowledge of the telegram?'

'Absolutely.'

'Interesting. Especially in view of what subsequently happened to the lady.'

'You're not suggesting Paul could have sent it, are you?' the Earl said suddenly. 'Sort of way of luring her down here, so he could kill her? That's ghastly. Would mean he planned the murder days in advance.'

'Seems highly unlikely my lord, but it would depend what his motive was. Any idea about that?'

'None at all. I've been assumin' it was some sort of brainstorm.'

'My men suggest robbery as the motive.'

'Robbery? But nothing's missing, is it?'

'Oh, yes, my lord. According to Signorina Lorenzo's maid, a very valuable mink coat, worth about two thousand pounds, has disappeared.'

'Disappeared? But how could it have? Paul didn't take it with him.'

'All we know, my lord, is that the lady was wearing it when she went upstairs after arriving home with your lordship at about one a.m. She wasn't wearing it when the body was discovered. It's not in her room, nor in her maid's room—she insisted on my men searching it. Their hypothesis is that Carter crept into Miss Lorenzo's room in the dark while she was asleep, and threw it out of the window to a confederate he'd previously arranged to have waiting outside. Then, before he could get out of the room, she awoke and he had to shoot her to silence her.'

'But she hadn't been to bed. She was dressed.'

'Well, the Countess told my men that before she went upstairs Miss Lorenzo told her that she had a headache. She might have lain down on the bed, meaning just to rest for a few minutes before getting ready to turn in properly—which, I imagine, is quite a procedure with a lady like that: lotions, creams, and so on—and then dropped off.'

'Seems extremely far-fetched to me.'

'Mm. Must admit it does to me, too, now I come to think about it.' Wilkins sounded surprised.

'Odd about the mink, though, I agree.'

Wilkins finished his coffee, put down his cup, reached into his pocket and brought out a grubby piece of folded paper. 'By the way, my lord, last time I was here I made a little sketch map of the first floor, showing which room every one occupied. I dug it out this morning. Could you just look over it with me and point out where everyone is accommodated?'

For the next few moments Wilkins scribbled in names on the plan at the Earl's instructions. Then he studied it for another minute before putting it away and saying,

'Now another point, my lord: the murder weapon.'

'I gave it to your men.'

'Yes, my lord, I've seen it. Had a job opening the

168

box without forcing it—Carter took the key. I understand the gun came from your collection?'

This was a moment to which the Earl had not been looking forward.

'That's right. Recognised it immediately. Checked in there since, just to make sure. Afraid six rounds of ammo are missing, too.'

'Now, you always keep the collection room locked, as I remember, my lord. So presumably he broke in.'

'No. He got hold of a key.'

Wilkins looked reproachful 'Oh, my lord.'

'I know what you're going to say: I should have been careful with them. Well, I have been—especially careful since that other affair. There are two keys. One I keep always on my watch chain. Here it is.' The Earl lifted it for Wilkins to see.

'And the other?'

'That I keep in my study safe. But when I went to the gun room I found it in the lock. I looked in the safe—just to be certain somebody hadn't somehow got a third key made—but no. There was no key there.'

'The safe was locked?'

'Yes.'

'And the key to that?'

'It has a combination lock.'

'How many other people know the combination, my lord?'

'As far as I know—knew—only my wife and daughter.'

'Lady Geraldine, then, could have told Carter?'

'She could have. Don't see why she should.'

There was a knock on the library door. Lord Burford called, 'Come in,' and a tall, cheerful-looking young man entered.

'You remember Sergeant Leather, my lord?' Wilkins said.

'Yes, indeed. Good morning.'

'Good morning, my lord. Excuse me.' He spoke to Wilkins. 'Just had a message, sir, that Carter walked into Swindon police station an hour ago and gave himself up.'

'Did he indeed?'

'Said he'd been driving round in circles in a dither all night, trying to decide what to do. He's being taken to Westchester. And, my lord, they've arranged to have Lady Geraldine's car brought straight back here.

'Oh, fine.'

Wilkins looked at his watch. 'Better get along to the station shortly, I suppose. No rush, though. They won't be making much speed with the roads as they are. Radio in and tell them I'll be on my way soon, Jack.'

'Yes, sir.' Leather went out.

'Er, there wouldn't be any more coffee in that pot, would there, my lord?'

'Yes, of course. Help yourself.'

'Thank you, my lord.' Wilkins did so.

'You will be charging him, of course,' Lord Burford said.

'Well, I really mustn't announce that in advance, my lord, if you understand—not before I've even seen him. At least, I won't have to arrest him, thank goodness. That's a thing I hate doing.'

'A policeman who doesn't like making arrests? You must be unique.'

'I daresay, my lord. But handcuffing people, locking them in cells—it always depresses me.

When I joined the force, I never saw myself out of the uniformed branch—perhaps a sergeant, at best. And in a peaceful place like Westshire, thought that poachers and the odd petty thief would be the extent of my contact with criminal types. But who could have anticipated the crime wave that's broken out among the English upper classes in recent years?'

'Crime wave? Put it as bad as that, do you?'

'Oh, my goodness, your lordship, yes. Never a week goes by without a nobleman being murdered in his library—oh, beg pardon, didn't mean to alarm you—or a don in his study, or an heiress in her bath. And where's it left me? Oh, I've made Chief Inspector, true—'

'Chief Inspector, now, eh? Congratulations.'

'Thank you, my lord. Could say you're responsible, in a way. It was your bit of bother here that finally got me promotion. But I can't honestly say I'm happy in my work. I'm out of my element. And I'm always scared the next case is going to stump me.'

'Oh, come on, Wilkins, you underestimate yourself. If you could solve our last case you could solve anything.'

'I had a lot of luck, my lord.'

'Luck? Poppycock. I'll tell you something, Wilkins. I lunched at me club in town with Peter Wimsey a couple of months back.'

Wilkins eyes bulged. '*Lord* Peter Wimsey?'

'That's right. I told him all about that business— he'd been abroad at the time himself. He was most interested, and said it sounded as if you'd put in a first-rate bit of detection work. Said he hoped he'd run into you sometime; he'd enjoy swapping case

171

stories with you.'

Wilkins was looking dazed. 'Really, my lord, that's quite a compliment. I don't know what to say.' With some reluctance he stood up. 'Better be making a move, I suppose.'

The Earl rose, too. 'Will you be coming back?'

'There may be a few more questions, my lord. It all depends, mainly on exactly what Carter's story is. I'll see you're kept informed of developments.'

CHAPTER FOURTEEN

The police constable unlocked the door and Wilkins went into the small, bare, windowless room, with its whitewashed walls and single light. The only furniture was a wooden table and three upright chairs. On one of these Paul was slumped. His hair was awry and his face haggard. A rough blanket was round his shoulders. A thick white china mug that had contained tea was on the table, and Paul was warming himself at an oil stove which was giving off a rather sickly smell.

Paul glanced up as Wilkins and the constable entered. There was a momentary flicker of hope in his eyes, which faded when he saw who they were and took in the expressions on their faces. For a few seconds Wilkins surveyed the young man without speaking. Then he pulled out a chair from the table and sat down heavily on in. The constable sat in the other chair and took out a notebook and pencil.

'I'm Detective Chief Inspector Wilkins.'

Paul looked up with sudden interest. 'Wilkins?

I've heard about you from Lady Geraldine. You solved that other murder at Alderley.'

Wilkins didn't answer this. He took a packet of cigarettes and a box of matches from his pocket and lit up. Then he pushed the cigarettes across the table towards Paul. 'Want one?'

Paul shook his head. 'I don't,' he muttered.

'Oh, no, of course. You're an athlete, aren't you? Certainly helped you last night, didn't it?'

Paul looked at him sharply. 'What do you mean?'

'Getting away after the murder. They say you were off down the corridor like a scalded cat. No one had a chance to lay a finger on you. Why'd you do it?'

'Do what?'

'Run away.'

'Why do you think? A woman had been killed, almost certainly murdered. I'd been found standing by her body with a gun in my hand. The Earl was just going to call the police.'

'But you claimed to be innocent.'

'Never heard of an innocent man being convicted?'

'No.'

Paul stared. 'What do you mean?' he said again.

'I've never heard of an innocent man being convicted—not of murder, in this country, in modern times.'

'Well, let's say I didn't want to be the first.'

'All you did was make it much more likely that you will be. You made the case against yourself even blacker.'

'It couldn't have been any blacker than it was already.'

Wilkins considered this. 'Well, no, perhaps not,' he said unexpectedly. 'Do you want to make a statement?'

'What, now?'

'Yes. Shouldn't if I were you. See a lawyer first, that's my advice.'

Paul hesitated. 'But in that case, won't everybody assume I'm guilty?'

'Nearly everybody assumes that now.'

'*Nearly* everybody?'

'I'm told Lady Geraldine is convinced of your innocence.'

Paul's face lit up. 'Is she really? Still? Oh, bless her.' He took a deep breath. 'I'll make a statement.'

'Sure?'

'Sure. What's the point in keeping quiet? Even after I've seen a lawyer I can only tell the truth. So I might as well tell it now. What have I got to lose? So here goes. And I know all that stuff about everything I say being taken down and used in evidence, so don't bother. Now, this is what happened.

'To make everything clear I'll have to start at a point a bit earlier in the evening, when Gerry and I were on our way back from the party. I ran out of petrol—which is something I still can't understand, but that's by the way. I had to walk to the main road and wave down a truck to get some. When I arrived back at the car after being away twenty or twenty-five minutes, I found Quartus had turned up. We had a bit of a fight. First he tried to sock me, then I took a poke at him. But I slipped on the icy road and hit Gerry by mistake, knocked her out. We put her in her car. I drove home in my car, and he followed with her. We got home about ten to two.

'By then Gerry, naturally, wasn't too pleased with me. So I thought it would be better if I kept out of her way as much as possible until the following morning. I had a quick drink with the Earl and then went straight up. I was so cold and tired that when I got to my room I sat in the chair in front of the fire for about fifteen minutes, just getting warm. Then I decided to turn in. I took off my overcoat and left the room again, meaning to go to the bathroom. I went to the right, making for the one at the end of the main corridor, which I usually use. But as I did so I heard Lady Geraldine's voice coming from that direction. Well, as I explained, I didn't really want to see her again that night, so I returned to my room to wait until the coast was clear. Now, as a matter of fact, I'd forgotten about the other, smaller bathroom at the end of the wing—I don't think I'd ever been right to the end—but after five minutes or so I suddenly remembered hearing some reference to it once. So I left my room again and this time turned left.

'As you get to the end of the corridor the illumination isn't too good—the last light is about level with the door to the gallery. As a result, I particularly noticed a narrow beam of light being thrown across the corridor, which meant that Signorina Lorenzo's bedroom door was open an inch. But I thought nothing of that. Then, when I got a bit closer, I noticed a small object lying on the floor just outside the door. It wasn't until I was almost on top of it that I realised it was a revolver. I bent over it and thought I recognised it as being one of Lord Burford's. I couldn't think how it had got there, but naturally I didn't imagine there was anything wrong. However, I knew that the Earl was particular about keeping all his guns under lock and key, so I picked it up, meaning to return it to him immediately.

'Just then I heard a sound from Signorina Lorenzo's room, a sort of muffled groan. I hesitated a moment, then tapped on the door. There was no reply. I called out softly, just asking if she was all right. But still there was no answer. So I pushed the door open wide and stepped into the room. It was terribly hot in there, like a greenhouse. There was a huge fire in the hearth, and on the rug in front of it Signorina Lorenzo was lying.

'I started to move towards her. As I did so, someone gave me a tremendous shove in the back. It sent me staggering right across the room, nearly falling. At that moment I heard a gunshot in the doorway behind me. I managed to stop myself and spun round. But by then there was nobody there. For a few seconds I dithered—couldn't decide whether to run to the door or go to Signorina Lorenzo. At last I went to her and saw the bullet wound. I just stood there. I couldn't take it in properly. A few seconds later Lady Geraldine arrived. The rest you know. And that I swear is the truth.'

Wilkins dropped the stub of his cigarette on the floor, stepped on it, and with his toe flicked it out of sight under the table. 'What do you know about the lady's mink coat being missing?' he asked.

Paul looked bewildered. 'Missing? You mean stolen? It's the first I've heard of it.'

'Well, I assure you it is. And it provides a quite adequate motive for murder. If you'd decided to steal it—thrown it out of the window to a confederate, say—and the lady caught you in the act, you'd have had to silence her.'

'That's absolutely crazy! Why on earth should I want the woman's confounded coat?'

'It's worth two thousand pounds.'

'I don't need two thousand pounds.'

'So you say.'

'Check with my bank, my brokers. Get on to them now.' He broke off and looked at his watch. 'Well, it'll have to be Monday now, I suppose. They'll confirm what I say.'

Wilkins shrugged, 'If you say so, no doubt they will. But robbery isn't the only motive for murder.'

'But I didn't have any motive!' Paul said desperately. 'I'd never set eyes on the woman until two days ago. I talked to her for about ten minutes in the library on Friday morning, and apart from that I just made a few casual remarks to her, always with other people present. Check up as much as you like. Or do you think I'm just a homicidal sex maniac, or something?'

'Oh, no, this case doesn't bear the marks of that sort of crime.'

'Then please, please believe me. When I went through that bedroom door Laura Lorenzo was already dead.'

Wilkins regarded Paul silent for a few moments. Then, 'I believe you,' he said.

*   *   *

Paul sat motionless, his eyes fixed on Wilkins. It

177

was as if for seconds be could not properly comprehend what had been said. Then his expression changed. Care was magically wiped from his face.

He slumped back in his chair. 'Oh, what a relief! But why? I mean, what . . . ?'

'Oh, a number of reasons. Mainly because as things stand it's all too pat, too obvious. What's more, you, if I may say so, seem a highly intelligent young gentleman. I'm quite sure that if you were going to shoot somebody, you wouldn't be so careless as to let yourself be accidentally found standing over the body, holding a gun.'

For the first time in many hours, Paul grinned. 'Well, thanks.' He stood up suddenly. 'Can I go now?'

'Yes, sir. Do you want to go back to Alderley?'

'Well, I'd better collect my car and my other things. But I won't stay. Far too embarrassing, with all the rest of them no doubt still thinking I'm a murderer. No, I'll go back to London, until such time as you nail the real killer. Gosh, though, half an hour ago I never thought I'd be officially in the clear as quickly as this.'

'Now hold on,' Wilkins said. 'Don't get carried away. I don't say you're out of the woods yet.'

Paul froze. He stammered, 'But—but you said that, that you believe—'

'What I believe isn't really all that important, sir. As you said, there's a very strong case against you. To most people, including I strongly suspect my chief, and perhaps the Director of Public Prosecutions, it's likely to seem overwhelming. Then there's the question of public opinion. If no new evidence comes to light which either clears

178

you or points to someone else, then I—or one of my colleagues—may be forced by circumstances to arrest and charge you.'

'And you said no innocent man gets convicted of murder?'

'I don't say you'll be convicted. But you may have to go through a very unpleasant couple of months before you're acquitted.'

Paul ran his fingers through his hair. 'This is ghastly. What on earth can I do?'

'Well, in the first place, sir, I suggest you go back to Alderley and stay there, rather than return to London.'

'But why?'

'For one thing, it'll look good from your point of view—the open act of an innocent man, not like someone with a guilty conscience running away. Secondly, if you were framed, you were framed by one of the guests in the house. I discount the servants—they've all been there donkey's years—and of course the family. On the other hand, I can't ask *them* to report or spy on their guests.'

'Is that what you want me to do?'

'I'd rather not put it in those words.'

'But, look, they're convinced I'm a killer. They're not likely to be friendly, or to allow me to pump them.'

'No, but you'll *be* there. You see, I want someone who can watch people, can gauge reactions—both to your return and to the realization that the police aren't satisfied, that we're still investigating.'

Paul nodded thoughtfully. 'And as the person who was the victim of the frame-up, I'm the only one of the guests in the clear, the only one you can

179

trust. Yes, I see.'

'*Officially* you're still a suspect, mind you, though just one of eight or nine. You've been released, pending further enquiries into the feasibility of your story and the possibility of somebody else's guilt. Though if you want to tell them that I personally believe you, you can. Will you do it?'

'I haven't got much choice, have I? You've as good as told me that if I don't help you spot the real killer I'll be re-arrested.'

'Put in that way, it sounds like blackmail, sir, but I assure you it isn't that. You're free to return to London, if you wish. It's just that I need all the help I can get to have any hope of cracking this case. We're dealing here with a very good brain.'

'But you will get him eventually?'

'I'd like to think so, Mr Carter. But without help, frankly I'm not sanguine, not sanguine at all.'

*   *   *

It was just after one when Paul got back to Alderley and, his heart in his mouth, mounted the steps to the big front door. As he approached it, it was opened from the inside and Gerry stood in the doorway. For about five seconds she just stared at him. Then she ran forward and threw herself into his arms.

'Oh, Paul,' she said. 'Oh, Paul.'

He clasped her to him. 'This makes it all worthwhile,' he murmured.

She drew back and looked up at him, bewilderment mixed with her pleasure. 'But why? I don't understand. What's happened? They said

180

you'd given yourself up to the police.'

'I did. They let me go.'

She gave a gasp of delight. 'You mean they believe you?'

'Your Inspector Wilkins does.'

'Oh, good old Wilkins! I knew he wouldn't let me down!'

'I'm not completely in the clear yet, Gerry.'

Her face fell. 'What do you mean?'

'I'll tell you in a minute—inside. Listen, where is everybody? Having lunch?'

'Yes. I didn't want any.'

'So nobody else knows about my being free?'

'Not yet.'

'Well, I want to surprise them. But first I've got to clean up. Can I get up to my room without being seen?'

'I don't see why not.'

She turned, ventured just inside the front door, looked around the hall, then beckoned him. 'All clear.'

He went in and together they hurried upstairs and along the corridor to his bedroom. Once inside he gave a sigh of relief.

He said, 'First of all, sorry about pinching your car. It was a spur of the moment thing. It didn't seem a very good idea to take my own—not with the top stuck down, and less than a gallon of petrol in the tank.'

'Oh, that's all right, silly.'

'You got it back?'

'Yes, the police brought it. But forget the car. Explain what you meant about not being in the clear.'

He did so, ending by saying, 'So I thought if I

could spring myself on them, while they were all together, and didn't even know I was here, it would be a good opportunity to gauge reactions.'

'You mean while they're at lunch?'

'Yes; have I got time?'

'I should think so. They've only just started.'

'Good. So what I want now is a quick wash, shave and change of clothes. Then will you go into the room with me and help watch their faces?'

She shook her head.

'You won't?' He looked amazed.

'Not *their* faces, Paul. There's only one face *I'm* going to be watching: Arlington Gilbert's.'

*　　*　　*

'You let him go?' the Chief Constable of Westshire, Colonel Melrose exclaimed incredulously.

'Er, yes sir,' Wilkins said.

'Are you out of your mind, man?'

Wilkins shuffled his feet like a schoolboy before his headmaster. The Chief Constable gazed at him helplessly, his honest, if not very intelligent, face displaying a combination of anger and bewilderment.

Colonel Melrose was popular with his men. Though a strict disciplinarian, he was basically kindly, scrupulously fair, backed them to the hilt when they did their best, and never used his position to fix his friends' speeding tickets. Moreover, he mostly left them alone to get on with their cases without interference. Occasionally, however, when people with whom he was personally acquainted were involved in criminal matters, he did feel obligated to take a closer interest in the investigation than usual. This, though, was not to help them get off lightly; rather in fact the opposite. He was determined to insure that none of his officers went easy on friends of the boss. As a long-time acquaintance of Lord Burford, it seemed he was going to make the latest Alderley murder one such case.

Wilkins sighed inwardly. Admirable though his chief was in the most ways, criminal investigation was not his forte. The lack of imagination, stubbornness and slight stupidity that had prevented him reaching the highest ranks of the army became all too obvious in such cases. Wilkins could see trouble looming on this one.

'I don't think I'm out of my mind, sir,' he answered.

'Then why the blue blazes did you do it? Here's a bloke, found standing over the woman's body, the murder weapon in his hand—'

Wilkins interrupted adroitly. 'That's been conformed, has it, sir? I haven't seen the ballistics report.'

'Yes, I got a copy a few minutes ago. But surely, you didn't think the gun Carter was holding *wasn't* the murder weapon, did you?'

'Wouldn't be the first time something like that's happened at Alderley, sir.'

The Chief Constable fingered his moustache. 'No, point there. But Wilkins, this isn't a case like that one. It's open and shut. You can't let the chap go.'

'But I have, sir.'

'Then you can pick him up again.'

'I'd much rather not, sir, really.'

183

'But we'll be laughing-stocks—with the press, the other police forces. This case is going to get a shocking amount of publicity, once the papers hear about it. Italian actress, Olympic athlete, stately home. And to cap it all that blessed Yankee film star staying at the house at the time. We must get the killer charged and brought before the Magistrate quickly, so it becomes *sub judice*. There's no time to lose.'

'I'm aware of that, sir.'

'Then why don't you want to arrest the chap?'

'Because if I do, sir, I'm convinced I'll have to let him go again. And that *would* make us laughing-stocks.'

'But why should you have to?'

'Because sooner or later some new piece of evidence is going to turn up that would force me to.'

'But the shot, the gun in his hand . . .'

'I know all about that, sir. Carter says it was a frame-up.'

'You can't believe that.'

'I do, sir.'

'Great Scott.'

Colonel Melrose sat down suddenly, a blank expression on his face. After a few seconds he asked, 'Any evidence as to who might have been responsible for this—frame-up?'

'No evidence at all yet, sir.'

Colonel Melrose said quietly, 'I'm speechless, Wilkins.'

'I'm sorry about that, sir. But this is how I see it: frame-ups are very difficult things to arrange. There are too many imponderables, too much that can go wrong. They may hold for a while, but not for long. Sooner or later some fresh piece of information comes to light that blows the whole thing sky-high. That's what I expect to happen in this case.'

The Chief Constable sat silently for several moments. Then he said slowly, 'Do I take it, then, that you refuse to arrest Carter?'

Wilkins looked unhappy. 'Well, of course, sir, if you order me to . . .'

'I don't want to do that.'

Abruptly Colonel Melrose stood up again. 'How about a drink?'

'Oh, thank you, sir. I wouldn't say no to a Scotch and soda.'

Colonel Melrose crossed to a glass-doored cabinet and there was a clink of glasses for a few seconds. Then he came back, handed Wilkins a glass and raised his own. 'Well, bung-ho.'

'Down the hatch, sir.'

They both drank. When the Chief Constable spoke again it was with a confidential air. 'Wilkins, you've had a lot of these cases, haven't you—these involved, difficult murder cases, I mean?'

'Too many, sir.'

'Perhaps so. And I suppose one of the worst was that other business at Alderley, what?'

'It took a bit of unravelling.'

'Had some help there, didn't you?'

'Oh, yes, sir. I'm not trying to claim all the credit.'

'I didn't mean that. We all know the case wouldn't have been solved without you. Fact remains that the espionage element meant that that secret service fellow was *technically* in charge, if not openly. Nobody said as much, but he had

185

direct links with the Prime Minister and could have taken over at any time if it looked as though you weren't up to it. Luckily he didn't have to. But the possibility was there.'

'Yes, sir, but I don't quite see—'

'What I'm driving at, Wilkins, is that if anything had gone wrong the ultimate responsibility wouldn't have been yours—or the responsibility of this force. It would have been his and his department's.'

'True, sir.'

'Well, I'm chewing over the possibility of somehow getting ourselves in the same situation again.'

'You mean ask the secret service to—'

'No, no, the Yard.'

'Call in Scotland Yard, sir?'

'Yes. How does the idea appeal to you? Don't take it as a criticism in any way, old man, but—'

'I don't, sir. I'd welcome it.'

The Chief Constable gave a slight start. 'You would?'

'Yes, sir, I've always wanted to work under a top Yard officer. The idea of just acting as a kind of glorified messenger boy and letting him do all the brainwork—why, it would be heaven. But you've always been dead against it.'

'I know I have. But I think there are special circumstances in this case. If we hand it over to them and they arrest this Carter chappie and then have to let him go, then it's no skin off our nose, what? On the other hand, if, as I suppose is possible, they agree with you that he's innocent, and then it turns out I'm right and he's not—'

'Our noses are still intact, sir. If I may say so, it's

a fine idea, very subtle indeed.'

Colonel Melrose clapped his hands. 'Splendid, splendid!' He looked at his watch. 'I'll put through a call straight away and see if they can get somebody here by this evening. They have several men who specialise in these more bizarre mysteries, don't they—John Appleby, Roderick Alleyn, St. John Allgood. What's that name they've got for them up there?'

'The three Great A's, sir. If we can get one of them it'll be marvellous.'

'Yes, and with luck we'll have Car—er, somebody—charged before the story breaks publicly. If we don't, it's going to be grim, reporters all over us. Fortunate that phone at Alderley being out of order. Someone there would certainly have blabbed by now if not. As it is, the only people I've notified are the Italian Embassy. They won't make it public until her next of kin—whoever that may be—has been traced in Italy and informed. So we've got a day or two's breathing space, with luck.'

'I think perhaps we ought to notify her London agent as well, sir. Seems she was going to visit him today. According to Lady Burford's statement, Miss Lorenzo tried to phone him at one o'clock this morning to tell him what time she'd be arriving today. Of course, she couldn't get through, so presumably he won't be worrying yet at her not turning up. However, he obviously will start to get anxious before the day's out. We don't want him notifying the press of her disappearance, or anything like that.'

'Do you know where to contact him?'

'Yes, sir, we found his phone number in her

address book.'

'Very well, put through a call. But be sure and tell him to keep it under his hat. Then grab a bite of lunch and get back to Alderley, keep the ball rolling until the Yard arrives.'

He gave Wilkins a clap on the shoulder. 'And thanks for being so accommodating. I won't forget it.'

CHAPTER FIFTEEN

Gerry looked at Paul. 'Ready?' He nodded, tight-lipped. She opened the door of the dining-room. Everybody looked towards her.

Lord Burford said, 'Oh, hullo, my dear. Change your mind about lunch?'

Gerry didn't answer. She said, 'Look who's here.'

She stood aside and Paul walked into the room. Any variation of reaction he might have been expecting from the assembled guests was not forthcoming. On every face, as he looked quickly from one to the other, he saw the same thing: blank astonishment. He let five seconds pass before saying quietly, 'Hullo.'

It was Lady Burford who first recovered herself. 'What—what are you doing here, Paul?'

'I was hoping, if I may, to have some lunch.'

'But we were told you were under—er, with the police.'

Gerry said, 'They let him go. Isn't it marvellous?' It was clear this reaction was not widely shared.

The Earl said, 'But why?'

'Inspector Wilkins believes my story,' Paul said.

From the lower end of the table Hugh uttered an exclamation. 'I don't believe it!'

Paul gave the slightest shrug. 'Ask him. I'm sure he'll be back later.'

'Come on, Paul,' Gerry said, 'let's sit down.'

They did so, Gerry first pulling the bell for Merryweather. There was a strained silence. It was broken by Paul himself.

'I'd like to repeat now the account I gave to Inspector Wilkins of just what happened last night, the account he believed. If anybody afterwards still disbelieves me, I can only say I don't really blame you. I probably wouldn't believe it in your shoes. However, it happens to be true and I hope before long you'll all know that for a fact.' He paused. 'As one of you does already.'

*   *   *

Wilkins arrived back at Alderley at two-thirty. He asked for Lord Burford, but was told by Merryweather that the Earl was lying down, as was the Countess.

'Perhaps you'd care to see Lady Geraldine, sir?' he said.

Wilkins looked pleased. 'Yes, I would, very much.'

'Then if you will kindly wait in the library I will find her.'

When Gerry entered the library a minute later, Paul was with her. She greeted Wilkins warmly. 'Mr Wilkins, I knew I could rely on you.'

'Very kind of your ladyship.'

189

'Any developments, Inspector?' Paul asked.

'Yes, sir. Very shortly the case will be out of my hands.'

Their faces fell. Gerry said, 'But why?'

'The Chief's called in the Yard, my lady.'

Gerry gave a gasp. 'Oh, no!'

'Now don't fret, my lady. They're sending one of their very best men, Chief Superintendent Allgood. You want the real killer nabbed, don't you?'

'Yes, of course.'

'With Mr Allgood here, he will be. He specialises in this sort of case.'

'I've heard of him,' Paul said. 'Quite a character, isn't he?'

'I'll say so, sir. He's a real lone wolf. Doesn't even have a sergeant to assist him—only his own valet, man called Chalky White. Ex-cat burglar. Mr Allgood saved his life years ago, climbed up a high building and brought him down after a drainpipe broke. Then persuaded the judge to give him a reduced sentence.'

'When will he be here?' Gerry asked.

'In an hour or two, my lady. As luck would have it, he's been investigating a case not far away—the murder of the Dean of Cheltenham. He finally cleared it up this morning—arrested the Bishop, as a matter of fact. After the Assistant Commissioner of Scotland Yard received Colonel Melrose's request, he sent instructions for Mr Allgood to come straight on here. It'll be an education to work under him. I'm really looking forward to it.'

'What do you want to do in the meantime?'

Wilkins scratched his nose. 'Well, nothing, really, my lady.'

'Wouldn't you like to question the guests?'

'No, I don't think so, thank you. Better leave that to Mr Allgood. Unless there's been any development since you got back, Mr Carter—any noticeable reaction from anybody which ought to be followed up immediately.'

Paul shook his head. 'Nothing.'

Wilkins shrugged. 'Didn't really expect a lot in the first instance, sir. Murderers don't often give away anything by their expressions. But continue to keep your eyes and ears open. I'm sure there's one person in this house very much on edge.'

Gerry said, 'You're convinced the murderer is here, then?'

'I'm afraid so, my lady. True, an outsider could have got in, the burglar alarm being out of action. But he'd have needed an inside accomplice: somebody who knew which room Miss Lorenzo was occupying, the location of a suitable gun in the collection room, where the ammo for it was kept, the fact that there was a spare key in his lordship's safe, and the combination of that safe. And that's the man I want, even if—which I doubt—it should turn out he brought someone in from outside actually to pull the trigger. Incidentally, that business of the safe is a bit of a poser in itself. His lordship thought that nobody but himself, her ladyship, and you, my lady, knew it. Now, could you by any chance have mentioned it to someone else?'

Gerry looked at him. She licked her lips. Then she shook her head.

'Sure, my lady?'

'Yes. Yes, of course.'

Quietly Paul said, 'Thanks, darling, but it's no

good.'

'Paul!'

'Sweetheart, I'm convinced that Chief Inspector Wilkins is my best hope. We've got to tell him the complete truth. What faith is he going to have in my innocence if he finds out later I've been lying to him?'

'There's no way he could have found out,' she said sulkily.

'Maybe not. But it'll be more comfortable if everything is open and above board. Fact is, Inspector, *I* know the combination of that safe.'

'But I virtually forced it on him,' Gerry put in.

'How come, your ladyship?'

'It was months ago. We were playing roulette at a place in London. Lord, I suppose that was illegal, too. Anyway, I was betting on the numbers of our birthdays. Paul was pulling my leg about being superstitious, and I said it must run in the family, because Daddy's birthday is on the eleventh, Mummy's on the eighth, and mine on the twenty-third, so he'd had the combination of the safe made eleven right, eight left, twenty-three right.'

Wilkins nodded slowly. 'Was anybody else present at the time?'

'Of course. We were in a night club.'

Paul said: 'But there was nobody we knew standing close enough to have heard.'

'Oh, really, you are the most utter chump!' Gerry spoke exasperatedly. 'You seem to be going out of your way to paint as black a picture against yourself as possible.'

Wilkins raised a hand. 'With respect, your ladyship, Mr Carter is doing absolutely the right thing. I suppose you didn't mention the combination to anyone else, sir?'

Paul gave a sigh. 'It would be so easy, wouldn't it, to say yes? But, frankly, if a good friend happens to mention the combination of their safe, it's not the sort of thing one goes around blabbing to all and sundry. No, Mr Wilkins, to the best of my recollection I didn't mention it to a soul.'

'I still say somebody could have overheard me,' Gerry muttered.

'Apart from that, you've mentioned it to no one else, your ladyship?'

Reluctantly, she shook her head.

'Well, his lordship is certain neither he nor the Countess has told anybody else.'

'And it's so easy to remember, he's never written it down anywhere,' she said. 'Oh, dear, everything seems to make it worse for Paul than before. I suppose you have got to tell this Yard man, have you, Mr Wilkins?'

'Afraid so, my lady, but I'll also tell him Mr Carter freely volunteered the information. It'll count very much in his favour.'

'Thank heavens something will. In spite of your releasing him, I'm sure everyone's going to think he's guilty once the murder becomes public. Unless you and Scotland Yard can find the real killer first.'

'You just leave it to Mr Allgood, your ladyship.'

'Don't you want to do anything until he arrives?'

Wilkins looked doubtful. 'Suppose I ought to do *some*thing. Don't quite know what, though.' Then he brightened a little. 'Oh, I know. I'll interview the servants.'

'Is there any real point in that?' she asked. 'I'm sure they won't be able to tell you anything. They

193

were all in bed at the time.'

'I agree, your ladyship. It's probably a waste of time, but it's something that's got to be done.'

'In all the hundreds of detective stories I've read,' Paul said, 'the Inspector always leaves that job to his sergeant.'

'No doubt, sir, but I've got to find something to do. And it's a nice, uncomplicated job, as a rule. Just right for me.'

*   *   *

The stable clock was striking four forty-five when a white Bentley swept up the now slush-covered drive of Alderley and skidded to a halt outside the great front door, with a fanfare on its horn. The driver—a dark, sharp-faced man, with a toothbrush moustache—jumped out and opened the rear door. The man who emerged was tall and broad-shouldered. The driver ran up the steps in front of him and rang the doorbell just a few seconds before it was opened by the imperturbable-as-ever figure of Merryweather. The tall man strode in without being invited.

He was wearing a stylish full-length vicuna motoring coat, a grey Homburg hat, grey suede gloves and grey spats. He had a large Roman nose, piercing dark eyes, and an upturned waxed moustache. He removed his hat to reveal curly black hair, saying as he did so, 'Allgood of the Yard. Kindly inform your master that I have arrived.'

Merryweather turned. 'Oh, here is his lordship, sir.'

The Earl bustled forward, Wilkins at his heels.

'Chief Superintendent Allgood?'

'St. John Allgood, yes. Of Scotland Yard.' He pulled off his gloves and held out his hand. 'How do you do, Burford? We haven't met, but I believe we have several mutual friends—Tubby Charrington, Pongo Smith-Smythe, Bertie Bassington.'

'Oh, yes, yes, of course. Delighted to meet you, my dear chap. How de do?'

Allgood snapped his fingers, and his driver hurried forward and helped to divest him of his coat. Under it Allgood was wearing a superbly cut grey pinstripe suit, with an Old Etonian tie. 'Understand you've been having a spot of bother here, Burford.'

'You could put it like that.'

'Ah, well, we'll soon clear that up.'

'I sincerely hope so. I don't know what you'd care to do first . . . ?'

'First I must meet the local man and get the facts. I take it he's around somewhere.'

Wilkins, on whose face had appeared an expression closely resembling that on Lord Burford's when he had met Rex Ransom, cleared his throat nervously. 'That's me, sir.'

Allgood stared. 'You? Oh, I didn't realise. Don't exactly look the part, do you?' He chuckled, revealing a great many large and very white teeth. 'Wilkins, is that right?'

'Yes, sir.'

'Right. Where can we talk?'

'Well, his lordship has kindly given us the use of the small music room.'

'Excellent.' He turned back to the Earl. 'I'll talk to you in due course, Burford. And the rest of your household.'

'Oh, yes, of course. If there's anything you want
...?'

'Yes, tea; China, please. And muffins.' He
addressed his driver: 'Chalky, bring my cases in
and take them up to my room.'

'Yes, guv.' Chalky hurried out.

Lord Burford looked a bit taken aback. 'Oh, er,
you stayin'?'

Allgood turned slowly to face him again. 'I
thought that was understood, It's the usual thing in
cases like this. Much more convenient. Means the
trouble gets cleared up far quicker. Only be for a
couple of nights. Of course, if it's not possible, I
suppose there's a hostelry of some sort in the
village.'

'No, no, that'll be quite all right—pleasure and
all that.'

'Good. What time do you dine?'

'Eight, as a rule.'

'Better make it a bit later tonight—nine, say. I'll
dine in my room. Right, Williams, lead the way.'

*   *   *

In the music room Allgood threw himself down
into the only comfortable arm chair and put his
feet on a pouf. 'Very well, fire away, Chief
Inspector,' he said.

'I'd like to say first, sir, what a privilege it's going
to be to assist you on this case.'

'Yes, you should learn quite a lot. I must
congratulate you, though.'

'What for, sir?'

'Knowing your limitations. I was told you were

196

all in favour of your C.C. calling me in. It's refreshing to find a man who knows when he's out of his depth and it's time to call in the expert. It's disgraceful the way some of these provincials cling to cases they haven't got a dog's chance of solving. And you won't lose by your attitude. I have no intention of grabbing all the glory. I'll see you get full credit with everybody, just as though we were equal partners. Now, tell me everything you know about this case. And I mean what you *know*. I want facts, and facts *only*.'

'Very good, sir.' Wilkins perched himself on the edge of an upright chair and took a deep breath. He had been mentally rehearsing this moment, and he was able to give a clear yet concise account of the events leading up to the murder. Then he picked up a briefcase from the floor and extracted from it a cardboard folder.

'As to the crime itself, sir, I have here a list of all the occupants of the house; a sketch map showing where everyone was sleeping; the reports of the officers who were first on the scene, including statements from Lord and Lady Burford and all their guests; ballistics and medical reports, etc. And a transcript of the statement made at the station this morning by Carter. Perhaps you'd better read them.'

Allgood snatched the folder from him and began casting his eyes over its contents at an enormous speed. While he was doing so a footman entered, wheeling a tea trolley. Without looking up, Allgood said, 'Thank you, my man, we can serve ourselves.'

The footman departed. 'Pour me a cup of tea, Wilton,' Allgood said. 'And butter me two muffins.'

'Oh, yes, sir.'

By the time Wilkins had completed this task and was wiping his fingers on his handkerchief, Allgood had come to the last page of the folder. He threw it down on the table, picked up a white linen napkin, shook it open, spread it on his knees, took the plate which Wilkins proffered him, and began devouring muffins hungrily.

'That's all right, as far as it goes,' he said. 'Now let's have your personal report.'

'Well, sir, first I had an interview with his lordship.'

'Tell me exactly what he said.'

Wilkins complied to the best of his ability. When he'd finished, Allgood said, 'Is that all you got out of him?'

'Just about, sir.'

'Hm. I'm sure that's not all he can tell us. Who else have you spoken to?'

'Well, Carter, of course. Lady Geraldine—though that wasn't a formal interview. And the servants.'

'The servants? Couldn't you have let your sergeant deal with them?'

'Well, sir—'

'Never mind. Tell me what you learnt from the servants.'

'Nothing of any great significance. I'm sure they're OK.'

'Of course they are! Once it was always the butler who did it, but not these days. That's very old hat.'

'For what it's worth, one of them—the third footman, William—confirms that the deceased did go straight up to her room last night. He was on a sort of patrol they've organised, since the burglar alarm is out of order at the moment. He came up the stairs at the far end of the eastern corridor at five past one, and she was just coming round the corner at the near end. They passed each other about halfway along. He looked back just before he turned into the main corridor, and saw her go into her room and close the door after her. That's all I got from the resident servants. I did have hopes of learning something about Signorina Lorenzo from her French maid, Eloise. But no luck. She'd only been with her mistress four weeks, and knew hardly anything of her private life. All she was really able to tell me is that nothing is missing, apart from that mink coat. She's struck up a friendship with Lady Geraldine's maid, a very reliable French girl called Marie, who's been with Lady Geraldine six years. They sat up very late chatting in Marie's room last night. Were together from about midnight till two-thirty, when they were told about the murder. Except, that is, for a few minutes at about twelve-thirty, when Eloise went along to her mistress's room to make the fire up. So she wasn't really much help at all.'

Wilkins paused for breath. Allgood swallowed his last portion of muffin. 'Well, go on, man.'

'Oh, right, sir. What else is there? Let me see. Ah, yes. I telephoned the signorina's London agent and told him what had happened. She'd been going to visit him at his home today.'

'What did he have to say?'

'He was naturally terribly shocked, but he couldn't tell me anything important. He hadn't seen her since she'd arrived in London on Wednesday. She booked into the Savoy and phoned him on Thursday morning, saying she was coming to Alderley to see Mr Cyrus Haggermeir, the film producer. She'd be back in London on Saturday and would call at his home and tell him all about it. The only odd thing is that late last night it seems she tried to phone him, only the line here was down. She told Lady Burford that she wanted to inform him what time she'd be arriving today, and she also mentioned that he kept late hours. Well, firstly, he says he told her that he'd be in all day today, and she could visit any time. Secondly, he does *not* keep late hours—he's invariably in bed by eleven. So it seems—'

'—that the ostensible reason for the phone call last night was false, that she had something important she wanted to tell him. Interesting.' Allgood sipped his tea ruminatively. Then he said, 'This mink coat: if nobody's left the house, and you reject the idea that Carter threw it out of the window to a confederate, it must be still here. Have you had a search made for it?'

'No, sir.'

'What about that telegram, the one which brought Signorina Lorenzo here? Made any inquiries about that at the Post Office?'

'Not yet, sir.' Wilkins took a sip of tea, grimaced, and quickly put the cup down.

'Hm. What about the other guests? What can you tell me about them?'

'Very little, really, sir.'

'Just the ones you've interviewed.'

'I haven't actually interviewed any of them.'

'None of them?'

'No, sir.'

'I see.' Allgood was silent for a moment before

200

saying, 'Wilkins, I'm baffled.'

'Are you, sir? I'm sorry. Still, I'm sure you won't be for long. You must have cracked tougher cases than this one.'

'No, man. Not by the case. By you.'

'Me, sir?'

'Yes. A murder is committed. A man is found standing by the body, a gun in his hand. He runs away, then later gives himself up. You interview him, and then release him. From those reports I just can't see why. I have to regard him as the chief suspect. But—all right. That was your privilege. What I can't understand is, having concluded Carter is innocent, you then do virtually nothing. You believe a murderer is at large, yet apart from a fifteen-minute interview with the Earl and five minutes with his daughter, you waste a couple of hours questioning the servants—something that a sergeant or constable could do quite well. You don't institute a search for the missing coat, make no inquiries about the telegram, and don't question the other people who were staying here. Surely you must realise that *if*, as you believe, Carter is innocent, he was cleverly framed—and plainly by one of the other guests. Yet you haven't spoken to any of them. Haven't exactly covered yourself with glory, have you?'

'Probably not, sir. But then I never expect to. As to the mink, well, Alderley's a big place. A fur coat would roll up very small, and I haven't had men here. An exhaustive search would take an age. Besides, if I might just explain my theory about that business, the matter of the telegram, and what you said about Carter being framed, I—'

'No, Wilkins, you may not. I don't want to be

201

cluttered up with other people's theories. They're almost invariably wrong, and I'm quite capable of formulating my own. So I'm not interested in what you *think*. Only in what you know. Clear?'

'As you wish, sir. But about interviewing the guests. Frankly, I'm not very good at interrogating the gentry—uneasy, as it were. I knew you'd do that much better than I could.'

'Naturally. All the same . . . Oh well, perhaps you're wise not to attempt too much.' Allgood spoke in a more kindly tone. 'And I don't suppose any great harm's been done by the delay.'

'Very good of you to say so, sir.'

Allgood put down his empty cup and wiped his mouth. 'However, what I must do now is find out about all these people: what they're like, what their relationships are to each other, just what's been happening here for the past two days. I need an objective account of things.'

'Where will you get that, sir?'

'Well, I won't get a completely objective one, of course. But the nearest thing to one will certainly come from their host and hostess. I take it you have no grounds for suspecting either of them of complicity in this crime?'

'Oh, no, sir.' Wilkins sounded quite shocked.

'Well, we're agreed on something. Not that it would have been the first murder committed by either an Earl or a Countess, but certainly neither Lord nor Lady Burford would murder a guest under their own roof. So we can rely on their testimony. They may not tell us everything they know, of course. But they won't lie. We'll get the truth and nothing but the truth, though maybe not the whole truth.'

202

'You'll see Carter first, I expect, though, sir, as you consider him the chief suspect?'

'No. Before I tackle him I need more information, more background. Otherwise I'm not likely to get any more out of him than you did. So go and find the Earl, give him my compliments, and ask him to come along here, will you?'

'Very good, sir.' Wilkins left the room.

CHAPTER SIXTEEN

Lord Burford came into the room a minute or so later, accompanied by Wilkins.

'Ah, Burford, come in,' Allgood said.

'Er, what can I do for you?'

'Just sit down and tell us all about this house party.' He indicated the armchair, which he'd vacated in favour of an upright chair he'd placed behind the room's only table.

The Earl blinked. '*All* about it?'

'As much as you can remember: the reason for it, how this particular combination of guests came about, anything you can tell us about them— especially, of course, every conceivable thing you know of Laura Lorenzo—any unusual incidents, conversations, and so on. Anything at all.'

'Good gad. Could take hours.'

'No matter. That's why I'm here.'

'Don't quite know where to begin.'

'Suppose we start off by my asking questions?'

Immediately he began interrogating the Earl. Allgood's manner became quite different from what it had been until now. He was less formidable, gentler and quieter, drawing the Earl out bit by bit, seeming almost to mesmerise him into remembering details he thought he'd completely forgotten. After three quarters of an hour nothing of significance which had happened in Lord Burford's purview since his guests had arrived was not also known to Allgood and Wilkins. He left the room in somewhat of a daze, promising to ask the Countess to step in.

'Anything particularly strike you, sir?' Wilkins asked.

'A number of things. Chiefly that business of the broken window in Ransom's room. Had the effect of putting the alarm out of action, which meant the windows could be opened at night—more than the inch or two they could otherwise have been raised. If the mink *was* thrown out, that accident was highly convenient. It might, as you said, roll up small, but not small enough to go easily through that sort of gap.'

Just then Lady Burford entered.

With the Countess Allgood's style was again subtly different. Exquisitely polite, he was however rather more incisive: sharper and quicker in putting his questions. Lady Burford had entered the room determined to say the bare minimum she could get away with. Her attitude was that the crime was nothing to do with her. None of her family or relations was involved, and *she* had not invited Laura, nor any of the other guests (apart from her cousin Cecily and her husband), to Alderley. If a member of the house party, other than Paul, was guilty, then it was plainly one of the film people. She had had little to do with any of them and so could not help in any way.

204

In spite of this resolve, however, the Countess found herself gradually revealing more and more. She was almost reduced to gossiping. The fact dismayed and astonished her. But such was Allgood's technique that she seemed unable to help herself, even relating conversations she had had with Cecily—not to mention those with Maude Fry and Jemima Dove. At last Allgood thanked her and she departed, looking more than a little shaken.

The Chief Superintendent sat with his brows furrowed, staring down at the table and drumming on it with his fingers. Then he looked up.

Wilkins said, 'Carter now, sir?' He sounded apprehensive.

Allgood smiled. 'Not just yet. I want to see the scene of the crime. Take me up.'

Wilkins led him up to the second floor, and Allgood made a quick but thorough examination of Laura's bedroom. He glanced in the bathroom opposite, and with the help of Wilkin's plan familiarised himself with who occupied each of the bedrooms. They then went back down to the music room and Allgood said, 'Right. Now for Carter.'

Paul came warily into the room. He was very pale. Allgood eyed him keenly from under his bushy eyebrows, his eyes seeming to burn into Paul. Paul gazed back unflinchingly.

'Sit down,' Allgood ordered curtly.

Paul did so. Allgood said, 'Now, Carter, I have to tell you that I have absolutely cast-iron proof that you shot Signorina Lorenzo.'

From his position behind Paul, Wilkins stared at Allgood in amazement. Paul drew in a quick, sharp breath—but didn't move.

205

'So,' Allgood went on, 'further denial is useless and will only make things worse for you. Far better to plead manslaughter, or even call it an accident. So tell the truth now and I promise the police won't press for a murder charge. You won't hang.'

Paul looked at him long and silently. 'You're bluffing,' he said.

'What do you mean?'

'About having cast-iron proof. There isn't any. There couldn't be. Because I didn't do it.'

Allgood was quite unabashed. 'All right. I was bluffing. But if you did do it, there *is* evidence—somewhere. And I'll get it. And you will hang. You've got one more chance now to change your mind. The promise stands. Understood?'

'Yes.'

'Well.'

'I'm changing nothing.'

'As you wish. Then give me your version of what happened.'

'I've already given it to Wilkins.'

'Now give it to me.'

'Well, in the first place, Gerry and I didn't get back from the party until nearly two a.m. last night. That was because I ran out of petrol.'

Allgood cut him short. 'No, no, start much earlier.'

'At what point?'

'At Signorina Lorenzo's arrival on Thursday afternoon.'

'Are you serious?'

'Perfectly. Recount to me everything you can remember about what people said and did. Then tell me about the talk you mentioned to Wilkins, which you had with her on Friday morning, and go on to an account of the events of Friday evening—up until the time you left this party at Sir James Needham's.'

'Well, I'll do my best.'

Paul's account, though hesitant and somewhat abbreviated, was accurate in all essential respects. When he'd finished, Allgood gave a nod.

'Very good. Now you can revert to the point at which you were going to start earlier.'

This time Paul's narrative was virtually identical with that given to Wilkins at the police station. Then began one of the toughest and most searching interrogations Wilkins had ever heard. Drawing solely on memory, Allgood went over the whole of Paul's story, throwing question after question about every conceivable aspect of it, trying to make him slip up or contradict himself. Wilkins found his admiration for Allgood's technique growing every second.

At the end of twenty minutes Paul was sweating. But he hadn't budged from his story. It was a display as impressive as Allgood's own.

Eventually Allgood said, 'Now tell me about your relationship with the other people in this house.'

'What, all of them?'

'Start with your fellow guests.'

'Well, there isn't one—a relationship, I mean. I didn't know any of them except Hugh Quartus before Thursday, and my conversation with most of them has been limited to small talk. I've had a couple of yarns with Rex Ransom.'

'And what about Quartus?'

'I'd met him a few times.'

'And you don't get on?'

207

'Not really.'

'Was last night the first time you've come to blows?'

'We didn't come to blows.'

'That wasn't for want of trying, though, was it?'

'Well, nothing like it has ever happened before. We were just cold and tired and irritable. And I suppose he was a bit jealous.'

'Of you and Lady Geraldine?' Paul nodded. 'You're in love with her?'

'Yes.'

'And she with you?'

'I—I think so. I hope so.'

'And Quartus resents this?'

'Naturally. Wouldn't you?'

'Are you suggesting he resents it enough to try and frame you for murder?'

'Of course not! He wouldn't do a thing like that.'

'Yet you're saying somebody did.'

'The frame-up needn't have been set specifically for me—just for anyone who came along the corridor at the right time.'

'I see. Very well, Carter, that'll be all.'

'Aren't you going to charge me?'

'When I decide to charge you, you'll be the first to know.'

Paul got up a little uncertainly, threw a glance at Wilkins, crossed to the door, and went out. Wilkins looked at Allgood, who'd started writing busily, and cleared his throat.

'Well, sir?'

Allgood looked up. 'Well, what?'

'What do you think about Mr Carter? Was I right not to—?'

'My thoughts remain my own, Wilkins, until I've

208

seen everybody. Next, I want to see—' He broke off as a knock came at the door and barked, 'Come.'

The door opened and Sergeant Leather came in. He addressed Wilkins. 'Sorry to interrupt, sir. I've been waiting outside for you to finish with Mr Carter.'

'What is it?' Allgood asked.

'I thought you'd want to see this straight away, sir.' He brought his hand from behind his back and for a split second Wilkins thought he was carrying the body of a drowned cat. Then he realised the truth. 'The mink!'

'Yes, sir. Sorry to roll it up like this, but I thought you mightn't want Mr Carter or anyone else to spot it before you saw it.'

'Where was it?' Allgood snapped.

'Outside, sir. Right underneath Miss Lorenzo's window. It's soaking wet. Must have been there since about the time of the murder. Thrown out of the window, if you ask me.'

'I don't,' Allgood said. 'Why wasn't it spotted before?'

'Covered in snow, sir. There's been quite a little drift there. The coat was spread out as though it had sort of floated down. It lay on the snow drift and then another layer formed on top of it. It's been thawing during the course of the day and gradually the coat was exposed.'

Wilkins nodded to himself in a satisfied way. 'I had a kind of feeling it would turn up of its own accord sooner or later.'

Allgood glanced at him sharply before saying to Leather, 'You should have left it where it was.'

'I would have, sir. But one of the maids spotted

it when she went to draw the curtains in one of the ground floor rooms. Slipped straight out, picked it up and brought it to me. I was having a spot of tea in the kitchen at the time.'

'Looked in the pockets?' Wilkins asked.

'Yes, sir, but there's nothing. There is something curious about it, though. Take a look.'

Leather gave a shake to the wet bundle of fur and the folds fell open. He held the coat by the shoulders and raised it high. 'See what I mean, sir?'

Allgood and Wilkins both stared.

In four different parts of the coat jagged holes had been cut.

Allgood's eyes narrowed. 'Extraordinary! Why the deuce . . . ?' He stopped and was silent for a few seconds before saying, 'Lay it down on the floor.'

Leather did so. Allgood knelt down by it and examined the holes in turn. Each one was of a different shape, but all were about four or five inches across. Allgood remained kneeling, staring down at the coat without speaking for a full minute before suddenly getting to his feet, picking up the coat as he did so.

He said, 'I want to see where these holes come when the coat's being worn. Wilkins, it'll fit you better than the sergeant or me. Put it on.'

Wilkins took the coat gingerly. 'Bit wet, sir.'

'Only for a minute or so, man. You're not made of sugar!'

Leather helped Wilkins into the coat and he stood, looking rather absurd, as Allgood walked slowly round him.

Two of the holes were in the back: one up high

in the left shoulder, the other about six inches from the bottom, in the centre. The third was also low down, in the front, while the fourth was in the left breast.

Leather said, 'Just sheer vandalism, do you think, sir? Someone venting their hatred?'

Allgood made an impatient gesture for him to be silent. His brow was furrowed in thought. Eventually he gave a shake of his head. 'It's no good. I'll need time to work it out. Get it off, Wilkins. All right, sergeant, take it away. But mind you keep it safe.'

'Right, sir.' Leather went to the door and opened it. Then he stopped. Gerry was standing outside.

She said, 'I want to see Mr Allgood.' She came into the room.

Allgood said, 'Ah, Lady Geraldine? What can I do for you?'

'I want to say I don't think it's fair, the way you're treating Paul. Mr Wilkins has cleared him once. Why can't you accept that—or at least tell him exactly where he stands? The suspense is killing him.'

'It wasn't suspense that killed Laura Lorenzo.'

'But Paul didn't do that.'

'You have evidence for that assertion?'

'No, but the idea's absurd. I know him.'

'Then who do you think did do it?'

'Arlington Gilbert.'

'Why him?'

She took a deep breath. 'I'll have to tell you rather a long story. It's a little embarrassing, I'm afraid. It all started with a silly and impulsive practical joke.'

                    *   *   *

'It's obvious what he was after in the study,' Gerry concluded, a few minutes later. 'The key to the gun room. I don't think he got it *then.* When I disturbed him the safe was definitely locked. Perhaps, though, he'd just been checking that the key actually was there, ready for the following night, and had already re-closed it. There'd have been lots of opportunities to go back on Friday and get it. Though don't ask me how he knew the combination.'

'And you say that on Friday morning Signorina Lorenzo seemed very anxious to speak to him?'

She nodded. 'And she stayed with him quite a long time.'

'Do you have any corroboration for any of this story?' Allgood asked.

She stiffened, 'No.'

'Pity.'

'I'm surprised you think it's necessary.' Her voice was cold.

'Corroboration is always useful if I'm going to question someone about alleged suspicious behaviour.'

'Oh, you are going to do that, then?' she said sarcastically.

'Naturally. But with nobody else involved, he has only to deny the whole thing.'

'Nobody else was involved in my encounter with him, but he was mixed up in some other funny business.'

'What precisely?'

'You'll have to ask—' She broke off.

212

'Ask whom?'

She hesitated. 'I was going to say Rex Ransom. But it won't do any good. He'll probably deny it.'

'Why should he?'

'I don't know. But, well—I hate to say this, because I like him—but in the circumstances I suppose I've got to tell you. He really behaved very oddly.'

'Can you be a bit more specific?'

She recounted first Rex's request for her to let Gilbert stay on, then their conversation while out riding, and finally told about her visit to his suite the previous night.

'What time was this last conversation?' Allgood asked.

'About ten past two. I looked at my wrist watch just before I left my room.'

'And you left Ransom how long before you heard the shot?'

'About five minutes.'

'And then you ran the full length of the two corridors and found Carter holding the gun?'

'That's right.'

'Very well, Lady Geraldine, rest assured I shall look into all these matters. Now, is there any further information you wish to give me? Any other unusual incidents you can remember? Anything you learnt about the other guests that might be significant? Any interesting conversations?'

'No.'

'Anything you can tell me about Laura Lorenzo?'

'I don't think—' She stopped.

'You've thought of something?'

'It's very trivial.'

'I'll be the judge of that.'

'It's just that when I went to her room to tell her we were ready to leave, she was writing a letter. She put it out of sight in her writing case—rather furtively, I thought. And she was over-eager to tell me quite unnecessarily that it was a reply to a fan.'

'Which you don't believe?'

'No. Paul said it was probably just a love letter to a boyfriend back home, but I think it was to her agent in London. Then, when she discovered she'd missed the post, she decided to telephone him that night. But our phone was out of order. It must have been important.'

'What did she do with the letter?'

'Put it in the dressing-table drawer, still inside the writing case.'

When Gerry had left, Allgood said to Wilkins 'Your men went through the deceased's effects?'

'Yes, sir. There was no letter among them.'

'Then where is it?'

'Presumably the murderer took it, sir.'

'Possibly. Which would mean it was incriminating to him in some way. But let's not jump to conclusions. The lady might have burnt it herself. After all, if Lady Geraldine's right about it—and it seems a plausible theory—the signorina was expecting to see her agent before any letter could reach him. Why she should *bother* to burn it, I don't know. However, let's assume she did throw it on the fire when she got back—'

Allgood broke off in mid-sentence. Slowly he stood up. The expression on his face had suddenly changed. It was as if a great light had dawned.

'Thought of something, sir?' Wilkins asked.

214

Allgood didn't answer. 'The fire in her room. It was a big one, wasn't it?'

'Yes, very big, by all accounts, sir. Several people mentioned how hot it was in there.'

Allgood strode across the room, jerked open the door and gave a yell. 'Sergeant!'

A rather alarmed-looking Leather arrived within seconds.

'Where's that fur coat?' Allgood barked.

'Locked in the car outside, sir, waiting to be taken to the station for—'

'Fetch it, quick!'

Leather hurried away. Allgood went to the piano, switched on a lamp that stood on it and took from an inside pocket a powerful magnifying glass. Leather arrived at a run, carrying the mink. Allgood positively snatched it from him and—holding it close up under the lamp and using the glass—carefully scrutinised the material round one of the holes. Wilkins saw that it was the one in the left breast.

Thirty seconds, then nearly a minute, passed. Allgood lowered the glass and raised his head. There was a strange gleam of triumph in his eyes. He addressed Leather.

'Sergeant, go and fetch Carter here immediately.'

'Yes, sir.'

Wilkins' face was suddenly pale. Quietly he said, 'Don't say—don't say you've found proof, sir.'

'Yes, Wilkins. I think I can say I have.'

Wilkins sat down slowly. 'Oh,' he said.

A minute later Leather returned, accompanied by an angry-looking Paul followed by Gerry. Allgood turned to face him. His expression was

215

grim.

Gerry said, 'Look, how much more of this is he expected to put up with? It's disgraceful.'

'Please be quiet,' Allgood said.

He moved close to Paul, and unobtrusively Leather edged round to stand between Paul and the door.

Allgood spoke heavily. 'Paul Edward Carter, as you are aware, I am a police officer. I am inquiring into the murder of Laura Lorenzo. It is now my duty to—' He paused.

Then, utterly unexpectedly, he smiled. '—my *pleasant* duty to inform you that you are no longer suspected of the crime.' He held out his hand. 'Congratulations.'

*   *   *

At Allgood's words, Gerry gave a whoop of joy. Paul, however, said nothing. His face was white. He swallowed, then like an automaton slowly reached forward and took Allgood's hand.

'You mean that?' he said thickly.

'I do. You're a very lucky chap.'

The colour was slowly returning to Paul's face. He said, 'You're a cad, you know, to frighten me like that.'

'Sorry. Just my little joke. Couldn't resist it. If you want to sock me on the beak I shall quite understand.'

Paul managed a wan smile. 'It's tempting, but no. I'm just too grateful.' He turned to Gerry, who came up and took his arm. 'Well, sweetheart,' he said, 'looks as if the nightmare's over.'

She nodded happily. 'So Inspector Wilkins was

right?'

'Yes, and I give him full credit for it,' Allgood said. 'Unfortunately'—he smiled '—he was right for entirely the wrong reasons.' He crossed to Wilkins and put a hand on his shoulder. 'Wilkins, you have a natural flair for detective work. You're what I call an instinctive or intuitive detective. Take my advice: learn to reason, to use logic. I think in time you could become quite an effective investigator.'

'Thank you, sir,' Wilkins said.

Allgood redirected his attention to Paul. 'Want to apologise, old man, for putting you through all that cross-questioning. Unfortunately it was essential. By the way, understand you were at Eton. What years? Wondering if we overlapped?'

They moved to one side a little. Gerry looked closely at Wilkins. 'You all right, Mr Wilkins?'

'Oh, yes, my lady, thank you.'

'You don't look well.'

'I expect that's just reaction, as they say.'

Her face cleared. 'Oh, I see. *You* thought he was going to arrest Paul, too?'

'Yes, my lady, for a minute or two there I really did.'

'Which would have made you look a bit silly, I suppose. Well, he didn't. You've been vindicated. Congratulations.'

'They're not called for, my lady.'

'But you were right! Oh, you mean what he said about the wrong reasons? But the reasons aren't really important, are they? Besides, it's only a matter of opinion. I bet your reasons were just as valid as his. What were his reasons, anyway?'

'I'm not quite sure, my lady.'

217

'Well, I'll soon find out.' She turned back to Allgood. 'Chief Superintendent, may we know how you came to the conclusion that Paul was innocent?'

Allgood hesitated. 'Well, I suppose it won't do any harm. After all, if we let the story get around, it'll show the real killer what he's up against it. Well, it all swings on this.'

He picked up the mink for them to see and briefly ran through the circumstances of its discovery. Then he said, 'Let's see if Chief Inspector Wilkins can explain my reasoning.'

Wilkins blushed. 'Well, sir, you were examining the fur round that hole in the front. You found something. I would guess traces of blood?'

'Right. And plainly Laura Lorenzo's blood— though, of course, we'll have to get that confirmed by the lab. Now, what does that tell us?'

'That she was wearing it when she was murdered. The killer removed it from the body and threw it out of the window afterwards.'

'Precisely. There you are: you see, Wilkins, you can do it. Go on. What about the hole?'

'You mean, sir, that he cut the fur away just to remove the bullet hole?'

'Of course. And no doubt burnt it. It could only have been done after she was shot. Carter couldn't conceivably have done it in the time that elapsed between the shot being heard and Lady Geraldine arriving. Which means that, as Carter said, *that* shot was a blind, and she was really killed earlier. It's not this which proves Carter's innocence, of course, since he could easily have fired both shots himself. What really clears him—as the murderer must have realised at the last moment—is the

218

mere fact that the lady was wearing the coat when she was killed; a fact given away by the existence of the bullet hole and the blood.'

Paul frowned. 'I'm sorry, and maybe I'm dense, but you'll have to explain that.'

Allgood was positively beaming by now. He said, 'Well, Wilkins, can you oblige the gentleman?'

'I'm afraid not, sir. It's got me beat.'

'Listen, in that bedroom there was a very big open fire. Several people commented on the heat in there, even with the door open. And we know that at about twelve-thirty the maid Eloise went in to make up the fire. Then, at about five past one, a footman saw Signorina Lorenzo enter the room and close the door after her. By then it must have been like an oven in there. Now, even granted that the lady was used to a warm climate and liked heat, it's inconceivable she would have kept her coat on for more than two or three minutes after going in. One of the very first things she would have done would be to take it off.'

Gerry said excitedly, 'Which means she must have been shot almost as soon as she went in!'

'Exactly, Lady Geraldine. Or before one-ten, at the latest, a time when Carter was still four miles from the house, stuck at the side of the road out of petrol—a fact vouched for by you, Lady Geraldine, and by Quartus.'

Wilkins was nodding slowly. Almost to himself, he said, 'Yes, I see. That's it. Very clever indeed.'

Allgood looked amused. 'Thank you, Chief Inspector,' he said, and there was irony in his voice. 'I assume you concur with my findings?'

'Oh, yes, sir. The murder was committed before ten past one, all right.'

219

'Most gratified.' Allgood gave him a mock bow.

'But what exactly happened?' Paul asked.

Allgood, now in high good humour, was eager to explain. 'The murderer got to the room before Signorina Lorenzo, and waited for her. He shot her almost as soon as she came in, took that letter—the one she'd been writing—from the drawer, and put the gun outside in the corridor. He had a second gun ready, to fire the alarm shot. He left the door open an inch and waited to give a groan as soon as he heard someone come along the corridor, stop and pick up the gun.'

'Someone?' Paul said. 'Not me specifically?'

'I don't think so. He couldn't have known you'd use that bathroom—though maybe, on the other hand, he didn't realise you usually went to the other one. I would say he just thought it inevitable that *somebody*—most likely you or Quartus or Miss Fry—would come along. But time passed and nobody did. You, Carter, had been delayed, and Quartus had gone out again to look for you. According to her statement, Miss Fry had entered her room before Signorina Lorenzo came upstairs, and didn't leave it again. We can imagine the murderer becoming more and more frantic as no one came, and then suddenly realising the point about the bullet hole in the coat giving away the actual time of death. His attempt at a frame-up was ruined, but his mind must have worked like lightning. There was a pair of scissors on the dressing-table, and it wouldn't have taken him more than a couple of minutes to cut the holes. No doubt he burnt the pieces he cut out. Then he threw the coat out the window.'

'Why?' Gerry asked.

220

'Well, the best way out of the coat problem would really be for it to disappear entirely. Perhaps he thought that if he got it out of the house temporarily, there was just a chance he might be able to dispose of it the following day. Failing that, however, then at least the holes would conceal the fact Laura Lorenzo was wearing it when she was shot. And they would have, had he not been a little bit careless in cutting round the bullet hole and left traces of blood. But, of course, he was working under great pressure.'

'Why cut four holes?'

'Camouflage, Lady Geraldine: to draw attention away from that particular hole, to disguise the reason for it.'

There was silence for a few seconds before Paul said, 'Isn't it odd that nobody heard the first shot?'

'I don't think it is,' Gerry said. 'The walls and doors here are so thick and solid that sound just doesn't carry. We found that out last time, didn't we, Mr Wilkins?'

'Yes, indeed, your ladyship. In addition, of course, the next door room is that of Mr Quartus, and he was out of it at the time.'

'There is another possibility,' Allgood said. 'He could have used a silencer. I must ask the Earl, if he owns a silencer for that gun, to check if it's still there.'

Paul said, 'That second gun—the one that fired the alarm shot—you think that was the killer's own?'

'Well, there are no other guns missing from the collection, so it must have been. But obviously, it won't still be in his possession.'

'You mean he'll have hidden it in the house

somewhere?' Paul said eagerly. 'Well, surely, if you search for it . . .'

'Oh, we will, in time. But it won't do a lot of good to find it, except to provide additional confirmation of your story. Plainly it won't be one that can be traced to the killer, since he could easily have stolen a second gun from the collection if he'd needed to. And he won't have been such a fool to have left his prints on it.'

Gerry was frowning. 'Where did that second bullet go? The window in Laura's room was closed, and so was the one at the end of the corridor. Or did he use a blank?'

'He might have, though I doubt it. If he brought blanks with him it would probably mean he'd planned the scheme before he arrived, which seems highly unlikely. No, remember the door of the bathroom is almost across the corridor from the bedroom, and the window in the bathroom is opposite the door. What's more, the window was open when I was up there a short while ago. Probably he opened it in advance. That wouldn't cause any comment, as people tend to open bathroom windows even in very cold weather, to let steam out. So all he would have had to do, after shoving Carter in the back, was stand in the corridor and fire his gun through the open bathroom door and out of the window. Then he could slip down the stairs, or actually into the bathroom itself, closing the door after him. A few seconds later he could quietly join the crowd which had gathered in the doorway. He could rely on nobody else looking anywhere but into the bedroom, though even if somebody did spot him coming out of the bathroom it would hardly cause any comment.'

Gerry gave a little shiver. 'He sounds awfully clever, doesn't he?'

'Yes, we're dealing with a very smart and ruthless criminal. However, one perhaps not quite as smart as he believes himself to be. Part of his scheme's gone wrong already. And he's one of a very small circle of suspects, some of whom will probably have alibis. So it shouldn't be too hard to root him out.'

She stared. 'You mean that?'

'Oh, yes. I expect to have him under lock and key by Monday. But if not, on Tuesday we'll start digging into the backgrounds of all the suspects— and Signorina Lorenzo—checking for past connections, possible motives, police records, and so on. The truth is bound to come out then.'

'I hope you're right,' she said. 'Incidentally, will you be starting your questioning tonight? Mummy was wondering about dinner.'

Allgood looked at his watch. 'I had meant to begin interviewing this evening, but all these developments have made it a bit late for that now. So tell them they can relax tonight, or at least the innocent ones can. I shall go to my room and spend a couple of hours in intense thought. I'll start my interrogations in the morning.'

'May I also tell them Paul is in the clear?'

'By all means.'

'And what you've discovered about the actual time of the murder, the mink and everything?'

'I don't see why not.'

She gave a grin. 'Spiffing. Come on, Paul, this is going to be fun.'

She took his hand, hurried him to the door and

223

opened it. Then she stopped. Leaning up against the wall outside, his hands in his pockets, was Hugh.

She said, 'Oh, isn't it marvellous? Mr Allgood's completely cleared Paul of the murder.'

'Really?' He cocked an eye at Paul. 'Congratulations.'

'Thanks.'

Hugh sauntered into the room. Gerry said, 'She was killed much earlier than anybody thought— almost as soon as she got home. Paul was out with me then. So he's got an alibi.'

'I see. And that must mean I have, too.' He gazed coolly at Allgood. 'Is that right? Am I cleared, also?'

Allgood said, 'You're Quartus, correct?'

Hugh bowed his head.

'Let me see. You were downstairs, in full sight of the Earl and Countess when Signorina Lorenzo went up to her room. You left the house almost immediately, drove four miles, found Lady Geraldine and Carter, and brought her back with you, arriving here at about one-fifty. Is that right?'

'Hundred per cent.'

'Then, yes, Quartus, you're in the clear.'

Hugh nodded casually. 'Good.'

'That's wonderful!' Gerry said excitedly. 'Thank heavens Paul ran out of petrol!' She took Hugh's arm. 'Come on, we're going to tell the others.'

He shook his head. 'You go on. I want to talk to the law.'

'OK.' She and Paul left the room.

'I've been wanting to speak to one of you all day,' Hugh said, 'but thought I'd better wait until I was sent for. However, if I wait any longer it won't

224

be worth bothering at all.'

'To do what?' Allgood asked a little coldly.

'To report a stolen motor-bike.'

CHAPTER SEVENTEEN

'A motorcycle?' Allgood looked annoyed. 'I am hardly the person and this is hardly the time to—'

'No? All right, I'll go and report it to the village bobby. Only as it was taken Friday night, shortly before the murder, I thought you might be interested.'

'Stolen from here?' Allgood was suddenly alert.

'Yes.' Hugh explained the circumstances.

'And the thief left the sidecar?' Allgood frowned. 'What an extraordinary thing. But I can't see any possible connection with the murder.'

Hugh said, 'The talk at first was of the motive being robbery and the fur coat being thrown out of the window to an accomplice. Although I see the coat's been found'—he nodded towards the piano, on which Allgood had put it down—'it occurred to me that that might have been the original plan and they took my bike as a getaway vehicle.'

Allgood looked dubious. 'Well, it's a possibility, I suppose. Anyway, thank you for telling us.'

'I want it back, so put out an all-points bulletin, or whatever you call it, won't you? It's a jolly good machine.'

'That'll come under my jurisdiction, sir,' Wilkins said. 'I'll see to it.'

'Thanks.' Hugh went out.

Allgood sat silently thinking for a minute or so,

until there came a knock at the door. It was Paul again.

Allgood said, 'Ah, Carter, how was Lady Geraldine's announcement received?'

'Oh, reasonably well. Everybody was very nice to me. The Earl apologised first, and then all the others—even though I'm far from certain they're all convinced. Particularly as it gradually sank in that if I'm innocent, they now understand they're all suspects. And when Gerry told them what you said about probing into their private affairs if the case wasn't solved by Monday, the atmosphere became a little strained.'

'Excellent! That should make all the innocent ones very eager to cooperate.'

'Lady Burford, of course, backed up by cousin Cecily, now maintains that the murder must have been committed by some passing tramp, who is now miles away. I think we're all going to pretend to go along with that, for the sake of normality. To admit openly that one of your companions is a murderer would make the situation intolerable. Why I came back, though, was to talk about silencers. Gerry told her father what you said. I offered to bring his reply. He has a dozen or more of the things. Seems he used to fit them to every pistol possible, so he could fire them without disturbing people too much. But since he's had that little shooting range put up, and the room is properly soundproofed, he's never bothered. They're all kept with the ammunition, and he couldn't possibly say if one is missing.'

Allgood nodded. 'I see. Well, it doesn't really matter. We know the shot was fired. Why it wasn't heard isn't vitally important.'

'Right. I'll tell him.' Paul started to turn away but hesitated.

Allgood eyed him keenly. 'There's something else, isn't there?'

Paul smiled. 'How did you know?'

'Why should *you* have brought the message about the silencers? It was a pretext. You wanted to see me again, and I would guess without Lady Geraldine being present.'

'Doesn't anybody ever fool you?'

'Not for long. Well, what is it?'

'It's a bit awkward, actually. But you said you wanted to be told of any unusual incidents.'

'You've remembered something?'

'I never really forgot it, but my own troubles sort of drove it from my mind. I'm not at all sure it's relevant.'

'Never mind.'

Paul collected his thoughts. 'Yesterday morning I discovered I'd lost my fountain pen.'

*   *   *

'And that's all I heard,' Paul concluded. 'Suddenly the voice just faded and there was silence. I waited for a couple of minutes, then opened the panel and stepped into the room. There was nobody there.'

Allgood shook his head. 'Remarkable.'

Wilkins said, 'Mr Carter, could you explain why you didn't tell us, or anybody else, any of this before?'

Paul wriggled uncomfortably. 'Well, dash it all, it was a bit tricky. I'd been eavesdropping. Quite unintentionally and all that, but it seemed hardly the done thing to take advantage of the situation.'

227

Allgood nodded sympathetically. 'Yes, one can understand that. But surely you couldn't have just ignored the matter altogether. You obviously had some sort of obligation to the family.'

'Of course. I didn't know what to do. I mentioned to Gerry that I'd heard something very odd, but not what it was. She advised me to wait. Then, as you can imagine, the murder put it out of my mind. When I did start to think about it again, I couldn't decide if it had anything to do with the murder.'

'Well, you can rely on me to look into it fully, Carter. Please don't say anything about the matter to anybody from now on.'

'Right. It's a weight off my mind.'

At that moment they heard the faint sound of the dinner gong. Paul said, 'I must go. An event unique in the annals of Alderley is about to take place: we're not dressing for dinner. Whether Merryweather will ever recover I don't know.' He went out.

'What do you make of that, sir?' Wilkins said.

'Well, assuming he's telling the truth, and I'm sure he is—'

'Yes, I agree, sir.'

Allgood frowned. '*If* I may finish, Chief Inspector.'

'Sorry, sir.'

'And if he heard and understood correctly, it opens up an entirely new aspect of the case. His allowing himself to be overheard by Carter like that suggests to me that our friend may be a little careless. After all, everyone knew of the existence of the passage, it seems. What's more, we know that the murderer can be careless, too. So it might

228

be worthwhile having a search of his room.'

'Now, sir?'

'Yes, while everyone's in the dining-room. Wait here.'

He left the room. Wilkins thankfully lowered himself into the nearest chair and lit a cigarette.

It was ten minutes before Allgood reappeared. There was a gleam of triumph in his eyes. He opened his pocket book and extracted a piece of paper about four inches square. 'No incriminating documents, or anything of that kind—all been burnt, without doubt. But this escaped. It was down behind the coal scuttle.'

He held the piece of paper out for Wilkins to get a closer look. It was charred all round the edges and covered with writing in ink. Wilkins read this and nodded slowly.

'Suggestive, isn't it?' Allgood said.

'Yes, sir, but ambiguous.'

'Of course; there are only, what, forty words altogether?'

'Do you know whose writing it is, sir?'

'It'll have to be checked by an expert, of course. But there's no real doubt in my mind that it's Laura Lorenzo's. It means that that letter she was writing wasn't intended for her agent, after all. And it provides us with a real motive at last.'

'So do you intend to make an arrest now?'

'Good heavens, no. It's far from certain yet. There are lots of loose ends. I'm going to keep this in reserve, produce it at an opportune moment.' He put the piece of paper away again.

'Should be a most interesting moment, sir.' He coughed. 'Is that everything for tonight?'

'Want to knock off?'

229

'Well, it has been a long day.'

'That's all right. You toddle off home to your beans-on-toast and cocoa. See you in the morning.'

'Actually, sir, I was going to ask if you'll need me tomorrow.'

'Need you? No, of course I won't *need* you. If you've got another case in hand you have to deal with, by all means do so.'

'It's not that, sir. Matter of fact, it's my day off.'

Allgood looked as if he couldn't believe his cars. 'Day off? You're not serious.'

'Yes, sir. And as you said you don't actually need me, I thought I'd get my feet up for a bit—take it easy, you know.'

'Ye gods!' Allgood looked up at the ceiling in despair. 'You'd actually stay home, taking it easy when you could be here, assisting me in a murder inquiry?'

'Well, I don't get all that many days off, sir.'

'But what about what you called the privilege of assisting me—all you were going to learn?'

'I've seen you at work now, sir. I've assisted a bit. It'll give me something to talk about for the rest of my life. As to what I'd learn, well, you can't teach an old dog new tricks. I'd never be able to conduct a case like you do. I'll probably blunder on in my own way, whatever happens. Of course, Sergeant Leather will be here all day, to assist in any way you want. He wouldn't miss it for the world. But, then, he's ambitious.'

Allgood shook his head in disbelief. 'All right, you take it easy tomorrow. I'll solve your little murder for you, without your help.'

'Oh, thank you, sir. That's very kind of you. In that case I'll say good night—and good luck, sir.'

230

He went out. Allgood stared at the door as it closed after him. He gave a sigh. 'Pathetic,' he said to himself.

*   *   *

'I say, my boy, what's all this about a missing motorbike?' Lord Burford asked the question over coffee in the drawing-room later that evening.

Hugh shrugged. 'That's all there is about it, Lord Burford. My motorcycle's missing. From your stable yard.' Somewhat reluctantly he recounted the story to the room at large.

When he'd finished the Earl shook his head. 'Very odd. 'Course, we're insured against theft here, if you're not, so no need to worry from that point of view. Deuced annoying for you, all the same.'

Jemima Dove, who was sitting nearby, said, 'Er.'

The Earl glanced at her. 'Yes, my dear?'

She went a little pink. 'Well, this may sound silly, but I suppose it wouldn't be your motorcycle that's up in the picture gallery, would it, Mr Quartus?'

Everybody in the room turned to stare at Jemima, as though she were crazy. She gazed back out of big grey eyes, and her pinkness suddenly intensified.

It was Lord Burford who broke the silence. 'The picture gallery, Miss Dove? Do you—I mean, you quite, er . . . ?'

She showed the first real sign of animation since her arrival. 'Yes, of course!'

'You're saying there's a motor-bike in the picture gallery?'

'Yes, down at the end. Nearly hidden behind a

231

sofa.'

'But how did you come to know?'

'I—I was looking round there. I wanted to stay out of everybody's way as much as possible today. People kept using the library, and it was a bit boring in my room. I'm fond of pictures, so I decided to have a look in the gallery. I didn't see the motor-bike at first. It's not noticeable until you get quite close.'

'But you didn't say anything about it,' Hugh exclaimed.

'No. Why should I have? It was nothing to do with me.'

'But weren't you surprised to find a motor-bike in a picture gallery?'

'I thought it a little odd. But I decided there had to be some good reason for it.'

Hugh got to his feet. 'I'll go and take a look.'

Jemima jumped up, too. 'I'll come and show you.'

'Oh, there's no need.'

'I'd like to.' Her face was still very red, and it was obvious she only wanted an excuse to get out of the room. So he didn't argue and they went out together.

'Well, that's certainly my bike,' Hugh said. 'But what maniac brought it up here? And why the dickens didn't anyone else spot it?'

Almost apologetically Jemima said, 'Well, one doesn't really notice it unless one looks directly at the sofa. I didn't see it until I'd been in the room a few minutes. And I don't suppose many other people have been in here last night or today.'

'Well, better get it downstairs and back outside, I suppose.' He stepped towards the bike.

232

'Oh, do you think you should?' she said diffidently. 'I was wondering if this could possibly have anything to do with the murder.'

'It might have, I suppose, though I honestly can't see how. Why?'

'I was thinking perhaps—though I know nothing about these things, really—whether, if there is the possibility of a connection, the police would want to test it for fingerprints.'

He looked thoughtful. 'Hm, maybe you're right. Though I imagine most criminals know enough to use gloves these days. Still, I suppose it may be advisable not to touch it until we've spoken to the police. And it's probably better off here than anywhere.'

They turned to leave. Hugh's eye fell on a long, stout wooden plank, about fifteen feet by twelve inches, which was lying on the floor against the side wall. 'Wonder what that's doing here.'

'I wondered about that, too. I thought perhaps decorators. They put them between step ladders.'

'Possibly.' He glanced round. 'Not that it looks as if they've had decorators in here lately.'

'Perhaps they're coming soon and brought the plank in advance.'

'Perhaps.'

They walked to the door. 'Will you tell that policeman tonight?' she asked.

'No, our great detective apparently needs several hours of undisturbed meditation. Tomorrow will do.'

They were about to leave the gallery when Hugh stopped. Jemima glanced at him curiously. He said, 'I knew there was some little thing wrong with that bike. The penny's just dropped. The petrol

233

cap's not on properly.'

He walked back to the motor-bike. Jemima waited by the door until he rejoined her a minute later. 'Someone's put petrol in the tank,' he said.

'Really? How odd. I mean why, if they didn't intend to ride it away?'

'Your guess is as good as mine. Anyway, many thanks for finding it. Come on.'

They went out. Hugh closed the door and made to lock it. Then he paused. 'Oh, no key.'

'Is that important? It's been unlocked all day.'

'Agreed. But I would like to be able to assure old Allbad that the bike hasn't been tampered with since I found it. Look, sorry to bother you, but I wonder if you'd mind going and asking the Earl if he's got a key to this door. I'll wait here, just to be on the safe side.'

'Oh, yes, certainly.' She walked off.

It was ten minutes before Lord Burford came along the corridor, carrying a large key. 'Sorry to keep you waiting, Hugh. Had to find this.'

'That's all right. Before you lock up—it's none of our business, really, but Miss Dove and I were wondering about this.'

He went back into the gallery and pointed at the plank. The Earl stared. 'Great Scott! Where did that come from?'

'We thought about decorators—recently departed or imminent?'

'No, no plans that way at all. It's another mystery. Oh, lor', I'm getting so fed up with them.'

They left the gallery again and Lord Burford locked the door and pocketed the key. Saying he wanted an early night, Hugh then went to his room, while the Earl rejoined his guests

234

downstairs.

It turned out, however, that none of them was in the mood for sitting up very late. Nobody had got a lot of sleep the previous night, and mentally it had been an exhausting day for everyone. It was, therefore, almost as a group that the entire party shortly afterwards went upstairs. Paul remained very close to Gerry and walked with her to the door of her bedroom. She was just going in when he took her hand.

'Sweetheart, do me a favour: after Marie leaves, lock your doors.'

She gave him a startled look. 'Why?'

'There's a murderer in the house, Gerry.'

'But he wouldn't want to kill me.'

'I expect that's what Laura thought. Will you, darling? Promise?'

'Oh, all right, you old fusspot, if it's going to keep you happy.'

'Thanks.' He gave her a kiss. 'And before Marie leaves make sure there's nobody hiding in there.'

'You know something,' she said, 'you couldn't be more protective if we were man and wife.'

'Gerry, darling, you know—'

She put a hand on his lips. 'Not tonight, Paul. Plenty of time for that when this is all over. Sweet dreams, darling.'

She went into her room and shut the door. Paul made his way to his own room with a song in his heart.

CHAPTER EIGHTEEN

At ten o'clock the following morning St. John Allgood seated himself behind the table in the small music room. He had moved it since the previous day. His back was now to the window, through which the light from a pale, wintry sun streamed in, waiting to strike straight in the face anyone sitting in the chair opposite him. On the table in front of him were the preliminary statements that had been taken from each of the guests the night of the murder.

Allgood addressed Leather, who was standing submissively by the door. 'Ladies first, I think. Go and tell Miss Fry I'd like to see her.'

*   *   *

Walking a little hesitantly, Maude Fry crossed the room, stumbling slightly as her foot caught the edge of the rug. She sat down, folded her hands placidly in her lap, and gazed at Allgood with a calm, uninquiring expression. Her eyes behind the blue-tinted glasses, were almost invisible, but she gave the impression of being prepared to sit there until kingdom come if it was required of her.

Leather sat down in the corner and unobtrusively picked up a notebook.

Allgood said, 'Miss Fry, how long have you worked for Mr Gilbert?'

'Only a matter of weeks. Before that I was personal secretary to Sir Charles Crenshaw, the company promoter. But he retired.'

'I see. That's a pity.'

'That Sir Charles retired?'

'I meant that you haven't been with Mr Gilbert very long. You can't know him all that well.'

'Quite well enough.' For the first time there was a note of emotion in her voice.

'Really? May I take it that he's not a very satisfactory employer?'

'You may. But I would prefer not to elaborate upon the subject.'

'Come, Miss Fry, that's hardly fair. It may mean that he works you too hard, that he fails to pay your salary on time, or that he makes improper advances.'

Maude Fry flushed slightly. 'Nothing like that. The work actually has been quite light. But he's insufferably rude to everybody, all the time— behaviour which, of course, tends always to rebound on the secretary—is invariably late for appointments and thoroughly disorganised. But the last straw was when he brought me here uninvited. It was a most invidious position, and one with which I was not prepared to put up.'

'Ah, yes, Lady Burford told me you'd been intending to leave on Saturday morning.'

'That is so, but naturally in the event I was unable to do so.'

'How did Gilbert react when you told him you were intending to leave his employ?'

'He wasn't pleased.'

'Why do you suppose he wanted you along in the first place?'

'To type the script of *The King's Man*.'

'But isn't it very early days for that? As I understand it, the film is only in a provisional

237

planning stage: no contracts have been signed, no firm decision has been made about shooting here at Alderley. Would one normally start typing a screenplay without a lot more discussion and preparation?'

'Well, I have never worked in films before, but I can see his reason for that: he wants to establish himself at the earliest possible moment as the writer of the film—make himself one of the team from the start, so that there can be no question of the job being given to someone else.'

'I thought he had the copyright.'

'Apparently the position is legally a little uncertain. However, if he actually started the script and was able to supply Mr Haggermeir with some good material, as they call it, before he left here, then they'd be far less likely to drop him.'

'Quite astute.'

'Mr Gilbert is no fool. Of course, the murder has changed the situation for everybody.'

'Speaking of the murder, what can you tell me about it?'

'I can tell you virtually nothing. I think the only words I spoke to Signorina Lorenzo were 'How do you do?' when we were introduced.'

'Did she speak much to Mr Gilbert?'

'They did have a private talk on Friday morning. I don't know what about. But then, she seems to have spent most of the day seeking out the various men and engaging them in conversation.'

'Is that so? Now, what about the night of the murder? Tell me just what you saw and heard, and what you did.'

'We'd been playing bridge—Lady Burford, Mrs Everard, Miss Dove, and I—until we heard the others arriving home. I was anxious not to see Mr Gilbert, and Miss Dove seemed eager to be out of the way before they came in, so we went up together. It was about one a.m. By ten past, I was in bed. I was very drowsy and fell asleep almost immediately. The shot woke me about an hour later. I got outside in time to see Lady Geraldine rush past, stop in the signorina's doorway, then go into the room. Mr Quartus emerged from his room and followed her. I joined them, and you know what I saw.'

'Can you tell me the order in which the other people arrived?'

She frowned. 'I'm afraid not. They just suddenly seemed to be all around me. And it's rather dim at that end of the corridor. Besides, I must admit I only really had eyes for what I saw in the bedroom.'

Allgood then questioned her about her activities since her arrival at Alderley. She gave painstakingly thorough replies. However, when he asked her about things said or done by the other guests, or any impressions or feelings she may have had about them, he might have been questioning somebody deaf, dumb and blind. He let her go, requesting her to ask Jemima Dove to come in.

*   *   *

Jemima sat on the edge of the chair, very pale in the harsh sunlight, her eyes flicking from Allgood to Leather as if she was fearful of a murderous attack being launched on her by one of them if she didn't keep a close watch on them. Allgood didn't speak, just gazed at her until eventually she let her

239

eyes settle on him. Then at last she blurted out, 'I don't know anything.'

'Oh, I'm sure you do, Miss Dove.'

'But I don't honestly. I only arrived a little while before it all happened. I never even saw Miss Lorenzo alive.'

'We only have your word on that.'

'But it's the truth! I went upstairs before she and the others came in.'

'Which gave you a perfect opportunity to go to her room, wait for her, and shoot her. You could have then put the pistol outside, waited for Carter to come along, groaned, to lure him in, pushed him in the back—it would have required no great strength—fired the alarm shot with a second gun, hidden in the bathroom for a minute or so, and then joined the others in the doorway.'

Jemima gave a squeak of dismay. 'But the gun, the murder weapon. When could I have got that? I mean, everybody's been saying that the murderer had to get the key to the collection room from the safe in Lord Burford's study first.'

'Are you saying you couldn't have done that?'

'Of course I am! Listen, no one could have got into the study while there were people about in the hall, could they?'

'No.'

'Well, from what's been said, after Miss Fry and I went up, somebody was there all the time until at least ten minutes after Miss Lorenzo went upstairs. I'd have then had to come down, open the safe, take the key, go to the gun room, open it, find and load the gun, and go to Miss Lorenzo's room. By then she would have been in her room at least a quarter of an hour. But according to Lady

240

Geraldine, you deduced from her still having her coat on that she'd been shot two or three minutes at the most after she went in.'

'That's correct. But what about when you first arrived? You were left in the hall while the butler told Lady Burford of your arrival. You might have had time to slip into the study then.'

'Wrong!' she said triumphantly. 'I was only kept waiting for about two minutes. And there was a footman there the whole time. He was winding the clock.'

Allgood bowed his head and spread his hands. 'Miss Dove, you have just cleared yourself of suspicion of murder.'

She fell back in the chair with a little gasp. 'Oh, my, what a relief!' She looked at him, and was aware of a slight smile playing round his mouth. She sat up again, suddenly indignant. 'You'd worked all that out yourself, hadn't you? You never suspected me at all.'

He drew back his lips, revealing his big teeth in a wolf-like smile. 'Perhaps not.'

'Oh, Mr Allgood, I do think that's very unfair! Why put me through all that?'

'Shall we say to stimulate you mentally, get you thinking about that night and talking about it? I think I've succeeded. Now tell me, what was the first you knew of the murder?'

'I heard the shot. I was in bed, but not asleep. Then I heard other noises—voices, footsteps—and I thought I ought to go and see what was happening. I put on a dressing-gown and went outside. I walked along to the main corridor and saw a man making his way towards the east wing. So I followed him. It was Mr Gilbert, I think.

When I reached the east wing I saw the crowd and joined them.'

'Everybody else was already there?'

'I think so, but they were mostly strangers and I wasn't really looking at them. And of course it was rather dark.'

'I see. Well, then, I think you can go. Unless there's anything else you want to tell me, anything you've seen or heard that strikes you in any way as odd or significant.'

She puckered her brow. 'No, I don't think so. Except the motor-bike in the gallery, of course. They told you about that?'

'Yes, the Earl mentioned it. Most intriguing. All right, Miss Dove, thank you. Ask Mrs Everard to join me, if you will?'

*   *   *

Cecily Everard was cool and calm and answered Allgood's questions crisply. She knew nothing of Laura Lorenzo, had never even heard of her before Thursday afternoon. She had spoken to her hardly at all, except for a few minutes when she'd been giving Laura a lift back up to the house. She related that conversation. Her knowledge of the other guests was no greater, only having engaged them in small talk. She had spent most of her time on Thursday and Friday talking over old times with her cousin. She had neither seen nor heard anything strange or unusual. As to the murder itself, she had not even heard the shot. Her husband had awakened her to tell her of it. They had gone outside, seen the Earl and Countess hurrying round the corner to the east wing, and

242

followed. She thought that Mr Gilbert and Mr Haggermeir had arrived in the doorway just behind them, but hadn't really noticed.

Allgood let her go. He asked her to send her husband in.

*   *   *

Sebastian Everard was by far the most relaxed member of the house party whom Allgood had yet spoken to. He wandered vaguely into the room, smiled amiably and said, 'Colder again today, what?'

'Sit down, please, Everard.'

'Oh. All right. If you like.' He eyed the chair doubtfully. 'Mind if I move this a bit? Sun in the old peepers, you know.' He pulled the chair to one side, plumped himself down onto it, and took a bag of brightly coloured sweets from his pocket. He held them out to Allgood. 'Like one?'

'No, thank you.'

Sebastian turned to Leather. 'How about you?'

'No, thank you, sir.'

'Sure? They're very good.' He took one, unwrapped it, and popped it in his mouth. 'I can make one last over twenty minutes,' he said indistinctly.

Allgood decided on shock tactics. 'Everard,' he snapped, 'did you kill Laura Lorenzo?'

Sebastian slowly transferred the sweet to his cheek. 'You've got to ask that, have you? In the jolly old book of rules, sort of thing?'

'No, I—'

'Ah, your own idea, is it? Don't everybody say no, always?'

243

'Mostly, but—'

'Seems rather pointless, then, what?'

'Answer the question, sir!'

'Oh, sorry. Er, what was it again?'

'Did you kill—?'

'Oh, yes, of course. Well, as a matter of fact, the answer's no, actually. Sorry. Is that all?'

'No, it is not. How well did you know the deceased?'

'Who?'

'Miss Lorenzo.'

'Oh, her. Hardly at all, more's the pity. Quite a corker, what?'

'So you were attracted to her?'

'Who wouldn't be?'

'Was your wife aware of this?'

'Cec?' He frowned. Then his face cleared. 'Oh— see what you mean. I say, don't get me wrong: happily married man and all that. Fellow can look, though, can't he?'

'You contented yourself with looking?'

'Eh?'

'You didn't perhaps make advances to her, advances that were repelled?'

'Golly, no. Never have the nerve for anything like that. Nor the inclination, really. Such a drain, all that sort of thing. These married chaps who have a little bit of fluff on the side live on their nerves, if you ask me. Not worth the effort. All for the quiet life myself.'

'Do you know anything about the murder?'

Sebastian scratched his head. 'Been trying to make sense of it, actually. Everyone seemed to think young Carter'd done it, then Gerry said he hadn't and Lavinia said it was a tramp, and Gerry said you'd said somebody'd cut up a fur coat because the room was too hot, and she was really shot through the bathroom window with two different guns, and the chap was going to get away on the motor-bike, but couldn't because the ignition key was locked in George's safe, so he hid it in the art gallery. I only heard one shot, though. I expect it was the Mafia.'

Allgood blinked. 'Mafia?'

'Yes, you know: Italians and Sicilians and all that.'

Allgood was silent. Clearly it would be an utter waste of time to try and get from Sebastian any coherent account of the events leading up to the murder, or ask if he'd seen or heard anything untoward. He sighed. 'All right, Everard,' he said. 'You can go.'

'Jolly good,' said Sebastian.

Allgood sat quietly thinking for ten minutes before sending Leather to fetch Hugh.

*   *   *

Hugh said, 'Look, I thought I was in the clear. My alibi—'

'It holds. But there are things I want to talk to you about. First, your motor-bike. The Earl gave me your message. Odd affair, I agree. However, I shan't bother to have it dusted for prints: there'll obviously be dozens of strange ones on it, impossible to check; in addition anybody here could have touched it quite innocently while it was parked outside, so their fingerprints on it would prove nothing.'

'As you wish. But there is a bit more you ought

to know. Somebody's put fuel in the tank. When I went out to check it after the garage chap brought it back Friday midday, I found it was practically dry—not more than a cupful in it. I was irritated that I hadn't told them at the garage to fill it up, or that they'd not had the sense to do so without being told. Now there's—well, not a lot, but a pint or two at least.'

'Which cars were parked nearest it on Friday?'

Hugh thought. 'Everard's on one side and Carter's on the other.'

Allgood nodded. 'And Carter ran out of petrol Friday night. He was surprised. He knew he didn't have much in, but had been sure he had enough to get back here.'

Understanding came into Hugh's eyes. 'You mean someone siphoned fuel from his tank and put it in mine? I see. But why? If they were going to steal the bike, yes. But why put petrol in, just to take it to the picture gallery? It doesn't make sense.'

'There's a lot that doesn't make sense so far, Quartus. But everything will soon. And you may be able to help. You had the room next to Laura Lorenzo's. I want you to think very carefully if you mightn't have seen or heard something that night which could help this investigation, something you may not have considered important at the time.'

'Do you think I haven't racked my brains about that? The answer's no. On Friday night I went straight up to my room after bringing Gerry home and threw myself down on the bed fully dressed. I was in a bit of a temper and wanted to think. I just lay in the dark, smoking. I heard nothing until the shot.'

246

'As you went along the corridor towards your room, did you happen to notice if Signorina Lorenzo's door was open?'

'No, I didn't. If it was, then the light was off in her room. I'd certainly have noticed if it hadn't been, as the corridor was rather dimly lit.'

'So you were unable to see if there was a gun on the floor?'

'Perhaps if I'd been looking for something there, I might have seen it. But I wasn't.'

'What did you do after you heard the shot?'

'Went to the door and got it open just in time to see Gerry's back as she sprinted past. I joined her in the doorway of Laura's room.'

'Didn't it take you rather a long time to get your door open? Lady Geraldine ran the full length of two corridors while you merely crossed your room.'

'Well, I was scared.'

'Scared?'

'Yes, I admit it. Gunshots are no doubt an everyday part of your life, Allgood. They're not of mine. I did what I think most people would do if they heard a shot outside their door: sat tight and wondered if it was safe to investigate or if someone might take a potshot at me.'

'You definitely thought the shot had been fired with criminal intent and wasn't just an accident or horseplay?'

Hugh looked a little surprised. 'Yes, now you mention it, I did. My immediate assumption was that someone had been shot—deliberately.'

'Signorina Lorenzo?'

He nodded. 'I believe so.'

'Do you know why you assumed that?'

'Just because she was in the next room, I

247

suppose. I know now the shot was actually fired in the corridor, but I didn't realise that at the time. It was just a shot, close at hand.'

'But Miss Fry's room was equally close at hand, and Carter's was only a short distance away.'

'What are you getting at?'

'Trying to find a reason for your instinctive assumption that it was Signorina Lorenzo who had been shot at. You see, I believe you had more to do with her than anybody else here.'

'Well, I speak Italian, you see.'

'Precisely. And I'm wondering if she said anything which might have subconsciously led you to believe she was in danger.'

'No, no, I'm sure she didn't.'

'What did you talk about?'

'Films, art. She asked me to paint her portrait. So you see, it wouldn't have really mattered if I hadn't had an alibi. I could have made quite a considerable sum, by my standards, for that painting: money I urgently need. I had every reason for wanting her alive. Apart from the fact that she was a beautiful woman, a great actress and a very charming lady.'

Hugh's voice was suddenly soft. He was silent for a few seconds. Then he looked hard at Allgood. 'You'll get him, won't you? I want that swine to hang.'

*   *   *

'Gerry,' Paul said, 'I've been thinking of that second pistol. I fancy, in spite of Allgood clearing me officially, that there are still people here who don't believe in that other gun. I'd love to find it

248

and prove I wasn't making the whole thing up.'

'It would be rather fun.'

'Then let's have a go. Where would *you* hide a pistol here?'

'Oh, that's easy. Among the guns in Daddy's collection.'

'I thought of that. But I think it would have been too risky for the murderer to have gone back there. It would be obvious your father would be going in to investigate the taking of the murder weapon. Where else?'

'Dozens of places.'

'Name one. Look, you're a murderer. You've got a gun in your possession which would point to you as the killer. What do you do with it? And remember, you don't know the house too well.'

She frowned. 'I suppose one place that springs to mind would be where the gun was hidden when we had our last murder here—how awful that sounds!—in the secret passage. Everybody here must know that story.'

'I say, that's an idea. All right, let's try there first.'

They went up to the linen room and Paul opened the panel. 'Do you want to look?' he asked.

'You bet.' She stepped into the passage, reached for the flashlight, switched it on and shone it round on the floor. Then she gave a gasp. 'It's here!'

'No!'

She bent down. 'Don't touch it,' he said. 'Prints.'

'I know! Got a pen, or something?'

He handed her his fountain pen and a moment later she emerged with the pen inserted into the muzzle of an automatic pistol.

He gave a whistle. 'First time lucky! Congrat,

darling.'

She looked modest. 'You started me on the chase.'

'But you thought where to look. Come on, let's take it to Allgood.'

*　　　*　　　*

'Thank you very much, Lady Geraldine,' Allgood said.

'That was extremely smart of you. And you, Carter.'

'It is *the* gun, I suppose,' Paul said.

'Oh, indubitably, I should say. One shot's been fired from it.'

'Does it tell you anything?' Gerry asked.

'Not just by looking at it, not even me. I'll have it checked for prints, of course, but it's a forlorn hope.'

'It's not a lot of use to you, then?'

'It confirms the hypothesis I'm working on.'

'And ought to convince everybody I *am* innocent, don't you think?' Paul said hopefully.

'All except the most bigoted, certainly. There's no conceivable way you could have planted this in the passage after the shot was heard. Now, if you'll excuse me, I must get on with my interrogations. Be so good as to tell Ransom I'm ready for him, will you?'

They found Rex in the library and passed on Allgood's message. He stood up. 'Oh, right. I suppose this is the time I ought to draw my sword, shout "Back, you villainous dogs!", and leap out of the window. Unfortunately, I didn't bring my sword with me.' He sauntered from the room.

Gerry wondered if he was aware of the beads of the sweat on his brow.

CHAPTER NINETEEN

'Sit down, Mr Ransom,' Allgood said.

'Thanks.' Rex sat.

Allgood pulled a sheet of paper towards him and picked up a pen. 'Your full name is Rex Ransom?'

'Yes.'

'And your age?'

'I refuse to answer on the grounds that it may incriminate me.'

'We have no fifth amendment over here, Mr Ransom. But I'll put "over twenty-one".'

'I'll settle for that.'

'Are you married?'

'Not at the moment.'

'And your occupation?'

Rex stared. 'You're kidding!'

'Oh, of course, I believe somebody did mention it. You're an actor, is that right?'

'As you know perfectly well, Mr Allgood. Do you have any more questions?'

'A few. How well did you know Laura Lorenzo?'

'Not at all. I only met her last Thursday.'

'Did you converse with her much?'

'Very little.'

'Isn't that rather surprising? Two film actors meet in a strange country, staying under the same roof with the likelihood of soon appearing together in a film, and they talk very little?'

'We didn't have a lot in common, I'm afraid. Her movies were—or had pretensions to being—intellectual. She tended to look down on my kind of picture.'

'You resented that?'

'Not at all. It's an attitude I'm used to. It means nothing. Most genuine intellectuals thoroughly enjoy my stuff.'

'In spite of her attitude toward your type of film, she was planning to take a part in one. Why, do you suppose?'

'I don't know, of course, but I guess she needed the money. I've no idea how well her recent pictures have done in Europe, but they've grossed zilch in the States.'

'But couldn't she have made more money with one of the bigger studios than with Haggermeir?'

'Maybe, but she'd turned them all down in the past, you know. And the moguls don't take kindly to rejection. She might have figured she'd get the brush-off if she went back to any of them now. Could be, too, she thought she'd carry more weight with Cyrus than with a Goldwyn or a Zanuck—get her own way easier, have the script adapted to her requirements, and so on.'

'That couldn't have been a pleasant prospect for you.'

Rex smiled. 'I think she would have found Cyrus a tougher proposition than she imagined. He's a mighty canny bird, knows exactly what the public wants and gives it to them. I doubt Laura's ideas would have coincided with that. And while he might have liked the idea of the prestige he'd get from signing her, when it came to a choice between kudos with the critics and bucks at the box office he'd choose the latter every time. Which is why I doubted from the start she'd ever appear in this picture, and why I wasn't especially worried. Certainly not worried enough to murder her to prevent it.' He paused. 'Besides, I must be in the clear, anyway.'

'How do you make that out?'

'Well, she was killed between five and ten after one, right?'

'Yes.'

'And according to what Gerry told us, your theory is that the killer waited in Laura's room until Carter came along, and then the alarm shot was fired. Well, I was talking to Gerry in my sitting-room ten minutes before that shot was heard.'

Allgood shrugged. 'I may have been wrong about the murderer remaining in the room all the time. It could have been you. Say you couldn't stand the suspense of waiting any longer and crept out to see what was happening. Or perhaps suddenly realised you'd forgotten something—the second gun, say—and hurried back to your room to get it. While you were there Lady Geraldine knocked at your door. That would explain your odd manner when you were talking to her. As soon as she left, you ran silently back to Signorina Lorenzo's room, getting there just a minute or so before Carter left his room a second time and provided you with your fall guy.'

Rex said, 'Plausible, but completely untrue.'

'Oh, I'm not accusing you. I'm not accusing anybody—yet. I'm just pointing out that you're not in the clear. Suppose you tell me exactly what you did see and hear?'

'Hardly anything. When we got home I went

straight up to my room and stayed there. I was undressing later when I heard what sounded like a shot. I put on a robe and went outside. That's it.'

'That was surely over an hour after you first went up. What were you doing in the interim?'

'Just sitting, smoking. Reading a bit. Oh, and Gerry stopped by briefly.'

'Ah, yes. Now, can you explain your very odd manner at that time?'

'You said something about that just now. I don't know what you mean.'

'Oh, come, Ransom. Lady Geraldine's given me a full account of your conversation. She said you seemed embarrassed, dazed, that your speech was disjointed, and that when she asked if you were all right you laughed hysterically.'

'Aw, that's baloney. Frankly, I was embarrassed at her coming to my room like that, so late.'

'Really? That embarrassed *you*, a famous film star? Surely you must be used to girls doing that sort of thing.'

'Not English aristocrats. This was in her family home, and I was a guest of her father. Don't get me wrong: I don't think for a moment she was trying to snuggle up to me. It was just the look of the thing.'

'But you *had* arranged for her to call?'

'Yeah, but much earlier, immediately we got home. And it wasn't all that important.'

'It was about Arlington Gilbert, I believe?'

'I was just going to advise her not to take his ill manners too seriously, that he's a decent enough guy at heart.'

'But you told her he'd been prowling about your room.'

'Gilbert? No. Oh, wait a minute. What I think I did say was that he'd been *scowling* about my room: i.e., that it was a bigger and more central one than his. Presumably she misheard me.'

'Presumably. But you can imagine why she thought it was important to talk to you.'

'Yeah, of course. But I didn't realise that. I was just mighty anxious to get rid of her in case somebody saw her and got the wrong impression. I *did* laugh, because it suddenly struck me as funny: the idea of *me* trying to give the bum's rush to an attractive chick.'

Allgood asked him a few more questions, similar to those he had put to all the others, then said, 'Right, thank you, Ransom.'

'That's it?'

'Yes, you can go.'

'Thanks.' Rex got up and walked to the door.

Allgood said, 'Oh, by the way, Ransom.'

He stopped and turned. 'Yes?'

'You've starred in thirty-five pictures, the first being *The Rapier* and the most recent *Prince of Baghdad*. Your most successful was *The Fifth Musketeer*, co-starring Maureen Garland. My personal favourite, however, was *Swordsman of Sherwood*, directed by Larry Main, which also starred Veronica O'Brien, and for which the cinematographer, Herb Nelson, won an Oscar. Ask Gilbert to come in, please.'

*   *   *

Arlington Gilbert lounged into the room, a pipe in his mouth and his hands in his pockets. Superficially he looked relaxed, but whereas with

Sebastian Everard this had seemed genuine, in Gilbert's case it looked definitely forced.

Allgood said, 'Ah, sit down, Gilbert.'

'I intend to.' He plumped himself down and gazed around.

'May I have your full name?'

'You'll find it at Somerset House, with all the other birth certificates, which will also give you my age. If you wish, that is, to waste your time on such irrelevancies.'

'I agree they are irrelevancies, but they help to put people at their ease.'

'I am always at my ease.'

'How fortunate. Where were you when the murder was committed?'

'I can't say. I don't know when the murder was committed.'

'Between five and ten past one.'

'At that time I was in my room.'

'In bed?'

'No.' He was silent.

'This isn't a film script, Gilbert. I suggest you stop trying to be funny.'

'Trying to be funny? Do you really think if I was trying to be funny I couldn't do better than that?'

'If you weren't in bed, where were you?'

'In the armchair.'

'Doing what?'

'Just about dropping off to sleep.'

'You were asleep in the chair?'

'Oh, well done, sir!'

'May I ask why?'

'You may.' Again he was silent, waiting.

Allgood breathed hard. 'Why?'

'Because I was a bit tipsy when we got home.

Haggermeir took me to my room. When we got inside the whole place was swaying. I decided to sit down in the chair for a few minutes to get my bearings before undressing. That's all I remember before the shot woke me. Couldn't think what it was for a few seconds. Staggered across to the door, found I'd left it open a couple of inches, went outside, heard a bit of commotion, went along to see what was happening—last one on the scene, I think.'

'Apparently not. Miss Dove says she followed you.'

'Oh, did she? I didn't see her. Of course, I was unaware of her existence, then. Everybody I *knew* was there before me.'

'Of course, she didn't follow you all the way from your room. When she first saw you, you were already in the corridor.'

Gilbert shrugged. 'So?'

'So there's no witness to the fact that you were actually in your room when the shot was fired.'

'What of it? Have the others got witnesses?'

'No, but they were nearly all in their night attire. You were still fully dressed.'

'So was Quartus. And Carter, of course.'

'Yes, but they'd got in only twenty minutes before. You'd been in your room well over an hour.'

'I've explained that.'

'You were "tipsy", or so you claim. But Lord Burford said he was surprised by your condition when you arrived home. You didn't appear to drink all that much at the party, and you didn't seem tight at all.'

'It hit me when I went out into the cold night

257

air.'

'But it passed off again quite quickly, apparently.'

'When I'd had an hour's sleep. Look, what precisely are you driving at?'

'Just this: a couple of minutes passed from the time Miss Dove heard the shot to the time she saw you. You could have murdered Laura Lorenzo, shoved Carter in the back, fired that shot, slipped down the stairs at the end of the corridor, and gone back up by the main staircase within a minute or so.'

'You buffoon,' Gilbert said distinctly.

'Now, wait a moment—'

'No, you wait. Do you honestly think that I, Arlington Gilbert, spent Friday night running about the corridors of this house, pushing people in the back, firing guns, committing murder? You're out of your mind.'

'Like it or not, Gilbert, you are a suspect.'

'Balderdash. I refuse point-blank to be a suspect. The idea is ludicrous. Why on earth should I shoot the woman? She was a virtual stranger to me.'

'Yet on Friday morning you had quite a long private conversation with her. According to Lady Geraldine, Signorina Lorenzo seemed very keen to speak to you alone.'

'Well, naturally. I'm a famous writer. She was hoping to play in one of my films. In those circumstances actresses are always all over one.'

'What did she specifically want?'

'For me to adapt the script so there would be a good part in it for her. Apparently Haggermeir had said I wouldn't be willing.'

'And were you?'

'Perfectly willing to consider it. I don't consider my work sacrosanct. I just won't have it butchered by fifth-rate hacks.'

'And is that all you talked about?'

'All? If you mean was that the sole subject of our conversation, the answer is yes. Now listen, Allgood. I'm not prepared to talk about my own movements and conversations any longer. I have given you a clear and truthful statement, which is all I am obligated to do. I came in here to offer you my assistance in solving this case. Do you want it or not?'

'What sort of assistance?'

'I know who committed the murder.'

'Who?'

'Lady Geraldine.'

Allgood showed no surprise. 'Really? You have evidence of that?'

'Not exactly. But the girl is a psychopathic schizophrenic.'

'Is she indeed? That's as may be. However, as it happens, we know she didn't commit this particular murder.'

Gilbert stood up. 'If that's your attitude, I refuse to stay in this room another minute. And I will answer no more questions. You, sir, are a pompous, incompetent ignoramus. Good day.'

Gilbert stalked from the room.

Allgood sat quite still. Then from Sergeant Leather's corner he heard a strange muffled, grunting sound. Allgood looked towards it suspiciously. But Leather's head was bent low over his notebook and though there seemed to be some kind of odd movement of his shoulders, the sound had now stopped.

Allgood realised he hadn't asked Gilbert for an explanation of his nocturnal visit to the Earl's study. But that would keep.

*   *   *

'George,' said the Countess, 'I'm worried about Geraldine.'

'Are you, Lavinia? She looks fit enough to me.'

'I don't mean that.' She lowered her voice. 'There's a murderer in this house, George.'

'There's always a murderer in this house, if you ask me.'

'Don't be flippant, George. Geraldine could be in danger.'

'How do you make that out?'

'Suppose this murderer is a maniac, a man who kills young women?'

'Don't think that's very likely. Men like that don't usually shoot their victims.'

'Perhaps they don't usually have access to guns. You have to admit it is possible. I must confess the danger hadn't occurred to me until she told me Paul insisted she lock her door last night. So he must think there's a risk. I think we should get her out of the house as soon as we can.'

'But the whole business may be cleared up tomorrow.'

'*May* is the operative word, George. Personally I don't think the police have the first idea who did it. It could drag on for a week or more yet. And I don't suppose they'll want the suspects to leave here until it's all over. I'd be much happier if Geraldine wasn't here.'

'Hm.' Lord Burford rubbed his chin. 'Maybe you're right, Lavinia. But she's not the only young woman in the house, remember.'

'I've spoken to Merryweather about the maids. I told him that if any of them wants to go home to her family until this affair is over she may do so, and that those who decide to remain should stay together as much as possible, do their work in pairs, and lock their doors at night. I don't think I can do more than that.'

'What about the little Dove?'

'Well, she's a free agent. She can leave any time she wishes, as far as I'm concerned. But that's a matter between her and the police. Whether they still consider her a suspect I don't know, but I cannot imagine they believe a woman did it. Either way, however, they have accepted Geraldine's alibi, and she's given them all the information she can. So I cannot see they can have any objection to her going away.'

The Earl looked dubious. 'Maybe not, but that doesn't mean *she* won't have an objection.'

'I want you to persuade her.'

'Oh, Lavinia, you know I can never persuade Gerry to do anything she doesn't want to. I could order her out of the house, I suppose, but it seems pretty drastic.'

'Maybe I could persuade her, sir.'

They turned. It was Paul, who had approached them without their hearing. He said, 'I'm sorry, I couldn't help overhearing the last part of your conversation. You'd like Gerry to go away?'

The Countess nodded.

'I think that's a very good idea,' he said.

'Why do you think you could persuade her,

Paul?' Lady Burford asked.

'Well, I'm in the same position as she is with reference to the police. They've told me they've finished with me, and frankly I've been through quite a lot the last couple of days. *I'd* rather like to get away for a bit now. If I tell Gerry that, she might be willing to come away somewhere with me for a short while.'

He went a little red. 'Of course, I know in normal circumstances you wouldn't countenance her going off alone with a fellow, but naturally I'd take great care to see that the situation couldn't be misconstrued. I'm terribly fond of Gerry, and I wouldn't do—do . . .' He tailed off.

The ghost of a smile touched Lady Burford's lips. 'I'm quite well aware that you want to marry her, Paul.' His eyes widened. She went on, 'Also, that until this weekend it was very much a toss-up between yourself and Hugh. Now, however, I'd say you've got the field to yourself. It's remarkable what a little adversity can do for a young man's chances.'

He said, 'I say, Lady Burford, I'd really no idea that you—I mean . . .'

'Normally, although I trust her implicitly, I would, as you say discourage any plan of hers to go away alone with a young man. But the situation is not normal, and I do want her out of the house. I'm quite sure she'd refuse to go to one of her relatives, but an invitation from you might be a different matter. So if you can persuade her, I would consider it a personal favour.'

Paul's face lit up. 'I'll speak to her now.'

'I fancy you'll be unlucky,' the Earl said. 'She'll want to see this thing through to the end. Try, though, by all means.'

*   *   *

'Now, Mr Haggermeir,' Allgood said, 'you presumably know more about Signorina Lorenzo than anybody else here.'

'I doubt it.'

'But you had several long conversations with her.'

'Sure, but only about the picture, her contract, and so on.'

'You didn't touch on her personal life at all?'

'Nope. Never let an actor or actress start on their personal life or you get tied up for hours.'

'It must have been a blow to you when she died, though, all your plans being dashed?'

'Not so you'd notice. I was already figuring the broad was gonna be more trouble than she was worth. She was aiming to squeeze every cent she could out of me, for giving me the privilege of employing her! She figured on getting her own way with the script, not to mention billing, publicity, the whole caboodle.'

'You say she gave the impression she was doing you a favour by signing with you. Yet she came from London especially to see you. And I understand you didn't send that telegram yourself.'

'I sure didn't. She sent it, or had someone send it for her.'

'But why?'

'So she could come and talk turkey without seeming to be offering herself, make it look like she thought I'd made the first move.'

'Which would indicate that she was in fact eager

263

to work for you. Again, why? If she was so much in demand, she didn't need to resort to such subterfuge.'

Haggermeir shrugged his beefy shoulders, 'I was available, and in England the same time as her. She'd said nix to most of the other studios in the past. I guess she figured that I'd be so hot to sign her I'd be a pushover when it came to the contract.'

'And you weren't?'

'Listen, pal, Cyrus S. Haggermeir wasn't born yesterday. No one hustles me into giving a contract I don't like. If Garbo herself was available I'd only sign her up on my terms.'

'You were eager to sign Laura up, though, at first.'

'Sure, tickled pink. *At first*. Then I got to thinking perhaps it wasn't such a lulu of an idea, after all. Oh, I hadn't turned her down. We were still talking. But there'd been no firm agreement, even a verbal one. Don't get to thinking the chick had gotten me tied into something I couldn't get out of without bumping her off.'

'Then why do you think she was killed?'

'When a good-looking dame gets croaked, ninety per cent of the time it's sex.'

'A crime of passion? It has none of the signs of that.'

'Well, you're the cop.'

'Then let me begin talking like one. Your movements on the night of the murder, please.'

'Got in about one, took Gilbert upstairs and left him at the door of his room. Went to my own room. In bed by about one-fifteen. Couldn't sleep. Read for a bit. Just dropping off and heard the

264

shot. Went outside and saw the Earl and Countess hurrying towards the east wing. Followed them.'

Allgood questioned him for another ten minutes about himself and the other guests. But he learnt nothing new and let him go.

*   *   *

'How about it?' Paul said.

'Daddy's right in one way. Normally I would want to stick this out to the end. Or I would if I hadn't been through it all before. In a way it's exciting, as it was last time. Naturally I want to know who did it. But the end of it all last time was rather horrid. I certainly don't want to see anyone arrested for murder again. I'd just as soon find out afterwards who it was. So, OK, I'll come.'

'Oh, that's absolutely topping!' He gave her a kiss.

'Where shall we go?'

'Oh, anywhere. Let's talk about that later.' He looked at his watch. 'It's a bit too late to get away today now. First thing in the morning, all right?'

'Fine.'

He thought. 'I suppose I ought to clear it with the police first, just as a formality. I'll slip in and have a word with Allgood now.'

He made his way to the small music room. He arrived just as Haggermeir was leaving, tapped at the door, and went in. Allgood looked somewhat surprised to see him. Paul explained his mission.

'As far as I'm concerned,' Allgood said, 'you can both clear off whenever you like, though I'm sure Lady Burford's fears are quite groundless. It's no maniac we're dealing with.'

Paul smiled. 'Don't tell her, for heavens sake. She might change her mind.' He went out.

Allgood yawned and stretched. 'All right,' he said to Leather, 'that'll be all for today. I'm going to your police station shortly to send some telegrams and make some phone calls to various sources in London and elsewhere, have some inquiries set in motion. How long it'll take to get results I don't know, but certainly not before midday tomorrow. So you needn't return until then.'

'Very well, sir. Thank you.' Leather stood up and gathered his things together. 'Good night, sir,' he said as he went out.

Allgood raised an arm in a dismissive move but didn't speak.

*   *   *

Allgood returned to Alderley at eight o'clock and again had dinner served in his room. Then he slept for a couple of hours on his bed. At ten forty-five Chalky arrived with coffee and awoke him.

'Well, I've 'ad a kip, guv, as you suggested,' he said. 'What's the program?'

'I want you to take up position on the corner of the main corridor and the east wing,' Allgood told him. 'From there you can keep an eye on all the rooms except those in this corridor. There's a cupboard there you can slip into if you need to hide.'

'What about this corridor, guv?'

'I'll watch it from just inside the door. Move that chair across there, will you?'

Chalky complied. 'Expecting chummy to try

266

something else, are you, guv?'

'I wouldn't be at all surprised, Chalky. We're reaching a crucial point in the investigation, and somebody—other than the killer—hasn't told us the full truth, I'm sure of it. It's probably for a quite innocent reason. But it could be vital, and they could come out with it any time. If the murderer knows this, tonight could be his last chance to stop that person talking.'

*   *   *

That night when they went upstairs Paul again took Gerry to the door of her room. They stood discussing their plans for the next day, then he kissed her good night. He waited until she'd gone in and he heard her talking to Marie, then made his way thoughtfully to his own room.

He was worried. Things had really worked out incredibly well, far better than he had ever hoped two nights ago. So in fact he oughtn't to have a care in the world. Nonetheless, something was wrong. The trouble was he couldn't put a finger on what it was. There was just this nagging sense of unease. If only he could think what was causing it.

He reached his room, opened the door and stepped inside, pushing it behind him and stretching out the other hand for the light switch at the same time. He pressed it down. But the room remained in darkness.

Paul swore mildly. The bulb must have blown. Now, where would they keep the spares?

At that second he gave a slight start, as immediately behind him he heard a tiny sound. The next moment the room was dimly bathed in the cold glow of a flashlight.

Paul started to swing round, but be was too late. With a blaze of light, his head seemed to explode. He felt his legs turn to jelly under him. The floor lurched crazily beneath his feet. Then he was vaguely aware that his face was pressing against the carpet.

After this he knew no more.

CHAPTER TWENTY

It was eleven a.m. on Monday when Wilkins alighted from his little car outside Alderley. It was considerably colder again this morning, and all around the slush of the previous day had been transformed into treacherous patches of ice.

Wilkins was admitted to the house and went in search of Allgood. He found him, pale and weary-eyed, poring over his notes in the music room.

'Ah, Wilkins,' he said. 'Decided to give us the benefit of your cooperation today, have you? I trust you enjoyed your day of rest?' Then before Wilkins could answer he went on. 'They told you what happened here last night?'

'No details, sir. Just that Mr Carter's been attacked. How is he?'

'He's come round and he's going to be all right, though he'll have a nasty headache for a while yet. The doctor insists he stay in bed for a few more hours yet.'

'Do you have any clues, sir?'

'As yet, none. Strictly speaking, the only people in the whole house we can clear are Lady

Geraldine and her maid. Carter had just left them in Lady Geraldine's room.'

'Might I know exactly what happened, sir?'

'You may well ask, Wilkins. I put Chalky on guard of the corner of the main corridor and the east wing. When he got to his post he noticed the door of Carter's room was open a little. He didn't think anything of it for a while, but after about fifteen minutes he decided to investigate. He found Carter unconscious on the floor. He fetched me, we sent for the doctor, roused the household, searched the place. But nothing. I must admit I never expected our friend to try anything so early in the night. I thought he'd wait until everybody had settled down. It was a very bold stroke that meant he was able to get back to his own room before Chalky or I had started our watches.'

'Any idea why Carter was the victim, sir?'

'Either he's been keeping something back—probably quite innocently, something of which he doesn't realise the full significance—or someone was searching his room and wanted a chance to search his person. But I went through his things while he was unconscious and it got me nowhere. I'm waiting to have another word with him as soon as he's up to it.'

A minute or two later a footman arrived to tell them they could see Paul. They went upstairs. Chalky White was seated on a chair outside Paul's bedroom. 'I'm taking no chances, you see,' Allgood said.

They went in. Paul was sitting up in bed. He looked pale but he summoned up a smile as they entered. 'Hullo, Allgood—Wilkins. Listen, tell this stubborn young lady there's no earthly reason why

269

we can't start off on our trip this afternoon.' He indicated Geraldine, who was standing at the other side of the bed.

'There's every reason,' she said firmly. 'You're very lucky. The doctor said that if that blow had been a fraction harder or in a slightly different position you could be dead now.'

'But I'm not dead. I feel top-hole, apart from a bit of a headache.'

'Listen, you pig-headed chump, you are not leaving this house today. Tomorrow, if the doctor says so. And you're staying in bed until after lunch at least.'

'Feel up to answering a few questions?' Allgood asked.

'Sure,' Paul said, 'but I can't tell you anything. I've explained I didn't get a glimpse of the bloke.'

'Not about that. What I want to know is whether you've told me everything you can tell me about this whole business. Has there been anything you've seen or heard that's made you slightly puzzled? Anything, or any face, that's momentarily struck a chord in your memory?'

'I swear, nothing.'

'Very well. And are you absolutely certain you know nothing that I don't know about any of the other guests here? If so, I appreciate you may have had an honourable reason for not speaking out, and I won't hold it against you. Well?'

Paul looked at him. For a second it seemed to Allgood that his eyes flickered. Then he took a deep breath. 'I'm quite certain.'

Allgood made a gesture of resignation. 'All right. I won't press the point.'

'Is there anything else?'

'No.'

Gerry said, 'Good. In that case, I can start my reading?'

'Gerry, there's really no need for you to read to me.'

'It is my duty, Paul, and I intend to fulfil it. Now I have some detective stories, which I know you lap up. Ariadne Oliver's *Death of a Debutante*, *The Screaming Bone* by Annette de la Tour, Richard Eliot's *The Spider Bites Back*.'

'I've had enough of crime to last me a lifetime.'

'Then,' she said, 'it will have to be *Eric*, or *Little by Little*. Are you ready?'

Paul groaned.

Allgood and Wilkins went downstairs again. In the hall Allgood said, 'Oh, by the way, that telegram which supposedly brought Laura here. In the post office they think it was handed in by a small boy. Didn't know him. Probably given sixpence to do so. Now I must—'

He broke off as he saw a figure hurrying towards them.

It was Lord Burford and his face was excited. He said, 'Ah, I've been looking for you chaps. Got some information.' He looked round conspiratorially. 'Come into me study.'

When they were all seated in the study the Earl said, 'I know how the bounder got hold of the combination of the safe.'

Allgood sat up. 'Do you, by Jove?'

'I do. Ten minutes ago I had a telephone call.'

'Your phone's working again then?'

'Yes, just this morning. Seems a line was down near the edge of the estate. Anyway, the first call I got was from the manager of the company who

271

made and installed the safe. Now, it seems that late Friday afternoon, after he'd left the office, they had a call from someone who claimed to be my secretary, and who said I'd lost the number of my safe and could they remind me of it.'

'They surely didn't just give it over the phone?'

'Hang on. He told me they've got a system in such cases, because they realise it's just the sort of trick a burglar might try. So what they do is hang up, look up the customer's number in the directory and call it themselves. If the customer answers and confirms that he has in fact just telephoned them—'

Allgood interrupted. '—they know the call was genuine and happily give him the combination of the safe.'

Lord Burford looked a little disgruntled at not being allowed to finish the story himself. 'Precisely.'

'And that's what happened in this case?'

'Yes. Same voice answered, confirmed the original query, took down the number and hung up.'

Allgood nodded admiringly. 'Very smart. Why did the manager phone you today, though?'

'He doesn't work Saturday mornings, and the first he knew about the incident was when his assistant told him about it this morning. Now the manager knew what the assistant didn't: that I have the family birthdays as the combination. He didn't see how I could forget those, so he called me up to check that everything was all right. Of course, I told him it was, but that we'd had a practical joker playing a few tricks lately and we'd like to find out who it was, so could his assistant describe the

272

voice.'

'And?'

'All he could say was that the caller was an educated-soundin' type, but spoke very softly, almost in a whisper. Couldn't even be quite sure of the sex. He thought it was a man, but it could have been a woman disguising her voice.'

'Did they say exactly what time the call was put through?'

'Near enough to five-fifteen.'

Allgood turned to Wilkins. 'Right. There's your job for the next few hours: find out if anybody was seen using the phone at that time.'

'My job, sir?'

'Yes. I'm going down to your station again for a while. I'm hoping for a number of important messages and I've arranged to receive them there. I should be back by mid-afternoon.' He started for the door.

Wilkins said, 'Sir, please, before you go, there is something I ought to say. You see, thinking about the case last night and having spoken to Leather on the phone and learnt much of what happened here yesterday, I came to the conclusion—'

'Wilkins, please.' Allgood raised both hands. 'I've told you repeatedly that I don't want to know. Your conclusions would just cloud the issue for me. Now, carry on with your assignment, there's a good fellow.'

Allgood hurried from the house.

*   *   *

Allgood arrived back at Alderley at three o'clock. He had a word with Chalky—who, with Paul now

273

up and about, had been able to abandon his guard duty—and then went to the small music room. Here he found Wilkins, who'd been joined by Leather, waiting for him.

'Oh, there you are, sir,' Wilkins said wearily. 'No luck, I'm afraid. I've questioned everybody in the house. Nobody saw, or at least will admit to seeing, anyone on the phone at five-fifteen on Friday.'

'Oh, you needn't have bothered,' Allgood said airily. 'The case is solved.'

'You mean you know who did it sir?'

'I do. Took a bit longer than I expected, thanks to those nitwits in the criminal records office at the Yard, but I'm almost ready to make an arrest.'

'May we know of whom, sir?'

'You may.' He told them.

Wilkins listened, his eyes growing wider and wider. When Allgood had finished he said slowly, 'That's remarkable, sir. An amazing piece of deduction, if I may make so bold.'

'Elementary, my dear Wilkins.' Allgood rubbed his hands together. 'Now, I want everyone gathered on the landing at the top of the stairs right away. Arrange it, will you?'

*   *   *

Allgood looked round the ring of faces. They gazed back, some anxious, some curious, some impassive. Paul looked quite fit and remarkably cheerful, perhaps because Gerry was standing next to him, holding his hand.

Allgood said, 'I'm glad to say that the ordeal, for most of you, is almost over. But first I need everybody's help in conducting a little experiment.

274

When the shot was fired on Friday night, you all, except Lady Geraldine—and Carter, of course—stated that you were in your rooms. I'd like you to go to them now, shut the door and do whatever you were doing at that time. If you were in bed, lie down on the bed. In a few minutes you will again hear a gunshot. Then I want you to re-enact what you did that night. Allow as much time as you think you took for getting out of bed, putting on dressing-gowns, slippers and so on. Then come out and make your way to the scene of the murder at the same speed as the other night. Will you all do that?'

There was a general nodding of heads. 'Go now then, please,' Allgood said, 'and be sure to close your doors.'

All those present except Gerry, Paul, Wilkins, Leather, and Allgood himself moved in the direction of their rooms. When they'd gone, Allgood said, 'Lady Geraldine, if you would kindly go and stand in the bathroom and when you hear the shot run as you did the other night.'

She nodded and walked away. Allgood went on, 'Wilkins, you wait here. Leather, you go to the corner of the main corridor and the west wing and remain there. Both make a mental note of everything you see.'

Leather moved off.

Paul said, 'What about me?'

'You come with me.' He strode in the direction of the east wing with Paul following meekly behind.

Allgood turned on the light in the east corridor and at the far end he drew the curtains across the window. Then he opened the door of Laura

275

Lorenzo's room, turned on the light, and drew the curtains in there, too. 'Must get the lighting conditions as identical as possible,' he said.

'Do you want me to do what I did the other night?' Paul asked.

'That won't be necessary. I want you to play the part of the person who pushed you.'

He opened the bathroom door and looked inside. 'Good, the window is open.' He unbuttoned his jacket to reveal a shoulder holster, holding a 38-caliber revolver. He drew it and passed it to Paul. 'When I nod, stand in the middle of the corridor and fire that through the open bathroom door and out of the window. Then immediately step into the bathroom, close it all but a crack, and peer through. Whenever you think you can slip out without being noticed, do so, and join the crowd jostling in the doorway.'

'OK.'

Allgood took from one pocket his notebook and pencil, and from another pocket a stopwatch. Then he gave Paul a nod. Paul raised the pistol, took careful aim for the bathroom window, and squeezed the trigger. The report rang out, echoing through the corridor. Paul hastily stepped into the bathroom and pushed the door nearly to. At the same moment Allgood started the watch.

Within ten seconds Gerry appeared round the corner at the far end. She sprinted along the corridor. As she arrived Allgood said, 'All right, look into the room, see Carter and the body.' He glanced at the watch and made a jotting in the notebook.

Only a few seconds passed before Hugh's door opened and he joined Gerry, followed almost

276

immediately by Maude Fry. Rex was the next to arrive; then the Earl and Countess, Sebastian and Cecily together, and Haggermeir. Allgood continued to make notes, all the while urging them into the doorway.

It was after Haggermeir's arrival that Paul opened the bathroom door wide, took a quick glance along the corridor and then, obviously unnoticed by the others, joined the gathering. It was a further thirty seconds before Gilbert arrived, followed at last by Jemima Dove.

Allgood stopped the watch and drew back the curtains. 'Thank you, ladies and gentlemen. Now, can anyone—' He broke off. 'No, we can't talk here; it's too crowded.' He addressed the Earl: 'Burford, do you think we might move into the gallery for a while? I don't want to go all the way downstairs again. There may be one or two other points I want to demonstrate up here at the scene of the crime.'

'Oh, of course. Gladly.' Lord Burford led the way to the gallery doors, saying as he did so, 'Still locked, actually, but think I've got the key here.'

He fumbled in his pocket, found the key, opened one of the huge double doors, and stood aside. The others trooped. As they were doing so, Chalky came along the corridor and whispered to Allgood for a few seconds. Allgood gave a satisfied nod. Then he and Chalky followed the Earl into the gallery and Chalky closed the door.

Allgood said, 'Those of you who'd care to sit, please do. We may be here some little time.'

Lord and Lady Burford, Cecily and Sebastian, Jemima Dove, Maude Fry, Gilbert, and Haggermeir moved to various of the sofas and

277

upright chairs placed by the walls and sat down. Gerry, Paul, Rex, and Hugh remained on their feet, the latter ostentatiously strolling across to a Reynolds portrait of the fifth Earl and studying it lazily, his hands in his pockets and his back to Allgood. Wilkins and Leather took up position, sentry-like, at each side of the doors, with Chalky a little further along. Allgood moved to the centre of the room and surveyed his audience.

'This has been a quite interesting little case,' he said. 'Teasing, without being too baffling. It was complicated by a number of strange incidents which preceded the actual murder, and I intend to start by looking at those. First I'd like you to begin, Lady Geraldine, by telling everybody about your adventure Thursday night.'

Gerry looked a little aback, but collected her thoughts and gave a concise account of the struggle with the prowler in her father's study. When she'd finished and her parents and the others were still staring at her in amazement, Allgood said quietly, 'Lady Geraldine, do you know who the prowler was?'

She nodded.

'Tell us, please.'

She gulped, then said, 'It—it was Mr Gilbert.'

'What?' Gilbert leapt to his feet with a roar. 'That's a lie! I've never been near the study.'

She said doggedly, 'You admitted it to me Friday morning in the music room.'

'I did no such thing!'

'I told you it was I who scratched your face.'

His eyes bulged. 'That wasn't in the study. That was up here, near the top of the stairs.'

She gave a gasp. 'I never struggled with anybody

278

there.'

'Well, I did. And I'm pretty sure it was a woman.'

'I suppose that was after you'd finished skulking about in Rex's room, was it?' she said bitingly.

Gilbert looked as thought he was going to burst. 'Skulking about *where*?'

'You heard what I said. And don't try to deny it. Rex told me about it.'

'Jupiter's teeth, it's a conspiracy!' Gilbert turned to Allgood. 'There's not a word of truth in any of this.'

Gerry said, 'I'm sorry, Rex, but I'll have to ask you to back me up.'

All eyes turned suddenly on Rex. He smiled a little nervously. 'Back you up?'

'Confirm what you said about Gilbert being in your room. I know the other night you said I'd misunderstood you, but we both know I didn't.'

Rex took out a cigarette case and lighter, lit up and inhaled deeply. He said, 'I'm sorry, Gerry, but Gilbert's never been in my room, as far as I know.'

Gerry gazed at him coldly. 'You're lying,' she said quietly. 'I thought when it came to the crunch you'd have more guts.'

Paul put his arm around her and addressed Allgood angrily, 'I don't know what's going on here, but Gerry's about the most truthful person I know. And she's certainly not crazy. I believe her implicitly.' Allgood just shrugged.

Gerry dashed a sudden tear from her eye. She said, 'I don't have to stay and put up with this. Take me out, Paul. Let's go away at once, after all. When we get back they'll all be gone.'

'Yes, of course, darling.' He started to lead her

towards the door.

'Stop!'

The voice rang out like a whipcrack. It came from Rex. Under his tan his face was pale. He said, 'It's no good. I could never stand to see a woman cry. Sorry I let you down, Gerry.' He looked at Allgood. 'It's true. Gilbert was in my room Thursday night. We had a bit of a scrap.'

Gilbert raised both arms skywards and gave a howl of rage. 'It's a frame-up! I'll have you all in court! Slander! Libel! Defamation!' He pointed a finger at Allgood. 'You put them up to this, you—you—guttersnipe.'

'Kindly keep a civil tongue in your head, sir. If there's any conspiracy I'll get to the bottom of it. Now sit down and be quiet.'

Gilbert stared at him silently for a moment, then subsided, muttering, on to a sofa.

Allgood said, 'Ransom, why did you deny this just now?'

Rex inhaled deeply on his cigarette. 'Because—because I'm being blackmailed.'

'Blackmailed?'

'Yes, a photo was taken in my room Thursday night. I've since received a copy of it and a note demanding two thousand pounds for the negative. I was going to pay up. But I've changed my mind.' Suddenly his chin rose and his voice rang out proudly. 'In the immortal words of your Duke of Wellington, "Let them publish and be damned".' It was a beautifully delivered line.

'Hear, hear, sir. Well said.' This from the Earl. For a moment Gerry thought he was going to clap. Rex made him the slightest of bows.

'We'll look into this later,' Allgood said. 'But

first tell me one thing, Ransom: what evidence do you have that the intruder was Gilbert?'

'I punched him in the eye. Gilbert had a shiner the next morning. He said he'd bumped into the closet door.'

'Was that true, Gilbert?' Allgood asked him. 'If not, I strongly advise you to tell the truth now, for your own sake.'

Gilbert hesitated, then shook his head. 'No, it wasn't. The man I struggled with near the top of the stairs did it.'

'The man? I thought you said it was a woman.'

Gilbert's eyes flickered. 'Both,' he said gruffly.

Allgood stared. 'Both?'

'Yes,' Gilbert snapped. 'First a man ran into me and blacked my eye and then a minute later a woman scratched my cheek.'

'Oh, for Pete's sake!' Rex gave a groan and looked at Allgood. 'You surely don't believe that, do you?'

'I neither believe it nor disbelieve it for the moment. But let's for the sake of argument suppose it's true. It means that apart from yourself and Lady Geraldine, another man and another woman were prowling about the house that night. Unlikely, but perhaps a little less unlikely if they weren't acting independently of each other, but were a couple, working together. Well, apart from the Earl and Countess, there was only one couple here.'

Allgood looked directly at Sebastian. 'Well, Mr Everard?'

Sebastian's mouth fell open. 'Me? Us? Walking about in the dark? Oh, no. Never. Both asleep. Cec and me. Sorry and all that.'

281

'You and who?'

'Cecily. My wife.'

'Ah, yes, of course.' Allgood suddenly swung round to face the Countess. 'Lady Burford, when did you last see your cousin, Cecily Bradshaw?'

'Before this weekend? Oh, twenty-five years ago, I should think.'

'You have not seen her this weekend, Lady Burford. I regret to say that Cecily Bradshaw was killed eight years ago in a car crash, in Australia.'

Every eye in the room turned on the woman they'd known as Cecily. She'd gone deathly pale and didn't speak.

Allgood said, 'I should add that her second husband, Sebastian Everard, died in the same crash.'

He stepped across to where Sebastian and Cecily were sitting and looked down at them. 'If you have an explanation I would like to have it now.'

Sebastian stood up. Suddenly he looked different: less limp and languid, harder and tougher altogether. When he spoke his voice was different, too. The foppish drawl had gone completely.

'Yes, we're impostors. My name is Ned Turner. This is my wife, Mabel. And let me say first that this is absolutely nothing to do with her. I talked her into it, much against her will.'

'Talked her into what exactly?' Allgood asked in a silky soft voice. 'Into—murder?'

'No! We had nothing to do with that. I mean talked her into coming here and posing as Sebastian and Cecily Everard.'

In a bewildered voice, Lady Burford addressed

282

his wife: 'But I don't understand. You knew everything about our family and the old days, people and places. And you look like Cecily.'

Mabel Turner nodded. 'That's the reason Cecily and I happened to meet in the first place. I was her understudy.'

'In Australia?' Gerry said.

'Yes, over twenty years ago. It was her first big part—well, really the only big part she ever got. Unfortunately the play folded after about a month and we were both out of a job. Well, I'd been a singer and dancer before, and she'd been in the chorus, and we looked so much alike that we got up a sister act. We toured the music halls and vaudevilles all over Australia for a couple of years. As you can imagine, we got pretty close. In some of those little towns there was just nothing for respectable girls to do when we weren't performing but sit in the boarding house and talk. I was fascinated by Cecily's background. It was so different from my own, and I used to make her talk to me about it for hours. After a couple of years I knew as much about her family and friends as she did herself. Then she met and married a Philip Brown, a sheepfarmer, and gave up the stage. She'd told me so much about England that I decided to try my luck over here. Well, I didn't make the big time, but luckily I did meet Ned. We fell in love and got married. Cecily and I kept in touch, however, and I knew about Philip dying and about her marrying Sebastian three years later—though, of course, I never met him. Then eight years ago they were both killed. I doubted very much if any of her English relatives were aware of it, though, because I knew she'd had nothing to do

283

with any of them for years. So when this—this business cropped up, I thought I'd stand a fair chance of getting away with it. And I did, until now.'

Lady Burford said, 'But getting away with what?'

'The silver, most likely,' Gilbert said.

Ned flushed. 'Nothing like that. We're not crooks. I talked Mabel into it because I wanted a chance to perform for Mr Haggermeir.'

Haggermeir sat up. 'Me? You're an actor?'

'No. I'm—I'm a stuntman.'

'Holy Moses.' Haggermeir looked baffled. 'Perform for me? I don't get it.'

'It's like this. I was one of the best stuntmen in Britain—'

'*The* best,' Mabel said quietly.

'Some people said so: cars, horses, planes, trains, falls, dives, anything. Then two and a half years ago I had my accident.'

Gilbert snapped his fingers. 'I remember. Some actress was badly injured.'

'What happened?' Gerry asked.

'It was a simple climbing job,' Ned said. 'The hero was supposed to shin up the outside of this building to rescue the heroine's cat, which was trapped on a ledge. The director wanted one shot of her on the ground, looking up at me—standing in for the hero, doing the climb. And when they were shooting that, I fell.'

'Were you hurt?' Lord Burford asked.

'Hardly at all. The lady cushioned my fall. I landed right on top of her. Her leg was broken. She was OK eventually, but the picture had to be scrapped. And I was black-listed.'

284

'Why did you fall?' Haggermeir asked him.

'They said I was drunk.'

'Were you?'

'No. Someone had smeared grease on one of my footholds. I knew who it was, but I couldn't prove it. It was wiped off before I could go and check. But the result was that I've never worked in films since, and never will in this country again.'

Rex said, 'How have you been earning your living?'

'Some circus and fairground work. But I hate it. I must get back into movies. I love them. They're my life. I thought my only chance was to get to Hollywood, where they probably wouldn't know of my trouble. I knew if I could get just one opportunity to prove what I could do I'd be OK. But we couldn't afford the fare. Then I read about Mr Haggermeir being over here and heard that he was actually going to stay with relatives of Cecily's, where Mabel could almost certainly wangle an invitation to stay if she could pass herself off as Cecily. It seemed too good an opportunity to miss.'

Haggermeir said, 'But how the heck were you figuring on giving me a performance?'

'I thought I might be able to pull off some spectacular stunt, which would impress you so much you'd want to give me a real chance in America. I spent the first two days here trying to work something out. Eventually I hit on something. And I have an apology to make.' He looked at Hugh, who had by now turned and was leaning against the wall. 'It was me who took your motor-bike. I'm very sorry.'

Hugh stared. 'But why on earth did you bring it up here?'

'The stunt I planned was to set myself on fire. I have a fireproof suit, crash helmet, and lots of other equipment in the car. Then I was going to ride the bike at full speed the whole length of the gun room, through the French windows, up a ramp formed by that plank, and leap off the balcony into the lake.'

There was a gasp in the room. The Earl said, 'But you'd kill yourself!'

'I don't think so, my lord. I've done similar stunts before. I carefully measured the distance and height and worked out the speed that would be necessary. I had to make the preparations on Friday. I played cards as badly as I could so the Countess and Miss Fry wouldn't want to go on playing with me for long, and as soon as Miss Dove fortuitously arrived I slipped outside and disconnected the bike from the sidecar. I put a little fuel in the tank, took the bike out to the road, and tested it. It's light, but it's got really tremendous acceleration. I brought it back and, while Mabel was making sure the other ladies were safely playing cards, I manhandled it up the back stairs and brought it in here. Naturally I never imagined Mr Quartus would be going out again that night and would notice it was missing. Then I fetched the plank, which I'd discovered in the stables earlier. On Saturday morning I intended to ask his lordship to let me have the key to the gun room, so I could take another look at the collection on my own. If he insisted on coming with me, I was going to tell him the whole story. I think he's keen enough on movies, and a good enough sport, to have gone along with me. Then, when Mr Haggermeir went outside to photograph the exterior of the house, Mabel was going to go with him, give me a yell when he was in the right position, and make sure he watched. And that would have been it.'

'And good-bye to my motor-bike,' Hugh said dryly.

'No, it could have been brought up and without being too badly damaged. I would have paid for any repairs. I could just about afford that. But in the end, of course, the murder stopped everything.'

'Why play the idiot fop?' Gerry asked.

'I guess it was partly the name: Sebastian Everard *sounds* foppish. And I wanted to adopt a personality as different as possible from my own. I thought, too, that if I made myself a silly-ass type, without too much to say for himself, I could avoid serious conversations and be less likely to get caught out. Of course, I didn't anticipate having to keep it up all through a police murder investigation. Must admit, though, I did rather get caught up in the part.' He gave a weak and sheepish grin.

Mabel said, 'I really am terribly sorry. I feel awful. Of course, we'll leave as soon as Mr Allgood says we may.'

'Not so fast,' Allgood said. 'You two have admitted being here under false pretences. A murder has been committed. I have every right to detain you for further questioning.'

Ned went pale. He said, 'We know nothing about the murder. We told you the absolute truth about that. There's only one small point. Years ago, before she became a star, Laura did appear in a couple of films in this country. I worked on one of them. She didn't positively recognise me this

287

time, but my face was obviously vaguely familiar to her. She was trying to remember where she'd seen me before and she went out of her way to talk to me. That's the only thing I didn't tell you, I swear.'

Allgood regarded him silently. At last he said, 'Very well. I believe you. Please don't leave yet, though.'

Ned gave a sigh of relief. He sat down beside Mabel, who was sobbing silently, and took her hand.

Allgood looked at Haggermeir. 'Tell me, if Turner had pulled off this stunt, would you have given him work?'

Haggermeir pursed his lips. 'Hard to say. Possibly. He'd have sure proved he knew his stuff. Trouble is, there are so many first-rate American stuntmen in Hollywood already.'

'How about the film you're making here, *The King's Man*? Couldn't you use him on that?'

'I, er, wouldn't like to commit myself at this stage.'

'Oh, come. I'm sure there'll be plenty of work for stuntmen in a Rex Ransom picture. If he proves his ability, can't you promise him work on *The King's Man* here and now?'

'Well, no, I'm sorry, at this stage I couldn't.'

'Is that because you have no intention of making *The King's Man*, and never have had?'

For long seconds Haggermeir just sat perfectly still, his eyes fixed on Allgood's face. Then: 'Don't know what you mean,' he said.

'Oh, I think you do, Haggermeir. The whole story of wanting to make a film here at Alderley was a ruse, a way of getting yourself an invitation to the house. You had your own private reason for wanting to spend a few days at Alderley.'

'Horsefeathers.'

'I don't think so. And I'm not the first to discover the truth, either.' He looked at Paul. 'Carter, I'd like you to recount the conversation which you inadvertently overheard in the breakfast room on Friday morning.'

At these words Haggermeir drew his breath in sharply.

Paul nodded. 'Very well.' He explained how he had happened to be in the secret passage and had suddenly heard the voice through the panels. Then he paused for a moment.

'The voice,' he said, 'was Mr Haggermeir's. He was saying he hadn't really come to Alderley to make a picture. That was merely an excuse to give him a chance to search the place. He said that just before she died his grandmother told him that as a young girl she'd been married in California to—to Lord Burford's grandfather, Aylwin Saunders.'

At this the Earl gave a gasp, Lady Burford's eyebrows nearly disappeared into her hairline, and Gerry gazed at Paul in amazement. Paul continued, 'Haggermeir said she'd told him that somewhere—probably here at Alderley—there was proof that he, Haggermeir, was in fact the rightful Earl of Burford.'

CHAPTER TWENTY-ONE

The Burford family seemed struck dumb by Paul's words. Nobody, in fact, said anything until St. John Allgood spoke quietly: 'Thank you, Carter. Well,

Haggermeir, what do you have to say to that?'

Haggermeir got slowly to his feet. His face was grey but his expression was defiant. He said, 'Yeah, it's true, it's all true. And I guess I owe you an apology, Earl, for fooling you as I did. To tell you the truth, if I'd known you were going to turn out to be such a regular guy, and the Countess and your daughter such, well, such *ladies,* I guess I'd never have done things in this way. Though that don't mean I ain't still determined to get what's rightfully mine.'

'I suggest you explain just what you mean by that,' Allgood said.

'Ain't it obvious? My grandma—her name was Martha Haggermeir—met and fell for Aylwin Saunders in California in 1850, when she was eighteen. That was just before he'd struck it rich. He told her all about himself, and that one day he'd be the Earl of Burford. The next year, after he'd made his pile, they got married. It was all legal. The ceremony was performed by a fully qualified Baptist preacher named Jones in a little town called Last Straw. The witnesses were Aylwin's manservant and a girlfriend of grandma's. Aylwin took her to San Francisco and for a year or so they lived it up and spent money like water: on furs, jewellery, art objects, you name it. Now, among the things he bought her was a little Chinese casket. Grandma was examining it one day when quite accidentally she discovered it had a false bottom. More for fun than anything else, she put her marriage license under the false bottom for safe keeping. Then she found she couldn't get it open again. She fiddled with it for ages, and decided eventually she'd have to take it back to the place where they'd bought it. She didn't say anything to Aylwin because at that time it seemed his manner to her was starting to change. She suspected he was tiring of her and he tended to snap her head off at the least excuse. He'd been very taken with the casket and had talked about using it as a cigar box. She was scared it might prove necessary to break it open to get the license out and that he'd be angry with her.

'Well, it turned out she was right about his feelings for her, because shortly after he left her. One day there was an English visitor for him—that lawyer Lord Burford told us about, I guess—and the next Aylwin just went out and didn't come back. He wrote her a letter from New York a week or two later, saying he was sorry and was returning to England. To give the so-and-so what credit's due to him, he did leave her practically all the cash he had left, together with the jewellery and stuff they'd bought. In fact, about the only thing he took with him was—'

'The Chinese casket,' Gerry put in.

'Yes, Lady Geraldine.'

'What happened?'

'Well, Martha wasn't the sort to sit at home, sobbing herself into a decline. She was a tough little broad. She said good riddance to bad rubbish, raised all the dough she could on the jewellery and stuff, and opened a rooming house in San Francisco, calling herself Mrs Haggermeir and telling people she'd been recently widowed. Something she didn't discover until a month or so after Aylwin left, and which he obviously hadn't known either, was that she was expecting a baby. However, that didn't stop her running the house

291

up to a week before my pa was born. That was on March 23rd, 1852. Incidentally, she gave him Saunders as a middle name.

'In no time grandma was back running the rooming house. It did well. She raised pa on her own. She let him believe his father was dead, though she always meant to tell him the truth one day. However, she kept putting it off. My ma and pa were married in 1881. I was born two years later, and also given the middle name Saunders. They both died of typhoid in 1886. That meant grandma had another boy to raise on her own. She did a pretty good job, too, except she could never make me go to school or get any sort of education. I got in with a pretty rough crowd, but that's by the way.

'Grandma was determined she wasn't going to die without anyone knowing the truth about her and Aylwin, and so when I turned twenty-one she told me the whole story. I guess it didn't really mean a lot to me at first, it was just a bit of a laugh to think I was descended from an English lord. But as the years went by I thought about it more and more.

'Grandma died at the age of eighty-one in 1913, and soon after that I started to make inquiries. I went to Last Straw, but it was a ghost town by then. The Baptist church had collapsed and there was no way of tracing a Reverend Jones after over fifty years. No doubt the marriage had been registered somewhere, but who could say where? Probably in Sacramento, the state capital, but two-thirds of the city was destroyed by fire in 1852, and there were devastating floods in '53 and '61. So there wasn't anything more I could do. All the same, some years later, when I could afford it, I consulted lawyers. They told me that a genuine, duly witnessed marriage license would be accepted as evidence by any court on earth.

'I checked up on the Burfords and learnt that Aylwin had succeeded to the title in 1854 and died in 1884. That meant that my pa had been the rightful Earl for two years, 1884 till he died, and now I was. I knew, too, that the only way I could ever prove it would be if I could get hold of that license. I was pretty sure it would still be in the casket, but as it was likely the casket was somewhere in this house there didn't seem any way I could lay my hands on it. I couldn't invite myself here, and I sure wasn't gonna be invited.

'All the same, I couldn't forget about it. I kept tabs on the Burford family, even arranged for a clipping service to send me everything that appeared on them in the English press. I don't know really what I had in mind. I was just always hoping that something might turn up. Then a couple of months ago it did. A clipping landed on my desk about the Earl. He'd become a movie fan and he wanted to meet Rex Ransom, my number one star. As Turner said just now, it was too good an opportunity to miss. I needed a good excuse for coming here, and thought of the movie idea. I had to have a script, though, and I searched through a lot of old screenplays until I found a suitable one. But because, as you said, I'd never had any intention of actually shooting the movie, I didn't bother to check up on the copyright, as I'd normally have done. So Gilbert turning up kind of threw me.' He paused. 'I guess that's about it.'

Rex addressed the Earl and Countess: 'Lady

Burford, George, I want you to understand I knew nothing about this. I'm as flabbergasted as you are.'

Lord Burford nodded abstractedly. 'All right, old man, understood.'

Gerry was still staring at Haggermeir. She said, 'And all the time you've been supposedly measuring and photographing the house, you've actually been searching for that Chinese casket?'

'Yeah.'

'Including my father's study, Thursday night?'

Haggermeir had the grace to look a little abashed. 'Sorry about that. Never figured on having to tangle with a lady. But I wanted to search the study as soon as I could, in case there wasn't a chance later. Thursday night I'd been working up on the top floor. I went back to my room to drop off my camera and found Laura waiting for me. We talked about the movie for a bit, and as soon as she left I went down to the study. I figured everybody'd be in bed. It was quite a shock when you burst in on me. I assure you I used the least possible force, but naturally I couldn't let you identify me.'

'I cut your face,' Gerry said.

'No, my forearm. I was in my roiled shirtsleeves and I had my arm up. It was quite a nasty cut.'

'I hope you don't expect me to apologise.'

'Not at all.'

Gilbert said indignantly, 'It was you who blacked my eye.'

'Yeah. After getting away from Lady Geraldine, I high-tailed it right up the stairs. Somebody'd turned the lights off and I ran slap into you. Didn't know it was you, of course.'

'And you let me take the rap for searching the

294

study! You're a bounder, sir!'

'Take the rap, baloney! No one was going to clap you in the jug.'

'My reputation could have been ruined.'

'Your reputation! A washed-up hack who hasn't written a screenplay in ten years. You're on your beam ends, so desperate to do *The King's Man* and scrounge a weekend's free board that you forced your way in here uninvited.'

Arlington Gilbert leapt to his feet without warning. He stepped up to Haggermeir. Then his fist shot out and caught Haggermeir squarely on the nose.

Haggermeir fell back for a moment, then launched himself at Gilbert, fists flailing. However, Leather grabbed him while Allgood stepped in front of Gilbert.

'That's enough,' Allgood snapped. 'This isn't a barroom.'

Haggermeir took out a handkerchief and clasped it to his nose. With a great air of dignity, Gilbert folded his arms and took his seat again.

Rex looked at Haggermeir. 'For years I've lived in mortal fear of offending you, Cyrus. But that's over. You've used me to try and trick these folks. Well, no one makes a sucker out of me. I've made my last picture for you. I don't work for thieves.'

'Thief nothing,' Haggermeir snarled. 'I want what's rightfully mine. That casket was given to my grandma. Aylwin had no right to bring it to England. I still aim to get it back, and what's inside it. And I don't give up easy.'

'I'm afraid in this instance you're going to have to give up,' Lady Burford said quietly. 'You certainly will get no more chances to search the house. However, if it's any consolation, I have never seen such a casket as you describe. If it was here, you'd be more than welcome to it.'

'Thank you, Countess. I'll bear that in mind. Maybe I can't search myself any more, but there are other means. And I'm determined—'

Allgood interrupted. 'Just *how* determined? Are you determined enough to have killed?'

Haggermeir swung round on him. 'Listen, cop, don't try and pin a murder rap on me.'

'I don't need to pin it on you. This does it well enough.' He took a piece of paper from his pocket. 'This,' he said, 'is a photostat of a fragment of burnt paper I found in the fireplace of your room. It was badly charred around the edges, but what remains is quite incriminating enough.'

He looked round the room. 'You see, Carter wasn't the only person to discover why Haggermeir was really here. Laura Lorenzo also did. And she wrote him a note, telling him so and threatening to expose him.'

'It's a lie!' Haggermeir shouted, 'She didn't find out.'

'Just be quiet while I read this. Then, if you've got an explanation you can give it to us.'

He unfolded the paper. 'We've had the original of this checked against a specimen of Laura Lorenzo's handwriting. She definitely wrote it. This is what it says.' He read aloud:

That the real reason . . . visit to Alderley is not . . . discuss making a movie . . . to expose a wicked . . . cruelly deceived a whole family . . . death at the age of . . . a young and innocent girl . . . married but he left her . . . having robbed her . . . valuable . . .

Allgood looked up. 'It's easy enough to reconstruct the gist of the message. It no doubt read roughly like this:

'I know now that the real reason for your present visit to Alderley is not as you claim, to discuss making a movie. I think it my duty to expose a wicked trick, by which you have cruelly deceived a whole family. I know that before her death at the age of eighty-one your grandmother told you that as a young and innocent girl in America she had married but he left her to return to England, having robbed her of a valuable casket.'

Allgood paused. 'Well, I needn't continue with what obviously followed. The implication is plain. After Haggermeir received the note he—'

Haggermeir gave a yell. 'I didn't receive it, I tell you!'

'Yes, you did, and you burnt it. But you were careless, and one bit remained. Laura was a threat. If she exposed you all your hopes of acquiring the title—a thing which has become an obsession with you—would be shattered. You planned to kill her.'

Haggermeir's normally ruddy face was ashen. He whispered, 'No, it's not true.'

'It's no good. You were the only person in this house to have a motive.'

'I didn't kill the dame. I swear it. You gotta believe me.'

Allgood stared at him silently for fully five seconds, Then: 'I believe you,' he said.

297

A gasp went round the gallery. Haggermeir gazed at Allgood and buried his head in his hands.

Allgood said, 'Oh, everything else I've claimed is true. Haggermeir was the only person here with the motive. But *he* didn't kill her. Somebody else saved him the trouble.'

Lord Burford said bewilderedly. 'But it doesn't make sense. If nobody else had a motive . . .'

'I'll explain. This is one of those rare cases: a motiveless murder. And the explanation of that is simple. Laura Lorenzo was killed in error.'

'You mean the gun went off accidentally?' the Earl said.

'Oh, no. Murder was intended. But Laura was killed *in mistake for someone else.*'

'But in mistake for whom?'

'The only person she could have conceivably been mistaken for: your daughter, Lady Geraldine.'

Gerry's jaw dropped. '*Me?*'

'That's right.'

'But—but that's crazy! Who could possibly have mistaken Laura for me?'

'The one person in this room who had never seen either of you before last Friday night.'

Allgood turned and his finger shot out. 'There's the killer of Laura Lorenzo.'

He was pointing straight at Jemima Dove.

Jemima Dove had gone white. For a moment she didn't move. Then she made a sudden grab for a small handbag she had with her and which she'd put down beside her.

Allgood's voice rang out. 'Don't bother to go for your gun. The bullets have been removed from it by my man Chalky.'

298

Jemima froze. Then she seemed to relax and slumped back in her seat, her face expressionless.

Lady Burford said disbelievingly, 'Miss Dove, is this true?'

'She's not Miss Dove,' Allgood said. 'The real Jemima Dove is at present working in Cambridge. I've confirmed that beyond doubt. She's planning to start work on your library next week, as arranged. This young women is another impostor.'

Gerry said weakly, 'But why did she want to kill me?'

'The story starts about two years ago, when she fell in love, desperately in love. For a time the man she was in love with was quite captivated by her. But gradually he began to notice clear signs of mental instability in her. At the same time he fell truly in love with someone else, and he broke off the romance. The grief and humiliation drove the girl right over the edge into insanity. Love turned to hate, both for the man and for the woman who'd taken him from her. She determined to take revenge on them both.'

Allgood looked at Paul. 'Carter, for a long time I've felt that you were keeping something back. I'm sorry, but I'm afraid you can do so no longer. You were that man, weren't you?'

Paul hesitated. 'Er, no. Well, in a way, I mean yes, but . . .'

'Carter, we've found a number of people who'll testify to the fact that before you met Lady Geraldine you were involved in a romance with another girl.'

'Yes, that's true.' Paul turned to Gerry. 'I'm sorry, darling. It was never really all that serious, and as soon as I met you—well, she was just

299

eclipsed.'

Gerry summoned up a shaky smile. 'That's all right, Paul. You never claimed I was your first love.'

Allgood said, 'And ever since this young woman arrived here, you've been concealing the fact that you knew her and knew she was an impostor. Though, of course, you did not know that she was also a murderess. Aren't I right, Carter?'

Paul's face was a picture of uncertainty and anxiety. Allgood said, 'Very well, I won't press you to answer. I admire your chivalry, and we don't need your evidence at this stage.'

Jemima Dove spoke harshly. 'You admitted yourself that I couldn't have stolen that pistol from the collection room.'

'Correct. And I was held up for some time by a preconceived idea: that the person who shot Laura must also have stolen the gun. What didn't occur to me at first was that two people were involved, working together.'

In a horrified whisper Gerry said, 'Somebody else wanted to kill me as well?'

'Yes, Lady Geraldine. And who hated Carter for exactly the same reason that this young woman hated you. As she had lost Carter to you, so he had lost you to Carter. Isn't that true, Quartus?'

Hugh was standing up, very stiff and very still. He was breathing heavily. He said quietly, 'You're mad.'

'No, Quartus, you're the one who's mad. You and your confederate. I don't know which of you planned it, but I would guess you, and I admit it was very clever: a way of taking revenge on the two people who'd humiliated you beyond endurance.

Kill her, and frame him for the crime. It was all carefully worked out. On Friday evening you, Quartus, rang up the safe company and obtained the combination of Lord Burford's safe. Later you got the gun room key from it, took the pistol, loaded it, and left it in some prearranged place up here on this floor. After you'd gone out, your accomplice arrived, passing herself off as Miss Dove. Before the party returned she came upstairs. She picked up the gun and waited. One thing you hadn't told her about, however, was the arrival in the house of Laura Lorenzo. As far as she knew, there was only one *young* lady here. Granted Laura was a few years older than Lady Geraldine, but she was so skilfully made up that that wasn't really obvious.'

Allgood turned back to Jemima. 'You saw this attractive and glamorous young woman coming up the stairs, and you naturally assumed it was Lady Geraldine. You followed her to her room and shot her. You claimed to have been in your bedroom when the second shot, the alarm shot, was fired. But it would have been impossible for you to have heard the shot from there, at the farthest part of the house and with your door closed. Just now I asked you all to go into your rooms and shut the doors. But *you* didn't. My man Chalky was watching from my room opposite and he told me a few moments ago that you left your door ajar and stood just inside it. It was essential you hear this shot, and you knew you wouldn't if you obeyed my instructions. But to revert: after murdering Laura, you just waited for Carter to come along. But he'd been delayed. Meanwhile, you, Quartus, were becoming anxious that Lady Geraldine and Carter hadn't turned up. The plan could be ruined. Naturally, you didn't know your accomplice had already shot the wrong person.'

He looked at Jemima again. 'You, in the meantime, had realised the point about the bullet hole in the coat giving away the actual time of death. And—well, I've previously explained what happened then, and we all know the eventual outcome.'

Allgood paused and looked round at his audience. 'And so the mystery is solved and my job is over. Chief Inspector Wilkins will handle the formal charges. So now—'

He broke off, for a *most* unexpected sound had interrupted. It was laughter. And it was coming from the girl they'd known as Jemima Dove. Allgood stared at her in amazement. Then he barked, 'You may think this is all highly amusing, but perhaps—'

She broke in. 'I'm sorry, Mr Allgood. Yours was a marvellous effort, it really was. I'm filled with admiration. Unfortunately for you, there's just not one word of truth in it.' She picked up her handbag. 'It's all right, I'm not getting my gun out—though incidentally I do have a permit for it.'

She reached into the bag and brought out a small folder of stiff cardboard. 'I *am* an impostor. My real name is Ann Davies. I'm an operative of the Tinkerton Detective Agency, as this will prove.' She handed him the folder and continued, 'I had never seen, or even heard of, Mr Carter or Mr Quartus until last Saturday. And I certainly didn't shoot Laura Lorenzo.'

Allgood was gazing at the identity card with an expression of utter disbelief. He looked up, stared blankly at her for several seconds, then suddenly swung round on Paul. 'Carter, this is the girl you knew, isn't it?'

Paul shook his head. 'No.'

Allgood gave what almost amounted to a screech of rage. 'You blithering idiot! Why didn't you say?'

Paul looked annoyed. 'I thought you didn't want me to say, that you wanted me to play along for a bit because you were laying some trap for her—or for somebody else. I didn't know what to say. Besides, you'd already accused her by then, so what difference did it make?'

Allgood's face was a study. He stammered, 'But—but she perfectly fits the description of your girlfriend, which your manservant gave a colleague of mine this morning.'

Paul looked amused. 'They've been talking to Albert?' He looked at Ann Davies appraisingly. 'Yes, I daresay she does. The colouring's the same, the height, the figure. But the girl I knew—her name was Jean Barnes, by the way—didn't look a bit like Miss Davies, really. As Albert, or any of my friends who knew her would confirm, if they saw Miss Davies. I haven't seen Jean for, oh, eighteen months. Last thing I heard she was in South Africa.'

Ann Davies bowed her head. 'Thank you, Mr Carter.'

Allgood rounded on her fiercely. 'All right, so you're not Jean Barnes. But you were here under a false name. And you wouldn't be the first private detective to commit murder.'

She shook her head. 'It won't do. If I'm not this Jean Barnes, where's my motive? And if Mr

Quartus and I have never met before this weekend, which I know he'll confirm—'

Hugh nodded. 'Absolutely. You'll never trace any connection between us, Allgood, because there isn't one.'

'So,' Ann Davies said, 'who stole the gun? You've admitted I couldn't have.'

Allgood made a valiant attempt to recover. 'Then if you didn't come here to kill why are you here under a false identity? What are you up to?'

Ann stood up. She seemed quite a different person from the timid Jemima Dove—brisk, assured, decisive. She said crisply, 'I came here on the track of one of the world's most ruthless and efficient professional blackmailers.'

Rex Ransom looked up sharply.

'My firm was hired,' she continued, 'by a wealthy businessman who'd been blackmailed and was determined to see his persecutor brought to justice. He gave us virtually unlimited funds. I've been on the assignment for two years, always just one step behind the blackmailer. I've travelled thousands of miles. Four times I've traced victims who were unwilling to cooperate, seven times I've lost track of my quarry completely. I was on the verge of giving up. And then I got one more lead: the next job was going to be at Alderley this weekend. How I found out about Jemima Dove isn't important. What is important is that at last I've succeeded.' She looked straight at Arlington Gilbert. 'Is it true what Mr Haggermeir said earlier, that you're washed up and on your beam ends?'

Gilbert bridled. 'How dare you! Of course it's—'

But suddenly the piercing gaze she was directing

on him seemed to make him think better of what he was saying. He stopped short and his eyes dropped. 'It's—it's true enough,' he muttered.

'In that case, how can you afford to employ a secretary?'

Gilbert seemed to come to a decision. He looked straight at her and spoke clearly. 'I can't.'

'You don't pay Miss Fry any salary, do you? In fact, *she* paid *you* to be allowed to accompany you here and pose as your secretary.'

This time he did hesitate, but only for a second before saying, 'Yes.'

'Would you be prepared to testify to that in a court?'

'I would.'

'Mr Ransom, are you prepared to give evidence and produce the photo and note that were left in your room?'

'You bet I am, honey.'

Ann Davies stepped across to Maude Fry and looked down at her. 'And that, Miss Fry—or Miss Robinson, or Miss Harris, or Miss Clark— means that after two years I've got you cold.'

When Ann had first mentioned her name, Maude Fry had seemed to freeze. But now she at least reacted. She jumped to her feet. 'This is monstrous! I've never been so insulted in my life. I shall leave this house immediately. And I assure you, Miss, that you will be hearing from my lawyers.'

'Then in that case, you'd better sit down again and listen until I've finished. You'll then be able to tell them all I said about you, won't you?'

Maude Fry's lips tightened. 'Well, really! I most certainly shall. I have an excellent memory.'

305

'Good.' Ann looked at Allgood. 'This woman's usual technique, though not in this particular case, is to obtain a post as private secretary to some wealthy business or professional man. It's always somebody she's heard some whisper of scandal about, and she has quite a network of informers. She's a first-class secretary and quickly makes herself invaluable. A confidential secretary has wonderful opportunities to dig out her boss's secrets. Then, sooner or later, she strikes. She leaves his employ, her bank balance considerably fatter, and usually with a good reference to boot. She's been intelligent enough never to go back with fresh demands, and so her victims have never been driven to prosecute. This time, however, she changed her technique slightly. She'd plainly learnt something about Mr Ransom who, he'll excuse my saying, must be a very rich man. There was little chance, though, that he'd want a secretary: the studio handles all his correspondence, and so on. However, when she heard he was coming to Alderley she did the next best thing. She got herself ostensibly taken on by a man who was going to be a member of the same house party.'

'I didn't get my lead on her movements until last week—how doesn't matter—and then I had to find a way of getting into the house myself. It took some time. On top of that I was delayed by the road conditions on Friday, so I didn't arrive here until the party was well under way. I'd never seen my quarry face to face, but I'd been given enough descriptions of her to recognise her as Maude Fry as soon as I clapped eyes on her. I didn't know what the situation was: whether she'd started to apply the squeeze, or even who her victim was. It

306

could have been any of the gentleman guests, or even the Earl.

'After I was introduced to Fry I was determined not to let her out of my sight more than I could help. When she left the room I went with her, but instead of going to my bedroom I waited a few seconds in the corridor and then followed her. I hid in this gallery and kept an eye on her door. It must have been after that that Mr Turner brought the motor-bike up. After a minute she left the room again, carrying a large envelope. She went into the Royal Suite, came out again almost immediately without the envelope, and went downstairs. I slipped in there myself. The envelope was propped up on the mantelpiece. I took it into the next-door bathroom and steamed it open. As I'd expected, it contained a photograph—which I did not, incidentally, look at—and an anonymous letter. This was cut from newspapers in the usual way and demanded two thousand pounds in cash for the negative. Otherwise copies would be sent to the press.'

'That's just about the amount of cash I have with me,' Rex said. 'How the heck did she know?'

'Oh, her research has always been excellent. She would probably have asked more, but that would have entailed a delay for you to get hold of the money.'

Ann addressed Allgood again. 'If Mr Ransom agreed to meet the demand, he was to come down the following morning wearing his watch on his right wrist. And he was then to leave the money in the roots of a certain specified tree in the park near the drive on Saturday morning. If he went out again in the evening he would find the negative in the same place. That way there need be no contact between blackmailer and victim, and Mr Ransom would not know who the blackmailer was. Fry, who had already prepared a reason for leaving the house on Saturday morning without causing suspicion, would simply slip back into the grounds later in the day and collect the cash.'

'But why do it this way?' Rex said. 'Why not wait until we'd both left here and she could have contacted me by post or phone? It would have been much less risky and, as you said, she could have squeezed me for even more money.'

'For the simple reason that she was in desperate need of the cash. She's made a great deal over the years, but she's gambled most of it away. She's in debt to several bookmakers, who are getting very nasty. She simply couldn't afford to wait. Of course, in the event, the murder meant she had no choice. One thing only puzzles me: why she didn't plant the envelope in Mr Ransom's room earlier on Friday. Before the party left for the village, I imagine, she was prevented by people constantly entering and leaving the other bedrooms all around, but I don't know why she didn't do it immediately after they all left.'

'I think I can tell you.' The words, unexpectedly, came from Mabel. 'I went to her room almost as soon as they'd gone and told her we were just going to start playing bridge. She more or less had to come straight down with Ned and me.'

'Thank you,' Ann said. 'Not that the delay really mattered. Mr Ransom would assume the envelope had been put there much earlier, while he was downstairs waiting to leave, and Mr Gilbert, as well as everybody else, was still upstairs, getting ready.'

Rex nodded grimly. 'That's just what I did figure. And all along it was *her* I tangled with in my room, not Gilbert at all. But I thought I blacked the intruder's eye.'

'You did,' Ann said. 'But it must have been a glancing blow and the bruising didn't show under these blue lenses. However—'

Suddenly her hand shot out and flicked the glasses from Maude Fry's face. 'You see? There's still a trace of a black eye there. She's been wearing these permanently since, and hasn't been seeing too well as a result—been tending to stumble over things. I fancy she only normally wears them for reading.'

'That's right,' Paul exclaimed. 'I remember her putting them on to write something almost as soon as she arrived and then taking them off again.'

Ann looked at Arlington Gilbert. 'It was after she left Mr Ransom's room on Thursday night that she cannoned into you.'

'I thought it was her,' he said in an unusually quiet voice. 'Until Lady Geraldine told me it was she who'd scratched me, that is. Even after that, when I'd had a chance to think about it, I decided Lady Geraldine had mistaken me for someone else. Because I became convinced it wasn't a knife I'd been scratched with. I couldn't prove it was Miss Fry, though.'

'I apologise for everything, Mr Gilbert,' Gerry said.

'But as a matter of interest, what were you doing walking about in the dark on Thursday night?'

'I'd been getting more and more worried about why Miss Fry had been willing to pay to accompany

309

me here.

She'd said she was hoping to wangle a job as Lady Burford's secretary, but I came not to believe that. I was determined to find out the truth. I knew she had a camera *and* a flash gun with her, and the most likely time to use that would be at night. I decided to keep a watch on her room. On Thursday night, I came along here and waited with the door open an inch. After about half an hour, however, there'd still been no movement from her room, and I realised I was being a bit of an ass and she might not stir all night. So I made my way back towards my room. But the lights had gone out, and just as I was groping across the landing somebody came blundering up the stairs and ran right into me. We struggled, and then he slugged me in the eye. So that bloody nose I gave you just now, Haggermeir, you had coming to you. I'd no sooner got to my feet, when almost the same thing happened again, only this time I got a scratched face instead. She must have gone into Ransom's room much earlier, before I'd ever started watching her room, and had been in there all the time.'

Ann nodded. 'The whole thing was well-planned. Even, I strongly suspect, to the extent of breaking the window in Mr Ransom's original bedroom.'

'She did that?' Rex exclaimed. 'But why?'

'She must have started snooping around as soon as she arrived and quickly realised it would be much easier to get a photo of you if you were occupying the Suite—three rooms with adjoining doors. If your first room was made uninhabitable, it was more than likely you'd be transferred to the

Suite: his lordship wouldn't want you relegated to a room at the far end of one of the wings. I won't press that point, though. I can't prove it.'

During all this time St. John Allgood had obviously been making violent efforts to get his thoughts under control. Now at last he spoke again. 'This is all very well, but it's Friday night, not Thursday, that concerns me. You weren't in your room when that shot was fired.'

'I admit it,' Ann said. 'I'll tell you what happened. After reading the blackmail note I replaced it in its envelope and put it back where I'd found it. I wanted the victim to have the shock of finding it. Then a little later I'd go to him, tell him the truth, and ask him to come to the police with me. But at that time *I still didn't know who the victim was.* I had no way of telling who was occupying the Royal Suite. There was no time to go through the occupant's things and get a clue. I had to hurry back downstairs for the bridge game. I could have asked the Countess who was in there, but it might have looked a bit odd. So when we later heard the others returning I went upstairs again with Fry, hurried to my room and put a dressing-gown on over my clothes—I thought it would look more natural if I was up for any length of time—then took up position in that linen room opposite the Royal Suite. About five minutes later Mr Ransom came up and went into his rooms. I decided to give him about ten minutes fully to take in the situation, then go across, identify myself, tell him I knew who the blackmailer was, and ask for his cooperation. Eventually I left my hiding place and tapped on the bedroom door. There was no reply. I was surprised, and I suddenly thought with

311

horror that perhaps he'd committed suicide. I went in. The room was empty. I crossed to the centre, looking fearfully round for a body. Then I saw the envelope where I'd left it—and heard Mr Ransom whistling in the next room. I realised he'd come in and gone straight through to his dressing-room without noticing the letter. The next moment I heard him coming towards the connecting door.

'In a flash it hit me that I'd made an awful blunder. If he came in and saw me there, he'd immediately assume he'd caught *me* in the act of planting the blackmail note. I was here under a false identity. I'd quite likely be accused of blackmail. I'd be able to clear myself eventually, but in the interim Fry would get away. It was vital he didn't find me there. There wasn't time to get to the door. I did the only thing I could think of— threw myself under the bed.'

Rex stared at her. 'When I found that envelope and opened it, you were under the bed? Good grief. I hope my language didn't shock you too much.'

'Oh, I've heard worse, Mr Ransom.' She addressed Allgood again. 'I stayed there for nearly an hour. I was more or less resigned to staying there all night. Then someone knocked on the door of the next room. It was Lady Geraldine. While Mr Ransom was talking to her I at last managed to get out. I'd heard her say she'd only be staying for a few seconds, which meant I might not have time to get back to my own room before she re-emerged, and as I didn't want her to spot me in the corridor I slipped into the bathroom next door. I waited there until I heard Lady Geraldine leaving, gave it another minute or two to be on the safe side, and then started back towards the west wing. I decided it would now be better not to talk to Mr Ransom until the morning. However, I'd only got level with the stairs when Lady Geraldine emerged from her own room again. I'm afraid this time I slipped into Lady Burford's boudoir. I was waiting there with the door open an inch when I heard the shot. Everything else happened exactly as I told you, Mr Allgood. There are just a couple more points and then I'll shut up. While you were questioning Miss Fry yesterday, I took the opportunity to search her room. It was, incidentally, the first chance I'd had, though I'd been hanging around in here for hours, waiting for a clear moment. In a locked case under her bed— I'm good at picking locks—I discovered a full set of developing equipment. Unfortunately, I couldn't find the negative of that blackmail photo. For safety's sake, she no doubt went out on Friday and hid it somewhere in the area so that she could retrieve it after she had Mr Ransom's money.'

'She went out in her car on Friday morning carrying an envelope,' Ned said. 'She said she was going to mail a letter.'

'Thank you,' Ann said. 'I doubt very much if she did actually mail it. However, it's not important. So long as Mr Ransom will prefer charges, we've got her where we want her.'

'Sugar,' Rex said, 'you've got yourself a deal.'

There was silence for several seconds. Everyone looked at Allgood. But he seemed incapable of speech. Eventually it was Lady Burford who spoke. 'Well, Miss Fry, have you nothing to say?'

Maude Fry burst into tears. 'I've never done anything like this before,' she sobbed. 'Whatever

313

this girl says. It was a sudden temptation. I knew Mr Ransom had all that money, and—and . . .' She tailed off.

A look of pure self-satisfaction appeared on Ann Davies's face. She said, 'My case is proved, I think.' She sat down.

Suddenly Allgood shouted angrily at her. 'Why didn't you tell me all this before? It's disgraceful!'

'I'm sorry. I suppose I should have. But as I knew nothing about the murder, other than what I've told you, I didn't think it would matter.'

'You lied about where you were when the shot was fired.'

'Yes, but it made no difference. I told you the whole truth about what I'd seen and heard. Of course, if I'd known you were going to pick on me as your number one suspect, I'd have told you the truth about that too. But yesterday you informed me I was no longer under suspicion. If you'd put to me the point about my not being able to hear the shot from my room, instead of rushing in bull-headed with a public accusation, I'd have explained everything and you wouldn't have made such a fool of yourself.'

Gerry thought Allgood was going to burst, as his face slowly turned puce. It was the Earl who asked him the question in everybody's mind. Very gently, he said, 'Tell me, my dear chap, do you have any idea at all who killed Miss Lorenzo?'

'What? Of course I have. It was—it was—well, if it wasn't her, it was . . .' He gazed round desperately. 'It was him!' He pointed at Haggermeir. 'As I said first. Or them.' He indicated Ned and Mabel. 'Or possibly all of them. Yes, that's it. It's a conspiracy. They—' He stopped

314

dead.

It was at that moment that Chief Inspector Wilkins cleared his throat.

CHAPTER TWENTY-TWO

Wilkins's intervention wasn't a particularly dramatic one. But it brought every eye in the room instantly round to him.

He stepped forward. 'I'm afraid Mr Allgood's rather got hold of the wrong end of the stick,' he said.

Lord Burford said, 'Wilkins, you mean you *do* know who killed Signorina Lorenzo?'

'Yes, my lord, I knew very early on in the investigation.' He turned his gaze mildly on Allgood. 'I did try to tell you, sir, but you weren't interested in my ideas, only in facts. I gave you all the facts I knew. I really thought you'd make the same inferences from them that I had, but you didn't. So all I could do was play for time until I could get hold of the proof I needed.'

He addressed the room at large. 'Miss Lorenzo came to Alderley to try and identify a man who some years ago caused the death of a cousin of hers, a girl who was more like a sister, and robbed the family of some valuable jewellery. I learnt that the family still had a snapshot of this man. I arranged yesterday for an enlargement of it to be flown from Italy. Ever since then I've been waiting for it to arrive. It reached the Westchester police station a short time ago and was rushed straight here. A few minutes ago it was handed to me

315

through the door by a constable. I don't think anybody noticed, as at that moment Mr Haggermeir and Mr Gilbert were engaged in their little fracas.'

Wilkins brought a glossy six-by-eight photo from behind his back and looked at it. 'As I said, it's only the enlargement of a snapshot, but I think it's quite identifiable.' Slowly he raised the photograph up for everyone in the room to see. The smiling face that confronted them was that of Paul Carter.

*   *   *

The first person to move was Paul. With one hand he caught Gerry by the arm and jerked her violently to him. The other hand flew inside his jacket and came out holding Allgood's revolver.

Only one man reacted as quickly. As the gun came up, Ned Turner threw himself at Paul, but he wasn't quite fast enough. The revolver barked. Ned fell to the floor, clutching at his leg. Mabel gave a cry and dropped to her knees beside him.

Paul shoved the muzzle of the gun against Gerry's head. 'If anyone moves, she dies.'

Halfway to his feet, Lord Burford froze. The Countess gave a strangled cry.

In a voice of disbelieving horror, Gerry gasped, 'Paul, are you out of your mind?'

'Shut up, you.' Then he snarled, 'Get against the far wall, all of you.'

'Do exactly as he says,' Wilkins ordered sharply.

The others began to back away to the wall adjoining the gun room, Ned being half carried by Rex and Haggermeir. When they were all lined up against it, Paul moved to the other door, pulling

316

Gerry with him. Just inside it he stopped.

'I want some handcuffs.'

At a nod from Wilkins, Leather took a pair from his pocket. 'Slide them across the floor,' Paul snapped. Leather did so. They stopped near Gerry's feet. Paul gave her a jab with the gun. 'Put them on.'

He kept tight hold of her arm as she bent down, picked them up, and awkwardly manacled her wrists with them.

Paul addressed Wilkins. 'How many men have you got here?'

'None in the house. There's a man at the lodge.'

Paul gave a nod and looked at the Earl. 'Where will the servants be now?'

It was Lady Burford who answered. 'Probably all having their afternoon tea in the kitchen.'

'That's fine.' He gave Gerry a prod. 'OK, let's go.'

Rex said, 'If you want a hostage, why not take me? I'm not worth as much as Gerry, but I'm quite a valuable property.'

'Nothing doing, buddy.'

Allgood said hoarsely, 'Carter, you can't think you can get away with this.'

'Maybe not. But I'm certainly going to try. And remember this, all of you: if the police take me I'll hang. Well, can't hang twice, so I've got nothing to lose by killing again.'

He opened the massive door, pushed Gerry through, slipped quickly out after her, and pulled the door behind him. A second later they heard the tumblers slide across.

Wilkins swung round on the Earl. 'Is there a bell in here for the servants?' Lord Burford shook his head. 'Then we'll have to try and break the door down,' Wilkins said. 'Jack! And some of you help him.'

He hurried to the nearest window and looked out. 'No drainpipe, creeper, nothing. And a flat stone pavement underneath.'

Leather, Chalky, Arlington Gilbert, and Rex Ransom had begun throwing themselves against the door. Leather called, 'It's like a rock, sir.'

Hugh said quietly, 'Why not shoot the lock out?'

Lord Burford gave a gasp. 'Of course! The guns!' Groping on his watch-chain for the key, he hurried to the door of the collection room.

Haggermeir and Allgood meanwhile had lifted Ned onto one of the sofas and were attempting to staunch the flow of blood from his leg.

Lady Burford was sitting very still, erect and pale. Her eyes were closed and she appeared to be praying.

The Earl had by now disappeared into the collection room. Ann Davies followed him. She saw the French windows leading to the balcony at the far end and started to run towards them, calling, 'Perhaps there's a way down from the balcony.'

'There isn't,' Lord Burford said tersely, but Ann didn't stop.

The Earl strode rapidly to the part of the wall from which was slung a heavy modern hunting rifle. He snatched it down and half-ran to the ammunition cupboard again fumbling for keys, this time in his pocket.

Ann reached the far end, unbolted the windows, threw them open and stepped onto the balcony. She saw immediately that there was no possible means of climbing down. And below was the flat terrace outside the ground floor ballroom. Beyond that was the wide path that ran right round the house, a steep grass bank, and the lake.

Then, round the corner of the house, appeared Paul's car. The top was still down. He was at the wheel and Gerry was beside him. But he was going much too fast for the conditions, and Ann gave a gasp as the car skidded wildly on the icy surface. It slid to a halt, facing back in the direction it had come. Paul started to yank desperately at starter and gear.

Ann gave a yell into the room. 'Out here! He's getting away!'

Lord Burford, who'd loaded the rifle and was on his way back to the gallery, stopped, turned, and then ran down the room towards her.

By the time the Earl had joined Ann, Paul had got the car moving again, but the surface was as treacherous as a skating rink. The car was sliding from side to side, its wheels spinning furiously.

Ann gripped the Earl's arm. 'Can you shoot a tire out?'

He shook his head. 'Daren't risk it, with Gerry in the car.'

There was the sound of running footsteps, and they were joined on the balcony by Lady Burford, Hugh and Wilkins.

'Why's he come this way?' Hugh panted.

'He's avoiding the drive, and the policeman at the lodge,' the Earl muttered. 'He's going to take the track to the home farm. That'll lead him out onto a lane that runs directly to the main Westchester road.'

As he spoke, the wheels of the tourer seemed at

319

last to find a dry patch. The car shot forward.

Just before the path reached a point opposite the watchers on the balcony, there was another bend in it. Hardly slowing at all to take it, Paul swung the wheel. At the same moment the car struck another patch of ice.

Its rear wheels skewed round, but the car continued in the same direction. It leapt from the path and over the bank, to land with an almighty splash in the lake.

The Countess gave a scream. The Earl dropped his rifle with a clatter on the floor. The car was slowly sinking beneath the water. They could see both Paul and Gerry struggling to extricate themselves.

In a matter of seconds Paul had got clear. He struck out strongly for the near bank. However, obviously realising that the steepness and slipperiness of it would make it almost impossible to climb unaided, he veered to his right and made for a point further away but where the bank was less steep. In his mouth, the trigger guard clamped between his teeth, was the revolver.

Lady Burford gave a cry. 'Gerry! Gerry, darling!'

Then they heard Gerry's voice. 'Help! I can't get out. The handcuffs—caught. Paul, help me!'

But Paul ignored the cries. He continued to swim for land.

The car was sinking even lower. The water was now only six inches below the top of the doors. 'When it gets to the top she'll sink in seconds,' Hugh whispered.

The Countess shouted, 'Oh, somebody do something!'

Lord Burford made a sudden lunge for the

320

balustrade. Wilkins grabbed at him, and the Earl tried to shake him free.

'It's no good, sir. You'll break a leg at the very least.'

Suddenly Hugh gave a loud shout. 'I've got it!' He turned and sprinted down the room.

In the gallery the three men were still working on the door. But now they'd taken up Ned's plank and were about to start using it as a battering-ram. Hugh yelled to them, 'Take that to the balcony! Lean it against the balustrade! Make a ramp! Quick!'

They hesitated only a second, then turned and started to run, carrying the plank between them.

Hugh dashed towards the end of the gallery. As he did so he snapped over his shoulder, 'Allgood, help me with this sofa!'

Allgood, who was sitting slumped on a chair, a picture of defeat, jumped up and ran after him. 'What are you going to do?'

'Try Turner's idea.'

'*What?* Don't be a lunatic!'

'Stop arguing. Move it!'

From where he lay, Ned called, 'You'll never make it, man. You'll kill yourself.'

Hugh, with Allgood's help, was already heaving the sofa to one side. Over his shoulder he shouted, 'You were going to do it.'

'I'm a pro, and I'd have had a helmet and protective suit.'

'It's either this, or Gerry drowns.' He threw his leg over the saddle and kicked at the starter.

With a roar that reverberated like a dozen engines round the gallery, the motor burst into life. Hugh rode it to the centre of the room, turned it to face the door of the gun room, and backed it until the rear wheel was tight against the outer door. Beyond the far door of the gallery the collection room stretched ahead, a sort of passage running between the display cases. The other men had done their job. The plank was in position. It looked a tiny target, yet at the same time absurdly close.

Hugh closed his eyes, said a silent prayer, squeezed the clutch, engaged bottom gear, and twisted the throttle to give maxirevs. The engine howled.

Hugh opened his eyes, put all his weight on the saddle, pulled up on the handle-bars to give optimum grip under the rear wheel, and let out the clutch. The bike rocketed forward.

For the first time Hugh felt the full power of the machine's engine. Accelerating at an enormous rate, he shot across the gallery and into the gun room. As he tore along it he kept his gaze fixed on the ridiculously narrow plank. Two inches out and he'd tilt it and go crashing into the wall or the balustrade. Then his front wheel had hit it—dead centre.

There was a jolt, and for a split second he was climbing the steeply sloping ramp. The next second he felt a blast of cold air on his face, and he was flying. For a moment he saw everything laid out below him like an aerial photograph: the terrace, the path, the grassy bank, and the icy waters of the lake.

He wasn't aware of the moment he parted company with his bike. He just knew that suddenly he was sailing through the air like a bird. He felt an instant of wild, insane elation, and then he was

322

plummeting feet first towards the lake.

Miraculously he managed to remain upright, and had the presence of mind to take a lungful of air. Then he was immersed in freezing blackness—sinking, sinking, sinking . . .

*   *   *

As Hugh hit the water every breath on the balcony was held. He'd landed seven yards from the car, in which Gerry was still struggling desperately to free herself. The water was now one inch from the top of the door. They waited, no one moving or making a sound. Seconds seemed like hours.

Then Hugh's head broke water. He stared, gasping, around him, spotted the car, and started a fast crawl towards it.

Lord Burford gave a gasp. 'By Jove, he's made it!'

But even while he spoke the car was continuing to sink. Then Hugh had reached it. He heaved the door open and water cascaded into the car. In seconds it had reached Gerry's shoulders. Hugh took a deep breath and once more disappeared beneath the surface.

Even though Gerry was straining upwards to the limit of her reach, the water had now got to her chin.

Then the horrified watchers saw her head suddenly vanish beneath the water like an angler's float. Lady Burford gave a little cry.

But the next moment they realised what had happened. Hugh had grabbed her by the shoulders and pulled her down, as the only way of easing the tension on the handcuffs and releasing her.

Further nerve-racking seconds passed. But then the two heads, the dark and the red, appeared together, moving slowly but safely from the car as it finally sank beneath the water.

Just then a sight never before and never again to be seen at Alderley was observed: Merryweather appeared—running. He came around the corner of the house and threw himself down on the bank, exactly as Hugh and Gerry reached it. Ten seconds later, with his help, they were out of the water.

Gerry fell against Hugh and he put his arms around her. They stood locked together, the water dripping from them. The countess let out a long shuddering sigh. 'Thank heavens.'

Meanwhile, however, Paul had reached the other bank and had been desperately trying to scramble out. But although the bank here was less steep, it was very slippery, and he kept falling back. He took the gun from his mouth and threw it up onto the grass. Then he made one final effort and at last managed to heave himself up out of the water, at almost the same moment as Merryweather was helping the others ashore. Paul lay gasping for a few seconds, then dragged himself to his feet. He looked up and saw Hugh and Gerry together. Abruptly his expression changed to one of malice and rage. He bent, snatched up the revolver, and aimed it straight at them.

In the nick of time, Hugh saw the danger. As Paul fired he threw himself flat, pulling Gerry down with him. Merryweather, too, dropped to the ground and the bullet passed harmlessly over them. Paul took aim a second time.

At that instant the Earl and Countess were deafened by a loud report from beside them. Paul

324

fell as though poleaxed. He made an attempt to rise, then collapsed again and lay still.

Lord and Lady Burford swung round to see Wilkins in the act of lowering the Earl's rifle from his shoulder. He gazed at them. Suddenly he looked very tired. Then he seemed to collect himself.

'Oh, I beg your pardon, my lord. Do forgive me for using your gun without permission.'

Lord Burford let out his breath in a long gasp. He put his hand on Wilkins's shoulder. 'Any time, Wilkins, any time at all.'

The Countess drew herself up. 'Well, everything seems to be over. Oh, dear, that girl! Always in some sort of scrape. George, you really must have a serious talk with her.'

CHAPTER TWENTY-THREE

'Well, Wilkins,' St. John Allgood said in the small music room later, 'that all ended very satisfactorily.'

'I suppose so, sir.'

Two hours had passed. Two ambulances and a doctor had arrived and departed, as well as more policemen. The body of Paul Carter had been removed to the mortuary. Ned Turner had been taken to the nearest hospital, Mabel accompanying him. Maude Fry had been arrested and escorted by Sergeant Leather to the police station. Arlington Gilbert and Cyrus Haggermeir, both strangely subdued, had retired to their rooms. After a hot bath, a deeply shocked Geraldine had been given a sedative and sent to bed, and the Countess was still with her.

'Yes, indeed,' Allgood went on. 'Nasty things, murder trials. Unpleasant for all concerned. Always a chance, too, of the prisoner getting off on a technicality. If not, hanging. Messy business. So, in a way, good thing he had that gun of mine, after all, eh?' Allgood gave a short, forced laugh.

'Perhaps Lady Geraldine wouldn't think so, sir.'

'Maybe not. But all's well that ends well. Good shot of yours. Unfortunately, I was out of reach of a gun myself, watching from a gallery window. But I had every confidence in you.'

'Very good of you, sir.'

'Not at all. Had from the start, of course. And realised you'd had quite a bit longer to work on the case than I, and were probably close to cracking it. So let you get on with it. Put on a bit of a show, false accusations and all that, in order to distract attention from you and your investigations.'

'Thank you, sir.'

'I, er, suppose you'll be making a statement to the press?'

'No doubt, sir. And you needn't worry. I've no intention of grabbing all the glory. I'll see you get full credit, just as though we were equal partners.'

'Ah. Yes. Very good. Er, thank you.' He looked at his watch. 'Well, must be getting back to London. Heavy case load waiting. It's been a very, um, interesting investigation.'

'I'll make sure you get a copy of my report, sir. And that your Commissioner does, too.'

'Oh, I don't really think there's any need to trouble—'

'No trouble, sir. I'm sure my Chief will want one

sent. They're old friends, I understand.'

'Oh, I see.' Allgood gave a sickly grin. 'That'll be something to look forward to, then. Now I really must leave. Chalky's waiting outside with the car. Bye, er, old man.'

He went hurriedly out. Wilkins shook his head and gave a sigh. 'Three Great A's, indeed!' he said aloud. 'Reckon he coined that himself. He's not in the same class as Mr Appleby or Mr Alleyn.'

*   *   *

Just as Allgood departed, Merryweather entered. 'His lordship's compliments, sir, and would you care to join him in the library for some refreshment?'

'Ah, come in, my dear fellow.' Lord Burford got to his feet. 'Toddle over to the fire and sit down. We want a full explanation of this extraordinary business.'

'We,' apart from the Earl himself, consisted of Rex, Hugh—a quite different Hugh, with a cheerful expression and a face flushed as a result of both a hot bath and the stream of thanks and compliments which had been showered upon him—and Ann.

'Very well, my lord, if you insist.' Wilkins sat down and stretched out his feet to the blazing fire.

The Earl pressed a glass of whisky into his hand. 'Now start talking.'

'Right, my lord. But let me say first that with both Carter and Miss Lorenzo dead, a great deal has to be surmised or inferred. The main outline's clear enough, but a lot of the minor details can only be guessed at.'

Ann said, 'But don't keep saying "I imagine" and "perhaps" and so on. Just give us the most likely outline, as though you actually *knew* all the facts.'

Wilkins collected his thoughts. 'I suppose the first thing to say is that Paul Carter was a professional villain of the nastiest sort. For years now he's been living by his wits, mostly off women. This case started about six years ago when he went to northern Italy to climb the Matterhorn. While he was there he met a girl called Gina Foscari. She was a nice girl, and she invited him home to meet her parents. Mr and Mrs Foscari took to him as well, and asked him to stay. They were a pleasant, middle-class family, not especially well-off. Virtually their only valuable possessions were some jewels, which had been in the family for several generations, and which eventually would have been Gina's.

'I needn't go into the story in detail, but one day the girl and Carter just disappeared, together with the jewels. Two weeks later the girl's body was found. She'd fallen from the third floor balcony of a hotel where she and Carter had been staying as man and wife. There was no sign of Carter, nor of the jewels. It was never known whether he'd pushed Gina off, or simply abandoned her and she'd killed herself. Mr Foscari had to identify the body. The shock was too much for him. He had a heart attack and died a day or two later.

'Carter, of course, hadn't given the Foscaris his real name. Moreover, he'd told them he was American. Police inquiries were therefore directed across the Atlantic and were naturally unsuccessful.

328

'The relevance of all this is that Mr and Mrs Foscari were the uncle and aunt of Laura Lorenzo. She was very close to them, and had been to Gina. Her own parents were dead and she had no brothers or sisters, so it was a personal tragedy for her. Now, it so happened that she had met Carter briefly, having paid the Foscaris a flying visit while he was staying with them.'

Rex said, 'So when she turned up here, he recognised her.'

'Not at first, sir. She hadn't made her reputation in those days. She was just a fairly small-time actress, and it's probable she was introduced to him by her family name, Laura Lorenzo being a stage name. Also, I imagine she's changed her appearance—hair style and so on—quite a lot since then. On the other hand, however, she herself did have an excellent memory for faces.

'Years passed. Then six or eight weeks ago, *The Londoner* magazine carried a highly complimentary article on Miss Lorenzo. Her London agent sent her a copy. In the society pages there was a photograph of Carter and Lady Geraldine at a charity ball.'

'And she recognised him from that?' Ann said.

'Not positively, miss. If she had, I think she'd have notified the police immediately. My belief is that she wanted a chance to study him closely and at length, in order to be quite sure. Mr Haggermeir's visit here gave her the opportunity. She arranged for that phoney telegram to be sent to her and just turned up here, knowing she'd almost certainly be invited to stay. She knew there was a good chance Carter would be staying here as well; but if he wasn't, she could no doubt make

329

friends with Lady Geraldine and meet Carter later through her. Well, at first she was lucky. He *had* been invited. Things, though, didn't go quite as she'd anticipated. She convinced herself that Carter was the man she was looking for, but she was put off by the fact that she also recognised Mr Turner, though wasn't able to place him. He denied knowing her, but she was certain. He was here under a false name and was therefore quite probably a villain. She must have asked herself if there could be any connection between him and Carter: had she years ago seen them together?

'Something else that bothered her was Mr Haggermeir's strange coolness. She'd expected him to be overjoyed at the prospect of signing her up. We know, of course, that her arrival embarrassed him intensely, because he actually had no intention of making a film here. Nevertheless, it must have been a blow to her ego. We must remember that she was first and foremost a professional actress. Although she came here to trace her cousin's killer, signing with Mr Haggermeir would probably be the necessary concomitant to that. It was going to be a big step to take. Hence her interest in the script, and in Mr Gilbert's attitude to adapting it, was quite genuine.

'I think it's possible that a further factor which unsettled her was uncertainty about Lady Geraldine: she didn't know if her ladyship was another of Carter's potential victims (in which case she ought to be warned against him); or if, on the other hand, she might conceivably be a partner in crime. According to Sergeant Leather, Mrs Turner told them yesterday that Miss Lorenzo questioned her quite closely about Lady Geraldine's past brushes with the law.

'As a result of all these doubts and questions, Miss Lorenzo dithered about what to do next. Then sometime on Saturday, probably around lunchtime, Carter recognised her. We can never know how—the odd giveaway word, the chance meeting of eyes. Perhaps, for all we know, she actually came out in the open: identified herself by her real name, and challenged Carter. But in whatever way it happened, she'd effectively signed her death warrant. He was playing for the biggest stakes of his life. For over a year he'd been exerting all his charm on Lady Geraldine, a lady who—begging your pardon, my lord—will one day inherit a huge fortune. And he believed he was on the point of winning her. Nothing, not the merest hint of a scandal, even if no crime could be proved against him, could be allowed to stand in his way. Whatever the risk, Miss Lorenzo had to be silenced.'

Wilkins drained his glass.

Lord Burford said, 'Well, that's all fascinating, Wilkins. But how did he do it, and when? How did he manage to convince you and Allgood that he was innocent?'

'He never convinced me, your lordship. I was careful never to say I thought him innocent—only, for example, that I believed him when he claimed that things weren't as they seemed, and that when he entered Miss Lorenzo's room a few minutes before he was found standing by the body, she was already dead. Actually, I was quite certain of his guilt within two minutes of the start of my first conversation with him.'

'Two minutes?' Rex exclaimed. 'You mean he

331

gave himself away somehow?'

'Not in the sense you mean, sir.'

'But then how?'

Wilkins leant back in his chair. 'It's like this. I'm a simple sort of fellow. When I hear that a man's been found standing over a body with the murder weapon in his hand, my overwhelming instinct is that he's guilty. In fact, in the dozens of murder cases I've investigated, and the hundreds I've read about, I've never heard of one in which a person found in such a situation was innocent. Therefore I arrived here with a strong predisposition that Carter was the murderer. Of course, it was just possible that he'd been framed. But to be framed for a crime in such a way, a person would have to be very stupid or naive. Two minutes' conversation with him, however, showed me that he was neither, and I was then certain that he'd been found in that incriminating position only because he'd *wanted* to be. Great Scott, nobody planning a frame-up would arrange such a haphazard one as this one was supposed to be. A dozen things could have gone wrong. How could it be known that when Carter or anybody else came along the corridor and found the pistol on the floor that they'd be alone, that somebody else wouldn't be in the corridor at the same time? What certainty could there be that he'd actually pick up the gun and obligingly step into Miss Lorenzo's room, and then allow himself to be pushed in the back, without seeing the pusher? No, it's the stuff of mystery stories, not real life. And Carter, I found out, was a great fan of whodunits.

'Having come to this conclusion, I saw the case as fairly straightforward: my only job was to nail him. I doubted it would be possible to get cast-iron proof, so what I had to do was provide strong circumstantial evidence—firstly by showing how he could have done it and secondly by discovering a motive. That was why I perhaps seemed half-hearted in questioning the other guests. I knew none of them was guilty, just as I knew that the other strange incidents were either camouflage or completely irrelevant. They could be looked into eventually, if necessary, but they weren't of the first importance.'

Hugh asked, 'But if you were so sure of Carter's guilt, why did you want Scotland Yard called in?'

'It was really a question of my Chief Constable, sir. Now he's a first-rate man, an officer and a gentleman. But to tell you the truth, he's not exactly very imaginative. I didn't think he'd believe for a moment in a man having framed himself. I didn't have the nerve to put it to him until I was able to make out a very good case for it. I needed time to do two things: first, to look into Carter's background and circumstances, and to a lesser extent into Miss Lorenzo's, to try and find some link between them; second, to work out just how Carter had done it. The delay caused by the calling in of the Yard gave me just the breathing space I needed. I was confident Mr Allgood would see the case in the same light as I did and play along with me. But', Wilkins looked sad, 'he didn't, and I had to go my own way. At first my main worry was that he might actually arrest Carter straightaway, which was the last thing I wanted. Fortunately, however, he came to the quite erroneous conclusion that Carter was innocent.'

'Why would it have been so bad if he had

arrested Carter?' Lord Burford asked.

'Because we'd have had to release him again. I was sure that he had a trick up his sleeve. Evidence was about to turn up which was seemingly going to prove he was innocent. I'd expected, from the fact that the mink was missing, that this evidence might involve the coat. And I was right, though Carter also had two other pieces of back-up evidence, just to be on the safe side.'

The Earl stood up and started to replenish glasses.

'Well, no doubt I'm dense, but I don't see why he had to go to the trouble of framing himself at all. Why not just bump her off and have done with it?'

Ann said, 'I think I have a glimmering. Was it that by being the first one to be suspected, albeit for false reasons, he could be the first one to be cleared?'

'That's it, Miss. You see, if we—the police—had arrived here and found a murdered woman and no leads to the identity of the killer, we would immediately have started checking up on all the guests, searching for a possible motive. We'd have looked into their backgrounds, sought a previous connection with Miss Lorenzo, investigated their financial situation, and so on. And it was vital to Carter that he not be put through such a probe. Firstly, although he'd made himself out to be well off, we'd have discovered that he was up to his ears in debt and was seriously overdrawn, which the bank had been pressing him about. It's true he did inherit quite a substantial sum from his grandfather, but he got through that years ago. We'd have immediately become suspicious, inquired into any sources of income he'd had, and who knows what we'd have turned up? He'd have been a major suspect, his movements would have been gone into minutely, and eventually—though it would have taken some time—we'd probably have discovered he was in northern Italy at the time Laura's cousin died.

'At all costs, he had to avoid that. He had to convince the police he was innocent. And the only way he could do that was to make it appear certain he'd been framed. Thereafter, everybody else in the house would be under suspicion and would have their backgrounds investigated—except, obviously, the victim of the frame-up.'

Lord Burford nodded slowly. 'I see . . . I think.'

Hugh said, 'Now, what I want to know most of all is how he did it. I thought he had an alibi for the time of the murder. Did Laura really die just after she entered her room, after all?'

'Yes, sir.'

Hugh banged the arm of his chair. 'But, Wilkins, he was out with Gerry then, four miles from here. I saw him.'

Wilkins gave a smile of deep satisfaction. 'There are two things which everybody overlooked: the geography of this area; and the fact that Carter was an Olympic three thousand meters steeplechaser.' He looked round. 'The point at which he supposedly ran out of petrol is indeed about four miles from here by road. In a straight line it's no more than a mile away.'

It was Rex's face which was the first to clear. 'For crying out loud, you mean he *ran it?*'

Wilkins beamed at him. 'Precisely, sir.'

Hugh said, 'Ye gods! So simple. But the petrol . . .'

'He had a full can in back of the car, sir. Of course, he didn't actually run out at that point, but he no doubt arranged things so that the tank was very low.'

'So Turner didn't siphon fuel from Carter's car into my motor-bike, after all?'

'No, sir, from his own car. Anyway, Carter walked back sixty yards towards the village, then climbed a gate into a field, left the can of fuel under a hedge, slipped into a pair of running shoes, and started off. There's a straight run of about three quarters of a mile across flat fields to the wall surrounding the park. He had a key to that door in the wall—I found it on a marked tab in his pocket—and then it was just another quarter mile to the house. He arrived just before the rest of the party got home. With a powerful flashlight it would have taken him no more than six or seven minutes all told. He scaled the drainpipe—remember he was a skilled climber—which took perhaps another minute. The lady arrived almost immediately. He shot her, stripped off her coat, and cut the fur partly away round the bullet hole—only being very careful, apparently, to mess up the job and leave some blood on the coat. Then he cut out the other holes and burnt the pieces. That was the trap he set for us.'

'Which Allgood fell into,' said Rex.

'Well, it was a very clever trick, sir; but I'm afraid when I said as much, Mr Allgood thought I was referring to him.'

'Next, Carter found the letter, which Lady Geraldine had, as she casually revealed to us, told him she'd seen Laura writing. He took her gun—'

'That was *her* pistol?' the Earl asked.

336

'Almost certainly, my lord. We found her prints, not on the gun itself—Carter wiped it-but on the cartridge clip. Where was I? Ah, yes. Carter went out of the window and down the drainpipe again, carrying the coat. He took a few seconds to make sure the coat was in a position where it would be covered with snow, then it was back to the car, stopping only to pick up the can of petrol and change into his ordinary shoes again. He could have done it all comfortably in twenty-five minutes, even if, as is a possibility, it was he who put the phone out of order, too. It wouldn't have taken him more than a couple of minutes to shin up a telegraph pole and pull down a wire; however, that might have been a lucky coincidence.'

Ann said, 'But what a chance he took! He could have fallen, broken his ankle on his way back, anything.'

'Not too great a risk, considering the stakes he was playing for, miss. He was, of course, familiar with the estate from his rambles on his previous visit, and no doubt he planned the route carefully and examined it for obstacles and hidden pitfalls during his supposed training run that afternoon. And in fact, everything went perfectly for him until he got back to his car and found you there, Mr Quartus. That must have been quite a nasty shock.'

'Why?' Hugh asked.

'Firstly, I'm pretty sure he had you marked out as the fall guy, as they say in America. Now, though, you had an alibi. Secondly, you might have realised that the point at which you found them was only a mile from here.'

'Oh, there wasn't much likelihood of that. I'm not at all familiar with the area, and I just kept my

337

eyes on the road one way and on Carter's taillight on the way back.'

Wilkins nodded. 'It must have been a great relief to him, and an added bonus, when you confirmed his car had been stranded four miles away. But before that, the real emergency arose when you hurt your hand and suggested Lady Geraldine drive home.'

Hugh frowned. 'I don't understand.'

'Well, sir, his scheme depended on Lady Geraldine not knowing exactly where they had stopped. If she did, she would be much more likely than you to realise how close she actually was to home, and later that Carter's alibi wasn't valid. So long as she remained slumped in her seat and didn't look out of the windows much he was safe. But if she drove home, it obviously wouldn't be very many minutes before she got her bearings. So he had to think quickly to stop that.'

Hugh gave a gasp. 'You mean he deliberately socked her on the jaw? He wasn't aiming for me?'

'That's my guess, sir.'

There was silence for several seconds before Rex and the Earl both started to ask a question together. Rex gestured to Lord Burford to proceed, and he said, 'I was only going to ask you when he took my gun.'

'Some time early on Friday evening, my lord, probably when you were dressing to go out. It would have been easy enough to slip unseen into the study first, to get the key. And he could be virtually certain you wouldn't be going into the gun room again that evening before you went out. Mr Ransom?'

'After we got home that night, how could Carter

338

have been sure Laura would go straight upstairs, that she wouldn't have some refreshments first, say? Working on such a tight schedule, that could have botched his plan.'

'She must have made a prior arrangement to go straight up, sir.'

'An arrangement with Carter?'

'Yes. Perhaps she'd challenged him earlier and he'd claimed to have a full explanation for what had happened in Italy and begged to be allowed to give it to her before she took any further steps. She might have told him to come to her room immediately they got home that night—remember she had to leave here the following morning. That's only a guess, but I think it's indicated by her obvious wish to contact her agent that night before she went upstairs; and by the fact, as I discovered when I phoned the gentleman myself, that she gave a false reason to her ladyship for wanting to make the call and told a lie about his keeping late hours. So that call was for a private reason, and was obviously important. She wanted somebody, not a stranger but somebody she knew and trusted, to have the facts as to why she was really here.'

'As a sort of insurance, a lever to use against Carter?' Rex said.

'That's right, sir. She'd started to write a letter to her agent earlier, but had left it too late to catch the post. So instead, at the last moment, she tried to telephone him. But she was unsuccessful. She had no choice but to go up to her room all the same. Carter was waiting for her, and shot her.'

The Earl said, 'No wonder he was in such a hurry to get upstairs when he got back, knowing the body was up there all the time.'

'Yes, my lord. He just took a minute or two for a quick drink with you, which no doubt he badly needed. Then he had to go up and put Miss Lorenzo's gun in the secret passage, making sure you didn't see him when you went up. After that, he hurried to his own room, took his coat off, came out again, and then probably heard the voices of Lady Geraldine and Mr Ransom in the main corridor. That must have been a last minute stroke of luck for him—provided a plausible reason for his supposedly having gone to the far end of the corridor and found the gun on the floor.'

'Why put the gun in the passage?' Hugh asked.

'He must have wanted to be sure it would be found—though not by him. From what Leather tells me, Lady Geraldine's account of its being found makes it pretty clear Carter led her on to look there. That gun, you see, was one of the other things that were apparently to prove his innocence. We were to believe it had been used to fire the alarm shot. One bullet had gone from it—no doubt he fired it in the air when he was a good way from the house on his return to the car—and, of course, as Carter hadn't had a chance to conceal it in the passage *after* the shot was heard, this would back up his story that the alarm shot had been fired by a second person.'

'So it was really fired from my revolver—which was also the murder weapon?' the Earl said.

'Yes, my lord. He must have put another bullet in the same chamber after the murder. And it was very important you didn't discover the fact that it was the same gun that had been used twice. That was why he was quick to lock the gun in a box. If you'd sniffed it you would have realised it had just

340

been fired—which would have really spoilt his scheme.'

'I'd have certainly thought it confirmed that he had committed the murder a minute or so before. But isn't that what you said he *wanted* everyone to think?'

'Yes, my lord, but he only wanted it *thought*—not confirmed. If you had sniffed that gun, then later on, when it was known that the lady had been killed over an hour before, you would have remembered that the gun Carter had been holding had just been fired when you found the body. That would show that his story of the alarm shot having been fired by somebody else in the corridor, with another gun, was a lie. It was for the same sort of reason—though in reverse, as it were—that he left the body right in front of the fire: it had to be kept warm. Given the poor road conditions, and the telephone being out of order, he could be pretty sure the doctor wouldn't arrive soon enough to pinpoint the time of death with great accuracy. He wouldn't test exhaustively, anyway, time of death having already been established by a dozen witnesses. But if my lord, or anybody else, had touched the body and found it was cold, you would have immediately realised the lady must have died some time before.'

'And we would have thought, after all, that Carter was not guilty,' Hugh said. 'But isn't that what he wanted?'

'No, sir. With respect, you thinking him innocent would not be good enough. Carter had the sense to realise that when we—the police—arrived, it would make no difference to us if you all assured us he was innocent. We'd have to satisfy ourselves

341

of that. We'd have suspected everybody equally and checked into Carter's history and possible motives as closely as everyone else's. He had to arrange things so that we cleared him. But he wanted to be our number one suspect at first, so that we'd concentrate on him. He knew we wouldn't be able to find out much about his financial position, say, until today, when the banks and so on opened, and that by then the fur coat would have come to light, the second gun found, and his story would have apparently been authenticated. He believed that he would then be crossed off our list of suspects at once, that we'd concentrate on finding out who had framed him and that inquiries about him wouldn't continue.'

'And if it hadn't been for you, Mr Wilkins, that's just how things would have worked out,' Ann said.

Rex said, 'You referred to three phoney clues Carter had lined up that were supposed to clear him. You've only mentioned two: the mink and the second gun in the secret passage.'

'The third was more subtle. It was that phone call to the safe company. You see, Carter knew the combination because Lady Geraldine had told him. She urged him to keep quiet about his knowledge. But he couldn't have relied in advance on her doing that. Her knowledge that *he* knew might have made her suspicious. So by that phone call he gave the impression that somebody else had discovered the combination. Then he freely admitted his knowledge of it, in spite of Lady Geraldine's advice. It was a very smart move, making him appear thoroughly open and aboveboard. It was the one thing that, for a short time, did give me some small doubts about his

342

guilt. Then Mr Allgood discovered the fragment of letter in Mr Haggermeir's fireplace, and that re-established my conviction.'

'Why?' the Earl asked simply.

'I couldn't believe it had actually been sent to Mr Haggermeir. Firstly, it seemed obvious to me that the person Mr Haggermeir had been talking to in the breakfast room was Miss Lorenzo herself—though it had never seemed to occur to Mr Allgood to ask who the other person in the room had been, no doubt because once he'd decided Mr Haggermeir was not the killer the matter wasn't relevant. But I've since checked with Mr Haggermeir and he confirms it. He'd had a row with the lady the previous night. He'd naturally been unable to offer her a part in *The King's Man,* and she'd taken this as an insult and been very annoyed. But he couldn't throw up the opportunity of signing her. He had to convince her that his reluctance to give her a part in the film was no personal slight. He decided the only way to do that was to take the big risk of telling her the full truth. Which he did on the Friday morning. They started their conversation in the breakfast room, and then when they were interrupted by a maid they moved upstairs to Mr Haggermeir's room. He offered to commission a film script especially for her, and promised to top any other offer she got from Hollywood provided she kept quiet about his real reason for being here.'

'So Carter told you the truth about that incident?' Hugh said.

'Yes, sir. He overheard it by chance, but later used it very cleverly.'

'What made you so sure that note wasn't written

343

to Haggermeir?'

'Because if Mr Haggermeir had told Miss Lorenzo the facts, she wouldn't have written to him in those terms. She wouldn't have repeated in the letter things he'd already told her about his grandmother being deserted, and so on. She certainly wouldn't have bothered to mention the old lady's age when she died! She would have simply said something like, 'the story you told me this morning convinces me it is my duty to expose,' etc. Apart from that, though, I didn't believe Miss Lorenzo would have cared that much what Mr Haggermeir was up to. It was nothing to do with her. She certainly wouldn't have got so indignant as that fragment of letter sounded. Thirdly, if I was wrong and she *was* so concerned about what he was doing, why not tell your lordship or her ladyship the facts? As I said, after the Superintendent decided Mr Haggermeir wasn't guilty of the murder, he didn't give much thought to these points. But I asked myself this: if the letter did not refer to Mr Haggermeir, whom did it refer to? I decided that the most feasible explanation was that Miss Lorenzo was writing about herself. And, in view of her attempted phone call later, it was a fair bet the letter had been meant for her agent. Now, when Lady Geraldine interrupted her, she thrust it into her writing case. But either because she felt guilty about the way she was deceiving Lady Geraldine, or because she was still suspicious of her, her manner was furtive. Lady Geraldine innocently and casually mentioned this to Carter. And incidentally, that was another point against him in my mind. The killer had known about that letter and where Miss Lorenzo had put it. It was overwhelmingly probable that Carter was the only person Lady Geraldine had mentioned the incident to; they had driven together to the village a few minutes after it had happened, and it was just the sort of thing one might naturally refer to. On the other hand, it was extremely unlikely Lady Geraldine would have gone round talking about it at the party later. Obviously, though, I didn't want to ask her straight out.

'Anyway, immediately she mentioned it Carter smelt danger. So later, after he'd killed Miss Lorenzo, he took the letter away with him. He read it and saw how, with judicious editing, it could be used to frame Mr Haggermeir. He carefully cut it to shape, charred the edges, and planted it in Mr Haggermeir's room. Then he told Mr Allgood and me about the conversation he'd heard. It was a fair bet we'd then search Mr Haggermeir's room.'

'But how do *you* reconstruct that letter?' Hugh asked.

Wilkins took out his notebook. 'I copied down the wording of that fragment in here. Now, let me see. Something like this:

This is to state that the real reason for my present visit to Alderley is not, as I have said, to discuss making a movie, but to attempt to expose a wicked criminal who once cruelly deceived a whole family and caused the death at the age of eighteen of a young and innocent girl. He told her they would be married, but he left her, her reputation ruined, having robbed her of a valuable collection of jewellery.'

345

Wilkins closed his notebook. 'That would be the rough gist of it, anyway.'

Rex said, 'That's remarkable. But how did it lead you so quickly to the business of Laura's relatives? You said just now that in normal circumstances it would have taken a long time to trace Carter's connection with them. You did it in no time.'

'Well, given that the first part of that fragment referred to herself, the last part had to relate to people in her life. I've explained how I deduced that it had been intended for her agent. So yesterday, on my day off, I went up to London to visit him. Nice man, very helpful. Name of Cattin. He's only nominally her agent in this country, as she's never worked much over here. But they'd known each other many years, and she always looked upon him as a sort of adviser and father confessor. So naturally he was eager to help in any way he could.

'I told him a good part of the story, though not my suspicions of Carter, of course. I wanted to know if at any time of Miss Lorenzo's past life there'd been an incident concerning a family who'd been cruelly deceived, the death of a young girl, and the theft of some valuables. He told me yes, that she had talked about it years ago. But she'd never told him the name of the family and he was a bit hazy in his recollection of the details. However, he agreed to try and find out more. He spent much of yesterday afternoon on the telephone to Italy, speaking to various friends and relatives of Laura's. Eventually he pieced together the story, together with a description of the young man

346

direct from Laura's aunt. It fitted Carter.

'Then Mr Cattin came with me to the Savoy hotel, where Miss Lorenzo had left her luggage, and we went through it together. We found a copy of the edition of *The Londoner* magazine containing the article on Miss Lorenzo and, on another page, the photo of Lady Geraldine and Carter. Mr Cattin explained how he'd sent it to Miss Lorenzo. But, of course, this wasn't anything remotely resembling proof. I asked Mr Cattin to do one more thing for me: try and find out from the aunt if by any chance she had a photo of the criminal. Well, it turned out she had a rather blurred snapshot, I was told. I then arranged with the Italian police to collect the negative from her and put it on the first flight to London. After that it was just a question of waiting.'

'By Jove,' the Earl said, 'and it only arrived in the nick of time. Allgood was really floundering.'

Wilkins cleared his throat. 'Well, actually, my lord, it arrived quite early this morning. Unfortunately, when I saw it I realised what they'd meant by blurred. It was completely unrecognizable as Carter.'

They all stared. Rex said, 'But that photo you held out.'

'—was kindly supplied by the picture editor of *Athletics Weekly*. It was an unpublished photo taken just after Carter won the three thousand meters steeplechase at the British championships two years ago.'

The Earl slapped his knee and gave a roar of laughter. 'Wilkins, that's brilliant! You sly dog!'

'Thank you, my lord. I relied on the sudden shock breaking him down. These good-looking, charming, vain young criminals are almost always the quickest to show themselves up when things start to go wrong. And it worked. Unfortunately, what I didn't know, and what I don't think I could possibly have guessed, was that shortly before Mr Allgood had handed Carter a loaded revolver and not taken it back.'

Lord Burford said: 'Well, Wilkins, I must congratulate you and thank you for again gettin' us out of a very sticky situation. Rest assured, I shall write to the Chief Constable, praising your handling of the case in the highest terms.'

'Oh, no, my lord, please don't do that. The more commendations of that sort I get, the more cases of this sort I'll be assigned to. And I really don't like them. I'd much sooner be handling nice simple burglaries and car thefts.'

'Well, if you're quite sure . . .' The Earl broke off and called, 'Come in,' as there was a knock on the door.

It was Sergeant Leather. He came across the room. 'Excuse me, my lord.' He turned to Wilkins. 'Sorry to interrupt, sir, but you're wanted immediately.'

'What is it?'

'Murder, sir. At Meadowfield School.'

'Good gad,' Lord Burford exclaimed. 'I'm on the Board of Governors. Who's been murdered?'

'The matron, my lord. Found hanging in the gym, her hands tied behind her back.' He looked back at Wilkins. 'The odd thing is, sir, she was wearing a Red Indian headdress.'

Wilkins gave a groan and got to his feet. 'Oh dear, here we go again. I don't like school murders. So many people about, and all the teachers hate

348

each other and lie like troopers all the time.'

Ann said, 'Oh, come now, Mr Wilkins. I'm sure you'll clear it up in no time.'

'I doubt it, Miss. I'm not sanguine, not sanguine at all.' He sighed. 'Well, goodbye, my lord—and everybody. Glad to have been of service. Lead the way, Jack.'

They started for the door. Suddenly Rex said, 'Hey, wait a moment, Wilkins. There's something you haven't explained.'

Wilkins stopped. 'Carry on, Jack. I'll join you in a jiffy.' As Leather went out he turned, asking, 'What's that, sir?'

'Who in the world clonked Carter on the head last night?'

Lord Burford said, 'My word, I'd completely forgotten about that.'

Wilkins said, 'Oh.' There was a pause.

'Don't you know?' Ann asked.

Wilkins hesitated. 'Yesterday, I understand, her ladyship put forward the suggestion that some passing tramp had gained access to the house. I think that's probably the explanation for the attack on Mr Carter.'

'A hobo?' Rex exclaimed. 'You've got to be kidding!'

'I suppose you'll be putting out a dragnet for him?' Ann said quietly.

'Oh, I don't think so, Miss. As a matter of fact, he did me a good turn.'

'What the deuce do you mean?' Lord Burford asked.

'Well, my lord, I was very anxious about Mr Allgood's decision to allow Carter to go away. Leather told me about it when I telephoned him

349

after getting back from London yesterday evening. Let a criminal out of your sight and you might never see him again. If Carter had somehow spotted the fact that I was on to him—I didn't think he had, but I couldn't be sure—he might just disappear. But more important was Lady Geraldine's going with him. She's a smart young lady. It only needed him to make one tiny slip when they were discussing the case together and she might well jump to the truth. Then her life wouldn't be worth a brass farthing. So I started desperately trying to think up a way to prevent the trip. Do you know, I even went to the trouble of getting out my truncheon and driving up here last night? I don't quite remember what happened then. Think I must have fallen asleep in the car. Had rather a strange dream, might even have done a bit of sleepwalking. Anyway, when I woke up I just went home again. But when I heard this morning that Carter had been temporarily incapacitated I was mightily relieved, I can tell you. So you see why I say that this, er, tramp did me a good turn. Well, if that's everything, I must be going. Goodbye my lord, ladies and gentlemen.'

CHAPTER TWENTY-FOUR

'How is he?'

Mabel Turner paused outside her bedroom door at Alderley and turned to see that Cyrus Haggermeir had approached.

She said, 'Oh, he's going to be all right, thank you. They're keeping him in for a few days, that's all.'

'Swell. You just got back from the hospital?'

'Yes, I must pack our things and leave straight away. I'll stay in Westchester until Ned's released, though I saw Lady Burford just now and she asked me to stay on. I said no, of course, but I was very touched.'

'Well, I figure we were all impressed by his guts in jumping Carter.'

'That's what the Countess said. And they're not going to do or say anything about my impersonating Cecily. It's a great relief.'

'Can I come in a minute? I'd like to talk with you.'

She looked surprised. 'Yes, of course.'

They went into the room and she looked expectantly at him.

'Did you like him being a stuntman?' he asked.

She hesitated, then said, 'Frankly, no. It used to scare me stiff.'

'Ever try to persuade him to give it up?'

'Certainly not. He was a stuntman when I married him. I've no use for women who marry men with dangerous jobs and then try to make them change. It's thoroughly unfair.'

'All the same, you must have been relieved when he had to give it up?'

'In a way I was. But it made him so miserable.'

'But you wouldn't have wanted me to give him a job?'

'Oh, you're wrong, Mr Haggermeir. I would, for his sake. It's his one ambition to get back to work.'

'Well, I gotta warn you, I ain't going to.'

'I didn't think you would.'

'You see, I could find a couple of dozen guys in

351

Hollywood who could have pulled off that motor-bike stunt. Even Quartus managed it. Chiefly, though, Ned's too old. It's a young man's job.'

She nodded resignedly. 'I know. I only hope I can persuade him to accept that and look for some other line of work. But I'm not hopeful. Movies are his life.'

'Do you mean movies are his life, or movie *stunting* is?'

'I don't think that he's crazy about stunting as such. But he just loves the film world. Stunting was the only way he was qualified to earn his living in it.'

'I don't think you're right there.'

'What do you mean?'

'Honey, what I saw from him over this weekend was a terrific acting job.'

She smiled. 'He thinks he overdid the characterization.'

'Sure he did. He didn't have any direction. But he fooled a lot of people a long time, ad libbing the whole thing. I don't mind saying I'm impressed. I think he ought to take up acting.'

'At his age? With no experience? He'd never get parts.'

'I got a part for him.'

Mabel gave a jump. She whispered, 'What?'

'Now, it's a small one, but nice: English character in a movie that's scheduled to start shooting soon. Quite an important little role. We haven't been able to cast it. Couldn't find anybody just right. But it's Ned's if he wants it.'

Mabel's face was a study. 'Oh, Mr Haggermeir, I can't believe it!'

'Yeah, well, he's gotta prove himself. But if he

352

handles it OK—and I don't see why he shouldn't—there's no reason he couldn't carve a niche for himself as a character actor. Other stuntmen, like George O'Brien, have made the switch. I'll pay his fare out of course, and yours.'

'I—I don't know what to say. You're so generous!'

'Don't say things like that! I want him for the part or I wouldn't be doing it. Here.' He reached into his pocket and took out an envelope. 'I wrote him a letter, laying it all out, before I knew I'd be seeing you again. Take it and show him. If he calls at my London office when he gets out, we'll fix all the details.' Then, as she started to stammer out her thanks, he added, 'OK, take it as said. I gotta go now. I'll be leaving here soon myself, but there's sumpin' I must do first and before that I gotta find Rex. So long.'

He went out. Mabel sank down on the bed and started to cry.

*　　　*　　　*

'You saved my life,' Gerry said.

'Yes,' Hugh said simply.

'It was incredibly brave, what you did.'

'I know.'

'You mustn't say that!'

'On the contrary, I must. For about first time in my life I feel rather pleased with myself, and I shall no doubt keep talking about it for a very long time.'

'You're impossible!'

'No, I've *been* impossible. I know that. I've been a boor and a cad. I've behaved abominably, to you

353

and everyone else. But you know why, don't you?'

'I think so. But tell me, all the same.'

'I could see myself losing you to Carter. And it was making me utterly wretched. I'm crazy about you, Gerry. You know that, don't you?'

She nodded silently. Her eyes were bright.

'At one time I thought I had a chance. Then you seemed to be leaning towards Carter and I got terrified. I was always certain he was a rotter. When you invited me here for the weekend again, I couldn't believe my good luck. But then I found out he was here, too, and I had to watch you getting closer and closer to him and farther away from me. It was the most miserable few days I've ever spent.'

'I never intended it like that. I meant to treat you both exactly the same. For the first day or two it was your own fault. You were such a bear.'

'I realise that.'

'And then, of course, it seemed Paul was going to be falsely charged with murder, and naturally I had to spring to his defence. Nitwit!'

'You weren't a nitwit. He had a lot of charm. In fact, I have to admit that, except when he was murdering people or robbing them, he was much nicer than I am. Anyway, now you have at least seen me at my worst.'

'That's nice to know.'

'So Gerry, will you marry me? I'll make an awful husband, but I do love you very much.'

'To distraction? I could never marry a man who didn't love me to distraction.'

'Positively to distraction.'

'Aren't you rather taking advantage of the fact that I'm grateful you saved my life?'

'Of course I am. Do you blame me?'

She said slowly, 'I'm a little scared of you, Hugh. I always have been. And you frequently infuriate me. Probably I shall often hate you. We'll no doubt have the most awful rows. But, well, I've never been one for a quiet life. So the answer's yes, without any doubts at all.'

He took her in his arms.

A minute or two later she said, 'You don't mind people saying you're marrying me for my money?'

'Not in the least. Do you?'

'Oh, of course not! I think it takes an awful lot of guts and character for a poor man to marry a rich girl and not let it make any difference. But I must admit I do worry a bit for your sake, about what people will say.'

'Let the oafs say what they like.' He kissed her again.

'Young man, don't you think it's time you stopped teasing my daughter?'

They sprang apart and spun round. It was the Countess, who'd entered the room silently and was gazing at them severely.

Gerry said, 'Mummy! I—er—' She took a deep breath. 'Hugh just asked me to marry him.'

'And clearly you had the surprising good sense to accept.'

Gerry stared. 'You approve?'

'I do. It's high time you were married. And you're obviously in love with each other, which is always an advantage.'

Gerry nodded vigorously. 'Yes, but I thought perhaps you'd raise objections to my marrying someone who—who . . .'

'Object to your marrying the only son of the

Marquis of Gower? Why on earth should I? It's a most excellent match. His family owns five thousand acres in west Wales and a considerable amount of property in London.'

'*What?*' Gerry gaped. 'Hugh, is this true?'

' 'Fraid so. How did you know, Lady Burford?'

'Chiefly your name. Quartus was your mother's maiden name, wasn't it? She and I came out together in '05. Then again, you have her eyes. I haven't seen her for well over twenty years. How is she?'

'She's very well, thank you.'

Gerry said dazedly, 'But—but why didn't you tell me?'

'When we first met I didn't want it to look as if I were using my family position to get an unfair advantage with you over Carter. Oh, I knew it wouldn't make any difference to you, but I thought if I won *he* might think it had. I wanted to fight on equal terms without the privilege of rank. Besides, I'd put all that stuff behind me.'

'But why?'

'Because I was fed up with Society. All the trappings of the sort of life people like us lead was making me sick. Besides, I wanted to paint. Father wanted me to take over the running of the estate, so he could concentrate on his collection and his other hobbies. But I was convinced I had what it takes to make the grade as a serious artist. Father challenged me to prove it. Well, if I wanted to be a professional it was no good dabbling at it: I had to have a real incentive to get on. I'd never get anywhere if I could just stop painting whenever I felt like it, because I'm basically a very lazy person. If I was to succeed not just artistically, but commercially—I had to *need to* succeed. So I took just fifty pounds, went to London and started to paint. Father and I agreed that if I had not made the grade in six years I'd give up all my pretensions to art and go respectable again. I changed my name and cut myself off from all my old crowd. The last thing I wanted was a lot of chaps I'd been at Harrow with, and debs I'd taken to parties, finding out and buying my pictures or commissioning portraits, to help me.'

'But you pretended to be really poor.' Her voice was indignant.

'Pretended? *Pretended?* In six years I've sold forty-four pictures at an average price of a little over fifteen guineas a time. I've been living on about two pounds ten shillings a week! Unless I sell something else, I've got just twelve pounds four and sixpence to last me until the end of April.'

'Why April?'

'Because that's when the six years are up.'

'Oh, I see. And what are you going to do then?'

'What do you think? Give it all up, with great relief, go home to Wales and start running the estate.'

'I thought you hated Society and all the trappings.'

'Well, in spite of everything that's happened here, the last few days have made me realise that there is, after all, a great deal to be said for three square meals a day. I still don't approve of big houses and lots of servants, but I can happily learn to live with them again after six years of the other thing.'

'You're not going to be a great artist, after all?'

'Of course I'm not. I haven't got what it takes,

357

and I've got it out of my system. But I do know a lot more about painting than I did. Moreover, I know what it *does* take to become a worthwhile artist. I can recognise talent in others now. So I intend to become a patron, do everything I can to support and encourage good young painters, and also start a collection. Collecting can be an art in itself, and my collection will become world-famous. I shall, in addition, write: scathing criticisms of bad art. I shall use every ounce of pull that money, position, and powerful friends can give. I shall become the most influential, admired, and feared figure in British art. *That,* my lady, is what I'm going to do.'

Gerry couldn't speak. The Countess said, 'That sounds highly satisfactory. Be sure to repeat to George what you said about collecting being an art. That will put you very much in his good books.'

Hugh said, 'Heavens, I suppose I should speak to him, ask for Gerry's hand and all that sort of thing.'

Lady Burford nodded. 'Yes, I think it's pleasant to keep up the old customs. I shall go and find George now and prime him, so you needn't be apprehensive that he'll refuse his permission, or anything ridiculous like that. Come along to the library in fifteen minutes. You'd better telephone your parents, Hugh, and then we can put the announcement in *The Times* immediately. A June wedding, I think. I don't approve of long engagements. Here, or in town, I wonder? I rather favour London; it's so much more accessible for most people. St. Margaret's, Westminster, I think, and the reception at Claridge's.' She went out.

Gerry grinned at Hugh. 'Satisfied?'

'Completely.'

'Me, too. Who'd have thought this time yesterday that everything could turn out so spiffingly so quickly.'

'Things have turned out pretty well for nearly everybody. Ned Turner's got a new job.'

'And Jemima or Ann or whatever her name is got her woman.'

'And Rex Ransom got a blackmailer off his back.'

'You know,' Gerry said, 'I've been meaning to ask you: what do you think she was blackmailing him for, on what grounds? What was he doing in that photograph she took?'

'There's only one thing I can think of,' Hugh said. 'I'm afraid it must be drugs.'

Her eyes grew big. 'You mean he's an addict? Surely not!'

'I agree he doesn't look it. But what else could it be? He was alone in the room. She must have got a snap of him giving himself an injection.'

'Nothing so dramatic.'

The voice came from the door, which the Countess had left open an inch or two. It was Rex.

Gerry and Hugh stared at him in horror as he came into the room. Gerry stammered, 'Rex, I— I'm terribly sorry. I didn't—' Then she stopped as she saw that he was smiling.

'It's OK,' he said. 'You wouldn't be human if you didn't speculate. And I'd probably think the same if it was someone else. Like to see the famous photograph?'

Hugh said, 'Certainly not! It's your business.'

'It's all right. I'd like you to look at it.' He reached into his pocket, took the photograph from

359

it, and held it out to them. 'Here.'

Hugh took it and he and Gerry stared at it together. Expressions of bewilderment appeared on their faces.

The picture was of a man, wearing shorts and an undershirt. He was standing, holding a couple of strange, limp, shapeless objects in one hand. A large stomach bulged over the top of the shorts and he had a high domed, bald head.

Gerry said, 'But I don't understand. This isn't—' She broke off with a gasp. 'It is! It's you!'

Rex bowed. He raised a hand to his head, pulled at the thick blonde hair, and it came away to reveal a gleaming, egg-like pate. Hugh and Gerry goggled at him.

Rex jerked a finger at the photograph. 'The other object I am holding is, I regret to say, my girdle. I'd just taken it off.'

'All she was threatening to publish was this?' Hugh said incredulously.

'All? You're joking! Can't you imagine the effect that could have on my career? The romantic, swashbuckling hero wears a wig and a girdle? I'd be a laughing stock. It'd finish me.'

Gerry said, 'Yes, I can see. Golly, no wonder your manner was so odd that night!'

'I was in a terrible state. I could see my whole world crumbling. When I first had the brush with the intruder I couldn't be sure what was behind it. It might be blackmail, or just a hoax. Even when I discovered—as I believed—that it was Gilbert, I still hoped he might just be a pathological snooper. I confronted him, but I couldn't accuse him straight out. If he hadn't thought of blackmail, I didn't want to let him realise there were grounds for it. But he was apparently scared, too. Then he said he was leaving and it seemed important to stop him. I thought it less likely he'd have the nerve to apply the squeeze while we were under the same roof. I used a little blackmail myself, threatened to see he didn't script *The King's Man*. I even made up a lot of hogwash about Cyrus's attorneys questioning the copyright situation. All I really knew was that Cyrus had mentioned he'd forgotten to check on who held the rights. Anyway, it seemed to work. He agreed to stay, if you okayed it, Gerry, and apparently climbed down. I decided that I'd either misjudged his motive or that he'd thought better of it. By that night I figured I was in the clear, which made the shock of finding that photo and the note in my room all the greater. I was in a real stew. Even if I paid and got the negative back, how could I be sure that dozens of prints hadn't already been made? I could see myself paying through the nose for years.'

Hugh frowned. 'But now you're quite prepared to have the photo published. Why the change?'

'In the picture gallery earlier I suddenly got nauseous at the lie I was living. I decided to face up to what I am: middle-aged, fat and bald. I don't care who knows it. It's a tremendous relief.'

'But your acting career?' Gerry said.

'My acting career is finished. I'm getting out.'

'What will you do?'

'Something I've had a hankering to do for many years: direct. I've got a story all lined up, too. Arlington's going to do the screenplay.'

'Mr Gilbert?' Gerry exclaimed.

'Yeah. We've had a long talk. He's not at all a bad guy underneath the bluster. He started all that rudeness when he was successful, as a sort of gimmick. And he's had to keep it up so people wouldn't guess he'd fallen on hard times. Oh, and by the way, I've explained to him about you and your hoax, Gerry.'

'How did he take it?'

'He laughed. I think it was quite an effort, but he managed it eventually. Anyway, whatever his faults, he's a first-class screenwriter. I've spoken to Cyrus and he's willing to give us a chance.'

Hugh looked surprised. 'You've patched up your quarrel, then?'

'Heck, yes. That was nothing. We've both apologised and shaken hands. He even borrowed two hundred pounds from me, though I don't know what he wanted it for. He's quite enthusiastic about the story idea; particularly as he's gotten a sort of personal interest in it, as you have, too, Gerry.'

'Me? What *is* the story?'

Hugh said, 'Good heavens, it's not a murder mystery based on this weekend?'

'Not likely! Who'd believe it? No, I'm going to make a movie called *The Adventures of Aylwin Saunders*. And I've an old rival and buddy of mine in mind for the lead. I hear he's thinking of changing studios.'

Gerry whispered, 'Not—not . . . ?'

'Yes,' Rex said. 'Errol Flynn. Who else?'

*   *   *

'Gower?' said the Earl. 'Yes, know him slightly. Eccentric, naturally, like all Welshmen. Collects coins. And he's fanatical it seems. Can't see the appeal myself. And he gets these odd crazes for things, jazz or breeding rabbits or something. They never last, apparently. Strange way to behave. Vague sort of fellow, too, terribly absentminded. Nice chap, though. Very amiable. Fine old family, of course.'

'So you approve, George? And you won't put any obstacles in their way?'

'Whose way?'

'Geraldine and Hugh.'

'Oh, no, course not. When did I ever put an obstacle in anyone's way? Gerry'll get engaged to whomever she wants, whatever I say. But I suppose she could have done worse. He can be an arrogant young puppy, but he's shown he's made of the right stuff. Only trouble is, I fancy he'll actually expect to marry her.'

'What on earth do you mean? Of course he expects to marry her.'

'She assured me that wasn't the idea at all. Still, if I give him my permission to do either or both, that'll be all right, won't it?'

'I don't know what you're talking about, George.'

At that moment there came a tap on the door.

'Oh, he's a little soon,' Lady Burford said. 'I'll leave you.' She crossed to the door and opened it to find not Hugh, but Cyrus Haggermeir, on the other side. She said, 'Oh.'

'Sorry to interrupt, ma'am. Just wanted to say I'll be leaving shortly. Can I have a word first?'

The Earl raised his eyebrows. 'Yes, of course. Come in.'

Haggermeir did so, closing the door behind him. He said, 'I owe you both an apology.'

363

'Yes, you do,' Lady Burford said.

'Well, I make it here and now. I behaved badly. I admit it freely. And that's something Cyrus Haggermeir don't often do. I hope you'll accept the apology.'

The Earl cleared his throat. 'Well, that's very handsome. We'll say no more about it. Er, *bon voyage* and all that.'

'Thanks. But there's more. I ain't quite given up. I just been having a word with your butler.'

'With Merryweather?' the Countess said, surprised.

'Yeah. Told him I had reason to believe there may be something in this house that once belonged to my grandmother. I described the casket, told him that you knew nothing about it, but you'd said that if it is here I'd be more than welcome to it. I told him to put it round among the servants that there's a two hundred pound reward for anyone who finds it and brings it to me—either here and now or at my hotel. I'll be staying on a couple more weeks in England. I figured one of them might just have seen it around. Wanted to put you in the picture.'

The Earl said dryly, 'Suppose *I* offer four hundred to anyone who brings it to me?'

'Don't reckon you'd do that, Earl, not after the Countess said I could have it. Wouldn't be exactly, er, cricket, would it?'

'I'm not so sure I'd worry about that if I stood to lose the Earldom. However, I'm pretty confident I won't have to.' He chuckled.

Just then the door opened. It was Merryweather. He advanced towards them, bearing a silver salver. He said, 'Excuse me, my lady.'

Then they saw that resting on the salver was a small wooden box, brightly painted with an intricate design of Chinese dragons. It was about six inches by five, and four inches deep.

'Would this be the object you wanted, sir?' said Merryweather.

Haggermeir gave a cry of disbelief and sprang towards him. He snatched up the casket and turned it between his fingers. He whispered: 'It must be! It must be!' He opened the box and started desperately probing at the interior. The Earl and Countess watched with bated breath.

But nothing happened. Haggermeir started muttering angrily to himself. Then Merryweather gave a discreet cough.

'Might this be what you are searching for, sir? It was concealed in the false bottom.'

He took from his pocket a folded sheet of ancient, yellowed paper, which he handed to Haggermeir.

Haggermeir gave a strangled gasp. With shaking fingers he unfolded the paper. For a moment he stood perfectly still, his eyes scanning it. Then he suddenly gave vent to a deafening howl.

'Yippee!'

His face alight with triumph, he brandished the paper. 'Got it, got it, got it! I was *right*!'

Lord Burford gave a gulp. 'That—that's it?'

'You bet your sweet life it is, Earl. Marriage license: Aylwin Saunders to Martha Haggermeir, officiating minister Rev. P. Jones, solemnised at the Baptist Church of Last Straw, Calif., date 8th April, 1851. Take a look.'

He held it out for them to see. The Earl and

Countess stared at it. Everything Haggermeir had read out was correct.

Lady Burford looked at her husband. 'George, what does it mean? Can it mean that—that . . . ?'

The Earl sat down, a dazed expression on his face. 'I don't know, my dear. It certainly seems that my grandfather's marriage to my grandmother in 1852 was bigamous, and Haggermeir's father was Aylwin's eldest legitimate son and automatically succeeded to the Earldom. That means my father should never have had the title, and neither should I.'

Haggermeir nodded. 'That's about the size of it. Look, I know it's hard on you, but you gotta see the justice of it.'

'But George, surely you're not just going to accept this lying down?' Lady Burford was pale. 'You're going to fight?'

'Well, of course I'll see my solicitor. I honestly don't know what the legal position is, or who decides things like this. Heralds' College? The Courts? I should imagine it's a pretty well unique situation. Of course I'll fight, if I'm told there's a chance.'

'Earl,' Haggermeir said, 'that's exactly what I'd expect you to say. It's what I'd say in your position. But do we have to fight?'

'You're suggesting we should just hand over everything to you and impoverish ourselves completely?' The Countess had regained a little colour and there was a gleam of battle in her eye.

Haggermeir gave a snort. 'I don't want to impoverish you!'

Lord Burford glanced at him sharply. 'You don't?'

366

'Heck, no! I don't want your money or your estates. Or your London house. Why should I? I got millions. I only want two things. Now, can't we come to an amicable agreement? If we fight it through the courts it could drag on for years and cost us both a fortune. Why make the lawyers rich?'

'Just what are the two things you want?' Lady Burford asked him grimly.

'First, the title. I wanta be the Earl of Burford. Can't you just see it: *The Lord Burford Picture Corporation?* And on the movie credits: *produced by Lord Burford?* That'd make Goldwyn and Warner and the other sit up, eh? Guess I'd have to give up my American citizenship, become a naturalised Britisher. Or perhaps I am legally British already. That's a minor point, though. Anyway, what about it?'

The Earl rubbed his chin. 'Well, I daresay I could live without a title. Wouldn't make any difference to Gerry. Looks as if she's going to be Marchioness of Gower one day, anyway.'

'George, you can't just give away a title!' the Countess exclaimed.

Haggermeir said, 'But, Earl, if you stood up and admitted I was the rightful holder of it and you didn't want it, that'd be bound to make a difference.'

'I—I suppose it might,' the Earl said unhappily.

His wife was gazing at him in disbelief. 'George, you wouldn't do such a thing!'

'I don't know, Lavinia. Perhaps it would be the right thing to do, if Haggermeir's got justice on his side. I don't want to hang on to something that's not rightfully mine. Do you?'

Lady Burford didn't answer. She sat down very slowly beside her husband.

Haggermeir turned away and noticed that Merryweather was still present, his face as impassive as ever.

'Say, I was nearly forgetting.' He reached into his hip pocket, took out a thick wad of banknotes, and handed it to Merryweather. 'Here you are, pal. You sure earned this.'

'I am obliged, sir.' The money disappeared in a flash into Merryweather's waistcoat pocket.

The Earl regarded his butler sadly. 'Oh, Merryweather, what have you done to us?'

'I am exceedingly sorry, my lord. I did not realise until minutes ago just what the situation was. I would, of course, deeply regret causing the family any inconvenience.'

He bowed and silently melted from the room.

The Countess looked at Haggermeir. 'What was the second thing you wanted?'

Haggermeir took a deep breath. 'Alderley.'

The Earl and Countess looked blank. Lord Burford said, 'But you said you didn't want the estate.'

'I don't. Just the house. I aim to take it down brick by brick, ship it across the Atlantic, and rebuild it in Beverly Hills.'

*   *   *

Haggermeir's words seemed to strike both Lord and Lady Burford totally dumb. They sat motionless, their faces masks of utter horror.

Haggermeir went on hurriedly. 'It's technically feasible, I've checked into it. And I wouldn't leave

368

you without a house here. I'd build you a swell modern one on the same site, all electric, air-conditioned, with a pool—everything. No one can say I'm not generous. Now, Earl, this isn't something the law would have to decide. The house is yours to do what you like with. So, whaddaya say?'

'Never!' Lord Burford jumped to his feet, his face red. 'You must be mad if you think I'd let you do such a thing. I'd sooner lose everything else than let Alderley be taken away. Good gad, it's been here nearly three hundred years. What you're suggesting would be vandalism.'

Lady Burford was staring at him in admiration. 'George, I never knew you cared so much.'

'May not talk about it much, Lavinia but I care!'

Haggermeir's face had hardened. 'Get this, Earl. I've been pretty easy in my demands so far. I was prepared to let you off light. But force me to go to the law and I'll go for everything: the title, the estates, everything you inherited. I'll ruin you.'

The Earl took a deep breath. 'Then you'd better try. If we lose everything, so be it. At least we'll go down fighting.'

Haggermeir shrugged. 'Sorry you're taking it like, this, Earl. It's not the way I wanted it.'

The silence that followed this was broken by the return of Merryweather. 'Excuse me, my lord,' he said, 'but I wonder if your lordship would care to look at this?' He held out his salver, which bore a folded piece of paper.

The Earl waved him away. 'Not now, Merryweather. I haven't time.'

'With great respect, I do urge that your lordship find time.'

369

The Earl snatched the paper up irritably. 'What is it?'

'If you will read it, my lord.'

The Earl unfolded the paper and glanced cursorily at it. His eyebrows went up. 'It's a marriage certificate. What the deuce? Gretna Green? Good gad!'

Lady Burford asked sharply: 'What's the matter, George?'

'It says 'Aylwin Saunders to Mary Carruthers.' I don't understand. They were married here at the parish church.'

Merryweather said softly, 'May I suggest you look at the date on the certificate, my lord?'

'Date? Where? Good heavens! It says 1839.'

'Let me see that!' Haggermeir stepped to the Earl's side and stared at the paper in his hand.

Lord Burford looked up blankly. 'Merryweather, I don't understand.'

'I can explain, my lord. The accepted story of the elopement of your lordship's grandfather is incorrect in one particular. When the young couple were found by their fathers, they were not still on their way to Scotland, but on their way *back*. They had reached Gretna Green and *had been married*. But Lady Mary was so nervous at the thought of her parents' reaction that she persuaded her husband to say nothing about it. However, the fact remains that when your lordship's grandfather went to America he was already legally married. His so-called marriage to Miss Haggermeir was bigamous, and the issue of it illegitimate. The later marriage ceremony he went through with Lady Mary in 1852 was in law quite superfluous.'

A look of delighted disbelief had come over the

Earl's face 'So, my father was the rightful heir, all along?'

'Indubitably, my lord.'

It was now Haggermeir who, pale-faced, sat down suddenly in the nearest chair. He muttered, 'All these years . . . all these years . . .'

Lady Burford was on her feet again. With a surreptitious movement she dashed what looked suspiciously like a tear from her face. There was the merest catch in her voice when she said, 'We— we are really most grateful, Merryweather, most grateful. But you must explain how on earth you know all this, and where you obtained those certificates.'

Before Merryweather could reply, however, there was an interruption. A strange sound filled the room, a rumbling, gurgling sound as of a subterranean river. It was a noise that had not been heard anywhere for many years. Cyrus Haggermeir was laughing.

'My dear chap,' Lord Burford said, 'are you all right?'

Haggermeir nodded. He seemed to have difficulty in speaking. At last he said, 'Just seen the funny side of it. Grandma married to a bigamist! Thank heavens she never knew.'

The Countess said, 'But this means you've lost. Don't you mind?'

Haggermeir wiped his eyes with his handkerchief. 'Reckon not.' He sounded quite surprised. 'Not now I know the truth. It was the thought that I'd been cheated out of what was rightfully mine that riled me. But now I know I wasn't. So it don't hurt any more. In fact, guess I'm kind of relieved. Didn't really want to give up my

371

American citizenship, whatever I said.'

'Well, I must say, it shows a fine sportin' spirit,' the Earl said. He stuck out his hand. 'Will you shake, cousin?'

'Sure.' They shook hands.

'Don't ever let me hear anyone say Americans are poor losers,' Lord Burford said.

Haggermeir grinned. 'Maybe it's true as a rule. You see, we don't get a lot of practice at it.' He looked at Merryweather. 'Lady Burford asked you a question. I'd sure as eggs like to know the answer, too.'

'Both those documents and the casket were put in my possession very many years ago, sir, when I was little more than a boy.'

'But by whom, man?'

'The faithful servant John, sir. He also told me the story of the two marriages. He was a witness to both. The Gretna Green certificate was handed to him for safekeeping. He claimed his master had given him the Chinese casket as a present, but I consider it more likely he spied on your grandmother, saw her putting her license in it, and deliberately expropriated the box without his master's knowledge before they returned to England. Why he retained the licenses I cannot say. Probably he just hoped they would come in useful one day. He was of a conserving and secretive disposition. I was perplexed for many years to know what I should do with them. Eventually I decided to say nothing until such time as it seemed proper to speak.'

'But why in tarnation did he give 'em to you?' Haggermeir demanded.

'If you glance at the full name of the witness on

one of the licenses, sir, you will see that it is John Merryweather. My grandfather. Not an altogether estimable character. We have never spoken much of him in my family. Incidentally, sir, I feel that under the circumstances I should return this money to you.'

He held out the wad of notes.

Haggermeir hesitated. Then he chuckled. 'No, a bargain's a bargain. You earned it. You keep it. But thanks all the same.'

'Thank you, sir,' said Merryweather.

CHIVERS

LARGE PRINT

—direct—

If you have enjoyed this Large Print book and would like to build up your own collection of Large Print books, please contact

Chivers Large Print Direct

Chivers Large Print Direct offers you a full service:

• Prompt mail order service

• Easy-to-read type

• The very best authors

• Special low prices

For further details either call
Customer Services on (01225) 336552
or write to us at Chivers Large Print Direct,
FREEPOST, Bath BA1 3ZZ

Telephone Orders:
FREEPHONE 08081 72 74 75